SOUL REAPER

SOUL REAPER

D.B. SMYTH

BALANCE OF SEVEN
Newport, VT

For information, contact:
Balance of Seven
www.balanceofseven.com
info@balanceofseven.com

Cover Design by Lance Buckley
www.lancebuckley.com

Developmental Editing by Deana Wilson

Editing, Formatting, and Proofreading by TNT Editing
www.theodorentinker.com/TNTEditing

Proofreading by Roberta Templeman

Publisher's Cataloging-in-Publication Data
Names: Smyth, D.B. | Burns, Deborah, 1980- .
Title: Soul reaper / D.B. Smyth.
Description: Newport, VT : Balance of Seven, 2023. | Summary: After one thousand years of violence as an Angel of Death, Keres discovers the truth is not what it seems and her contract to reap souls is destroying her own. Uncertain who to trust, she seeks to escape the unbreakable contract before her next reaping becomes her last.
Identifiers: LCCN 2023944356 | ISBN 9781947012578 (hardback) | ISBN 9781947012240 (pbk.) | ISBN 9781947012257 (ebook) | ISBN 9781947012561 (itchio ebook)
Subjects: LCSH: Angels – Fiction. | Death – Fiction. | Magic – Fiction. | Empathy – Fiction. | Forgiveness – Fiction. | Faith – Fiction. | Baltimore (Md.) – Fiction. | Jakarta (Indonesia) – Fiction. | Jerusalem – Fiction. | BISAC: FICTION / Fantasy / Urban. | FICTION / Fantasy / Dark Fantasy. | FICTION / Occult & Supernatural.
Classification: LCC PS3619.M98 S68 2023 (print) | PS3619.M98 (ebook) | DDC 813 S69–dc23
LC record available at https://lccn.loc.gov/2023944356

27 26 25 24 23   1 2 3 4 5

To my own Joe,
who walked the Hall with me
and didn't run away.

CONTENTS

Contents

CONTENT AND TRIGGER WARNINGS

Keres was born of darkness and lives in the shadows, with experiences as bleak as her role as an Angel of Death. As a witness to the full range of human depravity, she is an angel steeped in trauma, burdened by violence, and hungry for redemption. Readers who may be sensitive to the following elements, take note, choose courage, and prepare to fall from grace.

Abusive relationships	Decapitation
Anxiety	Emesis
Assault	Emotional abuse
Attempted murder	Fire
Attempted rape	Gaslighting
Blood	Genocide (mentions of)
Bones	Gore
Branding	Gun violence
Burning/burns	Hostages
Child abuse	Kidnapping
Control	Manipulation
Death / graphic death	Mental abuse

Content and Trigger Warnings

Misogyny
Nightmares
Pedophilia
Physical abuse
Profanity
Prostitution (mentions of)
PTSD
Religion
Satan / the devil
Self-hate
Sexism
Sexual abuse

Murder
Sexual assault
Sexually explicit scenes
Stabbing
Suicidal ideation
Torture
Verbal abuse
Victim blaming
Violence
War (conversations about)
Weapons

ONE

Baltimore—my *damn* city.

Tonight, she hummed with the electricity of human emotion, shoving it into my personal space via blaring horns, racing engines, and screeching tires. An energy of excitement, exhilaration, anger, and frustration. "I hate you!" communicated through one long honk followed by one short and another long, in mutated Morse Code. "Suck this!" beeped right back, as cars screeched and zoomed between red lights.

I watched the interplay, fascinated by the expression of raw emotion humans displayed when separated by metal and machinery. Things they would never say or do over a coffeepot at work. People were different onstage: Polite. Accommodating. Raging emotions neatly contained in a box.

I hated boxes.

I glanced at the oily waters of the Chesapeake as I walked around Inner Harbor. The surface was still, its reflection of the city lights picture perfect, yet I could see the hidden current churning beneath.

You and me both.

I looked up as emotions exploded into the sky beyond Pier 5, and a mushroom cloud of pain and remorse lit the night. I closed my eyes as a blast wave only I could feel rushed past, its heat palpable against my skin.

Another murder.

Taking life was the only act strong enough to elicit such raw emotion, and suicide didn't produce the same tints of surprise—pink and crimson—that accompanied homicide. I studied the bright light with practiced indifference. Death lights were common in the city, and I had learned early on to ignore them and what they signified. I couldn't change anything; intervening was forbidden. One of the few laws that ruled my kind.

But when death didn't return darkness to the sky, curiosity overcame my better judgment and I *blinked* to the source.

The human man burned in white-hot flames of innocence and desperation. They curled around his outstretched fingers and licked the edges of his face as they rolled up toward the charcoal clouds. He clawed at the arm locked around his throat, twisting and turning, but his attacker wouldn't let go.

Across from the pair stood a young man, maybe fifteen, holding a knife already tainted with blood. His emotions mirrored the victim's—terror, shame, and remorse reflecting into infinity as boy and man stared helplessly into each other's eyes.

I watched from the shadows, shaking my head. The man should have known better than to cut through this part of town.

"Again," said the second attacker, the only person

enjoying the moment. He shook the man locked in his grasp and smiled, his dark aura so putrid, I struggled to separate it from the garbage smell of the alley. "Again."

"Please," the man begged. "I have a family." Images of a woman and baby girl—his wife and daughter perhaps—surfaced in the heat. His thoughts flickered around him like a silent film: A premature delivery, tubes, NICU, and machines ticking away heartbeats and breaths. Images of him holding the baby and carrying her on his chest, as well as improved test results. Hope broke through the grief before being swallowed again by despair and terror—not for his own death but for a wife he'd never be able to kiss again and a daughter he'd never be able to hold.

"Do it." Dark Aura jerked his arm against the victim's throat, and the man coughed.

The young man stabbed a second time. Pain shot through my abdomen, sharp and piercing, before I remembered to redirect the emotions flooding me. Feeling others' bodily sensations and emotions was a real bitch.

I cycled through the pain, breathing in and out in rhythm with the knife as the kid continued to stab and the man continued to scream for help. They were both crying now, and Dark Aura chuckled.

Anger stirred inside me, but I pushed it down. I couldn't chance an accidental reaping, even if this sadist did have "tear my soul from my body and splatter it across the universe" written all over him.

Walk away, Keres.

Before I could *blink*, the victim turned his face toward the opening of the alley, where I stood.

I froze, too stunned to shield myself from his sight. It was *his* face. "Abba?" The word came out a painful sigh—a man so long dead, his bones had been reclaimed by earth and time.

Dead because of me.

Walk away! I screamed inside my head. *This is* not *Abba!*

My feet refused to move.

"Please." This time, the boy begged, his words strangled sobs. "No more."

"You want family?" Dark Aura replied. "Us or him. Choose."

Tension built inside me, a heady cocktail of the young man's inner turmoil and my own as we both fought against the inevitable. The desire to *not* do what came next, knowing we would anyway.

Please, God, forgive me. I stepped forward.

Not-Abba's face twisted with concern. "Run!" he yelled. He tried to scream again but only coughed up blood as tears flowed down his paling cheeks. All eyes turned toward me.

Stalking forward, I gathered the darkness around me until my Shadow power thrummed against the Bloodlust—a precarious balance on a reaping night, when the monster hungered even while asleep. I flexed my power, and the shadows of the alley shifted around me, as if darkness emanated from my body. Unfurling the Shadow, I raised it above me like a pair of giant wings, thicker and darker than the night.

Only when the Bloodlust yawned did I pause. *Steady, Keres.*

As I opened my hand, smoky tendrils slithered across the ground toward the trio. They wound around Dark Aura and the young man, pulling their arms down to their sides. Not-Abba fell to the earth, his emotional flames waning as blood pooled beneath him.

I stepped toward the boy being forced to choose between two paths that both led to destruction. Fifteen, yet still so young. I understood him. I hurt for him. I'd made that choice; it didn't have a happy ending . . . or any ending at all.

Dark Aura grunted in protest, but the tendrils held him still while darkness filled his mouth. I positioned myself between him and the boy and placed one hand on the teen's shoulder. With the other, I gently took away the slick knife.

"This is not you," I whispered, planting images and impressions in his mind—small seeds that would grow into new choices. "This *cannot* be you. If you choose this path, I will rip your soul from your throat and reap it into nothingness before your corpse hits the ground." Fear rippled through him. "Run. Never look back. Find another city, another place, another start. Run. Because if I find you, you will die." I released him from the Shadow. "Go."

He fled as though death chased him.

I turned back to the man still held in my power. Violence leaked from him, his mind all warp and shadow. *Seeding* him wouldn't work. I was glad; he didn't deserve a second chance.

Smiling, I released Dark Aura from the tendrils. He screamed and lunged over Not-Abba, who raised his arm. Dark Aura stumbled into the dirt.

I watched, amused, but didn't move. "This is your one chance. Walk away."

Rage shot from him in spikes. He drew a switchblade and lunged at me a second time. Rather than dodge, I grabbed his wrist with my free hand, twisted his arm back with a crack, and sunk his own blade into his side. The man howled as I pulled him into me by his broken arm.

"Thank you," I purred. "I couldn't have done this without you." I slit his throat and let him fall.

Dropping the boy's knife on top of Dark Aura, I

stepped over his body and crouched by the man with Abba's face. I had to force myself not to stare too long or trace its lines with my fingertips. The differences were subtle, but they existed.

Not-Abba kept his gaze away from mine. I reached out to push his hair back from his forehead, and he jerked away, inhaling sharply in pain. His emotions were a mess: gratitude and hope warred with disgust and fear.

I glanced at the body behind me. "Don't worry. I don't know how I should feel either."

As I turned back, his eyes met mine and widened.

"I won't hurt you, friend. I promise." I *seeded* his mind with calmness, and he began to relax.

"You're so young." He coughed. "Barely older than him." He nodded in the direction of the young man's escape. "And so . . . sad."

I averted my gaze. Every human saw me however they wanted: young or old, innocent doe or evil jezebel. Their assumptions said more about them than me. Still, his reflection of sadness made me uncomfortable.

"I'm going to pick you up, so please don't fight me. It'll only hurt you more."

He nodded. As I gently lifted him from the ground, he cried out in pain.

"One more step, friend. Just one more. This isn't going to feel good."

He leaned his head against me, and I *blinked* us to Johns Hopkins. To an onlooker, the *blink* would appear as an instant disappearance and reappearance. But to me and the frail mortal I held, we were a needle pushing through the fabrics of time and reality. The pressure forced a cry from the injured man before he passed out.

I wished I'd had another choice, but waiting for an ambulance would have meant his death.

That isn't your concern, I reminded myself. I didn't save lives; I took them. I glanced again at the man in my arms. *Too late now.*

A cry of pain signaled his return to consciousness.

"You passed out for a moment. Normal."

"Where am I?" he asked.

"Hopkins. You're going to be okay."

"You don't know that."

"Actually, I do."

"Are you a . . . doctor?" I could tell it wasn't what he wanted to ask.

"There aren't healers among my kind."

"What are you?"

"Shh. Sleep now."

I passed him off to the EMTs outside the emergency room, *seeding* their thoughts with memories of a random cabbie, rather than a dark-haired woman in a dark, shimmering halter top, black skinny pants, and ballet flats.

Not-Abba fought sleep, slurring "What are you?" even as an oxygen mask was placed over his mouth. As the EMTs wheeled him through the sliding doors, he tried to sit up, but they forced him back down. He mumbled the question one last time before passing out.

"Death," I whispered once they were out of sight. Not-Abba would live, though it felt like I'd saved him over a thousand years too late. I walked away from the bright lights of the emergency entrance.

‹Keres.›

It only took the one word whispered into my mind—its tone promising retribution—for me to realize the crushing impact of what I'd done.

Oh shit.

Not-Abba's salvation would be my undoing. Steeling myself, I *blinked* to my waiting Xiiphronai.

TWO

Anxiety coated my tongue like vinegar. My Xiiphronai stood on the ledge of a commercial rooftop, looking out over the city in silence. The inky black ribbon of her ponytail whipped behind her, and her embroidered duster twisted around her thigh-high boots, silk rustling against leather. As always, she looked ready for a fashion photo shoot, but her appearance of lightweight femininity belied her true strength and power.

"Raven," I acknowledged cautiously.

She ignored me. Her straight back and tight shoulders screamed rage. As her sickle danced against her hip, I held my breath and listened beyond the *clink-clink-clink* for its distinct hum, which resonated within me, just as the hum of my khukuri would resonate within her. Every Angel of Death—or Aod, as we called ourselves—had a reaping blade, as unique a weapon as the angel who carried it. Though I'd crossed paths with other Aods, Raven's song was the only one I *knew*. After all, other than the Xiiphronai—the Aod ruling class—Aods were forbidden from interacting with each other.

Which left me only her.

"Raven." I stepped toward her, close enough I could have pushed her off the edge.

Part of me wanted to. I hated that she had the right to punish me and hated even more that I'd given her that right by bending the rules so far, they had almost broken.

Another part of me wanted to bury my face in her duster and cry like I had in the days following my transformation—when nothing had made sense and only her strength and assurance had kept me sane. We were ageless, indistinguishable as older or younger, but she was my mentor and the closest thing I had to a friend.

Right then, I needed a friend. I reached for her, my fingers brushing the silk of her coat. "Raven—"

She whipped around and backhanded me. Before I could recover, her knee slammed into my chest. As we fell, I saw everything in heartbeats: my body falling backward, her knee chasing me, her arms up and back from the knee thrust, her coat flying behind her like wings, and her warm-ivory skin caressed by moonlight. Magnificent.

We crunched into the rooftop and slid a few feet into an old AC unit. Pulling my head back by my hair, she drew my weapon from the scabbard on my back and pressed it to my throat. I lifted my chin, matching her rage with defiance, even as I chastised myself in my thoughts.

Stupid girl.

"Intervene again, Keres, and I will kill you myself. Not even the Guardians will be able to find the pieces."

Turmoil whirled from her like a tornado, each feeling so entangled with the next, I couldn't get a solid impression. Would she *really* kill me? Over a millennium together, yet I still couldn't be sure of anything when it came to Raven. Being an Aod was complicated, and tonight's impulsivity had only made it worse for both of us.

As the pressure of the blade increased, I kept my gaze locked on hers, willing my heartbeat to slow and my stomach to relax. We stared at each other for a seeming eternity, the rest of the world falling away. Finally, she screamed in frustration, drove the knife into the rooftop next to my head, and *blinked* back to her original perch on the ledge.

I rolled to my knees and stood, pulling my khukuri from where she'd left it. Turning it over in my hands, I traced the ancient markings, which flickered between plain charcoal and brilliant blue. The runes always glowed bright and constant right before a reaping, so she must have been conflicted tonight, equally committed to obliterating my soul and to saving it. Tomorrow, who knew? Guarantees only existed in yesterday.

The runes dulled beneath my touch. I slammed the weapon into its scabbard, double-checking the enchantments that encouraged human eyes to overlook it. Rolling my bare shoulders, which had already healed from our scuffle, I dusted roof debris from my clothing. In seconds, I looked ready for the hottest night clubs this city had to offer.

"Tell me why I called you here, Keres."

My shoulders tightened. I despised this game of hers. She never explained what I did wrong, not even in the beginning. Instead, she allowed me to act and then corrected me with pain and questions.

With anger burning through my caution, I *blinked* to the opposite corner of the roof and crouched, another gargoyle staring down on the city. It didn't matter how much distance I placed between us, though; I would hear Raven's whisper on the other side of the world if she wanted me to. Her power and abilities surpassed my skill and understanding. Her fierceness devoured my own.

"Keres!"

"You know why."

"Remind me."

I sighed. I knew exactly when and where I'd crossed the line, and I knew what Raven would do if I didn't tell her. Most of the time, it was repeated slaps to the face, stinging and humiliating, until I could answer the why to her satisfaction. But when my actions put her under the scrutiny of the Guardians—as tonight's transgressions no doubt would—she would dish out more pain: A knife here, a pressure point there. Piercing, crushing, twisting with the same agonizing intensity she claimed my failures caused her.

I love you, Keres, she'd said after the one and only time I tried to hide from a reaping. I wished she had told me it was impossible. Aods couldn't stop it or hide from it. Instead, she'd let me try and then punished me later. I'd already killed the mark, but that didn't seem to matter.

This hurts me, she'd explained. *Your failures hurt me. I want to see you realize your full potential. I am your mother now, a mother who wants the best for her daughter. I do this for you, to help you learn. This pain is nothing compared to what the Guardians will do if you fail your tasks.* She had even cried as she pushed the dagger farther into my side as I hung like a pig for slaughter.

I had learned quickly that immortals could endure a lot of pain.

I glanced across the roof at Raven, who stared right back at me, her eyes tight with anger. She wouldn't ask again.

"The Guardians don't like it when I play God."

"*Intervening* is forbidden. You shame me."

I dropped my gaze. "I gave him the chance to walk away. *He* attacked *me.*" Direct interference in mortal affairs without higher sanction was prohibited, but even Aods were allowed the courtesy of self-defense. I didn't say anything about the two men I had saved.

"A technicality and the only reason you're still alive."

"The Guardians are just pissed they weren't pulling the strings." The words tumbled from my mouth before I could think to stop them. Evil was evil, wasn't it? Why were the Guardians the only ones who could decide which evil to eradicate? I crouched lower on the ledge, muscles tight and ready to move if Raven decided to attack again.

Instead, she laughed, a chuckle that grew into a raucous cackle. "Yes, the bastards." She laughed so hard, even I cracked a shy smile.

Wiping away invisible tears, she *blinked* to my side and wrapped an arm around me, pulling me down to sit next to her. She leaned her head against my shoulder. "I needed that."

"So, I'm not in trouble?"

"Not this time."

We returned to gazing out across the city, seeing everything and nothing.

"Why'd you do it?" Raven asked.

I turned to study her flawless face. How much did she tell the Guardians? How much was ours? "Does it matter?"

"It does to me." Her soft voice held me as firmly as her gaze.

I hated Raven. Hated how she hurt me and made me need her. Hated how her gentleness had me spilling secrets I never wanted to share in hopes that maybe I could make her proud. Mostly, I hated that despite everything, I couldn't stop loving her—the woman who rocked me when I couldn't sleep, protected me from overzealous Guardians, and showed me how to live with so much pain.

Why, God? Why was it set up to be like this?

"What am I to you, Raven? You call me daughter, but . . ." I left the rest to choke in silence.

"You are dirt," she replied, almost to herself. "Because if you are more than dirt—"

"Then you can't do your job." One of the first lessons she'd forced on me. Not a rule of the Guardians but a truth every Aod lived by: Everyone was dirt. Everyone was meaningless. Everyone was expendable for the greater good of whatever the hell we fought for—even other Aods.

I sighed. "I know I should have left, but I couldn't." I closed my eyes and leaned into the warmth of her body as I pictured Not-Abba, his emotions so intense, they moved like flames across his skin.

I should have let him burn, only . . .

I looked into Raven's eyes, willing her to understand. "He had my father's face."

I'd lived more lifetimes than a hundred people, yet my *abba*'s face and his unwavering love continued to haunt me. It was my worst memory, even more than the violence. It reminded me of all I'd lost because I'd been too weak to save him. To save any of them.

I hadn't been able to leave my father again, not even his copy. Look where that had gotten us the first time: both of us dead in our own ways. The desire to jump from the roof tugged at me, though I knew it wouldn't do any good. Nothing but God's hand could free me from the Contract that gave me my immortality and power.

"Don't you ever get tired of this?" I asked.

"How could anything be more rewarding?"

"But the rules? The nightmares? What we *do*, Raven? It's horrible."

"You know the answer." Her soft voice pushed gently against my pain.

"But your answer doesn't help me."

"It's the only one you have."

Acceptance—Raven's miracle cure. It promised to ease the conscience and increase one's power. All I had to do was accept my role in God's war and that destroying the wicked, regardless of the method, was his will.

I tried. Every day, I tried. Raven knew. God had to know. Each filthy memory I acquired reminded me of the importance of my work: I killed for those who couldn't defend themselves—became their sword and justice! The violence was sanctioned and justified.

Yet my soul kept aching, ground down with each reaping, until I couldn't ignore the question any longer.

"Why does doing God's will hurt so badly?"

Raven wrapped her other arm around me and pulled me into her the way my *immah* used to. Her ability to consistently duplicate my mother's actions both unsettled and comforted me.

I've been alone for so long.

"Perhaps it's punishment for letting your family die."

Her words pierced my heart. She had to be right. What more proof did I need? I had brought death to my people, and even as I begged God for mercy, I knew I deserved this fate.

I pulled my knees to my chest and buried my head in my legs. I wouldn't cry. Ever. But I needed someone— anyone—to tell me it was going to be okay.

"*My* Keres." I melted beneath the possessiveness of her voice. I really was hers. "You are the most special dirt on the planet to me."

I grasped her arms, pulling her tighter to me. "I *am* trying, Raven."

She gently stroked my hair. "I know, but sometimes your best isn't good enough."

My soul shrank in shame, and silence stretched between us. Horns blared in the distance, our blades hummed a soft harmony, but I had no words of defense. Anything less than perfect, *willing* obedience was failure in Raven's eyes, and I would never be good enough until my obedience was absolute, regardless of how many souls I reaped. My brokenness cut like shattered glass, and I glanced again at the pavement far below.

"Spilt water can't be gathered," she finally said. Letting go of me, she leaned over the edge, searching for something far off. The wind whipped and tugged at anything it could. "Stop failing. Start succeeding. Prove yourself worthy of the blade you carry."

"Through tonight's reaping?"

"No, you have turned reaping into an art."

My throat tightened. Killing should never have been an art.

"No more whining about the sacrifices you think you make. This life is a gift. Accept it. *Appreciate* it. This job carries with it great rewards, but our submission to our calling must be absolute. We give *everything* we have and *everything* we are."

Questioning meant I hadn't given everything.

"Remember, daughter. Every moment in your life gives you an opportunity to impress or disappoint. I hope you choose to impress me. I will not be able to intercede the next time you fail."

Intercede, my ass. I looked away before Raven could see the fire in my eyes. She was quick to punish and slow to forgive.

Once I'd suppressed the spark of defiance, I turned back to Raven. "I can take care of myself."

Raven sneered. "Then it won't bother you to know that Luke has been assigned to watch you tonight."

"What?" I *blinked* to my feet.

"I thought you'd want to know."

"But he's banned from protecting me!"

She eased herself to her feet and stretched her body with feline grace, a smile playing at the corner of her mouth. "You broke the rules. Be grateful this is your only consequence."

"I can't, Raven. You know I can't." I shook at the memory of his touch and paced to quiet the tremors.

"You should have thought of that before you helped your friend."

"Damn it!" I dragged a hand through my choppy hair.

Raven stepped in front of me and grabbed my shoulders. "Remember, Keres, *yī lì lǎo shǔ shǐ huài le yī guō zhōu* . . . one mouse dropping ruins the whole pot of rice porridge."

"What is that supposed to mean?" I snapped.

"Some family members are malignant and should be removed. Don't be one of them."

"So helpful. Thanks."

Rage exploded from her, and she slapped me. "Don't make me decide you're not worth keeping."

She waited, fingernails digging into my shoulder.

Finally, I bowed my head. "Yes, Raven."

"Good." She released me and stepped back, making a show of straightening her flawless clothing. "Watch your back tonight." She patted my cheek and *blinked* away to other responsibilities. For the first time in centuries, I wished she didn't have to go.

The wind tugged at my hair and loose halter top, as if pulling me toward my fate, my future, and the next reaping. I stared down at the endless stream of cars and people. They had no idea.

I took a deep breath and stepped from the ledge.

THREE

The Warehouse District—where the nightlife pulsed like a beating heart and the bass of the music bleeding from doorways lured restless bodies into crowded rooms. I, of all people, should have been immune to the seduction of the rhythm or at least been able to resist it, but I wasn't and I couldn't. It pulled me through the crowds and into Club Oubliette, where flashing lights echoed the call of the bass.

My body pounded in time with the music as each beat thrummed inside me—sensual, seductive, *primal.* The perfect outlet for my anger. I rolled my hips seductively—an invitation quickly answered by more than one person. I leaned back into the woman behind me, letting her hands drift over my body in a close-but-not-quite exploration that had me tipping my head back with desire.

Her hot breath coated my neck as invisible tendrils of her lust climbed the inside of my thighs. I spread my legs, letting the man in front of me move close enough for his muscled thigh to answer the throb building between mine. Their desire reached for me, stroked me from the inside out in ways their hands never could, and for a moment, I forgot who and what I was. I became another me, a more powerful me—if that were even possible—brokering power with every thrust and touch not because I was death but because I was a woman and they wanted me.

Damn, it felt good.

Focusing on Muscled Thighs, whose gaze and groin were heavy with want, I searched for some connection beyond our bodies.

Nothing.

His body moved with mine, but the rest of him remained walled off. Same with the woman behind me.

My elation gave way to repulsion.

Humans might be the lifeblood of these clubs, their touching, bouncing, and rubbing culminating in a single explosion of ecstasy, but most of them were dead to their human experience. Zombies artificially reanimated by the thump of the bass and driven to quench their most basic thirsts for sex and beer.

They felt with their bodies, not with their souls.

If they only knew how quickly they could lose both.

I breathed in sex one last time and released the fantasy. Muscled Thighs and Ms. Wandering Hands didn't want *me*, the complex girl with emotional needs; they wanted me, the gyrating body with all the curves. I wouldn't be someone else's plaything ever again. An object didn't have power, no matter how you dressed it. Besides, I hadn't come for a one-night stand.

I let desire drain from my body, until the only lust I felt was for blood, and continued to grind between the pair as I searched the crowd for one very specific person. Guardian intel indicated he'd be near this club tonight, and the growing connection I felt with him told me they were right.

Sergio Ricci—a seemingly average guy participating in a seemingly average social ritual. Yet he was anything but average. Sergio stalked this world as a pedophile-sicko, preying on the helpless to quench his thirst for lust and greed.

I had the nightmares to prove it.

I hated my job, with its graphic backstories and violent endings. Things no decent person should have to know. Things no angelic creature should ever have to *do*. Even more, I hated the Bloodlust that fed on both. Its craving for violence and death only intensified the longer I lived. The Guardians—a sect of angels assigned to protect us from the devil, and humanity from us—said it was contained, only accessible *during* a reaping. But I didn't believe them. I'd had too many close calls of the Bloodlust waking *before* a reaping, and what that might mean terrified me.

One of three secrets I'd been able to keep from Raven.

Picturing how my earlier hunger to destroy Dark Aura had stirred the monster inside me, I shuddered. I *had* to be more careful.

The Bloodlust's hunger for my mark tugged me toward a back hallway, and I left the dance floor, forcing my way through the pressing mass of people. Muscled Thighs and Ms. Wandering Hands didn't even realize I'd left as other bodies poured in to fill my vacancy. One well-developed, tightly clothed form was as good as the next. Did that bother me?

Fuck. Why do I even care? They are dirt. They are dirt. They are dirt!

The louder I shouted the words inside my head, the tighter my teeth clenched, until I wanted to scream. I hated them. Hated these humans because I couldn't *be* them. I wanted the mundaneness of their lives: grocery shopping, nine-to-five jobs, drinks with friends, weekend phone calls with parents, and the luxury to ignore it all.

Dear God, I want to be human again! Can't I have a do-over? A chance to make a different choice back then? Or to choose differently now?

I waited. Nope. No response.

There never was.

Unwanted hurt trailed behind me as I made my way to the back hallway, my internal temperature warming with each step. My mark was close.

The crush of people thinned, giving me space to breathe. Some waited for bathrooms; others chatted. A few couples were pressed against the walls, not even trying to disguise their groping. I found an empty piece of wall and leaned my back and head against it, eyes closed. The sandpaper texture of the brick soothed my anger as I ran my fingers back and forth across it.

A man leaned over me, his lust pressing against me as tangibly as his hot, beer-soaked breath. I ignored him, thinking he would walk away, but the cocktail of too much alcohol and an abundance of testosterone seemed to produce excessive amounts of stupidity.

"Hey, angel, did it hurt when you fell from heaven?"

A drunk trying to pick up an Angel of Death with an angel joke? *Really?* I should have laughed, but something about falling from heaven hit too close to home.

My eyes shot open, and I stared into his clouded gaze. I didn't say a word; I didn't have to. My job had at least one perk: "look of death" took on a whole-new meaning. He paled, spun, and retreated up the hall to the little boys' room, where he almost knocked over a frat boy with tousled blond hair and shamrock-colored eyes.

Now *that* was funny.

A smile played at the corners of Frat Boy's mouth as he pushed himself away from the wall and looked at me. His eyes danced with mischief, and he winked, as if we'd shared some inside joke. For a moment, I thought he might pick up where the other guy had left off, but he gave me a slight nod and headed back toward the crowded dance floor.

I couldn't help but sneak a quick glance at his disappearing form. He looked over his shoulder in that same moment, and his lips widened into a full-blown smile—broad enough to reveal dimples. I almost returned the favor. Almost.

The crowd swallowed him and the moment, leaving me feeling . . . something. I couldn't grasp the emotion. It felt cold, as though I'd stood near a fire and then walked away. I shivered and forced Frat Boy out of my head.

I eased my way toward the emptiness at the far end of the hallway so I wouldn't have to deal with the advances of any more drunken gorillas or beautiful men. As I reached the last cluster of humans before the exit, my creep-meter shot past warm and straight into boiling lava.

I'd found him.

He stood off to the side of the black double door that led out back, talking with an overly sweaty man. They finished what looked to be a tense conversation, and the sweaty guy nodded and left, shoving past me on his way to the main room. Guilt wafted from Sweaty like bitter cigarette smoke, a smell he'd never be able to scrub off his soul, and I resisted the urge to hurt him. Raven wouldn't accept any more mistakes.

The man I came to reap now chatted on his cell phone. Normal guy, normal cell phone, normal conversation. Most people wouldn't look twice.

I closed my eyes as the details of his life exploded in

my mind: memories of children molested, then sold and molested again. For those brief moments, I saw it, felt it, lived it. It was the same for every reaping. Broken fragments of memory and sin downloaded into my brain the moment of "scheduling," to be absorbed and relived over and over again until only God knew when. Each nightmare a scathing indictment of my inability to protect the victims. I was their justice, not their savior.

I fought to hold back the Bloodlust's insatiable hunger. It hurt to contain, but once it was released, I'd have no control—no way to choose who lived or who died. They all would.

I had to get him alone *now*.

"Yes, tomorrow," he said. "Just finished with your guy. Package is ready. Wait, what? What? Hold on." He shuffled a few paces in various directions before giving up and exiting into the narrow street behind the club.

I paused for a moment, then followed.

As I shoved through the back door of Club Oubliette, I saw him enter a warehouse on the opposite side of the alley. A quick glance assured me I was alone, but I drew the Shadow around me anyway. I felt safer in the dark. Easing my way across the century-old cobblestone, I grasped the handle of the door my mark had used and turned it.

Locked.

"You planning on doing this one without me, *cher*?"

I turned toward the syrupy voice with its heavy New Orleans accent. Luke leaned against a previously empty wall, his arms crossed and head tilted down just enough for his longish bangs to shield his deep-turquoise eyes. I'd spent too many years adrift in the ocean of that gaze. Their seemingly tranquil depths belied his sadism.

From his $300 T-shirt to his tailored jeans, his clothes

hugged his muscled body to perfection, leaving no doubts as to the power of his physique. I shuddered at the memory of his stamina, and I had to stop my fingers from reaching for the tattoos that swirled beneath his shirt, over his chest and down his arm.

"What of it?" I demanded.

In reality, I'd been so intent on the mark, I hadn't thought about it. The Guardians assigned to me had been random and constantly changing since my stint with Luke. They would show up right before the reaping and *blink* away again once I'd finished. They were only there long enough to ensure I didn't get out and others didn't get in.

I had hoped he would do the same.

But I sure as hell wasn't going to admit that to Luke. The embers of a dying romance still smoldered behind the door I'd shut on him centuries ago, and I didn't trust anything, especially myself, when he was around. He was a thick New England fog that changed the autumn landscape and made me question everything I thought I knew: Breathtaking. Mysterious. Dangerous.

He stepped toward me, and my heart raced from the electricity carried on the air between us. I tried to force it to beat a steady rhythm, but it ignored me.

Traitor.

Luke's desire washed over me in tender, soft caresses, inviting me to come to him. A touch here, a brush there, as if his hands were already moving over my skin. He approached me, slow and careful, and didn't stop until we were breathing the same air.

My chest and throat tightened, forcing me to take shallow breaths as tingles raced up my skin and through my most intimate parts. Two desires warred within me: to turn off the emotion he stirred or to ride it to ecstasy.

This. This is what I'd been missing all these years.

My mouth parted to invite him closer, and my head tilted back ever so slightly.

Stop it! I forced my mouth closed, teeth grinding against each other. His effect frightened me.

And he knew it.

"Enough, Luke." I meant to sound strong, in control, but the words came out as a whisper.

"*Cher*, you know you're supposed to wait." His voice was velvet. He traced the edge of my ear with his fingers as his gaze devoured me, ending with a gentle tug on my earlobe. Shivers rippled across the skin his fingertips brushed. Shivers that reminded me of the pleasure and touches I had begged for.

I wanted to retreat, to run away from him and the confusion he caused, but I refused to back down from Luke, just as I refused to give into my hunger for him.

I'd given into that desire before. Huge mistake.

I batted away his hand and put on my most disdainful expression. "What I *know* is that I'm here to do a job, and an overdue Guardian is the least of my worries."

He smiled and leaned against the door. "Really?"

"I don't need you."

His countenance darkened and his eyes became roiling storm clouds, as his emotions crashed into me in wave after wave of lust, hunger, and raw power. My body began to give way beneath the assault. When he finally grabbed my arms and pulled me into him, I expected his embrace to be as fierce and crushing as his passion, but he denied me. Instead, he held me tenderly and brushed his lips against mine—teasing caresses that fueled my desire instead of extinguishing the flame. I could barely breathe.

Intoxicating.

"Fascinating," he whispered. "When did you become so powerful, you don't need a Guardian?"

His smirk doused my desire. Gathering all my anger, hurt, and fear, I pushed them toward him like a shield. Surprise flashed in his eyes, and he let go of me, taking the smallest step back. My chest rose and fell in deep breaths as I fought to regain control of myself.

Then he laughed. Deep. Throaty. *Annoying.* "You do need me, *cher.* Admit it."

"I can handle this wack job."

"You could handle an army of him. That's not the problem."

"I know. That would be you."

He shrugged. "I could leave. But who would protect the rest of the city if you decided to go for a walk while under the influence?" I remained silent because he was right, and he pushed his advantage. "Who would protect you from the other things that go bump in the night?"

"Please, like you care enough to protect me."

He grimaced. "Enough, Keres. I've played your games—"

"My games? *My* games?"

"Yes, *your* games. I loved you. Pleasured you. Showed you what *this* life could be. And you cried rape and demanded I be banned from your presence."

"I never used that word, you bastard. I was a child, and you took advantage of me. You deserved to be reassigned."

"Over a thousand years old, Keres. You can hardly call yourself a child."

"Damn it, Luke! What is a thousand compared to your tens of thousands? Yes, I easily call myself a child. *You* should have known better."

"And there's the truth. Always pushing the responsibility of your choices onto others, Keres. That is your real problem!"

"Bull—"

"God's fault you suffer, Gabriel's for giving you the choice to live or die, Raven's for not warning you sooner, mine for loving you when you weren't ready to be loved. Need more proof, *cher*?"

"To hell with you, Luke." I used my Shadow power to pop the lock on the warehouse door and opened it to find a long, dark hallway. A slit of light spilled across the floor about halfway down the corridor, and Sergio's muffled voice drifted from behind the closed door.

"Daemons," Luke said.

"What?"

"Daemons, Keres. They're why I'm here."

I let the door close and stared at its chipped paint. Daemons—Satan's band of assassins, tasked with destroying every one of God's angels, including the Guardians.

Including me.

Fear—thick and greasy—clung to my gut. The rest of me was ice. Luke may not have been able to read emotions like I could, but he couldn't miss my tightened shoulders and lack of breathing. I didn't even bother trying to hide them.

"Your little stunt tonight caught their attention, *cher*."

"How?" I glanced at him and immediately wished I hadn't. His usual swagger struggled against worry.

Nothing got to Luke. Ever.

He frowned. "Does it matter? They have you in their sights."

"Yet you came alone?" No need to ask about rescheduling the reaping. Once it was set in motion, there was no turning back.

"Why risk more than one Guardian for a broken Aod? Surely you don't think your life worth the risk of starting a battle we're not ready for?"

I remained silent, knowing he'd won.

"Face it, *cher.* I'm your best chance of surviving."

If the Daemons hunted me, I did need Luke. He held more power than any other Guardian I'd met, and everyone deferred to him, including Raven—mostly. I didn't know much about the inner workings of the group designed to monitor and protect us, but I couldn't fathom Luke anywhere but among the elite.

"Let's hope for a quick in and out before they get a chance to show up."

"Damn it," I whispered.

Grabbing my chin, he tilted my face up. "Silly girl, you brought this on yourself."

I yanked my chin from his grasp but said nothing, keeping my gaze fixed on a patch of wall. I *had* brought all this on myself—the day I accepted the Contract.

"Was he worth it?" Luke asked. "The man you saved. A new lover, perhaps? A friend?" His tone twisted on the last word. He knew better. Aods didn't have friends, only painful memories. Our lives were ones of solitude.

"He doesn't matter."

"Nothing you do really matters, but I'll let you answer anyway."

"You serve me, Luke, not the other way around."

The street darkened as his Shadow power churned and boiled around him. He gripped my arms again, this time pouring power through his hands. I clenched my teeth against the pain as melted flesh sloughed off, making way for new pieces to grow. At least he wasn't aiming the power at my soul; *that* was a punishment one never got used to.

I really am a silly girl.

"I serve one being, Keres. Only *one!*" His voice

dripped malice, his New Orleans accent gone. A millennium of walking the planet as an Angel of Death, and Luke could still make me feel like the girl I had been before I accepted the Contract—powerless and pitiful.

"Okay, Luke. Okay."

He held my gaze for a moment longer and then let go, returning to his smiles and Cajun inflections. Nothing but the smell of burned flesh indicated he'd hurt me at all.

"Then answer me. Was he worth it?"

"Yes. He was worth it."

I dropped my eyes to the cobblestone, too ashamed to look Luke in the face. I'd intervened and somehow alerted the Daemons to my presence. Now, Luke had returned to protect my sorry ass, all because of the stupid human sentimentality I had thought I'd shed centuries ago. What was worse, I would have done it again in a heartbeat. If that wasn't pathetic, I didn't know what was.

Luke sneered. "I hope you can say that after tonight." He grasped my hand and nodded toward the door.

I didn't move.

"Luke." I still couldn't look at him, not while I begged. "Please, help me stay in control during the reaping." Maybe if he helped, it wouldn't be so bad this time. I hated Luke, but I needed him, and I hated that even more.

"You are not a mindless weapon, Keres. I protect you; I don't control you. Whatever happens is of your own making."

Even with a Guardian at my side, I stood alone.

Luke's hand squeezed mine. "*Cher*, I can promise that no one else will hurt you." His words echoed a time when my body tangled with his, sharing his breath and his life. He promised me the same back then: safety for as long as I stayed wrapped in those arms.

A very small part of me wished I had listened.

I squeezed his hand in return. "Thank you, Luke." Bracing myself for the inevitable, I opened the door, and we stepped into the darkened hallway.

Pain exploded within the back of my skull—and with it, an instant burst of euphoria.

The Bloodlust.

Before we could make it to the room that held Sergio, everything went black.

FOUR

Open . . . close . . . open . . . close . . .

My vision cycled slowly between darkness and a dim light that revealed a room turned on its side. I tried not to focus on any one thing, preferring hazy shapes to sharp images, but the violence and death were inescapable. No matter how hard I wished, three clicks of my heels would *not* send me home.

They wouldn't even get me to the other side of the door, where I knew Luke waited for me in the hallway. That's where Guardians always waited: outside. They protected; they didn't get their hands dirty. That was my job.

And I've turned reaping into an art.

I clenched my fists, fingernails digging into my palms, as I inhaled slowly. I held the breath for a moment and then exhaled, pushing both the air and tension from my body. I stretched my fingers as wide as they would go and repeated the exercise. Staying calm was mandatory for my sanity. Breathing was mandatory for staying calm.

I peeled myself from the floor, instantly grieving the loss of the cold concrete against my cheek, and surveyed my surroundings. Any normal person would've been shocked. I was definitely not normal, but even this had me gagging.

It. Was. Everywhere.

Carnage—that's how they'd write it in the paper tomorrow because that's what they always wrote. Only this time, the media wouldn't need fancy wording to make a sale. It was the worst I'd ever seen—that I'd ever done.

Why was the reaping always so violent? And why the hell was it getting worse over time? I didn't even want to know what I'd be capable of in another century or two.

Four mutilated corpses littered the room. One belonged to my mark, and the remaining three were piles of collateral damage. Though could a soul really be considered collateral—a meaningless "oops," as if I'd accidentally broken a few windows instead of slaughtering unintended souls? No matter what Raven wanted from me, I couldn't accept that. The families would bury these bodies with prayers and hope, but there were no souls left to ascend to God or send to Hell. My blade had made sure of it.

Maybe these guys had deserved it, maybe not, but "wrong place, wrong time" didn't seem to justify obliterating their souls. It definitely didn't excuse the children I'd killed along the way.

My chest tightened, and I rubbed my sternum until the tension went away.

Of the three collateral bodies, one had been sliced vertically from sternum to belly button with the precision of a medical examiner beginning an autopsy. The other two had been ripped horizontally across the abdomen, their entrails spilling to the floor. At least the heads were still attached—mostly. They all seemed to be turned toward me, dead eyes filled with judgment and blame.

I *hated* this.

Sure, reapings had always been bloody. A mess was unavoidable when the only way to access a soul was through the throat. But any other slice? Excessive and unnecessary. I could eviscerate a human all day long, but that wouldn't let me grab the soul and pull it out for reaping. According to Raven, the body protected the soul until the human died, and at death, the soul would dissipate before we could do our job. We needed our humans alive and wriggling when we yanked their souls from their bodies and reaped them into nothingness.

My body shook, and disgust bubbled inside me as I fought to remain indifferent. How could *this* be of God?

Detachment will help, I promised myself. But I didn't believe it.

Four men massacred without any evidence of a struggle or self-defense. The papers would eat this up. A crime scene with more questions than answers always drove reporters into a frenzy, like sharks devouring scraps in recently chummed water. Simple murder was too dull for them nowadays. Events that would have rocked a community for weeks, months or even years were now announced with a shrug by Phyllis at Five: *"Violent crime in Baltimore has increased dramatically during the recent September heat wave, leaving fifteen people slain in the last week. Homicide rates haven't been this high for more than a decade. When asked about their plans for combating the recent rise in crime, a spokesman for the Baltimore Police stated, 'We are arming the city with information.' Head to WNV5.com for details. Now back to you, Bob, for to-morrow's weather."*

Disgusting. *Fifteen* slain by human hands in a week: a security guard, a cableman, a woman walking her dog, a young man returning from work, an elderly woman in her home, a church volunteer, a handful of children and their teacher at school, a brother, sister, mother, uncle. All of them reduced to a statistic. None of them more interesting than tomorrow's weather.

And I'm *the monster?*

I only had to look around me to know the truth.

Isn't it better that one person die, Raven had asked when she caught me mourning my hundredth reaping, *than allowing them to destroy the lives of innocent people? Wouldn't it have been better if they had died before murdering your family?*

Yes, I'd told her. *Yes!*

But now . . .

My eyes stung, and I pressed a hand to my tightening chest as my shoulders curled forward. It wasn't supposed to be like this. I was justice! I fought for God. I did his will. Why did I have to carry the burden of doing what *he* wanted? Why did I feel . . . remorse? The tightening shifted to my stomach, and I fought to keep my body from crumpling beneath the strain.

Breathe, Keres. Breathe.

I forced all the emotion back, stuffing it into whatever internal closet I could find, until I felt hollow again. With my walls firmly in place, I turned my attention to the last body—the only one I didn't lament killing.

My target was unrecognizable, a mass of flesh and bone that could barely be labeled remains. It would definitely be a closed casket ceremony. Not that anyone would care, except maybe his close family who still liked to believe he was a "good dad."

I hated when people said that about men like Sergio, as if it made every ugly thing he'd ever done okay. I'm sure the children he bought and sold in the sex trade didn't care. He wasn't innocent; he was barely even human.

The widow can cry all she wants. I won't be listening.

I collapsed into the closest folding chair and hung my head. Cheap cigars still burned in the ashtray on the card table next to me, but even their sour smell couldn't hide the stench of death; the killing was too fresh.

This one would be added to my collection of nightmares that drowned me in violence and death until I thought I'd never wake.

I used to think that if I kept my eyes closed long enough, I could escape it, but it didn't matter. Whether or not I looked, my brain always recorded and cataloged the reaping, ready to replay the most gruesome parts in vivid detail whenever I slept and even, sometimes, while I was awake. Looking helped me separate reality from the disjointed replay of dreams and allowed me to believe the reaping was over.

I buried my head in my hands. Even now, I saw the panic on his face as he witnessed the murder of his associates. I saw the terror on theirs. I tasted the fear that trembled from his limbs as I whispered death into his ear. I felt the khukuri slice through his neck like a quick chop through a raw carrot. I heard the gurgle of blood and air as they escaped from his exposed arteries and trachea.

I couldn't stop the onslaught of images and sensations. I couldn't turn them off.

I leaped from my chair and screamed long and hard, angry at myself and everyone and no one at all. The sound was primitive, animalistic, painful.

Why, God? Why?

I was going insane, wasn't I? I couldn't quit, but maybe the madness of it all would explode my brain like leftovers cooked too long in a microwave.

Not likely, but one could hope.

I turned from the carnage. It was time to leave. I

needed clean air and a brisk walk. I needed to fill my senses with something other than death.

I paused at the door and looked back over my shoulder. How long could eternity really be?

Dear God, I can't take much more. I won't ask you to forgive me—I know it's impossible—but please . . . please release me.

Redemption and release—it seemed I was exempt from both.

Lucky me.

As ready as I could be to face Luke and another night of someone else's screams, I reached for the handle.

The door exploded inward, throwing me across the room, where I slammed into the wall and crumpled to the floor.

"Keres!" Luke screamed. "Run!"

FIVE

Shocked, I stared across the room, where Luke fought a hulking man and a redheaded woman. I couldn't imagine what Guardians would ever take Luke head on. I glanced at their arms, searching for the tattoos that would indicate their clan.

Their arms were bare.

Oh God, Daemons!

I *blinked.* What else could I do? An Aod only had two options when it came to Daemons: run away and fight to run away. Guardians could barely hold their own against a Daemon; an Angel of Death didn't stand a chance.

So I ran far and fast, not caring where I went. I *blinked* like I had been taught, jumping from one place to the next in successively longer *blinks,* in hopes the Daemons couldn't follow. It wasn't until frigid water splashed my face that realized I'd *blinked* myself thigh deep into an ocean.

I stopped.

Large waves rolled up the shore, slapping against my

legs. The rhythm of the current pushed and pulled at me as the sand gave way beneath my feet. My world followed.

Daemons had always been just monsters in fairy tales, stories told to frighten disobedient Aods, never a *real* part of my world. But now I couldn't pretend. The two terrifying, beautiful monsters Luke had held back as I *blinked* away were anything but a fairy tale . . . and he'd just sacrificed his life for mine.

I hated me.

It was happening again. The raiding party. The scream to run. Images of my parents overlaid the image of Luke, like two movies playing one atop the other. In both, I ran. Ran because I was too weak to save the people I loved. Ran because I was afraid.

"Why are you so weak?" I pounded the water with my fists and pushed at the waves trying to topple me. The ground dropped away, and I slipped with it, ending up chest deep in the water. Another wave broke over me, its current pushing and pulling me wherever *it* wanted me to go until I found my footing again.

"Enough!" I screamed into the empty night and pushed back against the roaring force. I pushed and screamed, as if holding back the ocean could somehow stop the inevitable. Luke would die, as my parents had. Then I would die. The Daemons would find me as surely as the raiding party had. All those deaths, in a vain hope of preserving my useless, weak life.

"You're so damn helpless!" I grabbed my hair and pulled. "You're a waste of space!"

Anger and hatred sliced through me like a sword. I grasped it, reforged it, and wielded it like a shield, pushing it out of me and slamming it against the ocean again and again, until I was too weak to stand. I flopped to the ground and dug my clawed fingers into cold, wet sand.

Sand. I grabbed a handful and studied it. A full minute passed before I realized I shouldn't have collapsed onto anything but more ocean.

I stood slowly and studied the wall of water building in front of me. A trickle of ocean sputtered through the invisible dam, and I walked toward it, holding my hand out to catch the salty drops. Cool liquid ran down my fingers, which I rubbed against my thumb as I tried to wrap my brain around what I was seeing.

"Oh. My. G—"

The dam burst, and a huge wave toppled me in its race to the shore, bouncing me along the bottom of the ocean before pummeling me into the beach. I coughed up liquid as I fought my way free of the wave, my mind racing with questions and possibilities.

Any angel could prevent water from soaking their clothes. Barrier shields—like a second skin—were effortless and almost automatic. But holding back the ocean? Impossible.

The salt water sloshing around in my lungs seemed to indicate otherwise.

A flame, tiny and frail, burned in my chest. *If only I could . . .*

I drew from the well of anger buried deep inside me and forced it against the coming wave, which broke in a giant spray of water as if it had hit a solid rock. Exhaling, I looked up toward the sky. If I could hold back the waves, perhaps I could hold back the Daemons long enough to save Luke. Maybe one more person wouldn't have to die for me.

All an Aod needed for a *blink* was intention and direction, and I intended to save Luke. It wasn't the greatest plan in the world, but it was the only one I had.

I *blinked* again.

When I reappeared in the warehouse, Luke was on the ground, his hands bound behind his back. The massive Daemon stood nearby, reciting gibberish, while the strawberry-haired Daemon watched the door. Snatching a small utility knife from my belt, I *blinked* to Luke's side and sliced the cords binding him. He threw his power at the redhead before she could fully turn around.

The oversized Daemon stopped his chanting and began drawing in light the way I drew in shadow, creating a halo effect around his already glowing skin. As he focused on Luke, I launched myself at him, and we crashed into the table, creating a storm of cigar ash, face cards, and broken furniture. I tried to press my advantage, but I slipped in blood as I tried to stand.

The bulky Daemon leaped on top of me as I faltered, pushing me to my knees. He twisted my knife-wielding arm behind my back with one hand and grasped my hair with the other.

"Who are you?" His voice was not gravelly and laced with Satan, as I'd expected, but deep and lulling, reminding me of floating on the Jordan River with my *bat doda*.

I tried to kick out his knee, but he dodged and forced me all the way to the floor.

"I won't ask again, Fallen. Who are you?"

The way he said *Fallen*, as if it were my name, filled me with an overwhelming sorrow. Turning inward, I grasped for the shield I'd used against the waves. The anger flowed, instant and powerful.

"Death," I spat and slammed my shield of emotion against him. He flew back, smashing into the wall a few feet away as I unsheathed my hidden khukuri. The markings on my blade shone a brilliant blue, and its hum drowned the sounds of the world. If I could reach him, he would die.

I lunged, *blinking* midstride, but he caught me as I reappeared. His massive hand swallowed my wrist, stopping the blade before I could do more than nick the side of his throat. The wound oozed a thick, iridescent liquid instead of red blood, but it was little more than a paper cut, too small to pull a soul through. I'd missed my chance.

The Daemon pulled me up onto my toes as he examined the blade more closely, twisting my arm this way and that to see it from all angles. He touched a finger to his throat. When it came away coated in the clear liquid, his eyes widened, and he spat what sounded like a curse.

His distraction became my opening. With my free hand, I jammed the utility knife in between his collarbone and neck. It might not be able to kill him, but I hoped he would at least drop me.

Instead, the huge Daemon ignored the small blade, looking from the khukuri to me and back again. He shouted several words to Red in a language I didn't understand, and she grunted. Behind him, the room rippled and shimmered, like a heat haze in the desert, intensifying until it became a wall of liquid light.

"No peril in the fight," he called out.

"No glory in the triumph," Red replied.

He turned and stepped into the wall, still clutching my hand as if it were a poisonous snake. It didn't matter how much I kicked and pulled, nothing I did forced him to release me. When everything but the hand holding my wrist had disappeared, I tried to *blink* and failed. Our connection tethered us together and, because of him, to someplace beyond my reach. I cringed as my hand crept closer to the light, turning away as it touched my skin.

I screamed.

A thousand paper cuts tore at my flesh, and unseen

fibers of energy sliced through my soul. Was this how they killed us? Fed us to energy? Strained our souls into nothingness? The pain made my rebirth as an Angel of Death seem like cookies and chocolate milk.

And the Daemon kept pulling.

"Luke! *Luke!*" I screamed, over and over. I wanted to scream so many other things too. Mostly that I was sorry. Sorry for breaking the rules, for bringing the Daemons here, for telling him I didn't need him. I felt sorry for all of it. But only his name escaped.

He struggled to subdue the woman, their attacks and counterattacks a blur, their forms only distinguishable by her strawberry hair and his brown. Red, reeking of overconfidence, misjudged Luke's retreat and ended up on the ground instead of landing her kick. Luke's gaze flicked to mine long enough to shout his own apology before she attacked again. He'd survive, but he couldn't save me.

No one could.

I stopped screaming and exhaled slowly, gritting my teeth as I swallowed back the pain. Enough flinching. I wouldn't be the girl who begged for mercy until her last breath. Instead of pulling away, I shifted and pushed my free hand into the wall, until I faced the shimmering light head on, so close I could have licked it. Its brilliance intensified and stabbed my eyes, but I refused to shut them.

"Keres!" Luke shouted.

"Goodbye," I whispered and pushed one last time.

The wall devoured me, and I lost everything—Luke, Red, the room—as if someone had grabbed the entire universe and yanked it from beneath me, like the old magician's trick with a tablecloth and glasses. Only, I didn't stay standing. Perhaps I was the tablecloth, not the glass.

I lurched forward, reaching for anything to catch my balance, and landed in the arms of the Daemon.

SIX

Y ou—"

I collapsed, my khukuri clattering to the floor. Electricity rolled through my body in waves, shocking and contorting my limbs. Pinpricks of light stabbed my eyes, but slamming them shut did nothing to relieve the pain.

"Leftovers from the crossing gate." The Daemon half led, half carried me to a nearby chair. "The first time is the most painful. I can help, if you'll let me."

I opened my mouth to yell obscenities at him—I knew exactly what he could do with his help—but my teeth clenched as another round of whatever the hell this was zapped my body. I doubled over and used what little time I had in between attacks to breathe, quick and shallow.

He used one of the breaks between cycles of pain to push me back and tie me to the chair with wisps of light so thin, they must have been meant to hold rather than imprison me. "For your own protection."

"Bas—" Zap. Burn. Scream. Breathe. "—tard."

Liquid agony streamed down my cheeks while lightning burned me from the inside out.

Zap.
Burn.
Scream.
Breathe.
So the cycles continued, every nerve so overloaded and raw, I couldn't even pull against the bindings around my torso, wrists, and ankles, let alone break them. How long before the crossing zapped me into fine powder? I had no idea how they killed us, and I found not knowing to be as intense as the crossing.

"Please, Fallen, let me help you."

Please? *Please!* As if I had any control to grant my permission. Wasn't it enough he had me writhing in a chair? Must he mock me as well? His "request" burned hotter than the fire already consuming me.

"Go. To. Hell." I forced the words between clenched teeth. His shoulders slumped, and he turned from me. I could only see blurry shapes through the tears filling my eyes, and I couldn't feel anything beyond my own pain. I wondered what face went with his body language. Frustration? Boredom? Sadness?

Why had he said please? Why did I care? He was a Daemon, a minion of the devil. What did his plea matter to me? But my mind clung to the word. Refused to let it go. Chanted it amid the pain.

Zap.
Please.
Burn.
Please.
Scream.
Please.
Breathe.
Please, please . . .
"Please." I didn't mean it. I shook my head, even as

the word continued to race from my lips. "Please, please, please." More fire. More burning. More needles. A hundred thousand pricks of pain assaulting me at once, and all I could say was please.

"Please," I cried.

"I can help," he said.

"I don't . . . need you. I *can't* . . . need you!"

The cycles intensified, and I screamed his word. "Please!" The shock waves came faster and hit harder. I couldn't see anything but blinding light. Couldn't think of anything but my insides being ripped apart. Who was I? What was my name? Was I anything before this? Or had I always existed as pain? My body shook. The chair shook. The whole world seemed to tremble with me. And all I could think, all I could say, was one damn word.

"Please," I whispered. "Please."

"Shh. I'm here." He pushed my soaked, matted hair away from my face. "I will help. Can you let me in?"

I whimpered and nodded weakly. I would have let Satan himself climb inside me if he could have stopped the pain. Perhaps that had been his sick, twisted plan the whole time, but I didn't care anymore.

He pulled over a chair, sat in front of me, and laid his hands on top of mine. "Look at me, Fallen."

I looked.

He had one blue eye and one purple. Strange color for an eye, purple, but also soothing. Something about the way he looked at me—the way his eyes whispered that everything would be okay—made me believe him.

"That's it. Focus on my eyes."

I blinked away more tears, and his face became clearer. I'd never seen a Daemon before. He looked like other men I knew, human or Guardian, except he towered over me even while sitting. His white hair, a wild mess on top, tapered into short black hair at his nape. His tanned skin glowed slightly—not like sweat but like the sun still shone on it even in the dimly lit room.

Had the Daemon woman also looked dusted in sunlight? Is that how I could identify them in the future? I tried to reason it out, but my brain couldn't follow the thought. It hurt to think. It hurt to *be.*

Warmth crawled up my arms from where the man's hands rested on mine. It soothed as it spread, until my whole body sighed with relief. I tensed as another wave of electricity crashed down on me, but it broke against the wall he'd built, washing me with smaller and smaller tingles until, eventually, it receded into nothingness. Only the warmth remained.

And the presence of the Daemon.

My stomach twisted. I wanted him out, but already his essence was pressed against my consciousness like a safecracker listening for the sound of falling tumblers until—*click*—he found the right combination, opened the door to my soul, and stepped inside.

We were connected now, two intelligences sharing the same space.

He closed his eyes, and mine followed suit, my head falling forward in exhaustion. I felt warm and safe and tired. So very tired.

The Daemon's voice sounded within my head. ‹That's it. Relax.›

I receded to an empty space in my mind and allowed him to take control. It felt so natural, as if I'd done it a thousand times before. I floated in the void, barely aware of him as he poked around, opening doors and searching the various rooms of my mind. I'd compartmentalized everything—emotions, thoughts, memories—to make it easier to ignore the things I didn't want to remember. At least while awake. No amount of compartmentalizing could protect me from what came while I slept.

‹What's your name?› he asked.

‹Keres.›

‹Where do you come from, Keres?›

‹Everywhere and nowhere.›

‹Do you remember where you were born?›

‹In the desert. Twice.›

‹You were born twice?›

‹Once as a baby girl. Once as a monster.›

‹Is that what you are now?›

‹I am Death.›

‹So you've said. What does that mean, Keres?› His use of my name kept jarring me awake. It annoyed me. I liked floating in this place, so quiet and dark, it was easy to sleep and forget.

I pulled the emptiness around me like a blanket. ‹I reap wicked souls for God.›

‹Will you explain it to me?› His presence moved along the corridors of my mind as he chatted with me. I liked talking to him. His presence made me feel happy . . . and safe.

‹Who are you?› I asked.

‹A friend, Keres. A friend who's trying to help you.›

‹I've never had a friend. Just Raven.›

He paused for a moment before continuing. ‹You were telling me about reaping souls.›

‹I was? Oh yes. I slice open the neck and remove the soul. Did you know that is how you gain access to a soul? I didn't. Not until Raven showed me.›

‹Is that why you have this?› An image of my khukuri floated past me in the nothingness and disappeared. Realizing his awareness had interlaced with mine, I tried to guard my thoughts, though I'd forgotten why.

‹Yes. But I don't mean to cut off their heads. I never mean to be so violent. It's not me. It can't be me . . . can it?› I wrapped my arms around my torso, suddenly cold.

‹Do you know what it is, Keres? This blade of yours?›

‹A reaping blade.›

‹Hmm. Do you know what the markings mean?›

‹No. I'm not allowed to know.›

‹Do you know how old this is?›

‹No.›

‹Do you know who made it?›

‹No.› I frowned. I didn't like his questions, and I hated my answers. I wanted so much to please my new friend.

‹Where did you get the blade?›

Finally, a question I could answer. ‹He gave it to me.›

‹Who?›

I hesitated. No one was supposed to know who. Another of our laws. ‹I don't want to be punished again.›

‹No one will punish you. You're safe.› The warmth increased and nestled against me. I liked this nice man.

‹Safe,› I repeated.

‹Who, Keres?›

‹The angel Gabriel. He offered me the Contract and asked me to choose a blade. We all get one.›

‹There are *more* of you?›

I flinched, expecting to be hit or cut or burned. Intertwined like this, I sensed him sensing me. Our edges had blurred even further, making it increasingly difficult to know where he ended and I began. Peace flooded me, and I relaxed back into the darkness.

Once we both felt calm, he asked, ‹How many of you exist?›

‹I only know Raven. Though I've heard a couple other blades in passing.›

‹Heard?›

‹They each sing a song.›

‹Do you remember how many blades there were when you were . . . reborn?›

I shook my head. ‹I don't know.›

‹Try to remember. Even a rough number. Tens? Hundreds?› He paused. ‹Thousands? THINK.›

‹I don't know! Why won't you *believe* me?› I *wanted* to know, wanted to tell him.

He soothed me with his lullaby tones. ‹It's okay. It's okay to not know. I'm sorry for pushing.›

I tilted my head and pursed my lips, studying his part of our whole. ‹No one's ever apologized to me before.›

‹They should have. Every damn one of them.› His anger and sadness seeped into my awareness as he continued down the seemingly endless corridor of my mind in silence. Eventually, he returned to his natural state of peace, and I relaxed into the serenity, drifting into a light sleep while he explored.

‹Keres, what happens once you've found the soul?›

‹Hmm?› His question roused me, and I immediately noticed he was in a different part of my mind. He wandered uncomfortably close to the only door I didn't want him to see.

‹You said that when you reap, you slit the throat to gain access to the soul. What happens next?›

‹I remove it from the body and destroy it with my reaping blade.›

He stood quiet for a moment, only four doors from the end. ‹What happens to the soul's energy?›

I frowned. ‹I told you, I destroy it.›

‹Energy can't be destroyed, only transferred. Who

gets the power?› He stepped toward the next door and glanced inside.

My frown deepened. He wasn't making sense.

‹Do you take the soul?› he asked, continuing down the hallway.

Only two doors left. ‹I . . . no . . . I . . . I don't understand.› I tensed. Something felt off.

He pressed harder. ‹Who gets the soul, Keres?›

One door. ‹No one gets it! It dies. Forever.›

‹I'm afraid not. Reaping a soul, as you call it, builds power—I'm guessing *your* power—but how does that serve *him*? How will it play out in the war?›

I wanted him to stop asking questions, to stop moving forward, but I couldn't break free of the emptiness. The more I fought, the more solid it became, until I thought I would suffocate. I forced myself to relax, and the emptiness relaxed with me, until I floated again.

The Daemon reached the last door, sooty black and bolted shut. It looked carved, but really, the worst of my dark secrets had simply seeped into the wood in an attempt to escape. Bodies climbed over more decaying, twisted bodies, their faces turned up toward Heaven as their mouths hung open in screams that only I could hear. They covered the door—grasping, reaching, and clawing their way out of the madness I'd tried to contain.

My gut twisted, my chest tightened, and the emptiness began to solidify again, but I couldn't stop fighting this time. He had to go. He wasn't allowed behind that door. No one was.

‹Leave!›

‹Why does this door make you so afraid?› He pushed, but the door didn't move.

‹Out!›

‹It's okay, Keres.› He pushed again, harder this time.

‹*Out!*› The word echoed so loudly inside my head, it passed my physical lips in a whisper.

‹Shh, it's okay.›

He tried to soothe me, but I refused him. He wasn't allowed. He wasn't allowed!

He threw his full weight against the door.

The bolts gave way.

I pulled all my rage in, muscles and veins straining against skin, and then pushed it out in one guttural roar, exploding from the emptiness that held me as though I'd been encased in a concrete block. Shards flew in every direction, and I surged from my corner, fierce and unrelenting. I smashed into his presence before he could step over the threshold, and we tumbled over each other as if we were flesh and blood, my awareness pushing, heaving, and pulling his away from the door.

"No!" I screamed. "No!"

I evicted him from my body, but I was too late. He'd opened the door, and light raced down the dusty, darkened hallway behind it, illuminating everything I'd hidden for over a thousand years.

Please, God, don't make me see this. Please, please take it away.

I clawed my way back to full consciousness as a horde of memories tried to devour my sanity with their fangs. My eyes shot open, and I glared at the Daemon. He stared at me, his eyes wide and brow raised. He breathed out "Kahaiya" as though calling on the Virgin Mary.

"You," I growled.

He stood, knocking his chair over as he stepped back. I pulled against the wisps of light restraining me, but they held. I'd played the fool. He'd tricked me into saying too much, and now it was time to kill him or die trying.

"Keres—"

"Don't say a word." I held back my anger, letting it build behind an invisible dam.

"You have to know the truth."

"Truth? Truth! What truth can a spawn of Satan give me?" My gaze darted around the room, searching for my knives, and found both resting on the table.

"I'm not who you think."

"You pull me through hell, break my spirit, enter my mind, sift through my garbage, and you're *not* who I think!" The chair groaned as I pulled against the light holding me.

"I had to know. The blades—they were supposed to have been destroyed! We haven't had them since—"

"I don't care!" I screamed. "I don't care if God resurrects every last blade. Satan deserves to die. You all do!"

"I'm not with Lucifer!" he shouted. "You are!"

I stopped pulling for a second as my mind rebooted. It couldn't be. I shook my head. "Liar," I whispered.

"What you do, it's not of God."

"Liar!"

"You have to know, Keres. I speak the truth, and I can prove it to you."

"*Liar!*"

The blood pumping through my head roared so loudly, it drowned the rest of the words spilling from his lips. I couldn't hold it anymore. The dam burst, and the power I'd been gathering exploded into the room. The bindings of light evaporated, the chair exploded, the walls shook, and I lunged, grabbing my khukuri and smashing into the Daemon with my anger and my body.

He thudded against the floor, and I landed on him a second later, knocking the air from his lungs, then rolled into a crouch. "You and the rest of Daemonkind can burn in hell!" I raised my knife to strike. The markings cast a blue glow on everything within reach, and the hum of the blade sang in triumph.

"Keres, you must see the truth." His hands reached out to me in a plea to stop as he searched my face for something he would never see—a sign of hope.

"I already do." I plunged the knife toward his neck.

For the second time that day, he caught my blade and held it for a moment that felt like eternity. "Seek the truth." He shifted the aim of my khukuri and released the blade so it entered his heart instead of his throat. His face contorted with a grunt of pain as it slid into his body. "That was more uncomfortable than I'd expected."

I stared. Stared as the blade glowed brighter and hotter. As the ripple of heat moved over and through him. As I witnessed for the first time with my own eyes—instead of through nightmares—what happened to a reaped soul.

It was supposed to be instant, wasn't it? An explosion of light?

Instead, the energy shifted and the matter changed, as if millions of large, rounded insects crawled beneath his skin, eating him from the inside out.

I should've felt elated. I'd won. I'd destroyed a Daemon.

Instead, I felt sick.

Confused.

Stunned.

This was *nothing* like the reapings I'd seen in my dreams.

I crumpled beside him as his breathing grew more labored. He'd destroyed himself. In that one heartbeat, he'd had the power to stop me, but he hadn't. He'd allowed himself to be sacrificed.

"But I didn't slice your throat. I didn't take your soul."

"My body and spirit are one." Smiling slightly, he reached out and brushed his fingers against my face.

"I don't understand."

"Doesn't matter." He closed his eyes and grimaced. "Just remember . . . it's the same for Guardians."

"Why, Daemon? Why'd you let me do it?"

His eyes fluttered open. "The truth is more important than me." He held out his hand. A small token, like something from an amusement park, rested on his palm.

"Take this, Keres." He pressed the coin into my hand. "Show it to Adi at Oscar's in Jakarta. Blok M. He can help you find what you need most."

"And what is that?"

"To be free."

My mouth fell open, but I had no words. They seemed stuck in the place where my fingertips touched my throat. With a whisper from him, the wall of liquid light—what he had called a crossing gate—returned. I flinched as its light filled the room.

The Daemon chuckled softly. "Don't worry. It won't hurt this time. Tell Daliah I love her."

"Who are you?"

"Then you do not remember?"

"You never told me."

He groaned and closed his eyes as the movement beneath his skin intensified. I didn't know what to say or how long we had, so I repeated what I'd heard the two Daemons say before.

"No peril in the fight," I said.

He smiled. "No glory in the triumph."

Then he disintegrated into a million orbs of light. Their brilliance grew until I had to shield my eyes. They swirled around me—tightly at first, like a small galaxy orbiting a dying star, before they burst outward to fill the entire room. The orbs held the climax of their movement for a breath, before they raced back into me—the black hole consuming their life force.

The Daemon's energy filled me and melded with my own. I felt myself changing. Morphing. Assuming power that wasn't mine to have. His soul didn't disappear; my soul devoured it. And for a moment, I believed he'd told me the truth.

"What have I done?"

When the light burned out and the transformation was complete, I sat alone in an empty room next to a pulsating wall of energy. I looked at the token in my hands.

"To be free." Was this really the answer? I swallowed all the other questions and stuffed the coin into a hidden pocket on my scabbard before I could change my mind and throw it away. After sheathing my utility knife, I clutched my khukuri, took a deep breath, and stepped through the gate—back to Luke, the Daemon woman, and questions I wasn't sure I wanted to answer.

Crossing back was nothing but a stumble.

"Keres!" Luke yelled.

"Ielu?" Red—the Daemon woman he had called Daliah—searched the wall behind me with her gaze.

"Ielu." I rolled his name around in my mouth. "He's dead."

"Impossible." Daliah and Luke muttered the word at the same time and shifted away from me, their bodies saying what their lips didn't: *dangerous*. Before I could respond, Daliah fled.

Luke rushed to my side and crushed me against his chest. I didn't care that he held me or that I'd sworn to never let him close again. I clung to him and pleaded for him to never let me go. Terror didn't even begin to describe how I felt about the Daemons and myself.

What the hell am I?

"Don't let me go," I repeated.

"I won't. I promise I won't." He held tight for a moment and then pulled away to look into my eyes. His gaze seemed to reach through me. "What happened?"

I shook my head, too exhausted to make sense of anything, and collapsed. He picked me up, cradling me close, and I wrapped my arms around his neck. With my head buried in his shoulder, I let myself succumb to the darkness.

SEVEN

I follow a man into a darkened hotel suite, where moonlight spilling through an open window casts everything in a bluish hue. Drapery sheers flit and flick in the light breeze. The man grasps one of the panels and runs his fingers lightly along its edge. Though I'm not touching it, I can feel the texture: soft, pliable, and delicate.

The man smiles, ugly and twisted. "Just like the one I selected for my client tonight." I taste salt as he licks his lips. "He has very particular tastes."

Muffled cries drift from the far side of the room. I walk toward the sound and reach for the closet, but I can't open the door. It's a closet, so it's not locked; I simply can't grasp the handle.

"Just a moment, Emily," the man calls over his shoulder. "We can't leave yet. First, we have to clean up, clean up, everybody clean up." He sings the last few words as he stuffs a small pile of clothing into a child's backpack lying on the dresser, taking special care to make sure the roses next to the backpack look perfect. He even plucks a few drooping petals and tosses them into a nearby trash can.

"Open the door," I command, but he can't hear me. I am nothing but a ghost here.

"Aren't you excited, Em? Tomorrow, your special daddy will remember this beautiful night you had together. Tomorrow, he will giggle over the romance and the fun. You should feel so lucky! Tomorrow, all he will think about is being with you."

I don't like what the man is saying. It makes my stomach churn as I fight both the closet door and the desire to vomit.

"Oh, Emily! You are so special. So many daddies love you. Don't you feel sad for the girls who only have one daddy to love them?"

Something is wrong. Terribly wrong.

Why am I so upset?

Why can't I stay calm?

Why can't I open the damn door?

"Open the door!" I scream. I claw at the closet, but nothing moves, including the man. Seemingly satisfied with the flowers and bed, he grabs the backpack and makes his way across the room—checking this detail, touching that one—until finally he reaches for the closet.

He stops, distracted by a crumpled piece of clothing on the floor. As he picks it up, he shakes his head, tsking. "This should have been with the rest of the clothes. A simple yet potentially costly mistake."

The man looks vaguely familiar. Where have I seen him before?

It doesn't matter, though. Emily's cries increase, and my need to save her—even though I don't know her—burns hot. "Ugh! Open the door! You have to open the door!"

He raises his voice to Emily. "We don't like mistakes, do we, Em? Mistakes are bad, and we don't want to be bad, do we? No, we want to be a good girl so we can make Uncle Sergio proud."

He holds the cloth up to the moonlight. Tiny scallops line the waist and leg holes. They're cute undies decorated with hearts and jumping unicorns, size 3T.

"Something my daughter would wear." He presses them to his nose and inhales deeply. "They smell like money."

For the first time, his eyes land on me, and he grins, holding the underwear out to me. I take them reluctantly, the only thing I can touch in the entire room. They're heavier than the world.

Turning back to the closet, he opens the door—finally!—revealing little Emily cringing on the floor, hands, feet, and mouth bound, tears streaming down her face.

"There's my good girl. I'm so proud of you."

She stares past him, at me, her eyes begging, *Please don't make me touch him.*

Rage and pain twist inside me. I can't stand it. She's so little—too little. Where is the justice?

Then I realize *I* am justice.

I tear my reaping blade from its hidden scabbard and slice through Sergio's neck. His gurgles and her gagged screams sing a sick harmony as warm liquid splatters my bare arms and face. But I can't stop hacking. The more she screams, the more I chop away at the monster who locked her in the closet.

When I turn to reassure her, her wide eyes and pale face tell me I'm the monster now.

"I'm sorry, Emily." But I don't think she can hear me above her screaming.

Her underwear, still clutched in my hand, bursts into flame, and the hotel suite melts into a dirty warehouse room, where Sergio is whole again.

How is that possible? I killed him, strewing bits and pieces of him like petals around the hotel room.

Yet here he is with three other men, lounging in a folding chair, drinking dirty scotch, and smoking a cigar. They laugh together over Emily and Sarah and James—more children for more clients with *very* particular tastes.

Strutting to the table, I pick up a glass of scotch. Two of the men stand up in surprise, but their shock quickly turns to desire. I can feel it—all four men thirsty for me.

As I take a sip from my cup, dark tendrils of my Shadow power creep across the floor and wind around the men, taking control. I walk them like marionettes to the center of the room, standing them in a small circle so they all have a good view of the upcoming show. Draining my scotch, I force the three men I don't recognize to slice themselves open.

Their screams form a pleasing chorus of tenors and basses, as every man pleads for his own life. Laced through their song is the voice of one girl pleading for hers, sounding so much like me, I can't stand it.

I *blink* from man to man, carving each one's neck with a red smile that spills crimson laughter more suitable for Emily than any sound. Each soul clings to its body, but I rip it free and pierce its crystal center with my khukuri. Dim specks of light flicker within the fog that is my brain, exploding like muted fireworks from each soul before disappearing behind shadows I can't penetrate. I shrug, sure I imagined them.

Sergio—the man from the hotel room and my mark—is left for last. Left to watch his companions unwillingly cut open their own bodies. Left to hear their screams for mercy. Left to imagine what gruesome fate awaits him, and left to hope that perhaps he might be spared.

I love the moment I take that hope away.

I carve him up and give him a red smile, too, before yanking his soul from his body.

His soul scratches feebly at the arm holding him by his neck. "No!"

"Yes." I raise my khukuri to strike him. "Monsters. Must. Die." I plunge the knife toward the center of his broken soul, where a crystal glimmers darkly, and time slows to match my heartbeats.

Pound—the beat echoes in my ears.

Though the blade hasn't touched him yet, Sergio's soul turns his face to the ceiling and screams.

Pound—blood rushes through my veins.

His screaming stops. When he looks back at me, I am staring into the face of the Daemon Ielu. Instead of fear, his eyes are filled with sorrow.

"But who is the monster, Keres?"

Pound—pain presses against my eyes.

"No." I shake my head and try to stop the knife from moving toward him, but I no longer have control. It creeps forward. I can't stop it. Can't change direction.

"You, Keres. You are the monster."

Pound—terror strangles my heart.

At the last moment, the soul morphs again, and I stare into the face of a girl stuck somewhere between child and woman. One who's seen too much death to be innocent and not enough mercy to be wise.

I stare into her face—my face. My eyes, my lips, my sorrow-filled stare.

"No!" I use all my power trying to halt the forward motion of my weapon, but it isn't enough. It's never enough. All I can do is close my eyes as I drive the reaping blade into my own soul.

My heart stops. Silence.

"And monsters must die," the other me whispers.

EIGHT

My eyes flicked open, the only part of me not paralyzed by sleep. I choked on the screams my throat refused to release. A sharp pain stabbed at my chest where the khukuri had pierced my soul.

I hated dreaming.

And since I always dreamed, I hated sleeping as well. Raven liked to remind me I was given power over death, not sleep, but I should have had both.

Tears spilled from my eyes, gathering in uncomfortable pools behind my ears as I waited for my body to finish waking. Tears for Emily, me, and all of Sergio's memories I would relive for the rest of eternity. I wasn't crying, really, only expelling the images from my body. They had to go somewhere, and Ielu had broken my internal storage unit.

As soon as I could, I wiped away the pools and curled around my pillow. I glanced around. Luke had brought me to my place instead of his. He really did know me well. My room and bed, wherever I lived in the world, had always felt safest.

I wonder what it means, then, that we always had sex in his.

I released the thought. It didn't matter. I focused on my breathing, inhaling and exhaling slowly, as I stared at the clock on my nightstand: 4:03 a.m.

In less than eight hours, I'd saved a human, been threatened by Raven, reaped some souls, killed a Daemon, and then asked the one Guardian I loathed to never leave me.

Luke. What would he say about me reaping the Daemon?

Feeling his presence outside my bedroom, I reached out with my extra sense—another dirty little secret I'd managed to hide from everyone.

No one knew I was a Reader, a term I'd created to label what I could do: feeling, smelling, tasting, and sometimes even seeing others' emotions. Mild emotions were more like perfume clouds, impressions that wafted from mortals and immortals alike and dissipated like hookah smoke. Sometimes, that impression conjured images inside my head, like the way frankincense made me picture a full moon reflecting off desert rocks. The more intense the emotion, the more solid the image. Sometimes, like with the human I had saved, the image wasn't inside my head at all. It was outside, burning its owner alive, even if they didn't know it.

Reading seemed abstract and fluid, and what I experienced wasn't the same with every person. Just as one person might feel anger in their shoulders and another in their gut, the colors, images, and impressions I received were unique to the individual. I didn't know the rules or how I *read*, only that I could.

Only one thing remained constant: I felt every single emotion as if it were my own. From every person. All the time. Over the centuries, I'd learned to ignore the emotions, like the white noise of a dryer tumbling clothes, but the emotions were always present, ready to drown me if I let them.

Tonight, however, my gift proved useless. While Raven's internal conflict manifested as a whirling tornado, due to the raging storm she called her soul, Luke put up walls, shut off his emotional ties to the world, and hunkered down. Right now, he read like black granite: slick and impenetrable. What he could be conflicted over, however, I didn't know.

I'd have to work this out the good old-fashioned way: talking.

Before I could throw back the covers and head into the living room, the hum of Raven's reaping blade broke the silence.

"I summoned you hours ago." Luke's whispered words stepped slowly out on a tightrope.

"You're not the only one with responsibilities," Raven replied.

"Sit."

"Nǐ qù sǐ." I flinched, surprised Raven would tell Luke to go to hell.

"Sit!"

Raven grunted, and the chair closest to my bedroom squeaked against the concrete floor. Luke's breathing filled the silence.

"We have a problem," he finally said.

"I heard. Daemons."

"No."

Luke paused. His granite wall cracked, and from that sliver of a fault line poured emotions so strong, I didn't have to reach for them—anger, confusion, and *fear.*

"It's Keres."

My whole body tensed as my heart dropped into my stomach. Luke was never afraid. Ever. Yet now it clung to him like tar—not *for* me but *of* me. This was new territory, and I had no idea what to expect.

I reached for the comfort of my reaping blade, but my hand closed on empty air. My breath caught in my throat, and I opened myself to the familiar hum I normally ignored.

It was nowhere nearby.

I swallowed hard. I *never* left my blade farther than arm's length from me. Luke knew this; it had shared our bed all the years we were together. While Aods could reap with any reaping blade, we couldn't *be reaped* by any weapon but our own.

And now mine wasn't even in my room.

My abdomen twisted in a painful knot that reached up through my belly to grasp my heart. My knife rested in the next room, the keeper of all the secrets I needed to hide until I knew who had told me the truth and who had lied. I swallowed down the bile climbing up my throat.

"Any chance she's awake?" Raven whispered tightly. I tensed but kept breathing evenly.

"She passed out before we left the building."

"That doesn't mean—"

"She reaped a Daemon, Raven. *Alone.*" He stressed the last word like it meant everything, but I couldn't discern what passed between them. "*Ma cher* won't be waking up for a while."

Perhaps he should have been right. Reapings always wore me out, and this one had felt especially potent. Even now, my eyelids drooped. But he didn't understand the power of my nightmares. No one did.

"Isn't that your job? To be *with* her? How the hell did she reap a Daemon on your watch?"

"She came back. Launched a full assault before we even knew she'd returned."

"Unexpected."

Luke chuckled. "Surprised the Daemons too. Damn, she was amazing!" His amusement vanished quickly. "I thought we'd lost her when he pulled her through a crossing gate, but less than a minute later, only she emerged."

A minute? It had felt like hours. Where had Ielu taken me?

"Only a very powerful Daemon or Guardian can open a gate—"

"So how did she get back?" Luke asked. "The thought has crossed my mind."

"Then she's working with the Daemons." The hum of her sickle began to climb, and my breath caught. If she believed me a traitor, she wouldn't hesitate to kill me.

"He's dead. Her blade was still singing death as she came back through."

My head swam with exhaustion, questions, and confusion. Since when could Guardians hear the song? Then again, what had made me believe they couldn't? I tried, unsuccessfully, to catalog everything I knew to locate the holes. There was too much I didn't know, and with a millennium of experience as witness, asking direct questions would never get me direct answers.

"Was it enough time for the Daemon to . . . ?" Raven's unfinished question slammed into Luke's silence and fell to the floor. "Surely you'll tell the Conclave."

"Only when *I* decide." Luke's heavy footsteps moved away. "There's something going on with our girl, something I'm not seeing."

"The change crossing gates force on us?"

"More than that. This was the feeling of something . . . lost. I sensed it when she returned."

Holy shit, the token!

I willed myself to run to Luke, turn over the token, and confess everything. Would that save me? Or maybe if I stayed silent, they wouldn't ever know. I could toss the coin, pretend it never happened . . .

And always wonder if Ielu had spoken the truth.

I could be *free*. No more death, no more nightmares.

Guilt pressed against my conscience, hot enough to burn right through my skull and spill my wicked thoughts across my pillow. Could they smell the smoldering hair, or was it only in my mind? I curled tighter in my sheets and inhaled slowly, forcing my heart to beat a steady rhythm.

"How did it all go so wrong?" Raven asked.

"We underestimated them . . . and her."

"Or overestimated you."

"Be careful, Raven." His silky tone belied his dangerous nature. Raven was walking a knife's edge. Luke could be patient, but when pushed, his reactions were quick and painful.

"If you had been, we wouldn't be in this mess."

The screech of Raven's chair skidding across the concrete swallowed my gasp. No one talked to Luke like that. It seemed centuries as a Xiiphronai had made her reckless. Both the chair and her body gave a distinct thud as they slammed to the floor.

"Watch it, *ma fifille*," Luke said, his words slithering right outside my door. "You forget your place."

"What do you intend to do? Reaping blades don't work for you."

They don't? Did she mean just him or all Guardians? What the hell was going on? I *blinked* to the edge of my doorway and peered around the frame. Luke had Raven pinned to the ground with Shadow as he crouched over her body, holding her sickle to her throat. Her chin tilted up with the same defiance mine had on the rooftop, and her jaw clenched as if she were grinding Luke between her teeth.

"Someone's been poking her nose into Guardian business."

"What of it?"

"You should check your sources. Guardians may not be able to reap a soul, but I can still destroy the blade."

My eyes widened. Guardians couldn't reap?

"You *need* me." Fear tinged Raven's voice. I didn't understand the implications of Luke's threat or what destroying an Aod's weapon would do, but if Raven was afraid, I should have been terrified.

"And there is your mistake, Raven. I don't need anyone."

"*He* wouldn't allow it."

"All these years and you still doubt my authority. I don't need his permission." He whispered the last word, soft and slow. It sauntered through the air like a Louisiana gentleman strolling through the park on an idle afternoon. Luke twisted the sickle away from her throat and, instead, grasped her neck with his free hand. I felt the surge of power before I saw it, directed not at her weapon but at her body.

Raven cried out, and I watched in sick fascination as human skin spilled to the floor like bacon grease. Luke's smile and gaze turned feral, and I knew he wouldn't stop at mortal flesh. I'd been on the receiving end far too often to believe anything different.

I'm sorry, Raven.

Turning up the heat, Luke shifted the energy emanating from his hand to her *soul* skin, melting the gossamer layers of her spirit. It was his signature move. His touch burned so hot, it scorched the soul and left scars that lasted long after the mortal body healed.

That's when the screaming really started.

"Shh. We don't want to disturb our Keres. She needs her sleep."

She'd barely caught her breath before her body rocked again in pain. I touched my cheek—the last place Luke had burned me before I left him. The soul usually stayed concealed beneath the flesh, but whatever Luke did made it possible for other immortals to see his brand. I'd spent the better part of a century looking at his scorched handprint caressing my face, until it finally flaked away and healed. Now Raven would wear his blackened grasp strangling her throat. For how long, only Luke knew.

All I could do was breathe—inhale, exhale—and thank God it wasn't me.

I *blinked* back to my bed while he remained distracted and pulled the covers tight against my chin, trying to block out everything she felt.

"Are you ready to submit, *ma fifille*?"

"Yes." She cried out again and then gasped for air.

"Yes, what?"

"Yes, Aishah."

Oh shit. When Luke insisted on the use of his formal title, it was time to run.

"Don't forget your place again. I won't be so kind next time." Luke's boots clicked across the concrete away from my room. "Sit."

I heard Raven pick up the toppled chair and sit down. The silence stretched between them. I stared out my window, watching darkness shift as sunrise neared. My eyelids grew heavy. The reaping, the fighting, and now Raven—it was too much. My body began to shut down, my questions circling my head like water round a drain.

"What do you require of me, Aishah?"

"I can't stay, and Keres can't be left alone while she recovers. She's vulnerable, especially to a repeat attack. The Daemons were too well prepared for me to believe it was a random raid."

"I'd assumed they'd followed her from the human."

"Perhaps. But why wait for the reaping? Why not take her immediately?"

"So I'm to babysit."

"I thought that's what you did." He wielded arrogance like a whip, and its sting found its mark with a crack of satisfaction. Unseen daggers of hate stabbed at Luke, but Raven remained calm.

"Am I to ask her about the Daemon?"

"Talk, yes. Torture, no."

"I never torture."

"No punishments. I need answers."

"Trust me."

The room grew cold. "Don't believe for a second that you are anything more than a tool for my purposes. You are a sword for killing, not a scalpel for removing, shall we say, malignant tumors." Luke's echo of Raven's earlier words earned a small but audible gasp. "Obedience without question—it's the first law. I won't remind you again."

"Of course, Aishah." Fear swallowed the last of her pride and spit out submission. Their words drifted to me through a growing fog, muting thought and emotion.

"When I figure out who's behind this—"

"The Daemons."

"We will see. Your reaping blade, Xiiphronai." Raven's sickle clanked to the floor. He might as well have slapped her across the face. "Be delicate, Raven. I don't know what that kind of power will do to our precious Keres. She was already so close."

"To the Burn Cycle?" When he didn't respond, Raven added, "She will be obedient."

Will I? A pair of eyes, blue and purple, stared at me in the fog.

"Your life depends on it. Stay with her until I send word."

"I've always led her as you required."

Led . . . me . . .

My thoughts winked in and out like twinkling lights.

"I haven't risked everything to hide her only to lose her now."

Luke's lump of granite emotion disappeared, and the soft duet of Raven's sickle and my khukuri reclaimed the apartment.

I struggled against sleep. I needed . . . something . . . oh yeah, answers. But what were the questions again?

The tick-tick-tick of the nightstand clock lulled me even closer to the abyss, and I watched the second hand move methodically around its face. Only one motion, one way to go. Forward.

Obedience . . . led me . . . hidden . . . Burn Cycle . . .

The words tasted like vinegar. My tongue sleepily scraped against my teeth as if it could be rid of the flavor.

Dear God . . . if I am wrong . . . please forgive my choice.

I reached for the comfort of a reaping blade that wasn't there, closed my heavy eyelids, and listened to my clock.

NINE

Dull light filtered through my blinds—the sun masked by a fall storm. Staring at the exposed brick framing the window, I blinked slowly until the world came into focus. My clock still ticked away the minutes of my life.

8:30 a.m.

My body felt heavy, and I stretched to shake off the sensation. When I realized my clothes were missing, I shot to sitting and pulled the covers against me. My heart thudded as nausea and exhaustion washed over me.

"You seemed uncomfortable."

I snapped my head toward the voice to find Raven perched on my dresser, her back against the wall and her left leg folded up to support her elbow. She held my reaping blade, twisting it as she pressed her forefinger against its sharp tip. She nodded toward the armchair next to her, where last night's clothes had been flung over the back.

I exhaled audibly and raked my hands through my hair. "Removing my clothes wouldn't change that. When you figure out how to remove the dreams, call me."

She smirked. "You look like hell."

"I feel a lot worse." My gaze flicked to the scabbard resting on the dresser near her hip.

She smiled and set my khukuri down. "Worried about something?"

"I was attacked by Daemons. Wouldn't you be?"

She leaned forward, widening her eyes in feigned innocence. "Oh, so not this?" She lifted her hand to reveal the small circular object she held between her pointer and middle fingers.

I wanted to *blink* to her side and rip the damn thing from her hand. Instead, I shrugged and forced my heart to beat more slowly. "Just a coin some guy at the club gave me last night. Something to remember him by, he said."

I learned early on that if you mixed just enough truth into a lie, people wouldn't question you. I crossed everything inside me, hoping Raven counted as "people" today.

"Must have been some guy."

I thought of Ielu's blue and purple eyes, interesting hair, and glowing skin. I remembered his apology and his death. "I don't know yet."

Raven hopped off the dresser and held the coin out to me. Her waist-length hair, freed from its usual ponytail, fluttered around her. She wore a short, heather-pink dress that looked like a tailored double-breasted trench coat, complete with side pockets and an oversize collar that hid most of Luke's handprint. Its stiff structure and rigid angles were perfect for her personality and petite frame. Black knee-high boots topped with stiff ruffles and a velvet cabbie hat completed the ensemble.

She was perfection and luxury. I knew her dress had to feel like silk—an obsession she'd had since her transformation. *When one goes from wearing paddy-field manure and leeches to wearing the silk of emperors, one never lets go,* she'd told me once.

I thought of my own need to be free of heavy skirts and bulky head coverings; I even kept my hair cropped short. My parents wouldn't recognize me now. Some days, I didn't recognize myself.

I left the false safety of my covers and crossed the short distance to where she stood. Her emotions had settled since her conversation with Luke, but I knew to tread lightly. She'd returned to being "the friend," but one misstep could flip her switch to enemy, regardless of Luke's warning.

I kept my gaze neutral, focusing on her eyes instead of her throat. Raven wouldn't welcome any sympathy or pity. We'd become experts at pretending things like this didn't happen.

"Promise me you won't turn this into an obsession like you did with Luke."

I flinched.

She smiled and dropped the coin on my open palm. She couldn't read my emotions—if she could have, I'd have been dead a hundred times over by now—but she sure as hell knew how to push my buttons. I reached behind her, making a show of discarding the coin in my junk drawer with the rest of the castoffs Raven knew I kept there.

"You ready to be up, then?"

"I'm ready to not sleep anymore."

"How about breakfast?" My stomach grumbled, and she laughed. "Sounds like yes." She left the room.

Once she'd stepped out of my line of sight, I snatched up Ielu's token, shut the drawer softly, and *blinked* into the master bathroom. "I'm going to jump in the shower."

"Hurry. Your apartment's boring, and I need someone to talk to."

"Try reading a book sometime."

I turned the shower on before closing the door and bending down to remove a small piece of baseboard from the corner behind it. There was just enough space for the token. I didn't dare carry it on me or leave it floating in my drawer. Not if Luke could feel it and not with Raven watching.

I'd just replaced the baseboard and stood when Raven pushed the door back open, forcing me to jump out of the way. I grabbed my towel from the bar next to her and cast her a dirty look. If she thought I was annoyed rather than surprised, she wouldn't snoop any further.

When she smiled with satisfaction rather than curiosity, I knew it had worked.

She leaned against the doorjamb, whisking eggs in the bowl she carried. "Why read a book? They're written by humans, Keres. *Bor*-ing."

"We were humans once too."

"Yes, but we fixed that, didn't we?"

I smiled sweetly over my shoulder as I stepped into the shower. "Bacon's burning."

She frowned and *blinked* into the kitchen, cursing loudly. The louder she yelled, the faster I washed. I shut off the water only minutes later, sighing heavily. No time for soaking.

Silly Keres. Thirty minutes of hot water can't wash away last night.

"Keres! Help. Now!"

I threw on some fresh clothes, belted on my khukuri, and trotted toward the kitchen. One glance told me it was futile. Veering toward the large windows, I opened them to let the smoke out before it could set off the alarms.

"Take out?"

She looked ready to explode as she dumped baking soda indiscriminately across the stove. "I hate your kitchen!" After grumbling under her breath for a while, she finally said, "Fells Point?"

I frowned. "What about Daemons?" I should have said no, but she knew my weaknesses all too well. Fells Point held one of my favorite coffee-and-pastry shops in Baltimore—the closest thing an American could get to the European café experience, with the best pastries outside France. I could practically smell the heavy scent of bread mingled with chocolate.

"Going out for breakfast won't change anything. If they knew where you were, they'd have been here by now."

"It's only been a few hours."

"Try *days*, Keres."

I stared blankly.

"It's Wednesday, my love. You've been unconscious since the reaping on Saturday night."

TEN

I stared out the tall window of the pastry shop at the gray, swollen sky. Wednesday's sky, when it should have belonged to Sunday. *Days,* instead of hours, since I had passed out. Too much time lost.

"Luke." He was seventy-two hours closer to finding clues that pointed to my guilt, and I didn't even have a plan. My ribs itched where he liked to leave charred handprints.

"I don't know when he's coming back."

My gaze flicked to Raven, whose flawless brow had furrowed. "I didn't ask."

Her emotions churned like the roiling clouds outside, mirroring how I felt. But I couldn't decipher either of us as we sat across from each other, tucked into the front corner of the shop. She lounged in her seat, while I curled uncomfortably into my own squat leather chair. A Napoleonic soldier glared down from the painting on the wall behind me.

I returned to the oversize art pad in my arms and scratched red chalk against the paper. I planned on using oils for this piece, but brushes offered too much detach-ment to release emotion. I preferred chalk when I felt raw. I loved its tangibility. Hands-on art brought me release in a way painting never could, and if I'd had any knack for it, I would have become a sculptor, working in clay, stone, or marble.

"Must you do that here?" Raven drawled, sounding bored.

I scowled and finished my first layer of color, losing myself in the blending of reds, oranges, and yellows as my fingers and thumbs pushed through the dust. I blew gently every now and then to free the paper of the excess.

Raven picked at the remains of a chocolate croissant. "So you've been asleep for a few days. I don't get why you're upset."

How could I explain without implicating myself? Was Raven a pawn like me or one of the players? Either was dangerous. Zealous pawns could do a lot of damage before they were sacrificed, and players knew all the moves. I had to be cautious.

Grabbing the black and gray chalk, I returned to scratching out the kill scene of my nightmare. The blood, however, I left on the warehouse floor. My art mirrored the *essence* of my pain—a coping tool I had stumbled onto centuries ago; it didn't copy it in graphic detail.

I gently tore the page from the pad and set it to the side for later. It would look good in oils. Picking through my chalk, I considered what to draw next. Raven sighed loudly, grabbed my sketch pad, and tossed it to the floor.

"Stop ignoring me."

"What do you want from me, Raven? I'm tired, I'm raw, and I have no idea what to do about Luke, let alone the Daemons."

"Luke hasn't been honest with you, Keres."

"And you have?" When people turned to stare, I lowered my voice. "Raven, I saw it. I know what happens when I reap a soul."

No gasp. No curiosity or request for me to explain myself. She *knew*.

"He wants to keep you ignorant; I disagree."

"But you're so good at it."

Our respective anger danced like lightning around us. The electricity left me a little heady.

"When it's for your benefit," Raven said.

Remembering her comment about leading me wherever Luke wanted, I narrowed my eyes. "Or yours."

"A boat goes where the wind wills. You are nothing without me." Her anger spiked, and her emotional control slipped, my usual signal to tread lightly. But I was running out of time—and patience. Luke could be back any minute, and if he discovered the truth before I made my choice . . .

I shuddered.

Yet here was Raven, centering the world on her tiring role as the martyr-hero, as if she hadn't reminded me almost every day for the last 365,000-plus days how much she'd sacrificed for me.

"It's easy for the wind to control a boat with no rudder," I spat. "You keep me ignorant so you can keep me controlled."

"You complain of ignorance? Then stop being a child! I'm trying to tell you—"

"Tell me what? How awful Luke is? How big a mistake I made sleeping with him? I've heard it, Raven. Save it for someone who cares."

"I'm only trying to help—"

"All you've ever done is hurt me! You are nothing more than dirt."

The last word echoed around the now-silent pastry shop as the other patrons and employees stared at me.

Using her Shadow power, Raven yanked a display case off the counter. As everyone turned toward the crash, she hurled herself at me and *blinked.* I slammed into the brick-and-concrete wall of a nearby side street devoid of human activity.

The back of her hand crunched against my face. "All I've ever done is protect you, you stupid girl!" She grabbed my arms, nails drawing blood as she pulled me off the wall and shoved me back into it. My skull cracked loudly against the brick. "If not me, then who? Who will stand for you? Teach you? Guide you? Help you navigate this existence? Luke? God? You want to climb under the covers and nurse your wounds? Fine! But don't believe for one second that you've cornered the market on suffering. That your pain, your nightmares, your torments are any stronger than what I carry. You know nothing of pain."

"And you do?"

Before I could chuckle, Raven shifted her hold and pulled me down into her knee, which rose to meet my ribs. My amusement came out as a wheeze a second before her elbow hit the tender spot below my left ear. I collapsed to my hands and knees, vision blurring.

I'd had worse.

I stood to retaliate, to finally fight back. Rage flaring, I slowly reached for my reaping blade.

Until her EF5 tornado of emotion went perfectly still. The sudden void stole my air more effectively than anything physical she'd ever done.

"Enough," she whispered. Deep, ancient pain seeped from her in rivulets of blackened blood—emotional scars spilling old secrets. She dusted the backs of her fingers across my cheek and down my arm, and I half expected them to leave behind smears of blood.

"You reach back in time, and what do you have?" she asked. "Happiness. Parents who loved you. Family who rejoiced in you. Freedom to be yourself, to be a child. Some of us were not born to such luxury.

"You know nothing of being despised solely for being a girl. Nothing of working and digging and planting, of doing everything you can to prove you are as strong—as useful—as a son, only to be sold to a fat warlord to pay off your brother's debts. Have you ever had a wet mouth shower your body with hot, unwanted kisses that leave your skin coated and smelling of soured tofu? Have you been passed from guard to guard after he'd finished, to be used and discarded as the trash you were born to be?"

Raven scoffed. "Yet you want *me* to cry for you because you received the gift you asked for."

I started as I realized there *were* tears pooling in Raven's eyes, but they weren't tears of compassion. They were tears of anger—perhaps the only kind of tears she could cry.

"You were soft. You *are* soft. And I've only tried to make you stronger. To help you survive this life. Don't blame me when you're afraid to get out of the damn boat and swim."

I wanted to stare her down and yell my own rage, but I couldn't even hold her gaze. I *was* soft. My parents had given their lives for me. They had cherished me, and I had known it. I had never doubted their love or myself until they were taken from me. But Raven . . .

"I didn't know."

"Of course you didn't." She turned away to wipe her tears before they fell, and perched on the hood of a nearby car.

Not knowing what to say, I waited for her to speak, but minutes passed as she stared beyond the street sign and out into the bay. She was lost, reliving a life *no one* should have to experience. It fueled her dedication to the cause and her willingness to accept the life we shared.

Would all that change if she knew we served Satan instead of God?

"Raven—"

She turned her head, her gaze burning through me. "Never speak a word of this. Ever."

"Never." I tried to say more, but the fire in her eyes turned my words to ash.

She tapped her foot against the bumper of the car in front of her as her emotions whipped into the small tornado I was used to. "Luke is hoping that if you don't know, you won't get hurt. He wants to keep you ignorant."

"Of what, exactly?"

She stared at me, her hesitation coloring the air around her in blacks and grays with a hint of red. "The Burn Cycle."

Burn Cycle. I held it in my mouth, tasting it, before swallowing. It caught in my throat, preventing me from speaking.

"You already know what happens to a reaped soul," Raven said.

"Why didn't you tell me?"

"What would you have done if I had?"

"Stopped or run."

"You've tried both. Did they work?" She knew they hadn't. "Besides, what difference does it make?"

"Destroying evil is one thing; absorbing it . . ." I shuddered at the thought of all those disgusting souls blended with my own.

"Energy is energy. Whether it's expelled into the

universe or assimilated by you, the outcome is the same. That is all that matters."

"But the dreams?"

"A side effect."

I laughed. "Like nausea and vomiting?"

"And sometimes death," Raven added, but she wasn't laughing. My stomach did a somersault off the high dive that ended in a belly flop. "Every time we reap a soul, we take upon ourselves their energy and, to some extent, their power. It's why the nightmares and reapings become stronger over time. Most Aods don't survive."

"Explain."

Raven sighed and walked toward me. She grabbed my hand as she passed and pulled me over to a small bench that had *Baltimore, the Greatest City in America* painted across its wooden back. She removed her sickle from its place at her hip and twirled it. Her eyes and delicate fingers traced the ancient markings that curved around the blade.

"Many are offered the Contract."

"Hundreds? Thousands?"

She frowned at me. Clearly, she didn't want to be interrupted.

"Some accept and become Angels of Death; some decline. Of those who accept, few are strong enough to absorb another soul's energy; fewer still can hold that energy over time. It's why we keep you separated. We don't know if or when an Aod will die, and we can't control who you'll kill in the process. We call it the Burn Cycle."

"Have you known the whole time?"

More hesitation. "Since becoming one of the Xii-phronai."

Anger popped and boiled inside me. Always anger. Did I even have other emotions?

"Your power spikes. It manifests differently in each angel, but it manifests. Pompeii, Banda Aceh, Helike—I've seen Aods take out entire cities before they died. Eventually, the energy inside you becomes so intense that . . ." Raven made an exploding motion with her fingers.

"That's it? Poof, you're gone?"

"The Guardians take every precaution—"

"Damn the Guardians! Why didn't you tell me?"

"Would you want to know the moment you were going to die? Living to die rather than dying to live? What kind of life would that be?"

"What kind of life is this now?" I rose and stomped a few paces away, before sliding to the ground, anger wrestling with grief. I'd just been told I had cancer and it was terminal. All those years spent wishing for an end, and now that it was here, I didn't really want it.

What the hell is wrong with me?

Large droplets splashed atop my head, and I looked up as the sky tore open and rain descended. I glanced at Raven, who stared at me through a curtain of water, her bench sheltered and dry.

Unable to hold her gaze, I looked away and focused instead on a nearby car, where beads of water raced down the passenger-side window. Each cascading drop swallowed others in its path until, too large, it fell and splattered into nothingness.

Raven's boots entered my periphery before she slid down next to me, her dress repelling the water that had pooled on the ground. The rain danced around her but never touched her.

"Why wasn't I told *before* I signed the Contract?"

"You were. Everyone is. You were granted power, and in return, you promised your life—for eternity."

"Not as nothingness! As a piece of energy to be absorbed by someone else! He lied. He *lied.*"

"Even if that were true, you had the chance to clarify, and you didn't, did you?"

I refused to look at her, because she was right.

"Nope, not a single question. He gave you the chance, but all *you* wanted was vengeance, not fine print."

My fault. The only one I had to blame was myself.

My body ached under the strain of holding back the rage, and a taut beat thumped in the back of my skull. As I pushed my fingers against my temples, a thought exploded in my mind, and I snapped my head up to glare at Raven.

"Who gets the Aod's soul?"

"Keres—"

"You *saw* the angel take out a city. You were there! Who, Raven? Who gets it?"

She didn't answer for minutes that stretched into eternity.

"If the angel burns before we can reach them, I don't know where it goes." She put up a hand to stop my question. "Yes, it has to go somewhere, but not even my Guardian sources know."

"And if they don't . . . *burn* first?"

Raven stood, replaced her sickle at her hip, adjusted her skirts, and straightened to her full angelic height. She seemed to fill the entire street. "One of the Xiiphronai. We get it. We reap the soul."

I stared, my brain and mouth devoid of words. There were none that could capture what I felt in that moment.

"We're the only ones strong enough to hold it," Raven justified. "Our position grants us . . . immunity . . . to the side effects."

"Immunity?"

They get it—Raven or one of the other Xiiph—and they're *immune?* I wanted to laugh and scream as betrayal ground me in its teeth. I pulled my legs more tightly into my chest, curling into a ball on the cement as I tried to control the monster tearing at my internal organs. My gut twisted, and my chest tightened. I shook in rage, until the whole world seemed to move with me.

"Earthquake," Raven whispered.

I forced my eyes open. Roads and walls rippled like sheets in the wind. Car alarms blared, and lampposts and trees swayed in the rain. I held my breath, waiting to see if the world would fall.

It didn't.

The walls eventually stopped moving, and the ground quieted. When it was done, I lay motionless on the pavement, exhausted.

"Shit." Raven stared at me, eyes wide.

"When will I die?" I whispered.

"I don't know. We've been watching you for a long time, Keres. Only a handful outside of the Xiiph have lived as long as you, and none of them have reaped even a fraction of the souls you have, let alone a Daemon. I knew from the beginning you were different. I had to make you stronger, daughter. I had to help you survive." She pulled me up and back to the bench, sitting down beside me, graceful and beautiful. "I know you have questions, Keres. So many questions. But we're running out of time."

"Luke?" I asked.

"Luke, the Daemons, the reaping. The problems are compounding, and they're taking their toll on you. The power you gained from the Daemon must have increased yours exponentially. Luke is oblivious, too caught up in his own schemes to see the signs. If we don't do something soon, you'll burn . . . with or without a Xiiph to ease the end."

Ease the end . . . as if she were an angel of mercy rather than an angel of death. Still, I had to ask.

"Is there a chance, then?"

"I don't know, but I can hope."

"I haven't hoped for a very long time."

"Then trust me. I will hope for the both of us."

"What do I do now?"

"Breathe."

I took a breath and made a decision. I had to tell her.

Before I could figure out how, a man called Raven's name from the shelter of a nearby tree. I didn't know the Guardian standing there—not that I knew many—but the sharp, swirling tattoos down his left arm indicated he served with Luke. All Guardians had them. Slight differences indicated the Guardian's clan and rank. Luke's spread up his arm, over his shoulder, and covered the entire left side of his torso, front and back. I remembered tracing them for hours, following the intricate twists and turns that reminded me of fire, water, and air.

The Guardian held out his hand.

"Not a word," Raven mouthed to me, "until I get back."

I nodded. Raven joined the Guardian, and they *blinked* away to wherever Xiiphs and Guardians go.

As the downpour turned to a drizzle, thoughts saturated my mind as thoroughly as water did my clothes.

I could stay and eventually die at the hands of my terrifying surrogate mother.

Or I could leave and risk dying at the hands of strangers who supposedly hunted my kind.

One side worked for Satan and the other God, but which was which? And did it matter?

I shook my head. Only one question mattered now: was I willing to sell my soul to be free of the Contract?

And only one answer: yes.

I headed back to the pastry shop to gather my things and return home, my last stop before leaving for Jakarta. *Two* tokens were hidden there: one promised me a future and the other—a secret kept safe for a millennium—held the memories of my past.

As I crossed the cobblestone intersection, I rested my hand on the khukuri sheathed at my side. It hummed the song of death.

ELEVEN

I took a taxi home rather than *blink*, wanting to postpone my next, irreversible step for as long as possible. I even chose to climb the stairs. Sure, I'd made the decision to run to the Daemons, but making a choice and acting on it were two separate things. I needed more time.

As I turned the key in its lock, a wave of grief washed over me. I loved my apartment, with its two-story windows, exposed brick, and open concept. Renovated from an old factory, it spread across one quarter of the building like a splayed Chinese fan. It wasn't the place I'd stayed the longest, but it felt the most like home.

Perhaps one or two more hours with my paints and brushes wouldn't hurt?

When I stepped through my door and into a ransacked apartment, though, I realized I was already too late. The earthquake may have knocked my paintings off the hallway walls and made a mess of the entry alcove, but it wouldn't have sliced through the canvases and overturned the massive table in the dining room straight ahead.

Shit.

Luke came to mind first, but I dismissed the idea. Even if he'd figured out I had a Daemon token, this wasn't Luke's style. He took his rage out on people, not things.

Which left one option: Daemons.

I quietly dumped my sketch pad and supplies and drew my khukuri. My traitorous heart pounded. Could they hear it? Was I already dead and simply didn't know it yet? Electric tingles raced over my skin, memories of Ielu's energy wall surging forward, and I shuddered.

Keep it together, Keres. Keep it together.

Pushing aside my discomfort, I reached out for any emotions beyond my own. Nothing in the kitchen to my left or the main living space beyond. Stretching my senses farther, I searched my bedroom to the far left and then my art studio on the far right.

More nothing.

I was about to move down the hall when a horrifying thought made me freeze. What if I couldn't sense Daemons the same way I could Guardians and humans? What if they didn't even have emotions? Ielu had said he loved Daliah, but I'd met plenty of humans who believed they felt love when they had only given a name to the numbness filling them. And I'd been too busy fighting for my life to even try *reading* either Ielu or his woman.

Damn. I cursed myself silently for all the things I couldn't control and pushed away from the wall. I *had* to have the token—I didn't dare show up to that Adi person without it—and that meant I *had* to face whatever might be in here.

Deep breath.

Clinging to the hope that the token would give me sanctuary with any Daemon, not just Adi, I moved carefully down the hall, past the kitchen, and into the heart of the apartment, where I took in the full extent of the destruction.

Overturned bookcases bled first-edition novels, and smashed chairs littered the floor. My studio wasn't any better, with its broken easels and spilled paint. The whole place screamed frustration and anger. Whatever they'd been looking for, I don't think they'd found it.

What if they were looking for me?

I swallowed against the instant lump in my throat and wondered again if chasing down a Daemon was the right move after all.

"Ielu gave his life to save mine," I told the wrecked room. "I have to be willing to risk the same."

As I turned toward my bedroom, I noticed an ancient cup resting among shattered antiques. I eased over to it as the sight stirred darker images inside me: a small vessel tipped over, spilled liquid, shouting, crying . . .

I sank to the floor at the mouth of the hallway and reached for the broken cup.

I stare past the overturned cup, its wine already soaking into the rug, dark like blood. The blankets hiding me do not muffle my mother's screams; they only add to the weight I already carry on my slim shoulders.

It is my fault.

With my belly pressed against the hard desert floor of our tent, I can only see feet and hear voices as I peer beneath the goat-haired wall separating the women's room—my *immah*'s and mine—from the main room of my father. My mother's feet kick and twist. My father's dig into the dirt as he pushes toward her, but the other feet— the black-booted feet of strange men—hold firm, like the pegs that hold our tents against the wind.

So much yelling and screaming, both inside our tent and out. I cover my ears and stare at the cup as I count the seconds until they find me. All the boots are laughing, enjoying the cries of my people, as another set of boots enters and crosses to the opening between rooms.

Not enough seconds.

Abba tears himself free and lunges for the man at my door. For a moment, I believe he will save us, all of us. Abba, strong and fierce, has always protected us. He is indestructible. He is forever.

Then he falls, beaten to the ground, while the boots pull Immah out into the night. I cry for all of us.

Abba's face is so close, and he meets my gaze over the rim of the cup.

I am sorry, his eyes say.

"Abba," I mouth, tears spilling over my lips.

His eyes close, and he mouths, "I love you." When his eyes open, they are full of anger. He pushes from the ground, and his feet charge one black-booted pair.

"Run, Yaffa! Run!"

I wriggle out from under the blankets and quickly back toward the outside wall of our tent. There are no boots beyond, so I slide beneath the flap.

A man inside laughs and speaks our tongue brokenly, like a child still learning his words, but he speaks well enough for me to understand: my *immah* is dead.

Abba screams like the animals we guard our sheep against, and my heart breaks as I run. It tells me to go back and save my father, that there is no honor in running, but cowardice wins, and I press on toward anywhere but here.

Fear chases me with every step.

Our tents burn as our people die beneath the strangers' swords. Aunts, uncles, cousins—the desert drinks their blood as I run from the men who move like shadows of death among my kin. The horses are so close. I could take one. I could ride somewhere—anywhere. There has to be someone who can save me.

Please, God, save me.

I trip in my haste to reach the horses. My face slams against the ground, and I taste blood. I glance back and see a small body lying near the edge of a tent.

"Uri!"

I drop to my knees at the border between death and salvation and pull the small body into my lap. The horses are only steps away and I can already tell Uri is dead, but I can't let go. He is barely five, a cousin I helped raise from birth.

"Uri, wake up! Please, Uri, please."

My heart refuses to accept what my brain already knows to be true as I cry and rock and brush my open palm over his hair.

"I'm so sorry I did this to you." Despite the body in my arms, the words are really for my father.

I kiss Uri's forehead and close his eyes, so filled with terror even in death. Not wanting black-booted feet to trample my sweet Uri, I lean over to tuck him under the back wall of a nearby tent. Before I can finish my task, a rough hand grabs me from behind. My little cousin slips from my arms, thudding against the ground, and I scream.

The man laughs.

And I rise from the ground, ready to kill whoever touches me.

In one fluid movement, I stood, drew my khukuri, and pushed whoever had grabbed me up against the wall, blade to his throat. The gun he'd been holding skidded across the cement, and it took all my restraint not to kill him as I struggled to pull myself from the past and focus on the present.

Shamrock eyes widened.

So did mine as I stared at the dimple-faced man from Club Oubliette. "Frat Boy?"

I pressed my blade into his soft skin and drew blood.

TWELVE

I had always found it strange that supernatural beings were almost indistinguishable from mortals. We were so powerful, so . . . *more than.* Our differences should have been a beacon warning everyone away. A wolf shouldn't have been able to blend in with the flock.

Maybe that was what really set humans apart from the animal world: not their conscious thought but the ability of their predators to move and kill among the sheep, only to return to baaing while the blood dried on their teeth, no one the wiser.

Aods were distinguishable by our reaping blades, but Guardians and Daemons? More difficult to tell.

From what *little* I'd seen, both factions exuded confidence and an innate sense of authority, not unlike many charismatic humans, only turned up a few notches. Immortals also seemed more beautiful than humans. Even imperfections, like different-colored eyes, only added to their allure, making them unique, rather than ugly.

Guardians were always wrapped in tribal tattoos, and so far, Daemons seemed to have a near-imperceptible gleam to their skin, like models dusted with bronzer. Did they both bleed that strange iridescent liquid, or was that solely a Daemon thing?

Regardless, the thin crimson line forming along the paper cut I'd given Frat Boy spoke volumes about his humanity. I didn't know whether Daemons could turn off their glow, but I doubted they could change their blood.

Frat Boy was human.

"What the hell are you doing here?"

Though his tall frame stretched away from my blade, Frat Boy seemed completely at ease. He glanced around at the destruction of my apartment with a nonchalance that belied the situation. "You redecorating?"

"This wasn't you?"

"I just arrived."

I released him and then shoved him harder into the wall. "Why are you here? Did *they* send you?" I hated my lack of knowledge around the workings of the angels and demons who hid in the shadows of the human world.

Frat Boy touched a finger to the small cut. When it came away with a smear of blood, his gaze hardened, adding menace to his nonchalant smile. "I'd love to chat, but I have rules against negotiating with people who try to kill me."

"That was only a warning. Answer the damn question."

"Release me." The lucky shine of his eyes dimmed as he tilted his head down to look directly into mine, but he didn't raise his voice. Instead, it carried an authoritative inflection I'm sure most humans would have felt compelled to obey. "*Now.*"

Good thing I wasn't human. "You're not in a position to make demands."

"I'm not in a position to follow them either."

I reached for his emotions, which should have been wafting around him. Instead, I slid into the crisp dawn of a mountain morning, sun peeking over the ridgeline, its rays glittering on a glacier lake cradled within the basin. A sense of peace and safety lingered in the air, underscoring the tension of a forest devoid of animal sound.

No one felt like that. Ever. I shuddered and pulled back until I barely brushed the edges of his emotions.

A girl could get lost in that.

Instead of *reading* him, I decided to *seed* his thoughts, pushing the idea of cooperation toward his little human mind, adding images of him helping me, along with feelings of friendship. When he didn't respond as if I were his long-lost BFF, I used words. Some humans responded better to vocal commands.

"I am a close friend. You want to answer my question."

For the first time, Frat Boy eyed me as if I were a wild animal—unpredictable and dangerous. Then he did the most unexpected thing; tilting his head back, he laughed.

"Aren't you supposed to wiggle your fingers or something?" He waved his hand in front of my face.

I narrowed my eyes.

"No? Okay. I guess we do this your way. Who are *they?*"

Fine. If friendship wouldn't work, I'd try something more visceral.

Most Aods used *seeding* to manipulate a human's emotions, but my Reader ability allowed me to reach deeper, past the thoughts he so easily rejected and straight into primal reaction.

In this case, need.

I opened myself to his emotional aura again, immediately smelling fresh mountain air. This time, I shielded myself from anything that wasn't desire, until I reached the current of his sexual hunger. I allowed its electricity to fill me and pulse within me before I pushed it back toward him. I locked gazes with him, filling his vision with my face as I filled his body with desire.

His eyes took on a slight glaze. His pleasure rose like the sun, burning away the cool mountain morning. It grew hotter and hotter as I turned up the charge between us. Amplified it. Pressed the *idea* of me against him and wrapped it around him, as I might hook a leg around his hip. I kept pushing until . . .

Until I met resistance.

With Samson-like strength, he flicked away the deepening desire. I pushed even harder, pouring out images, stoking his fire, manipulating every string that should have made his pulse race and his hands yearn to touch my body. His cheeks flushed, he coughed slightly, and his hands fidgeted with the bottom of his suit jacket, but he didn't give in. Instead, as if he were shutting down an electric fireplace, he flipped a switch and turned off the flame.

"Your body should be aching for me!" I knew he'd felt it. Hell, *I* felt it!

An orange wash of embarrassment flashed around him, and his eyebrows stretched high above his eyes. I almost believed his innocent surprise until he smiled and winked. "As much as I like a forward girl—"

"That's not what I meant." I looked away, glowing with my own embarrassment. I eased up on the pressure with which I held him against the wall, but I didn't let go.

This was bad. Not only had he deflected my advance, but now I found myself noticing *his* body: The lean mass contained neatly within his button-up shirt and the subtle aroma floating around him. How, paired with a suit, his face lost its baby charm that had made me think he was a young college kid and, instead, took on a rugged freshness that spoke of zip lines, cave dives, and untamed adventures.

My pulse raced. *My* hands yearned.

"Are you okay?" He sounded concerned, but I refused to look at him, even when he timidly touched the hand holding a blade against his throat. He didn't push, only rested his hand on mine. "Please. Let me go."

Please.

"Did they send you? The Daemons?" I couldn't keep the fear out of my voice. I glanced back into his eyes, and the smart-ass remark he might have shared died on his lips.

He shook his head. "No. No one sent me."

Truth burned hot like a branding iron. He believed what he said.

So did I.

I let go of him and backed away, placing the breakfast bar between us as I sheathed my blade. He stepped toward me.

I reached for my reaping blade. "Don't."

He stopped and reached into his pocket instead, tossing his wallet on the counter in front of me. "The name's Fitz, but you can call me Joe."

I flipped it open and glanced at the contents: Joseph Fitzgerald, Fugitive Recovery Agent, and, in smaller letters, Private Investigator.

"Next time, lead with that. I almost killed you."

"You never asked."

"Yes, I did."

"You asked why I was here and if 'they' had sent me, never who I was. Kind of hurt, really. Usually, the first thing you ask another person is their name."

"What are you doing here?" I held up a hand before he could answer and pushed his wallet back across the counter. "Never mind. I don't care. Just go."

Walking into the kitchen, he scooped up his gun and checked it over—either for scratches or to make a show of things—before he holstered it. "I showed you mine." He nodded to his wallet. "How about you show me yours?"

I reached for his emotions, easing my way back into the mountainscape. Rather than images, he made me feel transported, as if I existed both here in Baltimore *and* on the shores of a glacier lake. I probed further, expecting the tension I'd sensed earlier. Instead, I found a forest alive with movement and sound. His lake shimmered with a calm that rippled here and there as winds blew across the water, teasing it into movement.

I got the sense he *enjoyed* this.

He made me want to smile, which in turn made me want to punch him. So I left him standing in the kitchen and headed to the bedroom. "Leave!" I called over my shoulder. I'd already wasted enough time.

My room was a bigger disaster than the living room. All my dresser drawers had been ripped from their sockets, the contents dumped on the floor and kicked around. All the bedding and even the mattress had been torn apart, covering the room in feathers and fluff.

I sprinted to the bathroom and pulled up the baseboard behind the door, sighing in relief when I found Ielu's token still hidden within. Tucking the token into the hidden pocket of my khukuri sheath, I returned to the bedroom.

One down, one to go.

Joe leaned against the doorway separating my room from the main living space. *Go away,* I thought, trying again to *seed* him, but he didn't move. Maybe broken powers were part of the Burn Cycle? I wished I'd had more time with Raven. So many questions.

"What's your name?" he asked.

I knelt to scour the mess. Feathers and crumbles of foam moved around me like sand. No matter how much I scooped, more of the same floated back in to fill the space. I settled on gathering the bigger things, like clothes, and then running my hands beneath the fluff to find the tiny piece I searched for.

"You don't look like a bounty hunter."

"Fugitive recovery agent." The correction sounded automatic, as if he said it a hundred times a day. "My suits blend in with the type of people I hunt better than leather vests and snakeskin boots."

I paused. "Am I your prey, then?"

"That depends."

"On what?"

"Do you like my suit?"

I turned to see a flash of dimple that implied a joke, but tension had returned to the mountain wilderness of his emotions. I returned to my search.

As I continued sifting through clothes, lace panties, shredded pillows, and mattress stuffing, Joe joined me on the floor. He gathered my clothes and underthings into neat piles, sorting and picking up the room as he moved.

"What are you doing?" I asked.

"Helping, though I could be more useful if I knew what we were looking for."

What was his endgame? "You really should go."

As should I, but . . . five more minutes. If I could not find it in the next five minutes, I would leave it behind. *I'm always leaving you behind, aren't I, Abba?*

I glanced at the human sorting and piling. "You don't want to be connected to me."

"I already am."

"What does that mean?"

"What do you know about Sergio Ricci?"

My stomach flipped. I wasn't prepared for that question. Questions about Ielu, Daliah, or even Luke, yes. But Sergio?

"What should I know?"

"Hopefully a name or face."

"You just gave me his name." If *seeding* wouldn't work, talking in circles might.

"I mean his killer."

"Murder? You think I know something?" I tried to sound innocent—however that was supposed to sound—but without the power of persuasion, I felt like a bad actor. Raven was right; I *was* soft.

He leaned forward on his knees. "Do you?"

I shrugged. "Sorry to disappoint."

Joe stopped searching. I felt his gaze on me, but I refused to look up. "I saw you follow him from the club into the alley."

Instead of answering, I pulled Ielu's token from the sheath and held it out. "I'm looking for an object about this size, only slightly thicker and with a small hole in the middle." I returned the token to its hiding place. "The outside will be dark and shiny."

"Your home is violated, you are willing to kill whoever walks through your door, and *that* is what you look for?" His eyes asked the question his mouth was too polite to speak: *Why?*

After a pregnant silence, I answered the unspoken question. "It belonged to my *abba* . . . my father."

It was a piece of his shofar, to be exact—a thin slice I'd sheared off the smallest end of the ram's horn before I buried it with my *abba*. To anyone else, it would look like a thin slice of rock or ancient wood. To me, it was, as my *abba* had always taught, an extension of his soul.

And to the Guardians, serious contraband.

Our final law: forsake everything. No ties to humanity, not even something as tiny as the piece I searched for. Raven claimed it was essential for accepting our new life as Angels of Death. Perhaps she was right.

Yet here I was, sifting through the destruction for the last remnant of my humanity.

I guess I never had been good at keeping the rules.

Please, God, give me time to find my abba *before I go.*

Our search seemed to take forever as I counted down the seconds to my self-imposed deadline. Just as I gave up, Joe held up the slim piece of shofar.

"Does it look like this?"

"Yes!" Closing the gap between us, I reached for the item.

Standing, he pulled it out of my reach. "Sergio?" His eyes begged for answers, a soft, pleading stare that spoke of long hours and late nights. For the first time, I didn't have to reach for his feelings; they drifted toward me.

Normally, I felt, saw, or smelled emotions—tar, daggers, heat, flames—but *this* carried the low sounds of a cello: deep, resonating, and humming grief. Images of children flickered within the music.

One I knew: Emily.

"Sergio was a sick man. Whatever happened in that building, he deserved it."

Joe leaned so close, I could feel the electricity of his body dancing along his skin. "I don't disagree, but he was only a stepping stone to a much bigger bastard. If I can find the killers, perhaps I can find who hired them, which might lead me to Quinn."

I grabbed his wrist and reached for my memento. I wouldn't lead him anywhere. "More than one, huh?"

Joe's eyes widened, but he flicked the piece to his free hand before I could take it. "Had to be. What can you tell me?"

I didn't have much, only flashes and brief memories. It wasn't like Sergio's complete history had been downloaded into my brain.

I twisted Joe's arm behind his back and slammed him into the wall near the door. "Give it to me. I'd prefer not to hurt you, but I will." This annoying dance of ours had to end.

He raised his free hand to face level, my shofar clenched within his fist. "What do you know?"

"Not enough. I'm sorry, but I have to go." I bent his arm back until he gave a short cry, but instead of handing me the item, he pushed it into his mouth and swallowed.

"Are you kidding me? What are you, two?"

I yanked him from the wall and swept his legs out from under him, sending him to the floor. I kept his head from hitting the ground but pressed my knee into his sternum until he grunted.

"Whatever it takes. You're all I've got."

"Find another bounty." I grabbed Joe's face, ready to force open his jaw and make him vomit up the shofar.

"Tell that to the kids being prostituted around the city."

Pain burned in my gut and pounded in my head as images of a little girl crying in a closet flickered in my vision. I pushed off him and stood, staring down at the idiot who'd placed himself in the middle of a situation he could not understand and probably wouldn't survive. He rose onto his elbows and returned my gaze, steady and calm.

"Idiot."

"I prefer persistent or dedicated. Besides, you'll get it back in about twenty-four hours—"

"For your sake, you better be right, or no Guardian law on this planet will save your soul, intervening be damned!" I grabbed a fistful of his jacket and yanked him to standing.

"Tell me." His eyes pleaded with mine.

I held his gaze. "*I* killed him. I killed all of them. And trust me, that doesn't lead you anywhere you want to go."

I'd finally shut him up. Leaving him to chew on my confession, I returned to the living room to take a final look at the bits and pieces that summed up my life. Books, furniture, my art—the totality of my existence to be left behind. Who was I? Who would I be?

Joe followed. "You're not lying—"

"I know."

"But what you're telling me is impossible."

I turned to him. "Hold on to that word, Frat Boy. You're going to be using it a lot where we're going . . . assuming you survive."

"And where is that?"

"To Satan himself if it will free me from my Contract."

"Fascinating. Do tell."

I froze as the hard, cold voice sounded behind me. I'd been so distracted by Joe, I hadn't noticed Luke's arrival.

Fuck.

THIRTEEN

I whipped around and placed myself between Luke and the human who held the last remaining piece of my *abba*. Drawing my khukuri from its sheath, I reached for Joe with my free hand and pulled him close. Any space between us would have left room for Luke, and I couldn't afford that.

Blinking was out of the question. Though I could jump from here to the moon in a heartbeat, piercing the fabric of time and space created a momentary disturbance that any good tracker could follow, like strings of beads swaying in a doorway after someone passes through. I couldn't outrun Luke on a good day, let alone with human baggage. Which meant I had to knock him out long enough for us to make our escape and hope to whatever part of God that still loved me that I could find a Daemon to protect us before Luke found me.

What the hell am I thinking? It was a terrible option, but it was the only one I had.

Watching Luke, I called over my shoulder, "You should have walked away, Frat Boy."

"*You* should have begged me for mercy, *cher.*"

Blinking closer, Luke backhanded me across the face so hard, I stumbled to the floor, my blade clattering across the cement. He picked Joe up by his perfectly tailored suit and threw him into the wall next to my bedroom door. The human crumpled like a discarded rag doll.

"No!" I scrambled for my reaping blade, and Luke followed, leaving Joe alive. Just as my fingers brushed the wooden handle, Luke grabbed my ankle and yanked.

"Did you think you could leave me again, *ma petite*?" He pulled me to my feet by my upper arms. His gaze grew distant, his eyes narrowing, as he cocked his head to the side. Refocusing on me, his eyes widened. "Where is it?"

Silence.

"*Where*?"

He usually started slow and worked up to the hottest temperatures, but this time, the heat from his hands was instant and intense. I screamed. Steam and the stench of singed flesh wafted up from my biceps as Luke scorched my body and soul. New skin formed as the charred tissue sloughed off, the regrowth as painful as the burning.

"Please, Luke."

"Give me a reason to save you, Keres."

When I refused to answer, his power raced across my body and gathered at my hip. Grabbing my neck with one hand, he felt around my khukuri sheath with the other until, jaw clenching, he found Ielu's token and removed it from its compartment. The token sizzled, burning Luke's fingers, and he threw it to the floor, his anger sharp and unrelenting.

"Tell me he forced that on you. Tell me you didn't know you had it!"

He searched my eyes for an answer I couldn't give him.

"No." His face flushed with rage, and he shook me. "NO!" Spittle flew from his mouth as he screamed like a broken, ferocious animal, and my screams echoed his. Two very different types of pain filled the apartment as a cycle of scorching heat singed my neck.

"Did you hope that because it belonged to a Daemon, I wouldn't sense it? I didn't recognize it at first, but I felt its power the moment you returned through the gate. Only I never guessed *you* knew about it. You should have told me!"

"Please stop." *Please.* But that word didn't hold any magic with Luke.

"I gave you every chance, and you betrayed me, Keres."

"*I* betrayed *you?*" Choking on pain and anger, I reached for a sliver of Shadow and cracked it toward Luke, slicing his cheek. It healed as quickly as it opened, but he released his grip on my throat and stumbled back. Shock rippled through his emotions.

"Careful, *cher,* you don't know what you're doing." His voice vibrated with the smallest trace of fear.

I whipped Shadow toward him again, gaining confidence with each of his retreating steps. "Tell me, *Aishah,* what is faithfulness and loyalty in our world? What is *truth?* Gates. Reaping blades. Protection. Daemons. Burn Cycles. LUCIFER! Where does your betrayal end? Prove to me I'm one of God's soldiers instead of Satan's pawn."

"You are as you have always been: a warrior for the right cause."

"Then why does it hurt so damn much?" I lashed out, but my power shattered against a shadowy barrier and dissipated into nothingness.

"I am tired of your impertinence."

A force crashed into me from behind, and I stumbled

to my knees. Smiling wickedly, Luke struck me in the face with his Shadow power. My bones crunched beneath the force, mending before I hit the floor.

"You are a stupid girl, Keres. Too willful for anyone's good. But lucky for you, I am good at breaking will."

Darkness slithered over my body, binding my arms and legs and gagging my mouth. I tried to fight it, but his power crushed my defenses and cut me off from the Shadow. I could *feel* the shadows just beyond my reach, but I couldn't manipulate them—like being trapped in a glass prison.

He stalked closer, crouching down to stare into my wide eyes. "You don't know a sliver of the truth, *cher.* Who will protect you if not me? Who will love you? You have nowhere to run."

I turned my face away, ashamed of the answer in my eyes: Daemons. That's where I would run. He grabbed my chin and pulled me back around to face him, but he stared at the token resting on the floor next to me.

"You think the Daemons will help you? You think they *can?* You are nothing to them . . . to *anyone.*"

The shadowy chains tightened around my body, creating a cacophony of snaps and pops as my ribs broke under the pressure. Luke ignored my muted cries and begging stare. He paced in front of me, his gaze becoming wilder and more distant with each turn.

"I've been too lax, but I can fix this. I still have time. But where to hide her?" He stopped and gazed at the token again. Whatever plan was forming in that head of his would not be good for me.

Behind Luke, Joe groaned and pressed a palm to his head. I met his blurry gaze and shook my head slightly. *Stay down,* I pleaded silently. Instead, he stood, using the wall to steady himself.

Luke looked at the mortal, then at me and grimaced. Crouching, he patted my cheek. "Let's get rid of this one, shall we?"

I gave a muffled yell and struggled violently against my chains. If I lost this human, not only would I have more innocent blood on my hands, but I would also lose the last piece of my father.

Luke rose and stalked toward Joe, his movements graceful and menacing. "You, I'll kill slowly."

Frat Boy's signature glass lake of emotion lay perfectly still as he drew his firearm and squeezed off a few rounds. His eyes widened as bullets hit an invisible wall and fell clinking to the floor. Instead of emptying his clip, Joe holstered his weapon, grabbed a piece of broken furniture, and stumbled forward to meet Luke.

Idiot!

Luke laughed as the human swung a chair leg at him. He grabbed the leg with one hand and flexed, shattering the wood into little splinters. Dropping the wood, Joe threw up his arms in a boxer's defensive stance, and the two men circled each other.

I turned my attention to the shadowy chains woven around me, which had stopped tightening once Luke focused on Joe. I scanned them for a weakness or a way out—anything—but I came up empty. The links held tight, more solid than steel.

Joe jabbed a quick right punch to Luke's face and winced as his hand connected with supernatural flesh and bone, which didn't give way as a human's would have. Luke rubbed his jaw and smiled but didn't return the hit. After a punch to Luke's stomach that did more damage to the human than the Guardian, Joe backed away, keeping broken furniture between him and Luke. Joe threw books, lamps, pieces of furniture—whatever he could get his hands on—and Luke batted each away without effort, playing with Joe to torture me instead of killing him outright.

"Could use some suggestions right about now, Angel Girl," Joe called out.

"I'm trying!" came out as "Hmm *hmm*hmm!"

Luke deflected another object and pounced. *Blinking*, Luke grabbed Joe's neck and lifted until Joe's feet stretched for solid ground. "You should never have come here."

Joe gasped for air, hands hammering at Luke's forearm as the Guardian turned so he could watch me watch Joe die. I kept my face expressionless as he squeezed the life from Joe and the last remnants of hope from me.

"Too bad she didn't tell you that everyone she touches dies."

I stopped fighting my chains, his words breaking me. Luke smiled victoriously.

Movement beyond Luke's shoulder caught my attention. Two men stepped from my bedroom door—a tanned ginger and a dark-umber man with piercing blue eyes. Both had the distinct sun-kissed quality to their skin that Ielu and Daliah had had. My eyes widened, and Luke glanced over his shoulder.

Joe used the distraction to punch Luke in the throat, and a surprised Luke dropped him. Joe coughed and inhaled gulps of air as he rolled toward me and away from Luke's reach.

Fury poured from Luke like hot steam, but he turned toward the greater threat—the Daemons. They struck in unison, a blur of attacks and counterattacks. Despite myself, Luke's skill impressed me. His fluid grace, his powerful blows. Power surged between the three men, shadow and light weaving an intricate tapestry. If Daliah had been here, Luke would have fallen, but this two-on-one seemed an even match.

Mostly. I could access my Shadow power again, which meant Luke needed everything he had for the fight.

"What can I do?" Joe reached for a shadowy chain and flinched when he touched it, eyes wide. "It's *solid.*"

I nodded, already searching the links with my power. I quickly found what I needed—a weak link. One that hadn't been there before. I poured more Shadow into that one spot, wedging the link apart until it snapped and Luke's chains dissolved, releasing me from my prison.

I *blinked* to my khukuri at the base of the breakfast bar, too close to the raging trio, and a third Daemon appeared only steps from me. He stood about Luke's height, with huge muscles and dark sandy hair, and he *reeked* of pride and overconfidence—a cheap cologne so bad, it had me blowing air out my nose. This guy *really* loved himself.

I snatched up my blade and backed away.

"You're late!" called Ginger.

"Looks like I'm right on time. They said you'd have one of those,"—Mr. Narcissist nodded toward the weapon in my hand—"but I didn't believe them." He shifted his weight to the balls of his feet and stretched out his arms like he might bear-hug me into submission. Joe tried to lunge in between us, but I pushed him back behind me. His fractured hand, bruised trachea, and major concussion would only hinder my efforts.

"Stay," I commanded. He frowned but nodded.

The Daemon inched closer. "Is he a toy, Fallen, or a pet?"

"I seek an audience with Adi. Can you take me to him?"

"Keres!" Despite everything he already knew, Luke sounded shocked.

Mr. Narcissist glanced at Luke still fighting the other two and then back at me. He smiled and straightened from his fighting position. "Sure."

The faint, putrid odor of deceit wafted from him like a dead skunk. Why hadn't I ever noticed it on Raven or Luke? Maybe they believed their lies? I shook my head. Things to think about later.

"On second thought, we'll take the train. I wouldn't want to intrude on the alone time you need for you and yourself."

"Cheeky little Fallen, aren't you?" He jumped at me, his expression dark with contempt, lips curled. I dodged but didn't use my blade. A rising body count wouldn't do me any favors when I asked this Adi person for help.

The Daemon *blinked* out of sight, and I backed up toward Joe. *Shit. He could be anywhere.*

Reappearing, he grabbed my right wrist and shook until my reaping blade fell to the floor, where it skittered and bounced toward the dining room table.

Mr. Narcissist smiled wide. "Surprised?" He leaned in close, the stench of cheap cologne intensifying. His little trick had made him recklessly confident.

I turned into him slightly and then stepped back out, using the whipping motion of my body to give power to my left elbow flying at his face. It struck hard near his left ear, and the Daemon released my arm, falling back into the stools at the bar.

I turned to check on Joe. He leaned one shoulder against the hallway wall behind me, studying the scene. His hands hung loose at his sides, one thumb tucked into a pocket. He was either the stupidest man I'd ever met or the calmest. Hard to tell which.

"Look out!" he shouted.

Fingers grasped my hair and yanked me backward. I

turned in time to catch the Daemon's knee before it connected with my head. I still took a hard hit to the side of my face, which made my eyes water, but I preferred it over a blow to the base of my skull. He forced me the rest of the way to my knees and, still holding me by the hair, attempted a second knee thrust to my nose.

I braced for impact as I gathered power inside me, amassing it behind an invisible dam. Instead of Shadow, I reached for the force I'd used against Ielu and the ocean. I tapped into my rage, my fear, maybe even some of my hope and kept pulling until I couldn't pull anymore.

A pop preceded a bullet crashing into the Daemon's skull. Simultaneously, a shadowy tendril whipped out and latched onto my attacker's ankle. Luke tugged, and the Daemon lost his balance, falling forward. Neither killed him, but they allowed me to land an uppercut to his chin, followed by a jab to his chest that I spiked with a drop of the power I'd been gathering. He flew back and slammed into Piercing Blue Eyes, knocking him to the ground.

All eyes turned toward me.

"Get up, fools!" Ginger shouted. "We need them both alive."

Both? Alive? I'd assumed they were hunting me and Luke had simply gotten in the way. Were they after both of us now because Luke had helped me before? Or because he was here now? Or because he was a Guardian? I glanced toward Luke, but the static in his emotional aura told me he was confused too.

Since I didn't know enough about either faction to draw a clear conclusion, *my* plan had to stay the same. These men weren't my ticket to Adi, but that was where Ielu had pointed me and that was where I would go.

I moved to Joe, who'd holstered his weapon and returned to leaning. A stance, I realized, that had less to do with cockiness and more to do with the fact that his body was giving out. He hurt more than he wanted to let on.

"Time to go," I said.

"You sure? I'm almost ready for the rest of round one." His smile turned into a wince.

Mr. Narcissist freed himself from his friend, murder written in his gaze, and I drew in the last remaining drops of power I could hold.

"You have a plan?" Joe asked.

"Sort of."

"Those are my favorite."

It wasn't really a plan so much as a hope. I only needed a small window and enough of a distraction to grab the coin and my blade and run. With Luke and the Daemons at each other's throats, I hoped they wouldn't be inclined to follow me.

Mr. Narcissist *blinked*. When he reappeared right in front of me, I released the torrent, making sure to project it away from the fragile human behind me. A shockwave tore through the room, throwing my attacker back again, knocking over the rest of the men like reeds in a hurricane, and blowing out the two-story windows beyond.

I hesitated, surprised by my own power.

"Umm . . ." Joe's voice snapped me back into focus. I *blinked* to my blade and then the token, snatching up both before returning to Joe. I felt . . . *winded* . . . almost too tired to *blink* again. I hadn't even known that was possible. I hoped I had enough left to get Joe and me out of here.

Keeping an eye on the unconscious men, I sheathed my khukuri and returned the coin to its hidden pocket. Luke stirred slightly, and part of me felt glad he was the first to move. I hoped it meant he'd have time to escape before the Daemons regained their senses. He could be hurtful, controlling, and downright scary, but love—even broken, dying, toxic love—made me want him to be okay.

"I'm sorry, Luke."

I wrapped my arm around Joe's waist and draped one of his over my shoulders. I tried to ignore how good he felt beneath my hands.

"Ready?" I asked, more for myself than for Joe.

Luke groaned, and Joe's arm tightened around me. "Thought you'd never ask."

"Be careful what you wish for, Frat Boy. We're probably headed straight to Hell."

"Too bad. I hear the Bahamas are nice this time of year."

"Kerrr . . ." Luke slurred.

"By the way," I told Joe, "this is going to hurt." Before he could even raise an eyebrow, I *blinked* us away.

Please, God, let me have made the right choice . . . and protect me from whoever follows.

When we reappeared in the rusted moonlight of Jakarta, I unsheathed my reaping blade and readied myself for whoever might be waiting and whoever might follow.

FOURTEEN

Putrid odors fused into a sour sweetness that wafted through the Jakartan slums. Houses with blackened windows hunkered together on stilts along a river of floating garbage. Some had large pieces of debris attached to their posts, creating single open-air "rooms" underneath.

With my khukuri at the ready, its runes glowing bright blue, I backed Joe into the closest structure covered in shadow, until he bumped into corrugated metal. Still, I pressed closer, as terror—of Luke—and heat—for Joe—warred within me.

Reaching behind me, I pressed my hand protectively against Joe's waist. His heart beat rapidly against my back, a match for my own, and the touch, however slight, addled my brain. At the same time, my chest tightened painfully as I considered the situation.

"Shit." There was no going back after tonight. I hadn't just disobeyed Luke; I'd weaponized my power against him. No way he'd leave me breathing long enough to repeat my mistake.

"You're crushing me," Joe breathed.

Releasing him, I stepped back into the hazy moonlight and peered around the small path between houses, trying to anticipate where pursuers might appear. "They should be here by now."

"I take it we're not in Kansas anymore," Joe said.

"Jakarta."

Joe's face remained impassive, though shock rippled through his calm. The man kept an almost inhumanly tight rein on his emotions.

"We're waiting for more of your friends?" he asked.

"I don't have friends." I'd always hoped that maybe, if I were good enough, obeyed strictly enough, I might someday be accepted, but . . . Guardians were still puppet masters, and I was just their doll on strings—a murdering, fighting, serial-killer doll.

"Too bad. I was beginning to like them." Joe coughed and felt tenderly at his throat. Drawing his Glock, he moved toward me, investigating the various openings beneath the houses. His movements were not as smooth as when he had tried shooting Luke but also not as awkward as I'd expected. He was good at holding both emotion and pain under control.

"What is taking so long?" The pit in my belly widened. Luke had called my name, which meant he had already been awake. Someone should have followed by now. The Guardians knew how to find me; they always had. Whether I went to Buenos Aires or the Nepal jungle, I couldn't hide.

Then why the hell did I run? My idiocy had no end. Daemons weren't the shield I'd hoped they'd be, and I'd attacked the one Guardian with the power to protect me.

Too many things I didn't know and people I couldn't trust. I prayed Adi would be different—that he'd be waiting for me at all.

"Did we lose them?" Joe asked.

"You don't lose Guardians."

"Then what?"

"I don't know." I hated those words.

"Maybe grabbing reinforcements?"

"I don't know."

"What next?"

I glanced at him, lips pursed, and refused to say the words one more time. "Let's move." I reached for his arm to pull it back over my shoulder, but he pushed my hands away and shook his head.

"I'll be in your way if we have unwelcome guests."

I couldn't argue.

We crept through the jungle of stilts and garbage. Joe occasionally pushed a quick breath out through his nostrils, either managing pain or trying to rid himself of the smell burning our noses. I moved quickly toward the city center that grew out of the landscape in the distance, marked by a cloud of light that drowned out the stars. The sooner I found Adi, the better.

"Baltimore to Jakarta, huh?" Joe whispered after a few minutes.

"We call it *blinking*. Surprised?"

"After what I saw in your apartment, not really. Just curious."

"Now's not a good time."

"Perhaps, but I might not get another chance."

"To what?"

"Know your name."

I stopped and looked at him over my shoulder. "Seriously?"

He smiled to his dimples and shrugged. "I always like to know who I'm risking my life for."

I studied him for a moment and relented. "Keres."

"*KEAR-iss*," he repeated, tasting the unfamiliar word. "Like the sisters from Greek mythology?"

I looked away, shame filling me. The name was a gift from Luke. I could still recall the slither of Luke's pride as it moved up my arm from our intertwined hands to caress my face: Cool. Smooth. Possessive.

You've earned it, he'd said after a particularly brutal reaping. *Plural for the amount of carnage you can reap even though you are only one angel.*

I shuddered. "Keep moving."

We crept between the stilts until they gave way to the crooked alleys of precariously stacked two- and three-story shanties. Everything seemed to be built of discarded remnants. I headed down the closest alley.

"And those . . . people?" Joe asked. "You used the term Guardians."

"How much do you want to know, Frat Boy?"

"Everything, Angel Girl."

I threw a questioning look over my shoulder. "That's the second time you've called me that."

He pointed at my back. "Your tattoo was kinda hard to miss."

I raised an eyebrow. *Right.* The halter top I had worn to the club had left most of my angel wings exposed. A joke from a few centuries ago.

Before I could comment, a clatter echoed nearby. Weapon in hand, I turned toward the noise and cursed the confined space. There wasn't enough room between the makeshift buildings to fight without risking human casualties, and Joe was in no condition for another *blink.* Then again, neither was I.

I hadn't felt this drained since I was human.

Before I could get a clear read on the source, Joe stepped in front of me, his gun leveled at the darkness.

Every muscle in my body tightened, and I pushed him out of the way as a sick animal that might have been a rat or a small dog tumbled out over the garbage.

"Idiot!" I hissed.

Joe's eyes widened.

"You can't protect me. You can't even protect yourself. Your guns and weapons are useless, human."

To prove my point, I grabbed his hand, pointed his gun at my chest, and pulled the trigger. The bullet burned my skin and drilled through a rib on its way through my body. I felt every rip and crunch as it passed through soft tissue and bone. My body healed right behind it, a painful reconstruction of skin, muscle, and bone weaving back together. I felt a pinch as the bullet entered my heart, and then it was gone. The regeneration process was so fast, it nearly caught the projectile inside me, but the bullet burst out my back and buried itself in the metal wall behind me.

"What the hell!" Joe whisper-shouted.

"I figured you needed a demonstration." I released his hand and continued down the alley. A few curtains swayed from hidden onlookers, but we were in a part of the city where people kept silent lips.

Joe caught up in a few pain-filled strides and jerked me around to face him. His trembling hands gripped my shoulders, and his eyes burned. Rage whipped the glassy waters of his emotional calm into stiff peaks, and fear shrouded the scene in a dark mist. Not fear *of* me, but fear of what might happen *to* me—a small nuance, but clear as it wafted from him. We didn't even know each other, and he was concerned for my welfare. What was I supposed to do with that? I felt grateful for the darkness that concealed the flush of my embarrassment.

"You need to know your limits, mortal, or you're going to get killed. This isn't the time for you to play hero."

"So you fucking make me pull the trigger?"

Was he angry that I'd surprised him or that I'd put myself in danger in the first place? I honestly couldn't tell and didn't have the mental or emotional bandwidth for his shit. Let the mortal figure out his own damn emotions.

I yanked my shoulders from his grip. "Let's go. We need to find shelter before sunrise. I'd rather not have any other visitors before I'm ready."

"That's too bad," said an unfamiliar voice.

As I whipped around, another body collided with my own.

FIFTEEN

The Earth fell away as my attacker rode me like a kneeboard skidding across the ground. As we slowed, he grabbed my khukuri and threw his body forward, tugging the blade from my grasp and rolling to his feet.

"You've finally come, then," he growled in Betawi, an indigenous language of Jakarta. He was shorter than me by at least an inch, if not two, with a boxy face. From his hooded, angular eyes to the cut of his jaw, all his features were chiseled from the same rich amber as the shoulders and biceps exposed by his tank top. He was too beautiful.

I stood slowly. The garbage and metal of Jakarta had faded into a gray landscape of dirt and outlines, like a 3D charcoal sketch of the world we'd just left. It made me feel like a bat using echolocation—disorienting and strange.

"Where the hell are we?"

"Your tomb."

"Then you've been expecting me?"

"Every day. I'm only surprised it took you this long."

No wonder Luke hadn't followed. He'd already set the trap and then waited to see if I'd spring it. *Damn.*

I glanced down the sketchlike alley. Joe's outline crept forward, gun drawn, while other human outlines closed in. I tried *blinking* to him, but it didn't work.

Fuck! I had no way to save him. No way even to save myself.

Jerking the small utility knife from its sheath and shifting my weight to the balls of my feet, I squared off against my opponent. My heart was beating so fast, I thought it would explode. "Who are you?"

"I shed my need for titles a long time ago, Aod."

I immediately ruled out human and Daemon. A human wouldn't have been able to transport us to wherever the hell this was, and he didn't have the sun-kissed glow of the Daemons.

Glancing at my khukuri, I flinched as I noticed the runes flickering between charcoal and bright blue. "Holy shit, you're an Angel of Death."

And he's holding the only blade that can kill me. I took a step back.

His eyes narrowed, but he remained silent.

I reached for the emotional power I'd become accustomed to using as a battering ram—and found nothing. I reached again, but I couldn't hold it. The energy in here felt different. Every time I pulled on what I thought was solid power, it poured from my grasp like sand.

"Whatever power you think you have, it's useless here."

He lunged and swiped at my body with my blade. I jumped back, and the khukuri sliced through air, but even if I hadn't moved, he would have missed. Was he toying with me?

Backing away, he tucked my blade in his belt loop but remained crouched, guarded, and ready to fight.

I opened myself to his emotions and frowned. I could

sense the boundaries of his emotional aura, but I felt nothing inside, like reaching into an empty fish tank.

This day just keeps getting better. I resisted the urge to throw my hands up in the air and stomp away. What good was this "enhanced" ability if I couldn't *read* the people I needed to the most? Luke and Raven hid their emotions behind walls and chaos, and now this guy felt empty?

Ugh!

I leaped toward the Aod, aiming a punch at his chest. I expected him to block and had a few countermoves planned. Instead, he deflected my punch neatly to the side and wrapped his opposite arm beneath my elbow—first over, then under—and pulled up until I found myself up on my toes with my back against his chest. He locked the hold with a grip on my shoulder and wrapped his free arm around my neck.

I would have to adjust my approach to counter his *silat* fighting style. My own was rusty at best.

"How did you find me?" he asked. The pressure at my shoulder turned into a cycle of tearing and mending ligaments, almost dislocating the joint.

I frowned. "What did you say?"

"You heard me, Aod."

I shook my head slightly. "*You* were waiting for *me*, remember?"

Uncertainty filled his fish tank before he emptied it to nothingness again. "If not me, then who?" He flexed his arm to add pressure to my windpipe and spine.

"Crawl back to your masters, dog." I stepped back between his legs and, grabbing the forearm around my neck, flipped him over my body. My right arm, pretzeled with his, snapped at both the elbow and shoulder joints, and I inhaled sharply as all the ligaments tore.

Arms were not meant to bend that way.

Once free, I twisted my arm back into place and let the healing process do the rest.

The Aod rolled out of my throw and back to his feet. "And beg their forgiveness? I don't think so."

He rushed forward, faster even than Raven. I tried a quick front kick, but he blocked it down and struck me in the chest with his elbow, followed by a quick strike high inside my thigh. My nerves screamed long enough for him to land an open palm to the underside of my jaw, cracking the bone in two, before he finished with two fists to my lower chest. My heart stuttered under the onslaught.

As I stumbled back, he jumped after me, wrapping one leg around my abdomen and the other behind my legs to haul me to the ground. Before he could follow up the scissor kick with anything else, I rolled out of his hold and scrambled to my feet.

My body might continue to heal with every break, but emotionally and mentally, I was exhausted.

As we began circling each other, he pulled my khukuri from his belt. "If you will not answer my questions, you are of no use to me." He rushed forward, forcing me into a silent-but-deadly dance of attacks and counterattacks, until I tumbled to the ground.

With no other choice, I rolled to my feet and ran.

SIXTEEN

Speed and distance didn't seem to matter in this space. I only had to will myself forward and the world slid past me like I was a bullet train. At first, I tried to steer clear of buildings and people, but I couldn't shake my pursuer, so I took a chance and cut through some of the outlines racing past me. It worked! Rather than running into a wall or a person, I slid through everything as if it were smoke and air. Tiny wisps swirled after me from the outlines I crossed, but they reset almost as quickly as they formed.

It gave me hope, and I pushed myself harder, gathering speed with each step. I raced through what looked like Singapore, Thailand, through China to Kazakhstan.

"You can't run, silly girl," the Angel of Death whispered.

But I did run. All over this shadowy world, trying everything I knew to open a space back to the other reality. Soon the streets and cities all looked the same. I turned down an unnamed road in an unnamed city and ran smack into *him*, back in the same alley in Jakarta.

"Impossible." I ran again.

Jakarta.

And again.

Jakarta.

Every road, every space led back to him. I shook my head in disbelief. Impossible!

"Who are you?" I asked.

"A man with no name and no people."

He *blinked* from in front of me and reappeared behind me. Rules didn't seem to apply to him. He kicked the back of my knees, and I fell forward, kneeling on the ground in defeat. His fingers laced through my hair and yanked my head back. I stared up into his dark-brown eyes, filled with the same eternal sadness I saw whenever I looked into a mirror.

The runes on my blade flickered. He hesitated. But why?

He brought the knife to my neck. "Why are you in Jakarta?"

I thought of the lights crawling beneath Ielu's skin and how he had exploded into a galaxy, only to be devoured by me. For all my attitude and rage, I feared that ending—any ending. I didn't want to be destroyed only for someone else to soak up the mess I called my soul. Yet all of it seemed completely out of my control.

"I am dying." I stared into his eyes, refusing to look away. "And I have so much shit swimming around in my head, I don't even know which way is up anymore."

The runes dimmed.

"The Burn Cycle." His tone was matter-of-fact, but fear and sadness swam around his fish tank, and try as he might, he couldn't seem to empty it.

I nodded. "Yeah, the Burn Cycle."

He let go and backed away. I stayed on my knees, trying to fight the fear of death clawing at my belly. I'd held it together through Daemons, Raven, and Luke, only to fall apart in front of some unnamed Aod who may or may not still kill me. My gut burned, and I fell forward, gasping in pain, one arm curling around my abdomen as I tried to keep myself up with the other. If only I could smash my emotional container to pieces and let all those feelings seep into the ground beneath me, but I didn't know how. Where was the emergency axe?

I shook violently, and my arm gave way, my face colliding with the ground as the convulsions twisted my limbs inward. I couldn't stop it or control it.

Breathe, Keres, breathe.

I gulped air and pushed it back out through pursed lips for what felt like hours. Once the shaking stopped, I stayed locked in a fetal position, cold and more exhausted than I'd ever been—even as a human.

The man watched me. "They come and go. All you can do is wait for the shaking to pass."

I would have raised an eyebrow, but I was too tired even for that. I closed my eyes and inhaled slowly. "Are you going to kill me?"

"I haven't decided. I may leave you here forever."

My eyes shot open. "You can do that?"

"One learns to do a lot of things when—"

He cut himself off and shrugged, sinking to the ground across from me and laying my khukuri on his legs. He braided his fingers together—except for his pointer fingers and thumbs, which pressed together in the shape of a diamond—and closed his eyes as he breathed deeply. Fear and sadness flowed away from him, draining his emotional container until nothing remained.

"Why Jakarta?" he asked without opening his eyes.

I gently sat up, hugging my knees for extra support. "I'm looking for the Daemon Adi."

He opened his eyes wide at the word *Daemon.* "Interesting move." His inflection made the word *interesting* sound more like *idiotic.*

"I was told he could help me break the Contract."

He frowned. "There is no end to the Contract. There is only death."

"Then why hesitate to kill me?"

"I do not take the destruction of any soul lightly."

His words felt strange and uncomfortable, especially coming from one of my own.

"Unless you have come to kill me or any of those I protect, you are safe. Otherwise . . ." My blade flashed an eye-stabbing blue in his hand.

"Then you're not with the Guardians?"

"I am with myself. No more, no less."

Are we destined to always be alone?

The runes on my khukuri faded to solid charcoal, and its hum returned to a whisper. For the first time since he engaged me, I realized I only heard one melody, not the dual harmony I would have expected.

"Where is your reaping blade?"

The Aod flinched but remained calm. "They destroyed it."

I remembered Raven's fear when Luke threatened to destroy hers. "W-what does that mean . . . for the angel?"

Instead of answering, he stood. "Time to go."

"But—"

He raised an eyebrow. "Would you rather stay?"

When I shook my head, he helped me up. Once I was standing, the world slid beneath our feet, stopping abruptly at the edge of the slums, where shadowy shanty homes gave way to the outlines of industrial parks and apartment buildings.

"What the hell *is* this place? Why can't I *blink* here?"

He stared at me. "This *is* the *blink*."

The sketch-like reality disappeared, and we reappeared in the world I knew, filled with color and substance. I seized the Shadow power surrounding me and almost cried out when it didn't slip away. I never wanted to feel trapped like that again.

I turned to the Aod. "How?"

"They taught you to act, not question. I questioned."

From the beginning, *blinking* had been simple. Any two places were separated by strands of reality, like hanging beads. I only had to reach between those strands with my thoughts, pull back the beads, and "step through"—no actual physical movement required. I didn't know how, only that I could, so I did.

But if the beads belonged not to one single veil of reality but two . . .

This time, I focused on *one* side of the *blink*. Just the space here, in front of me, and *not* a destination. Pulling the beads aside, I peered into the charcoal landscape I'd just escaped. My eyes widened. "This isn't Earth, right?"

The Aod shrugged. "I call it the Echo—a dimension just below this reality."

"And if I step in there, will I be trapped again?"

"Only take that step if you have years to figure it out. And *don't* take your human there until you do." He held my gaze until I released the beads and looked away.

"Speaking of . . . I need to find him." I held my hand out for my reaping blade.

Ignoring my silent request, the Aod pointed at the nearest cement building. "In there."

As we walked toward the apartment structure, confusion and questions festered within me. "Can an Aod accidentally stumble into the Echo?"

He shrugged. "Possible but unlikely. Whether human or immortal, we tend to accept our beliefs as truth. You see your *blink* as a doorway; therefore, it is a doorway, a single path between points A and B. All your intentions, power, and actions align with that truth, making it so. I see my *blink* as an entirely different world, with infinite pathways between two points, so it is. Remember, most things stay hidden until we go searching."

I nodded. I was beginning to see that. "So, man with no name, what do I call you?"

"Nothing. I don't exist."

"J-Man it is." When his brow furrowed, I shrugged. "Man-from-Jakarta is too long."

Once in the building, J-Man led me to a stairwell. Our footsteps echoed as we climbed, bouncing around the whirlpool of stairs like the thoughts in my head. Everything had seemed so simple before: Show up, reap souls, go home, wait for the next assignment. Wash, rinse, repeat. I had never needed to think for myself, and I surely hadn't needed to figure out how to stay one step ahead of people hunting me. I needed to be smarter to survive this life without Guardians.

I frowned. "How have you stayed hidden?"

"I don't have a blade."

My tired brain strained to connect the dots. "What does that have to do with it?"

"How do you think they track us? That hum we hear from our reaping blades? For the Guardians, it is a homing signal identifying each Aod's precise location."

When I stopped, J-Man glanced back at me and smiled wickedly.

"Pretty ingenious, huh? Feed us a hefty diet of obedience and fear, fill our minds with stories of boogeymen, and then make the one thing we cling to for safety and power a tracking device. What Aod would ever leave home without it?"

I glanced at my khukuri, still in his hand. "So, why haven't they found me yet?"

He turned fully to me, his emotional container shuddering. "The song of *your* blade is silent until it is too late."

Confused, I tilted my head to the side and listened. "It seems the same to me."

He shook his head. "I'm not talking about what *you* can hear, but what your superiors hear. Normally, the hum gets louder the closer the Aod gets. The point at which a Xiiph can hear an Aod's blade varies depending on the strength of the Xiiph. Guardians can find the signal at any distance. But yours? I couldn't even hear it when you entered my own *kota*. That should be impossible, regardless of my strength."

My eyes widened. "You're a Xiiph!"

He looked away. "Was."

Feeling the pain that cycled through his emotional container, I chose not to push. "If you couldn't hear my blade, how did you find me?"

A smile flashed across his face and disappeared. "Humans don't forget a person who gets shot point blank but doesn't die. Not very subtle."

"Pretty sure I left subtle on the living room floor next to the Guardian I blew up."

This time, J-Man's eyes went wide. "You *attacked* a Guardian?"

I shrugged.

He descended the stairs until he looked me straight in the eyes. "Have you ever been able to hide before?"

I thought of all the times I'd run—from reaping, from Raven, from Luke. "No. They've always found me."

"Until now?"

I nodded. "Maybe they aren't searching?"

"They're searching, little Aod. They're searching. I have reaped Aods for far less." He leaned forward until our noses almost touched. "You are more dangerous than you realize. Especially if you've learned how to mute the song of your blade. They can't allow you to survive."

I swallowed back fear. They had any number of reasons to kill me. In the last few days, I'd discovered a new power beyond Shadow, been dragged through a crossing gate, sucked up a Daemon soul right after accepting his token, entered the Burn Cycle (maybe), admitted my intention to find Adi, and stopped following Guardian rules. And now my reaping blade didn't have a signal.

Shit.

Too exhausted to deal with it now, I tossed this newest worry onto the growing pile labeled *Clusterfuck* inside my head.

The former Xiiph turned and began climbing again without a word. Silence stretched between us as I followed, compounding my tension with each step. We were taking too long. I needed to get to Adi *now*.

"Why not *blink* to the human?"

J-Man shrugged. "I have grown used to doing things the human way."

"I am in a hurry."

"You don't know what you are."

Before I could retort, we exited the stairwell into a short hall. Two doors down, an old man sat against the wall. When we reached him, J-Man helped him up and handed him some cash. "Thank you, friend."

The man bowed and left without a word.

"Friend?" I asked.

J-Man watched the ancient man retreat, his gaze tender. "He taught me I didn't have to be what I'd always done. I had a choice." A tingling warmth flashed through him before he tucked it away and opened the door.

The apartment was small, with a sliver of kitchen to the left of an open space crammed with a small table, two aging chairs, and a sofa that looked like cats had been nesting in it for the last century. Directly across from the front door was the bedroom.

Joe sat hunched over the table, facing us, his head resting in his good hand. Anxiety and anger wafted from him, jarring in its opposition to the calm he usually maintained. Glancing up from his gun, which lay on the table in front of him, his eyes locked with mine. He sprung from his chair, relief washing away his anxiety and drowning his anger. I drank it in, the heady flavor a balm to my volatile nerves. It was so different from anything I'd felt from . . . well . . . anyone else.

I breathed in again, deeply, but already relief had been replaced by a rapid succession of shock, frustration, longing, annoyance, and confusion. I halted the step I almost took toward him, unsure of Joe. Unsure of myself.

"J-Man, Joe; Joe, J-Man." I waved my hand back and forth between them, and both grunted their hellos. "Oh, and I'm Keres."

Joe glared at me. The heat of his mounting anger boiled away his other emotions, until only the glacier lake remained, steam rising from its surface. I didn't need to be a Reader to know he was pissed, but I wished it could help me understand why. Which part of tonight had finally pushed him over the edge?

"You're alive; I'm alive. Why are you so pissed?"

Ignoring my question, Joe sat back down and focused on the gun before him. His disregard echoed Raven's, which grated my final nerve. I'd saved this idiot!

You saved the shofar, I reminded myself.

"Look, you *chose* to come, so don't blame me—"

"You don't get it, do you?" He flicked a fiery glance at the bullet hole in my shirt.

I scowled. "Fuck. This again? I already told you. I. Can't. Die."

The muscle along his jawline bounced, and his anger exploded against me.

I smiled grimly. "Want to hit me?" I needed to be done with this conversation, and if it made him feel better . . . "Go ahead."

Joe's glacier lake went dark. No anger. No peace. Only a deep pool of some emotion I struggled to identify. Light strains of cello music reached for me from his aura. They brushed against me, begged me to see them, and then drew away, taking with them both warmth and light.

He swallowed hard, his shamrock eyes pained. "I don't know what kind of people you come from, but don't expect me to be one of them."

Hurt. Joe felt hurt, and I had no idea what to do about it.

I rubbed at the base of my throat, where an uncomfortable pressure built. I didn't like that he made me feel all twisty inside. Anger I could handle; constant derision was my norm. But this? I had had no idea that tenderness could undo me so quickly.

I turned to our host. "What next?"

J-Man stared at Joe for an uncomfortably long time. "Go rest. I'll give you an hour, but then you must leave. I don't want your problems here."

Angry, tired, and frustrated, I looked out the tiny kitchen window, where daylight crept up the glass. *Nothing* had gone according to my simple *blink*-to-Jakarta-and-ask-for-Adi plan. "I don't have time for rest. Give me my khukuri, and we'll go."

J-Man took two steps to his sofa and grabbed a tattered blanket hanging off the edge. He threw it at me, hitting me in the face.

"If you can't stop a blanket, how will you stop a blade?" I frowned. He had a point. "An hour will allow you to recharge enough to keep going."

"My blade?"

"Rest here or *there*. Your choice."

He meant the Echo. If I had had the capacity to hold even a drop of power, I would have slapped him with it, but now, even my body was shutting down. I really did need to sleep. Who knew even Angels of Death had a limit? I wondered if Guardians and Daemons did too.

I nodded and headed toward the bedroom.

As I passed Joe, he grabbed my wrist with his good hand but didn't look at me. Images flickered through his emotional turmoil like a silent film. I saw myself pull his gun to my chest and force it to fire. The barrel spewed a bullet into my heart and rocked back in slow motion as the slide expelled the leftover casing. My face flickered to another's, so fast, I couldn't be sure it even happened. Terror and despair engulfed the memories and pulled them beneath the surface of his calm, until all that remained was my reflection in his lake.

The intensity of the memory left me breathless. Shooting myself had meant nothing to me, but it had unraveled him. I had to remember that humans were frail.

"I need you to be sorry," he said—a plea, not a command.

I grasped his hand and gently pulled it from my wrist. "Okay, Joe. Okay. I'll try." I tried to mimic his relief and push it into him, to give him the same balm he'd given me when I first arrived. With his emotions locked behind a glass lake, I had no idea whether it worked.

SEVENTEEN

My khukuri sticks out of my chest, bathing my skin in brilliant blue light. Death stands above me, smiling sorrowfully. She looks like me.

"Monsters must die," she says.

Lifting my arm, I see a million bug-like lumps race beneath the surface of my skin. It hurts. I cry.

Hot streams of light burn down my face. My skin slips away, and I am a body of light, a billion dancing stars.

I am beautiful.

I am afraid.

"I don't want to die."

"Too late," Death whispers.

My eyes shot open. Even after I woke, the glowing orbs danced in my vision like fading fireflies. Terror pulled on every muscle, curling my hands and limbs inward.

Always too late.

I handed myself over to the shaking, too tired to fight and too broken to be strong.

Once the quaking passed, I went to the adjacent bathroom and threw water on my face. Glimpsing myself in the mirror, I gingerly touched the blackened handprint on my neck. "You have time," I whispered. "You still have time." Grateful Joe couldn't see my new scar and the former Xiiph hadn't mentioned it, I confirmed Ielu's token still rested in my sheath and stepped into the living area.

I ignored J-Man in his tiny kitchen and flopped into the dining chair closest to Joe, who lay on the couch with an arm over his eyes. The human had returned to his usual calm, the tranquility a drug I never wanted to quit.

"We've gotta go," I told him.

"Sleeping."

"No time."

He smiled. "Not since I met you, at least."

It was hard to believe this man could ever be serious, but with his dimple showing, I didn't care. His banter answered the question I didn't want to ask: were we okay?

Joe swung his legs off the couch and sat up, resting his elbows on his knees. "What's the plan? Or are we still working off the one from yesterday?"

"That plan has been shot to hell, but I don't really have a better one."

J-Man poured two mugs of steaming liquid. Placing one on the table in front of me, he handed the other to Joe. "Drink. You'll need it."

I reached for the cup but recoiled from its warmth. Heat and humidity seeped uncomfortably through the walls and my clothes. Joe had to be dying in his rumpled suit. He'd already removed his jacket and tie and unbuttoned the top two buttons of his shirt.

"Drink," J-Man repeated.

"You talk too much." I grabbed the cup and sipped. The hot liquid tasted awful. "Melted tires?"

"Fresh Jakartan coffee."

Joe choked it down with more grace than I could manage. He only coughed once. "Wow, that's potent."

"Nothing like bad coffee to get unwanted *bules* out of the house."

Joe smiled at J-Man, who returned the favor.

"I'm asleep for less than an hour and suddenly you two are best friends?" I definitely needed more sleep. Joe smiled to his dimples, and I downed the rest of my coffee like a shot of tequila, before taking my cup to the sink.

Following, J-Man pulled my khukuri from his belt and handed it to me.

Taking the blade, I reveled in the wholeness I felt, even as I raised an eyebrow. "What changed?"

"My desire to stay clean outweighed my desire to live. Holding this, the temptation to use it is too great."

"You make it sound like a drug."

"Isn't it? The killing, the power. Tell me you don't feel the rush."

I wanted to say something snarky; instead, I blushed. I *did* feel the rush every time I reaped—that euphoria right before unconsciousness, and sometimes in my dreams, that made me feel complete, whole, happy, and fulfilled. I didn't *feel* power; I *was* power. I was beauty. I was more than the sum of all good things, flawless and perfect.

Then I'd wake to the stink of death—happiness and wholeness so cloaked in carnage, I'd wonder if I'd even felt it at all. But it was there, aching and calling to me.

Just one more. Just. One. More.

I glanced at J-Man. It seemed the insatiable need for death made all Aods crazy in our own ways. It twisted our brains and squeezed sanity from our souls like water from a soaked cloth, until we lost track of ourselves as angels and became only death.

"I'll tell you what I'm feeling," Joe said. "Lost."

Jarred from my thoughts, I stepped around J-Man and sheathed my blade.

"Are there any more like us assigned to the city?"

"Not permanently. Blade hums come and go every so often, but nothing stays."

"At least that's working in my favor."

Joe grabbed his suit jacket and tie off the couch and headed for the front door. I *blinked* in front of him, blocking his path.

"Waste of energy," J-Man muttered.

Ignoring him, I focused on Joe. "You can't leave, Frat Boy."

"If you want me to stay, don't keep me in the dark."

"You coming along wasn't my idea, remember?"

"We'll explain on the way," J-Man said.

We both looked at him. "We?" I asked.

"You're most likely headed to a Daemon nest. Do you really want to *blink* into the middle of that?"

I hesitated. I wanted this to be over, but he wasn't wrong. "Fine. Let's go."

"Shotgun!" Joe laughed as if we were leaving on a weekend road trip, not driving our car straight off a cliff.

Humans.

What should have been a thirty-minute trip stretched longer than an hour as we inched our way toward Blok M. The roads were rivers of rusted metal; too many people crammed into not enough street, while mopeds and motorcycles wove in between the creeping cars.

J-Man's car should have been retired to a scrapyard years ago. With no AC, I prayed for a breeze to pass through the open windows and carry away the humidity coating me. Sweat trickled down my chest and back, collecting uncomfortably in my bra.

I should have made time for a shower.

Instead of a breeze, the sounds of the city drifted through the car. Where Baltimore sounded artificial with its clink and hum of metal and electricity, Jakarta seemed to have a human voice—the dull mumbling of millions of people shouting over each other to hawk their wares.

Joe sat in the front seat, turned toward J-Man so he could see me. He listened to everything I told him—Angels of Death, the Contract, marks, Guardians, Daemons, reapings, and reaping blades—and absorbed the information bomb I dropped on him without flinching. An eyebrow rose here and there, but no desires to throw himself from the car. His ability to remain unruffled was inhuman.

I glossed over some parts—my past, rebirth, training, and punishments—and left out others altogether: the Burn Cycle, my ability to *read*, Ielu's token. Information that could be fatal in the wrong hands, Daemon or Guardian.

"Questions?"

Joe shook his head. "Not yet, but I think I'm still trying to wrap my head around it."

"Fair enough."

After a minute of silence, he asked, "Sergio?"

"My mark."

"And the others?"

"Collateral damage."

Joe frowned.

"It sounds harsh, I know, but we do our best to minimize the damage."

His frown deepened. "These are people we're talking about. Is life so meaningless to your kind?"

I responded in rote. "All of us, including me, are dirt. Useful only as a tool to fulfill the will of God."

"And you believe that?"

My back stiffened, and I flexed my hands to keep from balling them into fists. "It's all I know."

"Doesn't have to be."

I turned my face away and looked out the side window. Overgrown trees in vibrant greens hugged the edges of the road, and beyond them, tall buildings fought each other for a piece of the sky.

"Leave her be," J-Man said. "The programming is absolute, and undoing it is almost impossible."

He glanced at me in the rearview mirror, and I held his gaze until he looked back at the road. His words held a challenge, one I refused to back down from. I could be different. I *would*.

Once I knew the truth. Once I'd freed myself of the Contract.

Joe nodded. "If Guardians are the good guys, why leave? Why run to the faction who wants you dead?"

I listened to the city while I chewed on his questions. I'd already made my choice and there was no going back, but I still doubted whether I'd made the right one. Was Ielu's death really a witness to the truth he claimed or the sacrifice of a zealot?

"I don't know who the good guys are anymore," I said. "I was always so sure I sided with right and justice and God."

"And now?" Joe's question felt arrogant and condescending, as if he held all the answers and was throwing me breadcrumbs to help me find my way to the truth.

"What do you want me to say? My world of us versus them has been smashed into pieces, and I'm trying to figure out how to put the damn thing back together!"

I didn't even know I was angry until I was halfway into the front seat. I released Joe's headrest and flopped back into my own seat, rubbing my temples as I inhaled deeply. Maybe he wasn't arrogant. Maybe I was just tired of not having answers.

"Sorry."

He nodded and gave a quick squeeze to my knee.

How the hell does he stay so calm?

"You're a *bule gila* if you think the Daemons will help you," J-Man said. "There's no such thing as black and white in this world. Good versus evil is a myth. There are only shades of gray, some darker than others, but those shades exist no matter which side you choose."

"So you choose none? Is that the right answer?"

He shrugged. "I don't know about right, but it is mine."

"Whatever."

We drove the next twenty minutes in awkward silence, each man emanating calm in his own way: Joe a picture of serenity and J-Man a vessel of emptiness.

Once we reached Blok M—a business-and-shopping quarter on the south side of Jakarta—J-Man pulled over at a drop-off spot inside. Joe and I would search for the "Oscar's on Blok M" Ielu had mentioned on our own. Although the other Aod and I had reached some form of neutrality, I wasn't comfortable sharing with him our exact destination, and he didn't ask. He could tail us, but I'd know, as long as I kept myself open to emotions rather than tuning them out. He would be the only silent spot in a world full of emotional noise.

"How do you do it?" I asked him after Joe had climbed out of the front seat.

"Do what?" J-Man asked.

"Stay so calm?" *So empty.*

"Practice. You must learn to control your emotions."

I rolled my eyes and reached for the door nearest the

sidewalk. J-Man grabbed my wrist, clingy tar pumping from his hand in rhythm with his racing heart. It climbed, wet and sticky, across my skin. I pushed against his fear, rolling it back onto his hand.

He didn't seem to notice.

"Listen, Keres. Our kind are used to masking and burying everything to survive, but that changes as your powers surge. Control slips away. Right now, you cling to the cliffs of sanity with a great abyss below you. Your emotions will determine how long you survive."

"It's inevitable, then?"

"The Burn Cycle takes all Aods eventually, even the Xiiph—"

"I thought the Xiiph were immune." Either Raven had lied or she didn't know. Both meant danger for me.

He shook his head. "We're promised immunity, retirement—power without reaping. I believed them, until they came for my soul." His grip on my wrist tightened, silencing my questions. "The rest doesn't matter. Only control. It allows us our humanity for as long as possible."

"But we're not human."

"We don't have to be monsters either. Now go. May God, wherever he is, keep you safe from Daemon hands."

I placed my free hand on top of his. "Thank you."

When I climbed out of the car, Joe was leaning against the post of a nearby street sign. "You good?"

"Yeah."

I watched as J-Man's car pulled away and disappeared into traffic. He took with him so many secrets I wanted to know and perhaps some answers I needed to have. But he couldn't free me from the Contract. He couldn't save my life.

"Let's go find Oscar's."

With hands in his pockets, Joe offered me his elbow.

The gesture was probably second nature to him. I'd seen humans walk like this often, usually couples strolling along Inner Harbor. It seemed intimate and familiar, a unique world of shared experiences and secrets. As much as I longed to, I hesitated to create that world with Joe. How much more would he twist me up before deciding I wasn't worth having? And yet . . .

Our humanity.

Did I deserve humanity?

Just as I decided to try, Joe shrugged and tucked his elbow back against his side. "Lead the way."

I did, all the while wondering about the small ache in my chest.

EIGHTEEN

Oscar's was unremarkable. Its door could have led to any business in any city in the world. The three-story building squatted along a deserted street that wouldn't be enticing Westerners or locals anytime soon. Four large windows flanked the locked door, which displayed a *Closed for Renovations* sign.

I stepped back to verify our location. *Oscar's Pub* was printed clearly beneath the image of a large red flower.

Joe stood at the window, hands cupped around his face as he looked through the glass. "This is it, huh?"

"Seems like it. I expected something . . . impressive." Stepping beside him, I peered inside. "And open."

Haphazardly draped tables lined the walls, and wires hung from metal beams above a large dance floor. An old wooden counter ran along the back wall, broken shelves framing the mirror behind it. Dust covered the whole place—dust not of construction but of time.

The pub had been abandoned.

Joe backed away from the glass and dusted off his hands. "Maybe there's a back office or something."

"Yeah, maybe."

"Worth looking, right?"

I nodded, and we headed around back to search for another entrance. My head told me to be angry—*Ielu lied*—but instead, I felt heavy, as if someone had severed the cord connecting my heart to hope. I followed Joe as he found the back door, picked the lock, and went inside.

Dust covered the back of the pub too. The kitchen, the office—everything looked discarded and forgotten. I sank to the floor, sliding down the doorframe that separated the back half of the building from the bar and dance floor we'd seen through the front windows.

Joe glanced at me. "I'll check upstairs. Don't go anywhere."

"Where would I go? This is it, final destination."

He squatted and lifted my chin with his uninjured fingers, looking me in the eye. "In my line of work, you can't accept dead ends. You hold on. You believe. You search for the clues that will lead you where you need to go."

"Sergio is a dead end," I told him. "I wasn't hired by that Quinn guy, so you have nothing."

The words tumbled out, mean and petty, even if they were true. His eyes tightened slightly, and he stood up.

"Sorry, Joe. I didn't mean it. Thanks. For helping."

He shrugged. "You may not know Quinn, but if your boys are keeping an eye on terrible people like you say, *they* will know him."

I pictured Joe strolling up to some Guardian fortress and demanding to look at their records. I laughed. "What are you going to do? Break into their records room and trace their phone calls?"

He smiled. "Probably not, but I don't believe in giving up either. Wait here. I'll be back."

As he headed up the stairs at the back of the kitchen,

I hefted myself off the ground. If not here, then where? Maybe Joe was right and we would find something to lead me to another location and another, until I found Adi.

We searched the building from top to bottom, emptying drawers, moving furniture. Joe even took pictures off walls and checked toilet tanks. He was certainly thorough.

Still, we came up empty.

"We'll find something," Joe promised. "Let's check outside. It doesn't look like they pick up the garbage very often. Maybe there's something out there." He headed toward the back door, but I didn't follow. Standing in the kitchen again, something felt . . . off.

"Coming?" he asked.

"We're missing something."

I expected him to roll his eyes and dismiss me as Luke always did. Instead, he returned to me and leaned against a dirty counter. "Okay. What are you thinking?"

"Where haven't we searched?"

"Better to start with where we *have* searched."

He listed every room and space, down to the last stall. We'd searched everywhere. Still, I couldn't shake the feeling we'd missed something. Yet every time I almost had it, the thought slipped away.

"Like it doesn't want to be seen," I said out loud.

"Say again?"

"I feel like there is something here that doesn't want to be seen. How do I explain it?"

"Like your khukuri."

"What?"

"I never noticed it until you pinned me against the wall in your apartment, and sometimes, I still forget you wear it unless I focus. But what you're describing, that's what it feels like around your knife. Like the blade doesn't *want* to be seen."

"You are too observant for your own good, Joseph Fitzgerald."

"Does that mean you will or won't explain what you left out of our chat in the car?" I kept my face blank and my tongue silent. "You didn't tell J-Man about the small coin that was so important to both you and your Guardian. And there's the Burn Cycle—"

Stepping closer, I clamped my hand over his mouth. "Some information could get us killed. Do you understand?" When he nodded, I let him go.

"Later?" he asked.

Ignoring his question, I moved back to the door separating us from the front of the pub. It had a little window in it, through which I could easily see the same wires, dusty tables, and empty dance floor we had seen from out front. If I craned my neck just right, I could even make out a corner of the dark wooden bar on the right.

I glanced at Joe. "Your list didn't include this area."

"No, it didn't." He walked up behind me and placed his hand on the door, but I stopped him before he could push it open. Extending my senses, I felt along the frame until I met resistance. Focusing on the point of resistance, I pulled in shadows from around the room. Dark tendrils seeped from the corners, slithered across the ceiling, floor, and walls, and flowed into that section of the door.

Crack. The suggestion shattered into tiny pieces.

"Done."

"Had no doubts," Joe said.

I let the shadows recede. "Do I ever surprise you?"

He smiled. "Every day."

"You've known me less than twenty-four hours."

"And so far, you're one for one."

Shaking my head, I placed my hand on the door and pushed.

NINETEEN

The room teemed with sun-kissed people.

Daemons filled the booths lining the room and surrounded the tables dotting the dance floor. Thankfully, the table closest to us was empty save a slender waitress wiping it down. Once finished, she hefted her tray full of glasses and turned, freezing when we made eye contact. She reminded me of a skittish doe—black eyes wide with apprehension, high cheekbones, warm-fawn complexion.

I swallowed hard, trying to stay calm. "I'm looking for Adi."

The tray slipped from her hands, and the resounding crash silenced the pub. All heads turned our way.

My reaping blade's hum intensified, but I forced away the desire to draw it. Putting a knife to someone's throat didn't exactly say, *I come in peace.*

A large man walked over from the bar and put his arm around the young girl, who had picked up her tray and now held it against her chest like a shield.

"Clean this up and head home. I'll take care of our guests."

Joe moved toward the waitress, and the bigger man stepped between them. Joe held up his hands in a gesture of surrender. "Only trying to help." He bent down and picked up the glass closest to us.

The waitress smiled—cute and grateful—and I wanted to stab her. Breathing slowly, I hooked my thumbs in my pockets to give my hands something else to do.

Dumb, Keres. Really dumb. Joe wasn't mine, and being with a human was ridiculous. I'd live forever, and he'd probably die before the end of all this.

The thought made me . . . uncomfortable.

I'd almost convinced myself I didn't care when he smiled back and helped her stand. Easing closer, I buried both hands in my pockets until Doe Girl had rounded the bar and disappeared down an out-of-sight staircase.

The man I assumed to be the bartender nodded a quick thanks to Joe before turning his gaze on me. He looked me up and down, a man sizing up his opponent before a fight. My hands came out of my pockets.

"Fallen. I believe you're looking for me."

I frowned. The word *Fallen* forced my hackles up. It didn't help that *reading* him hurt my head. Everything about his aura felt distorted and weird, as if I were seeing two different Daemons at once. I sensed a deep well of power within him—he was dangerous—yet a hazy film coated it, floating the idea that he was nothing and no one.

Harmless, it seemed to whisper.

The conflicting impressions extended to his physical form. His deep-brown skin with its golden undertones reminded me of the play of light and shadow on a banyan tree at dusk—a juxtaposition of dark recesses and caramel golds. His large, muscled arms exuded similar strength and serenity. Yet he also looked greasy and unkempt. His black hair clumped together, and slashes of fingerprints ran diagonally up his white apron, where he'd wiped his hands. Everything about him felt both natural and staged.

Whoever he was, he wasn't telling the truth.

"Look, Grease Man, either you're Adi and *I'm* wasting my time or you're some other lying Daemon and *you* are wasting my time. Either way, I'm in the wrong place." J-Man had been right. I was an idiot to seek Daemon help.

As I turned to leave, the man threw his head back and laughed, deep and guttural. "Feisty, huh. That'll make this interesting."

When he stepped toward me, I drew my reaping blade. I didn't want to use it, but I would if I had to. The blue light of the runes flickered and drew all eyes to me, eyes that widened as Ielu's had as they realized what I held. Grease Man stepped back from my blade as he raised his hands—half defense, half truce.

Tension poured from all directions, smothering me in everything from disbelief to anger. It reminded me of riding Mexico City's Sistema de Transporte Colectivo during rush hour, when the flow of people getting off crashed against the flow of bodies trying to get on and at least a dozen hands grabbed any female body part they could find. Only in this room, it wasn't dirty men trying to cop a feel; it was a group of immortals trying to process all their emotions in a breath.

And at least one of them wanted me dead.

"Who sent you?" Grease Man asked.

"Ielu."

Chairs scraped across the floor, toppling backward as their occupants stood too quickly. "It's her. It's her. It's *her*," raced through the bar. Some Daemons *blinked* closer, while others vanished altogether. Whispers rode the undercurrent of the crowd, one phrase rising to the surface, dripping abhorrence and fear: "Soul Reaper."

For each Daemon who disappeared, two *blinked* in to take their place. They pressed against the bartender, calling for my banishment—whatever that meant.

Grease Man struggled to hold back the angry mob, if only to keep himself away from my khukuri. It seemed everyone wanted my head, but no one wanted to be the first to get close. I needed to grab my human and go.

I reached for him without taking my eyes off the Daemon mob, but he wasn't there. "Frat Boy?" I called over my shoulder.

No response. I risked a quick glance and then turned in surprise. A Daemon held Joe in a headlock that had already drained the color from the human's face.

But it wasn't just any Daemon. It was Ielu.

My body and mind froze. *Impossible. Dead, dead, dead. You're dead. Stars, lights, black holes.*

I shook my head. "Ielu?" I wanted to cry and scream. What did this mean? What had happened?

Tree-trunk arms encircled my upper body, pinning my arms to my sides, while hands knocked my khukuri from my grasp. Once I was unarmed, my arms were pulled behind my back and my wrists tied together.

Only once I was bound did Ielu release Joe, and the human collapsed to the floor and lay still. My breath caught in my throat.

"Joe. Joe!" My calls turned to screams, and I writhed in the arms that held me. Joe had to be okay. He *had* to.

What if he's not?

I reached for Joe with my senses but ran into a wall. I couldn't grasp anything—Shadow, emotion, nothing. I couldn't even find them, and my wrists burned every time I tried. Panic clawed my insides.

Ielu stepped over Joe's body and grasped my left bicep. "Murderer."

The dam broke, and the mob surged forward. Too many hands pulled at my clothing and hair, and someone hefted me onto the bar, face down, and hog-tied me. I twisted to get a look at my bindings—the same golden cord I'd cut from Luke's wrists at Sergio's place—and then twisted further, looking for Joe.

I couldn't see past the crush of people. No Joe. No Grease Man either. The only face I recognized was Ielu's.

"Kai! Don't!" Grease Man's voice boomed over the yelling crowd.

"She killed my brother!"

Kai?

Ielu-called-Kai stepped in front of me, and shock stilled me as I got a better look at his face: both eyes blue, hair all white with only a streak of black near the left ear, and a shorter, leaner build.

This wasn't Ielu but an altered copy.

"Ielu's brother?"

"You don't get to speak his name."

Kai raised his fist, in which a dagger of lightning appeared. Instinctively, I reached for Shadow, but again the bindings denied me. My gaze jumped from face to face, pleading, but no one stepped forward in my defense. Why would they? I was an Angel of Death, sword of the Guardians, and Daemons existed to destroy me as I'd been told.

I am a fool.

Though I couldn't sense it, I reached for the calm of Joe's glacier lake and imagined resting at the water's edge. I wanted it to be the last thing I felt before I died.

Kai's weapon plummeted toward me.

"No!" Grease Man shouted.

"Keres!"

I almost cried at the sound of Joe's voice. *Thank you, God. Now please keep him safe.*

As Kai's dagger struck, an intense heat blossomed in my chest. Grease Man appeared behind the bar a breath too late, striking Kai with power that knocked him back into the crowd. I closed my eyes and waited for death.

Silence filled the pub.

I waited.

The whispers began.

"What is it?"

"What happened?"

"Glowing?"

"What does it mean?"

"Impossible," Kai said.

I opened my eyes. Kai was backing away from me, his eyes wide and mouth slightly agape. His body shook, until he could no longer contain his anger and screamed. Closing his eyes, he gripped his beautiful hair and roared again—stronger, more desperate.

The crowd pulled away from him as he struggled to regain control. Lowering his fists, he closed and opened them as he seemed to force the rage in instead of out.

Despite years of wishing for silence, I took it all back as I watched Kai struggle. The emotional silence I was experiencing now wasn't a blessing; it was blindness.

When he finally opened his eyes, his gaze was dark and murderous. He stepped toward me.

"Enough!"

Grease Man waited for Kai to look at him before he continued. Even without my *reading* ability, I could sense the tension between them. Anyone could have.

"You shame me." The large man scanned the crowd. "Every one of you."

Turning to me, he cut the rope tying my feet and hands together and freed my ankles, leaving my hands bound. Lifting me from the bar, he was just setting me on my feet when I caught my reflection in the mirror behind him, and my legs gave out.

A blue aura pulsed around me.

I looked up at Grease Man, who had kept me from falling. "What is it?"

"Where are you hiding it?" he asked gently but firmly.

I stared at my reflection and shook my head. I had no idea what he meant.

"His token, girl. It is the only way."

My reflected eyes widened above dark circles. "In my sheath."

He let go of my arm and reached for my scabbard.

Crack!

Still staring at the mirror, I watched a bullet hit Kai in the face. For an instant, his twisted, beautiful features became a Picasso—*The Weeping Woman*, tortured and breathtaking—before righting itself again.

I turned toward the crowd.

"Don't. Touch her." Joe stood on a chair, gun now aimed at the man reaching for the sheath at my waist.

Grease Man nodded, and two Daemons *blinked* to Joe, stripped him of his weapon, and tied his forearms together. When he kept struggling, the woman pushed him against the nearest wall and pinned his face against it.

"Sorry," he said to me, "you make me forget I'm human." He half smiled, as much as he could with his face being smashed by a Daemon.

I half smiled in return.

"Everybody leave!" Grease Man yelled. When only a few people at the back *blinked* away, he roared a Daemon phrase, and the rest fled. Only Kai, the two detaining Joe, and a woman holding my blade like a cobra remained.

"This is wrong, Talon," Kai said.

"Tell that to your brother, boy. He's the one who gave her his token. Even after death, he's saving your ass!"

Kai flinched. "You don't know that. She's a murderer."

Grease Man—Talon—*blinked*, finishing his step right in front of Kai on the other side of the bar. Although he stood a good six inches shorter than Ielu's brother, Talon's presence grew to fill the room.

"Grow up, boy! Tokens must be given with full intent; we don't lend them to each other like toys. She could not have stolen your brother's token any more than you could hide the sun in your pocket. Ielu gave her his token fully and freely." He looked back at me. "As much as we all hate that, it's hers, and it gives her the right to an audience with the Council."

"Screw the Council," I said. "I'm here to talk to Adi."

He shot me an exasperated look and turned back to Kai. "Unless you plan to challenge this Gatekeeper, go. Now."

Kai seemed to consider it, his fists flexing with angry restraint. In the end, he *blinked* away.

"Stupid kid," Talon muttered. "If he'd harmed you, the Council would have had his head. That's the problem with young people: they don't think with their brains."

I huffed my agreement.

He eyed me. "As for you! Pulling a forbidden blade in a room full of Daemons—what were you thinking?"

"*You* came at *me*."

"If by that you mean stepped closer so I could tell you we should find a more private place to talk, then yes, I came at you." Heat crept up my cheeks. Talon nodded toward Joe. "Bring the human. Let's get them to the Council before anyone else decides to be an idiot."

"What about the glow?" I asked.

"It's already gone."

"That's not what I mean."

He and the others came around behind the bar. Talon grabbed my bicep and led me down a flight of stairs hidden beneath the countertop at the far end. They were easy to miss unless you knew what you were looking for.

After a few steps, Talon spoke up again. "The glow comes from the token you hide in your sheath. Ielu gave you his most precious gift, equal to that of his life. What did he say when he gave it to?"

"To talk to Adi at Oscar's in Jakarta."

Even with superhuman eyesight, I struggled to see the steps in the dark and keep from falling. Joe clunked and tripped down behind me, his Daemon captors the only reason he didn't send us all plummeting to the bottom.

"Then you are safe from Daemon harm until after you have fulfilled his command."

I bristled. "Command?"

"The command is not for you but for the token. It allows you entrance into our city and, until you talk to Adi, shields you from any power we might use to hurt you."

"And then?"

"The only thing keeping Kai from sending your soul to Darkness will be the Council's decision and his ability to follow it."

"So not much."

Talon laughed. "I'd kill you myself, but it wouldn't do any good. Better to wait and see how things play out."

"That's reassuring."

The two Daemons escorting Joe chuckled. I needed to get a read on these people. Talon's voice held no malice; he even sounded playful. But he could have been as deceptive as Luke, and I wouldn't know until he plunged a dagger into my heart.

"You sure know how to make friends," Joe called.

"A real people magnet," I drawled.

Once we reached the bottom of the stairs, our party of Daemons guided us down a hallway to a small room, second to last on the left.

"What do you guys have against light?" I asked.

"Nothing, really." Talon opened the door, entered, and flicked on a light, revealing a small storage area.

Piles of fruits and vegetables littered the room, a too-sweet scent indicating some were beyond edible. On the far wall, a few strides away, stood another door. It seemed ratty and old, not worth looking at. But as I stared at the stone around it, an ornate mantel covered in intricate carvings and artwork materialized, like a 3D optical illusion.

I jerked my chin toward it. "I take it that doesn't lead outside."

Talon chuckled. "Surprised?"

I glanced at him, and when I looked back, the door's appearance had returned to the piece of old wood surrounded by scratched wall. "Very clever."

He shrugged. "Doesn't matter. After today, it will be moved." Then he nodded.

Suddenly, darkness engulfed my vision as something was pulled over my head. Cursing, I struggled against the arms holding me. They must have done the same thing to Joe, because I could hear him fighting as well.

I managed to land a solid roundhouse kick—a woman cursed, and my blade clattered to the floor—but without my blade, power, or sight, Joe and I quickly lost. An Aod and a human against four Daemons? I growled, frustrated.

Talon laughed. "So feisty. I can see why Ielu might have taken a liking to you. Don't worry, kid. We're not going to hurt you." The unspoken *yet* hung in the air. "This is for your protection as much as ours."

I continued to struggle. "A human won't survive a crossing gate."

"This isn't a gate; it's a doorway."

"There's a difference?"

"If you survive the Council, I'll explain it to you. Let's go."

The energy of the doorway we passed through felt more like entering J-Man's Echo than crossing whatever gate Ielu had pulled me through. What world was I being taken to? What other worlds existed beyond Earth, the Echo, and Ielu's grave? I swallowed against the dryness building in my mouth and throat.

"Nervous?" Joe whispered. His hand pressed against my back. The touch reassured me, which in turn made me uncomfortable.

"A little," I admitted. "You?"

"Feels like an indoor roller coaster. The unseen hill as we click, click, click our way to the top."

"And you like that?"

He pressed his hand harder against me. "Some rides you just have to experience."

"Quiet!" Talon barked.

"What if I don't like where it's going?" I whispered, ignoring the Daemon.

"Throw your hands up and scream," Joe said.

I could practically feel his dimpled smile.

"Enough." Talon whispered a few words in Daemon. Falling was my last sensation before blacking out.

TWENTY

I woke to darkness. Fabric still covered my head. My hands remained tied behind my back, pulling my arms around the back of a chair, and my shoulders ached. The ache would dissipate as soon as my bindings were removed, but until then, my ability to heal was fruitless.

Shifting, I tested the bands holding me to the chair.

"Finally awake, I see," Talon murmured from behind me. "You sure took your own sweet time."

Not knowing whether we were alone, I whispered, "I thought your powers didn't work on me."

"I said they can't harm you, and I didn't. It's tricky, but if you know what you're doing, even a greasy bartender like me can work around the right of the token."

"You are a very deceptive man, *Gatekeeper.*"

"Just a very old one. I've been around the block more than a few times. I'd even give you some advice to navigate this trial, but I don't think you'd follow it."

"Trial?"

"You killed a Daemon. Why did you think you were coming before the Council?"

"Interview, maybe?"

Talon snorted. "You're a funny girl."

"What about Adi?"

"Anger the Council and not even Ielu's token can help you."

"Do I still have it? The token?"

"In your sheath where you left it. It isn't ours to take."

I exhaled relief. The scabbard remained strapped to my side, a tiny comfort in a world of unknowns.

A heavy hand rested on my shoulder. "Good luck, Fallen. I only hope Ielu knew what he was doing."

"Me too." The room returned to complete silence, until I called out, "Talon?"

"Right here." He still stood right behind me.

"Where's the human?"

"Safe." Abruptly, light blinded me despite the cloth covering my head. "Ready or not." Talon pulled the fabric from my head.

His retreating footsteps echoed in what must have been a massive chamber, but I couldn't see anything beyond the brightness stabbing at my now-watering eyes. Even without a hood, I was blind.

"Fallen," a woman's voice called from my left. "You stand accused of the murder of Ielu Zavayasu—"

Murmurs drowned the rest of her words as they raced around me, growing steadily into a roar. The bang of stone striking stone echoed from directly in front of me, silencing the crowd.

"Do you accept or deny this accusation?"

"Keres," I said.

There was a pause before a man's voice asked, "What do you mean?"

"My name is Keres, and you will address me as such."

Behind me, Talon sighed, but I didn't care. Ielu had

made a promise, and I *desperately* wanted to believe the purity of his intentions. Maybe because he'd walked around in my head, I'd developed a fondness for him, a sense of connection that seemed to whisper back through millennia, not just days. I *needed* to know: Did Ielu stand with or against me? Was his intention to help or harm?

The lack of answers had me on edge.

"Your name is inconsequential, Soul Reaper," said the original voice, low and booming.

Tension crawled up my spine, through my shoulders, neck, and jaw, and spilled right out my mouth. "So is this questioning. I came in good faith at the request of Ielu."

"Do you deny that this is your weapon—a forbidden blade?" asked a second woman, her pitch higher and tone softer than the first.

Two Daemons stepped from beyond the wall of light. My reaping blade had been placed on a stand, encased in some transparent material that blocked its usual hum, and set on the rectangular tray that hovered between them.

"No."

"Do you deny that you used this weapon to reap Ielu's soul?" asked the man.

"I didn't know that's what would happen."

I focused on the waist-high railing I could finally see as my eyes adjusted to the piercing light—anything to block the memory of Ielu's final moments. The metal barrier encircled me, the delicate curve of its bars running in a horizontal motif that made them look like wisps of air, but the energy emanating from them was anything but deli-cate. It pressed against me, heavy and uncomfortable; I shifted in my seat.

"Then his death was an accident?" asked a second male voice. He spoke more slowly than the first, his voice carrying a slight whistle.

I hesitated, reliving the memory—the blade coming down, Ielu catching it and shifting its aim before letting it go. I hated the way his face twisted as it entered his heart.

Tears that had nothing to do with the stabbing light fled down my cheeks.

"No," I whispered.

Before I could explain, the room erupted into the buzzing chaos of an angry hornets' nest. Stone pounded against stone, louder and louder, until the spectators' voices lowered to an electric hum.

"It was Ielu's choice!" I shouted. "He could have stopped me, but he didn't." *Why didn't you stop me?*

"Lies!" Daliah stepped into view from the right. "Ielu would never—"

"Were you there?" I demanded. "Were you in the room? Did you see what happened?"

"I know my mate—"

"Were. You. There?" I screamed, and even the hum of the onlookers stopped.

She stared at me with burning eyes and silence.

"The Council requests that Daliah answer the question," said woman number two.

Daliah dropped her gaze, and her head fell slightly. "No, I was not." Whispers again began to build. "But Ielu would *not* have allowed himself to be murdered."

"He didn't consider it murder," I whispered, seeing his eyes, hearing his words in my mind. "It was his sacrifice for truth."

"What truth?" Man number three sounded sharp, his voice laced with arrogance.

"I don't know."

"Why send you to Adi?"

"I don't know."

"What did he know that we're missing?"

"What is he up to?"

"Why her?"

"Why now?"

Why . . . ? Why . . . ? Why . . . ?

I lost track of who asked what. Were they talking to me or to each other? I couldn't breathe as the questions piled on top of me and buried me alive. Too many questions, too many people, too many directions. I gasped for air.

"I don't know!" I shouted. I strained against the rope that bound me to the chair. I wanted to stand and yell. I wanted to tear the chair from the floor and throw it at the voices. I screamed and stomped my feet. "I don't fucking know! I don't know who I am or what I am or who I work for or what I believe or why I was created or what purpose I have on this Earth. I. DON'T. KNOW!"

I collapsed back into the seat, exhausted.

"Then have you come to die?" asked the first woman, sounding pleased.

"I'm already dying. I came for answers."

Whispers raced through the room.

"Lies," the arrogant man said.

"So Ielu told me. Too many to count."

"Liar," said Daliah.

"Believe whatever you want, but Ielu said the truth was more important than his life and I had to know it. He gave his life so I would find Adi."

"Liar."

I saw more words form on her lips but couldn't hear her over the crowd. Her back straightened, arms stiff and hands fisted at her sides, as fire filled her gaze. We held each other's glare for what felt like forever—hers hot with rage, mine cold with defiance—until something beyond the circle of light caught her attention. She cocked her head slightly back and to the side, listening as she stared at me. Finally, she nodded and faded into the darkness. It should have felt good, watching my accuser retreat, but instead, I felt sad. I'd taken someone precious from her. From my perspective, all my marks had deserved death. All but one.

When had I become the raiding party I so despised?

He came at me! I reminded myself. But the excuses and blame tasted like undercooked chicken.

The room continued to writhe with sound. Voices wrapping over and under one another as the onlookers tried to make sense of everything they'd heard. I sat at the epicenter of it all, ashamed and confused.

Hating Daemons was easy when you only saw them as monsters. But Ielu had a brother named Kai. Did he have a father and a mother? Other brothers and sisters? More relatives and friends who would be mourning his loss because he wanted me to believe him? Daliah called Ielu her mate. They were lovers and friends. Did they have children? A little girl like me whose father had been taken from her?

Oh God, what have I done?

The stone gavel continued to echo through the chamber. "Quiet," said the council member directly in front of me. I couldn't tell if they were a man or a woman, but when they spoke, the entire building listened. "A decision must be made. Based on the testimony given, I cannot recommend death." They banged their stone before the room could explode again.

The first woman spoke up. "But Daliah's witness—"

"Was nullified," said the second woman. "She wasn't in the room and cannot confirm the details for or against the defendant."

"And there is the matter of his token," man one said.

"It gives credit to her statement that Ielu gave his life rather than lost it."

"But if she had not tried to take it," man three said, "Ielu would not have had to give it."

The Council continued their discussion as if no one else existed, and the whole room held its breath.

Finally, the one at the front gave a small click with their stone. "Then it is decided."

"What's decided?" I asked.

"The Hall," they said.

"The Hall," said the first woman.

"The Hall," said the second, followed by a third woman who hadn't spoken at all during the trial.

"The Hall," said the third man, repeated by the first and second. The words echoed around the room as more people in the audience whispered "The Hall" in hushed, fearful tones.

"You will be brought to the Hall tomorrow. Pass, and the Council will grant your audience with Adi."

"And if I fail?"

The stone gavel clicked a final time, and the lights shifted, allowing me to see the mini coliseum in which I sat, surrounded by seven empty daises, where I assumed the Council had been, and beyond them, thousands of staring Daemons.

They watched me watching them. I opened my mouth to say something, anything—the need to explain myself rested heavily on my tongue—but the entire room exploded with sound.

TWENTY-ONE

Daliah and Kai glared at me with murder in their eyes as four guards released me from the chair and led me away from the growing chaos. The narcissistic Daemon who had attacked me in my apartment stood behind the pair, whispering into Kai's ear something that twisted Kai's already dark face into the monster I'd originally believed Daemons to be. When he noticed me watching him, Mr. Narcissist glowered and joined the flow of people exiting through another door.

I glanced at Kai, wondering if he or Daliah had sent the hunting party after Luke and me. Though, after what I'd seen in the bar, Kai didn't seem the kidnapper type. No, if he'd known I was in Baltimore, he would've come and killed me himself.

Which left Daliah.

I shifted my gaze to her, and she stared back, daring me to give her any reason to act. I dropped my gaze, ignoring the flush moving up my neck.

What would Abba have said if he were here? Raven's tart *He's not, you are, get over it* sounded in my head.

But "getting over it" wasn't ever as easy as it sounded. I didn't *want* my heart to hurt. I didn't want to feel the loss of Ielu burrowing a hole in my chest, making space for the lead weight of Daliah's grief and Kai's anger. What did I do with the shame constricting my lungs?

In Luke's world, I only had to receive whatever punishment he deemed necessary; feeling regret needed not apply. But Joe had been appalled when I'd suggested he hit me for upsetting him. Whose world did I exist in now? And what would be required of me for anyone—including me—to forgive me for taking Ielu's life?

I didn't know the rules here, which confused and terrified me.

We exited the arena into a maze of hallways, where, after several turns, we met up with another four guards. Two guarded my khukuri, still in its glass box, and two flanked Joe.

Joe's smile grew with each step I took, fully displaying his dimples by the time I reached him. "You didn't die! How great is that?" His smile made me feel like I'd stepped from shadow into sunlight, warm and safe. I coughed, surprised by the emotions his reaction elicited in me. Happiness, maybe? Something . . . more?

Whatever the feeling, it had to be mine; I couldn't *read* anyone in these bindings. Yet my emotions felt foreign, my labels inadequate. More troubling, did I feel this way because he was a familiar face or because he was *him*?

I pushed it all away and focused on the trial. Feelings were too dangerous for us both. As I killed the joy bubbling within me, the smile left Joe's eyes.

"Postponed until tomorrow." I related the highlights and the verdict as the guards led us deeper into the maze.

"What does that mean?" he asked.

"Hell if I know." I glanced down, realizing for the first

time that his hands were neither bandaged nor bound. "Your hands are healed . . . and *free.*"

He chuckled. "Pretty sure it's an insult."

He winked as I turned back to him, and I smiled despite myself. He had a way about him. When he wasn't annoying me, he was making me laugh—a lightness I hadn't felt since my days with Abba in the desert.

Joe feigned sadness. "It hurts, really, being treated like a pesky ant instead of the mosquito I am." The guard next to me shook with suppressed laughter. Joe smiled at him, then turned back to me, leaned closer, and whispered loudly, "Little do they know, fire ants bite."

The guard laughed out loud, and Joe joined him.

He amazed me.

The laughter spread among the guards until Daliah appeared in front of us, halting and silencing our procession. Lingering giggles bounced down the hallway.

"Ielu is dead, and you can laugh?" She looked each guard in the eye, but none showed embarrassment, their faces empty of anything.

The guard next to me spoke up. "Daliah—"

She held up a hand. "Don't. I am tired of excuses." She looked at me. The two forward guards stepped together, blocking her path but not her line of sight. "You may have fooled the Council into letting you off easy—"

"Didn't sound easy to me," Joe said.

"But I am not so blind," she finished.

I had nothing to say to her. She wasn't the only one tired of excuses. "Can we go?" I whispered to the guard next to me.

"Abomination!" Daliah lunged toward me, but the guards held her back. I shook my head at the absurdity of the situation. *Like a schoolyard fight.*

"Ielu had a message for you." Perhaps not the best

timing, but would I get another chance? "He said to tell you he loves you."

Daliah *blinked*. She materialized in front of me, fist swinging, and punched me in the face. Had she been human, the move would have fractured her hand. Instead, my cheek gave way beneath her supernatural power.

The violence numbed my guilt and shame. It made sense.

"Son of a bitch!" Joe reached for Daliah, but a guard stepped between them, pushing Joe back and pinning him to a wall. My guard grabbed Daliah and pulled her back.

She yanked her arm from his grasp. "Take the mortal and leave the Fallen with me."

"We can't do that." Daliah growled, but he didn't back down. "The Council has ordered her to the Hall, and Adi wants her for questioning."

She glared at me. "By the time I'm done, she'll tell me anything I want to know."

"Ielu couldn't find what he wanted. What makes you think you can?" Her punch had felt so good—soothing. "Ielu died trying. Will you?" *Punish me,* I willed. *Bury me beneath a mountain. Hide my shame.*

Daliah lunged for my throat, but a female guard intercepted her. "Daliah, no. That's not how things are done."

"How things are done? Ielu dying—is that how things are done? Letting a Fallen into our city—is that how things are done? Letting his *murderer* go free—is *that* how things are done?"

The female guard remained steady and unruffled. "You know it's not freedom that awaits this one."

"Where is *my* justice? *Ielu's* justice?"

I didn't have to *read* Daliah to know how she felt: the shattering of her world, the desperation to put it back together the same way, the realization she never could. I understood the pain in her scream. It mirrored my own—the shattering of a heart.

"I'm so sorry." The words slipped out, meaningless but true.

"Don't." Daliah's body shook. Golden strands gathered around her—not emotion but raw power. "You don't get to be sorry. You get to die."

"Monster must die," I whispered.

"No!" one of the guards called out. "You can't!"

"I keep hearing that word: *can't*," Daliah spat. "*Can't* be damned."

Three of the guards rushed her, while one held me and the others shielded Joe and my khukuri with their bodies. Good soldiers following orders to a tee.

After dropping the first two tenderly—her removal of them as obstacles without hurting them was a testament to her skill—she released all the light she'd gathered in a concentrated beam. The air crackled. The third Daemon, who could have moved into the beam, moved away instead, and the full force of Daliah's power hit me.

Ielu's shield absorbed it all.

"You can't hurt me," I whispered. The barrier didn't color my gaze, but the blue field curved over my shoulder at the edge of my vision. "He's still protecting me."

Daliah flinched, color seeping from her face. *Blinking* to my khukuri, she knocked over the case and grabbed the blade before anyone could stop her. Some of the guards moved to protect me, but she was faster and the blade sunk easily into my stomach, burning as she pushed it deeper.

"Keres!" Joe screamed.

"I can always hurt you," she whispered.

I stared into her eyes as shock rippled through my body. I had thought the token would protect me. Instead, my abdomen popped and sizzled with pain, and blood oozed from my wound. I sank to the ground, sliding off my blade as Daliah remained standing.

"I will repent to Adi," she said over her shoulder, eyes still on me. Dropping my khukuri to the ground next to me, she *blinked* away.

A female guard with wisteria-colored eyes shifted me onto my side, not bothering to untie my hands. She felt around the wound as I awaited my fate, wondering if it would hurt. I chuckled darkly. Of course it would. Everything in life hurt. Why should death be any different?

"It's too late," I told the wisteria-eyed guard. "It's a reaping blade."

"Don't be so dramatic." She pointed at Joe, who was thrashing in the grip of the guard who held him. "You! Your girl is fine. Hand me your jacket."

Once Joe stopped struggling, his guard let him go, and he stepped closer, handing his jacket to the Daemon woman kneeling at my side. She grabbed it and pressed it against my bleeding abdomen.

"Those blades don't work for us anymore. Not in the way you're thinking. In most hands, khyabadian only acts as a nonlethal poison to any immortal it's used against. Daliah might have given you a nasty wound, but she can't steal your soul. Seems only your kind can do that."

The woman lifted the jacket. The blood flow had already slowed. "You'll have to tend your wounds the old-fashioned way: with time." Placing a dry section of the jacket against the wound, she beckoned to a smaller guard. "Let's take them to the cell as planned."

The petite guard wriggled her hands beneath me and lifted me as if I weighed nothing. As we continued on, the wisteria-eyed guard kept pace with the one carrying me.

"Daliah is so impetuous. I am sorry."

I stared at her. "*You're* sorry?"

"Ielu was one of our best, a general from the War. *I* know you could not have killed him, but Daliah is still too hurt to see it. As angry as I am that he is gone—as we all are—he had his reasons for saving you."

"What if he was wrong?"

The prison was uncomfortable. Not because of its lack of size and amenities but because the walls themselves seemed to reject me. With my hands finally unbound, I lay on the cot and tried to run clammy fingers along the slate-like wall, but the material repelled me, as though we were two magnets of the same charge.

Encompassed by the material, I could hardly breathe.

Emotions had flooded me as soon as the guards removed the bindings from my wrists, but no matter what I tried—*blinking*, manipulating Shadow, pulling from my newfound power within—I was just as powerless as I had been bound.

The burning in my abdomen only added to my discomfort. The skin had finally healed, leaving a faint line where Daliah had sliced me. Dried blood caked the skin and cloth around it. Inside, the soft tissue continued to mend in the slow, painful rhythm of a sewing needle pulling thread through my organs. One internal tug in particular elicited a short grunt of pain from my closed lips.

"Let me look at it." Joe crossed from the chair he'd been perched on and reached for the hem of my shirt. I swatted his hand away. I didn't need to feel any more confused than I already did.

"I'm fine."

"Then looking won't matter."

I didn't have the energy to fight him off, so I gave in

and lifted my shirt. His hand traced the faint line gently, tickling my flesh. I sucked in my stomach to pull it away from his touch.

"See," I said. "No big deal."

"Sit up."

"I'm busy healing, Frat Boy."

"You'll feel better without all the blood. K, *please*."

Heat hit my cheeks. *A nickname.* Did he know what he was doing to me? He didn't press any further, but he also didn't go away. Relenting, I pushed myself upright.

Standing behind me, he eased my blood-soaked T-shirt up and off over my head. Pre-Daliah, I would have blushed and told him to stop. Now, though, I was tired and didn't give a damn who saw what.

Part of me, however, was happy I'd worn a black lace bra. His reaction—the instant tug-of-war between desire and restraint—made me feel better.

When different cloth draped over my shoulders, I turned, surprised. Joe had removed his button-down and crossed to the sink in the opposite corner. His undershirt hugged his torso, accentuating his lean muscles.

"I hate that you're still wearing this." Snagging a finger in one of the holes his bullet had put in my shirt, he ripped the shirt into several strips of cloth, discarding the pieces crusted in blood. After wetting the strips, he returned and slid his shirt off me.

"Sorry about this." He unhooked my bra, pulling the left side off my shoulder.

I shrugged, and the strap fell farther. When Joe shifted behind me, I smirked. "Don't tell me shoulders make you uncomfortable."

"I don't like the sight of blood."

I snorted. "You're a bounty hunter. I assume you've had to use your gun."

"Doesn't mean I like it." Pressing a rag against my back, he held it there for a few seconds before gently wiping away the crusty remnants of my little display in the Jakartan slums. His motion followed the contour of my wing tattoo—just the upper curve at first, but then his hand slid down my back, where the lower tip of the left wing disappeared beneath my waistband. His thumb brushed lightly—idly—against my skin, trailing heat in its wake.

"Like what you see?"

Coughing, Joe finished wiping my upper back, and refastened my bra. "Let's look at the knife wound. I think if you lie down—"

I glanced over my shoulder and raised an eyebrow, a teasing gesture meant to break the tension. He obliged by rolling his eyes, so I smiled and leaned back. When I winced from the pain burning in my belly, he caught my neck and carefully lowered me to the cot. He held me for a moment longer than he needed to, his body leaning over mine and his shamrock eyes staring into my utterly plain brown ones. I held my breath.

The cot squeaked as he shifted and turned his attention to my abdomen.

I watched his eyes intently, waiting for them to sweep up my slightly sunken stomach, over the bottom of my ribcage, and up to my breasts. But they never did. He kept them trained on the wound. Disappointment warred with gratitude. I didn't need any more complications, but that didn't prevent me from feeling rejected. Wasn't I beautiful? Wasn't I *desirable*?

Without thinking, I pressed desire against him as I had in my apartment. I pulled all the right strings and played all the right cords, until his heart beat so loud, I heard its rhythm—a rhythm that could rock us both into ecstasy. His desire wafted over me, gentle yet hungry, and

I sank into the glacier lake of his emotions. Reds and oranges burned the water as the sun set over the mountain peaks, casting everything in hues of fire.

My heart raced.

Yes. You want me.

I shifted slightly, and his hand brushed against my skin. He stared intently at the spot where his hand rested on my stomach but didn't move it away.

Explore me. Feel me.

So close. His hunger was only a push away from over-riding his desire to do the right thing. Just one more . . .

I hesitated. *Is this fair to him?*

But I couldn't stop myself.

. . . push.

Abruptly, Joe stood and carried the used cloths back to the sink, where he painstakingly rinsed each one. It gave him the time he needed to climb down from the edge of passion, to let the fiery sun of his inner landscape dip behind the mountains and return to a peace-filled calm.

As his desire receded into reason, my own desire died out. I felt cold.

I stared at the ceiling as he returned with fresh rags. "You don't have to finish. I know the . . . blood . . . makes it difficult."

"I'll manage." Kneeling back down, he continued to soak and wipe away the blood. After a few moments of awkward silence, he added, "You make being the good guy very, very difficult."

"Then don't."

He stopped wiping and stared at me, holding my gaze and my breath. The heat of his want crawled up my body, and my lips parted. As his desire touched my face, I closed my eyes and turned into it. I could almost feel the backs of his fingers brushing gently against my cheek.

Then the wave of desire receded, leaving behind tingles of warmth, but not lust. When I opened my eyes again, he was still staring.

"I think you've had enough of the other kind."

I bit my lower lip, studying his face as he continued cleaning. "Much, much too observant."

With that, the awkwardness passed.

He had to rinse the cloths once more before he managed to remove all traces of blood. He was right, though. It did help me feel better.

"I already hate it," I said.

"Being clean?"

"You being right."

His shamrock eyes danced and his cheek dimpled slightly as he helped me into his button-up. "Better get some sleep. I'm guessing tomorrow won't be any better."

"You want the pillow?" I had taken the only bed in the cell.

"Who said I was sleeping on the floor?" He raised his eyebrows suggestively, and I laughed. He laughed too, full and deep, like he hadn't almost died at least twice tonight, and for whatever reason, I pictured his hair being tugged by the wind.

He pulled a blanket over me before dragging a chair to the door of our cell, where he sat down and propped his feet up on the bars. "Tonight, I'll watch over you."

"Death doesn't have a watcher."

"She does now."

"Joe." I waited until he looked at me. "Thank you."

He nodded and turned back to the cell door to keep watch. I kept my eyes on him as I fell asleep, and that night, I dreamed of being the wind.

TWENTY-TWO

I yawned into the blanket Joe must have tucked beneath my chin and rolled over to find a fresh set of clothes lying on a chair next to me. Joe squatted near the bars of the cell door, on the other side of which stood a young boy, perhaps seven or eight years old. He could have been Raven's little brother, but in contrast to her silky black hair, pale-blond layers framed his face. His little hands clutched the bars, and his toe dug into the corner of the frame closest to the hinges.

"Who's this?" I sat up and stretched, curling and un-curling my back. While I still wasn't at a hundred percent, the few hours of sleep had gone a long way toward replen-ishing my tank and healing my wound.

The little boy ducked out of view. Peeking around the doorframe, he waved and then ran off down the hall.

Joe stood and brushed his hands together. "It's never easy for you, is it?"

I rolled my eyes. "No shit." I nodded toward the clothes. "Would you mind?" His gentleness last night had left me shy and uncertain.

Joe turned his back to me and even tried to fill the doorway with his body. Once dressed, I noticed we wore matching T-shirts and cargo pants that fit each of us perfectly. He looked good in casual.

When I gave the okay, he turned around and took a seat on the cot. "How's the stomach feeling?"

"Better than last night." I lifted my shirt. From the outside, everything looked great. Not even a scar. Inside, I still felt a pinch and tug if I moved in certain ways.

"You must be Keres."

I turned toward the sultry voice. A woman with peacock-blue hair stood just outside the cell door. She shared Ielu's sun-kissed glow and Daliah's contempt for me. Her anger battered me over and over until I wanted to scream, but I tried to ignore it. I didn't need any more problems. Adi was so close and, with him, the end of my contract.

"And you are?" I asked.

"To escort you to the Hall." Two men almost as tall and broad as Ielu stepped into view behind her.

"The hard way, huh?"

"Place your hands through the bars."

I walked over and slid my hands through the opening she indicated—a small rectangle that would allow her to bind my wrists without opening the door.

"Behind your back," she said.

I rolled my eyes and turned around. As she bound my wrists, I cursed the special rope they used. Being cut off from my power sucked, but losing my Reader ability was worse. My own emotions made for terrible company.

Once finished, Peacock nodded to Joe. "You too. Hands in front." She smirked at me.

As Joe approached the cell door, I stepped in front of him and glared at the Daemon. "He isn't part of this."

Joe lightly touched my shoulder. "It's okay."

I glanced back at him. "No, it's not."

"Step to the bars," Peacock repeated.

I blocked his path again. "You don't have to do this."

He smiled, sad but warm. "I know."

Stepping around me, he placed his hands through the opening for them to be tied. We all knew a human wasn't a threat, but Peacock seemed insistent on going the extra mile out of bitchiness.

Once we were safely tied, she opened the door and pulled us out into the hallway. Eight more guards surrounded us—men and women who looked battle-tested and ready for a fight.

"This is a bit excessive, don't you think?"

Peacock sneered. "We're always cautious when dealing with rabid animals."

Joe's face darkened. Peacock caught his expression and raised a questioning eyebrow. "Problem, human?"

Instead of answering, he turned to me. "Your fight. I'm just backup."

I shrugged. "Sticks and stones?"

He turned back to Peacock. "Unless we're waiting for others to join the party, I suggest you lead the way."

Her face turned three shades of purple. A smile tugged at my mouth. I would have to kiss that man.

Later.

The Daemon woman turned and led the procession back through the maze of underground tunnels. Glass doors and stairs appeared at random, and I couldn't keep my bearings.

I was already lost when Joe next spoke. "I'm going with you."

My brow wrinkled in confusion.

"Into the Hall," he clarified. I tried to respond, but he shook his head. "You're going to say no, I'll say yes, you'll put your foot down, and then I'll do something to piss you off. Won't matter; I'm going. So let's save ourselves the aggravation and agree ahead of time."

"I don't know what's in there, and I can't risk—"

"Me getting hurt? So you *do* like me." His dimples danced on his cheeks.

"You getting in my way," I finished.

He mocked being hurt, but his smile never dimmed. "I'm heartbroken, really." When I didn't respond, he added, "It's my choice."

"So far, none of this has been your choice. What makes you think you get one now?"

"It's always been my choice, K. You simply haven't realized it."

His gaze fell to his hands, and mine followed. Tucked between two knuckles gleamed the dark edge of my father's shofar. My heartbeat sped up, sending tingles down into my stomach.

"But—"

"You're not the only one with talents. Granted, I can't bend space and time, but a good illusion works well in a pinch." He winked.

"Then—"

"Yep."

"And I—"

"Exactly."

I reached for the shofar—awkward with my hands tied behind my back—but he pulled away. When he opened his hands, they were empty. "I'll return it to you after."

"Blackmail?"

He clicked his tongue. "Such a harsh term. I prefer insurance."

"You know how annoying you are?" I feigned anger, but my heart wasn't in it.

"Very."

I smiled. This human had balls *and* skills.

We exited the maze through one of the random glass doors, which was wide enough for us to pass through two at a time. Guards stood at attention on the other side, but they made no move to stop us as Peacock led us up a curving marble staircase and into a giant chamber crafted from the most ethereal of elements.

I wished I had a canvas and paints.

Light spilled in through two-story cathedral-style windows that lined the outside walls. Instead of stained glass, cascades of prisms filled the windows, scattering the light into a million dancing rainbows. Between the windows, faux pillars rose from floor to ceiling—so delicate, they must have been spun rather than carved—and benches that seemed to be made of water sprang up from the ground in random elegance.

Overall, the room held an energy of cleansing and new beginnings.

Perhaps the Hall wouldn't be so bad.

Peacock led Joe and me to the middle of the room, where we faced a gigantic pair of gold doors taller than even the windows. They were flanked on either side by a wide staircase: one that led back to the tunnels we'd come from and one that curved up and out of sight.

Talon descended the second staircase with the solemnity of a death procession. Cleaned up, the Gatekeeper looked impressive in his knee-length tunic coat, with its high collar and beautiful red-and-gold embroidery, and the accompanying red stole that hung from around his neck, draping over his chest. Even his weird aura had solidified into a single powerful image. He didn't have to hide himself here.

I whistled as he stopped and turned to face us, but he

didn't smile. Instead, he nodded toward Peacock, who snapped at the other guards. Two women approached us; one held my khukuri, the other Joe's holstered Glock.

I narrowed my eyes as they sheathed my blade and strapped Joe's weapon at his waist.

"For your journey," Talon said.

"That dangerous?"

"More than you can imagine."

"I've lived nightmares worse than you can imagine, Gatekeeper." His gaze softened.

With another nod from him, Peacock removed our bindings, and the three warriors closest to us quickly retreated. As they did, emotions slammed into me from every direction, and I nearly collapsed beneath the initial surge of not just feelings but images, crisper and clearer than I'd ever experienced.

Behind me to my left, Peacock exuded fear, in which played the image of me taking her soul with my bare hands. Her earlier anger had been not a weapon but a defense. It took all her energy just to stand still and stay calm. The same was true of the other guards, all of whom thought the worst of me.

Directly ahead, anxiety wound through Talon. What would it mean if I didn't make it through? What would it mean if I did? He was surprised to discover he cared about the difference, as hints of joy mingled with the image of my success, which in turn led to confusion.

At my side, Joe, who usually exuded tranquility, was a storm. Dark clouds roiled above his glacier lake, and harsh winds whipped the water into tumultuous peaks. He wasn't like any other human I'd met, but I was beginning to understand this place he used to center himself. Right now, it reflected fear, anger, and . . . power.

Something unexpected caught my attention then.

Other than the guards, Talon, Joe, and I, the room appeared to be empty, yet I felt seven others. Latching onto the strongest cord of emotion, I traced it back and . . . up. Above the windows on the back wall, almost hidden by the pillars, sat seven alcoves. I couldn't see anyone, but I could feel them.

The Council.

Talon motioned to the guards, who retreated down the staircase we'd come up. When the last guard exited, Talon fixed his gaze on me and stepped closer.

"Fallen. Soul Reaper. Keres." I seemed to be collecting a lot of names. "Why are you here?"

"To kick the ass of the next person to call me Fallen," I grumbled. He smiled slightly, and I shrugged, grateful he had a sense of humor. I had grown tired of all the stuffiness and formality among the Daemons.

He waited for me to answer in earnest.

"To speak with Adi. To find the answers I seek." I spoke loud enough for the onlookers high above us to hear. I felt stupid, but Talon nodded, so I assumed I'd done something right.

"Human. Joseph Fitzgerald. You've committed no crimes against the Council or its people. We free you from the Soul Reaper's path."

My chest tightened, and I held my breath. If Joe had any sense, he'd run far and fast—even if I didn't want him to.

"I choose to follow wherever Keres leads." When I glanced at him, Joe tilted his head as though to say, *I told you I was going.* The pain in my chest didn't subside.

What if I lead him somewhere he shouldn't follow?

"So be it." From Talon's lack of surprise, he'd expected Joe's response.

Behind Talon, the giant gold doors swung open to reveal an impossibly tall hallway that required mental gymnastics to figure out how it fit in the building. Golden light spilled out into the airy foyer, making the previously bright room feel dark and empty.

Talon grabbed my left hand and Joe's right and rotated them palm up, placing mine atop his. When he held out his hand expectantly, I tried to grasp it with my right, but he batted my hand away. "The token."

Blushing, I pulled Ielu's token from its hiding place in my sheath. Once it was out, I hesitated.

"This is the only way forward." Despite Talon's calm assurance, though, worry danced pins and needles across his skin and through the air to touch mine. I cocked my head to the side. Why did he care? Why worry about my outcome? It didn't make sense, but as this was the only way forward, I relinquished the coin.

Cupping it in his hands, he whispered words I could not understand, until a blue light flickered from the token—the same light that had protected me from Kai in the bar and from Daliah in the hallway. As Talon continued to chant, the token lifted into the air and spun in a circle, gaining speed until it looked like a solid sphere and the whir of its motion had risen to a whine. Just as I thought it might fly off into eternity, it stopped and dropped back into his hands.

When he placed the token onto our stacked, upturned palms, I felt its weight in my soul.

Talon's gaze flicked to the ceiling behind us. Uncertainty held him for a moment before he gave the slightest of nods. "Take the Gatekeeper's blessing." He blew gently on the coin, and blue fire erupted from its center. The flame expanded until it had swallowed both Joe and me, soothing rather than uncomfortable. Gasps and whispers showered us from the alcoves above. Joe turned to look for the source, but I didn't need to see them to recognize their shock. Even Talon hadn't expected the outcome.

My being connected to so many firsts among these Daemons didn't exactly feel like a good thing.

Only one person in the room didn't seem surprised by the flames encircling our bodies. I glanced over my shoulder at the center alcove.

We'll talk later, I thought in their direction.

‹I'll be waiting.› The reply sounded inside my head—the same genderless voice from the trial. Shocked, I began to turn, but Talon caught my arm.

"This protection will only last for a short time. When the fire dies, you'll meet your test."

"Wait, what test?" I demanded, torn between the speaker in my head and the one in front of me. What the hell had just happened?

"Time is slipping away. Do not let go." He released me and headed back toward the ascending staircase.

"What do you mean? What the hell is going on?" I moved to follow Talon, but Joe caught my wrist with his free hand.

"We have to move, Keres. The only way is forward."

I glared at him and then at the unseen figures in the alcove overhead.

"We're running out of time," Joe said. Already, the perimeter of the fire crept back toward the coin at an almost imperceptible crawl.

"Fine." ‹But this isn't over,› I projected to the voice. ‹Not even close.›

We hurried into the Hall. The doors closed behind us with a click that might as well have been a sonic boom.

TWENTY-THREE

We slowed. The sheer magnitude of the Hall was mind boggling, but it was the presence I felt that overwhelmed me. It coursed through the room—an unseen power pressing down on us and compressing the flames with every step.

"What the hell is going on?" I whisper-yelled.

"From what little I understand," Joe said, "this place is a gauntlet of sorts, designed to test your character, strength, and will."

I bristled. "To prove my worth to these bastards?"

"Yes."

I narrowed my eyes, but as Joe had neither flinched nor made excuses for the Daemons, I let the matter drop and turned my gaze to the far end of the hall.

"Then our goal is most likely the double doors at the other end." From where we stood, the doors appeared almost small, which spoke to the distance we had to travel.

Because nothing here was even remotely small.

The ceiling soared at least a hundred feet high, and canopic jars taller than the door behind us lined both sides of the hall on marble platforms. There were twenty in total, ten on each side.

"I'd assume so," Joe replied.

"How much do you know?" I demanded as we reached the first pair of jars. The force pressing against the flame intensified, but our barrier held. I glanced up as we passed. Etched into their golden surfaces were drops of water raining down upon upturned fish.

Strange.

"That's it," Joe said. "The boy only stopped to ask if I planned to go with you."

"Because I can't do it alone?"

"So you don't have to."

Five words and suddenly the tightness in my chest and belly wasn't about outrage.

We approached the second pair of jars in silence. Etched into the front of each was a pyramid of frogs. Again, power pushed against our shield. It let up for a moment and then hammered again.

"It's trying to break through," I said.

"It?"

"The Hall. I can feel it . . . pushing."

We traded a grim look and sped into a jog.

Joe stared at the closest jar as we passed between the pair. "I don't like this jack-in-the-box feeling. Like something insidious is waiting to spring out at us."

"Maybe it is."

"Can you *blink* us to the end?"

I tried, but there were no beads, no fabric. Nothing to grab or part. It was like being trapped in J-Man's Echo. "Nothing." I breathed slowly against the growing panic.

I couldn't hold it back, though.

"Why didn't the boy talk to *me*? You're not even supposed to *be* here!"

"I don't know, Keres."

"Did you even suggest it?"

"Of course I did."

"And?"

"He said he couldn't."

Joe refused to look at me as we passed the third pair of jars, which depicted a bald Egyptian woman sitting on a dais. At her feet lay piles of hair. The collective etchings nagged me, stirring a very old memory. But of what?

Joe's flickering indecision distracted me.

"What aren't you telling me, Joe?"

"I don't know that it matters."

"Your honesty matters."

He sighed. "Whatever this is"—he waved a hand to indicate the hall and the jars—"comes from you."

"What?"

"If I understood him, the Hall is different for every person who enters it. It's tailor-made to you."

"Which means being inhumanly strong and immortal won't give me an advantage." I exhaled a long breath. "Anything else I don't need to know?"

He shook his head. "That's everything."

The blue sphere continued to contract with each footstep. "How can I be sure?"

Joe's whole body tightened, and the muscle at his jawline danced. "Keres, I'm not one of them."

"Daemons? I know."

"The people who hurt you, used you. I'm not one of them. Stop expecting me to be." A shadow darker than black flashed from his core so quickly, I couldn't be sure I'd even seen it. I shivered.

We pressed forward, our pace increasing without either of us saying a word. At the fourth pair of jars—these carved with flies—the magic of the Hall slammed against our barrier again, and the fire receded beneath the pressure. At this rate, we'd be exposed by the sixth, maybe the seventh pair.

"Run?" I asked.

"Run," Joe agreed.

We sprinted down the corridor, falling into an easy rhythm. I could have run faster without Joe, but we had to stay connected for the fire to protect us.

"Ugh! Why didn't Ielu just tell me the truth and *blink* me to Adi?"

"Would you have believed him if he had?"

"Of course not."

I hated that Joe seemed to know me so well. Like Luke, like Raven, like this Hall—all of them taking advantage of the weaknesses I tried so desperately to hide. What did this place know about me? What was I missing?

As we approached the sixth pair of jars, it hit me. "The plagues of Egypt."

"Come again?"

I reached back centuries to the lessons my *abba* had taught me at the door of our tent. "My test—it's the plagues of Egypt. That wasn't water on the first jar; it was blood. Followed by frogs, lice, flies, and pestilence. Look!" I pointed at the people etched into the closest jars, small bumps rising from their flesh. "That has to be boils."

"Does that help us?" Joe asked between breaths.

"It tells me what they want."

"I'm not really the religious type."

"The plagues were sent to destroy the pride of Egypt and force them to let the Israelites go. It wasn't until Pharoah's heart broke that he agreed to release God's people. They mean to break me."

But they'll only succeed in pissing me off.

"Or change your heart," Joe said.

I ignored him and held onto my anger, allowing it to fuel my steps. The double doors grew bigger with every stride, but they were still too far away to be helpful. The fire receded again, and an angry buzz seeped through the protective shield. As we passed the plague of hail and fire, the blue flame sputtered and dimmed.

"Faster!" I didn't have to yell, but I couldn't help myself. The room felt alive, and I *knew* it didn't like me.

Seven down. Three to go.

We lengthened our strides. Sweat poured down Joe's face as we struggled to keep our movement in sync and the coin from tumbling out of our hands. But no matter how fast we ran, we weren't gaining ground any quicker.

As we reached the eighth pair of jars, the fire sputtered and withdrew, exposing half of each of us. The buzzing shifted into a deafening cadence that pierced my ears and threatened to explode my brain. Movement caught my eye, and I glanced toward the closest jar. It seemed to be melting. I glanced beyond Joe to see the other jar crumbling as well.

No. Not crumbling—*fracturing* into a massive army of locusts. My heart raced, pumping lead into my stomach.

Millions of insects tumbled over each other in their race down the disintegrating jars. We were caught in the middle as two tidal waves of golden locusts crashed together, swallowing us whole.

Closing my hand around the coin, I pulled Joe in as the insects swarmed. His screams echoed in my head, louder than the cries of the locusts. Beyond the protection of the fire, bugs swarmed my legs and arms, tearing at the flesh and burrowing into my limbs. They couldn't cross the fire, though, not even from within my body.

Figuring it was the same for Joe, I pulled him closer and centered the flame around him. My body would heal.

"Thanks," he heaved.

I grunted, trying not to let the pain show on my face, but he saw it anyway and pulled me into him. Holding each other like this, so close we could have been one, we fit within the sphere of flame, but we couldn't move.

How the *hell* was having him here helpful? What had that child been thinking?

I saw only two options: get eaten alive over and over for eternity—which might have been a fitting justice for my choices—or take the coin and leave Joe to his death.

He had a chance at a next life. I didn't.

Joe pressed his lips against my ear. "Keres, run."

He let go.

I'd spent a millennium trying to cast aside the human emotions of fear and concern for anyone but myself. Yet as Joe pushed away from me and the fire's protection, I felt it all and then some. Emotions I couldn't—*wouldn't*—name.

Fucking human.

I grabbed his wrist and pulled him back into me. "I don't need a damn hero." I pressed the coin into his hand, forced his fingers to close around it, and shoved him as hard as I could toward the door and his only means of escape. Annoyance flashed across his face, right before millions of hungry golden locusts blocked my sight.

They stripped my flesh like piranhas, chewing through muscle and down to the bone. In their wake, my flesh regrew—more for them to consume. I tried to keep walking, but I stumbled to the ground beneath their weight as they ate me from the outside in and the inside out.

Burrow. Heal.

Burrow. Heal.

Eternity would be a *very* long time.

Tucking my head into my chest, I swiped bugs from

the soft flesh of my eyes and face, refusing to give in to the pain and cry. Still, it didn't seem to matter what choices I made; they all turned out bad.

Through the pain, I became aware of something tugging at my arm, pulling harder and harder. A faint noise I couldn't identify joined the cacophony of the burrowing insects. As my body grew warm, I wondered if the insects had reached my brain.

The warmth grew steadily, until a bright blue flame enveloped me. Screaming, the locusts raced away from the flame's touch—even those inside me. They burst from my flesh, following their fellows to wait beyond the fire.

Grabbing my hand, Joe yanked me to my feet. I had no time to gape at the blue flames once again engulfing us both as he got in my face. "You may not need a hero, but who the hell said I didn't need you?" I couldn't tell if he was angry, as my own emotions played havoc inside me.

We raced through the locusts, not looking back until we reached the ninth pair of jars. When I did, I stumbled.

As Joe caught me and pulled me upright, I nodded toward the golden bugs, which swarmed against what appeared to be an invisible barrier marked by the end of their marble platforms. "I don't think they can follow us."

The blue flame flickered and shrunk.

Shit.

Joe stared intently into my eyes. "What's next?"

"Darkness," I whispered.

His fear broke through my turmoil, and I knew he felt it too—the *something* waiting beyond the fire. His jaw clenched. "Whatever happens, please don't let go of me."

"I promise." I held his gaze as darkness descended. His fear was the last thing I sensed.

Then there was nothing. No sound. No sight. My whole life extinguished with a single exhale.

TWENTY-FOUR

Where was I? Did I even exist anymore?

I took a tentative, fearful step and nearly wept when my foot settled on hard ground. Arm outstretched, I stumbled forward through tangible darkness. It brushed against my skin, filled my eyes, and infused my brain. I choked it down and breathed it out again, heavy and thick.

My chest, lungs, and throat burned as my body cried out for oxygen my brain believed I couldn't have.

Breathe. Inhale. *Breathe.* Exhale.

I ran a hand down my face, seeking the black cloth that must have been pressed against it. I found none, and my pulse quickened. I swung my free arm wildly, willing myself to feel *space*, to feel freedom, but the blackness stretched endlessly in every direction, disorienting in its stillness and silence.

So heavy. So thick.

If I screamed, would anyone hear me?

"Help me!"

My words fell beneath the crushing emptiness to quiver at my feet.

You're lost. Always lost.

Going the wrong way. Turned around.

Not enough. Never enough. You deserve this.

Whispers echoed around me, the same voice climbing over itself again and again. Panic ground into terror as my emotions unsuccessfully sought the right gear.

"Please!" I shook. "Please!" I tried to run, but something clung to my hand, tethering me to the nothing. I pounded and clawed at it, but it wouldn't release me.

A man's voice pushed through the blackness, tired from the journey. "Don't let go." It held reassurance and a *need* to hold on.

I held.

The whispers grew louder, tumbling over the plea.

You are weak, too weak to save them, to save him, to save yourself.

You are a monster.

You've done terrible things.

Who will forgive you? Who can?

The warehouse filled my vision. Like some macabre fish tank, it brimmed with human fluids, in which decapitated heads with razor-sharp teeth ate terrified children dropped in from above. Emily's screams assaulted my ears as whispers crashed over me in endless waves.

My stomach twisted, and I vomited.

Wouldn't death be better than this? Let go. Let go of living. There is peace in death.

No one would miss you.

You're a burden. Relieve the world of that burden.

Stop being selfish. Let go.

No one close to you ever survives.

The tank became a shelf lined with human bodies, propped up like dolls against the wall behind them. Their mouths gaped open as dead eyes stared ahead. Abba, Uri,

Immah, Emily, and so many more—all the people I'd been too late to save.

Ielu turned to me, recognition flickering in his dead eyes. Opening his mouth wide, he howled, and the rest shrieked in reply, blood leaking from their eyes.

I yanked at my tether. I had to run. I had to get away from the screaming. I clawed at my ears. I didn't have the strength for this. Life didn't exist here. Only death.

Death is better. No more pain. No more thought. No more emotion and doubt.

Death is better.

"Death is better!" I cried.

Death is better.

I opened my heart, ready to give in to the darkness.

"You promised." The voice was so distant, I had to strain to hear the words.

What did I promise? What was I doing here? I sifted through the fog in my brain, straining to remember what the whispers didn't want me to. Beyond the tank, beyond the dolls: a hand, a promise, answers, and . . . freedom.

I stepped forward again.

Come be with me.

I stopped, recognizing the voice this time. "Abba!"

Yaffa, come be with me. I miss you.

"Abba!" I had to get to him. I had to save him, hold him, keep him close. Every part of me cried out to be with him. "Where are you? Where *are* you?" I used my free hand to push against whatever held my wrist. "Let me go! Let me *go!*"

"Don't let go," the man said. "Keres, don't let go."

Yaffa, come with me.

"Keres, don't leave me."

Yaffa. Keres. Two names, one person. Who was I?

"Keres—"

The darkness devoured the rest, but it was enough. I stopped fighting, stopped screaming, as awareness broke through. Yaffa died a millennium ago. I was *Keres* now.

Yaffa, don't go.

My shoulders slumped forward, and tears streamed down my face. "I'm sorry, Abba. I have to."

But you left me before, and I died.

I stumbled over the painful memories. "You told me to run!"

You killed me.

I sobbed. "I loved you."

You should have stayed.

"I know, I know! I hate myself every day."

I hate you too.

My legs gave out, and the blackness pressed me to the ground. I fell, clutching my chest. I wanted to die.

"I'm sorry, Abba, so sorry." Tears streamed down my cheeks as I wailed and rocked myself.

You are stronger than this, said a new voice, female and familiar.

I laughed, tears and snot dripping off my face. I didn't feel strong.

You deserve freedom.

"Does a monster deserve anything?"

You are worth the price.

"Am I?"

Only you can decide. Don't let go.

I decide? I wiped my face with my shirt and pushed myself from the ground. *I decide.* I focused on the woman's voice and walked through the darkness.

You are strong, she repeated. *You deserve freedom.*

"I am strong." The darkness roiled around me as I tried the words for myself. I loved their taste even if I didn't believe their truth. I was a monster.

Yes, a monster, the whispers chimed in. *Monster, monster, monster.*

A burden.

Burden, it echoed.

I deserved to die.

Yes! Death. Death!

The whispers, I realized, were all my own. They echoed the secrets I kept from everyone but myself. This darkness and everything in it reflected the ugliness of my soul. What right did this darkness have to exist? What right did I?

Yet there had to be hope.

Yes, hope, the familiar, female voice said. Memories of saving Not-Abba, releasing the young man, and protecting Joe flashed like lightning in the dark.

I clung to her truth. "I can change!"

No, the darkness responded.

"I deserve another chance."

Lies.

"It isn't too late," I promised myself.

It's always too late.

I tightened my grip on the hand holding mine and willed us forward. I had to move while I had clarity, while I could tell the difference between the darkness and myself. We were separate, and if we could be separate in here, then maybe I could be rid of the blackness entirely.

Believe it and never let go, called the woman's voice.

My voice—the part of me that wasn't darkness, wasn't awful, and perhaps, didn't deserve to die. My words were sharp and clear, no longer hindered by the blackness.

"I choose life," I said. A soft breeze blew across my face, and the darkness swirled. Ghostly hands with long nails scratched my face, and the whispers screeched in pain. "I choose life!"

A gust blew through the Hall, and the blackness receded, until nothing but light remained.

The breath of life.

Joe and I stumbled to a stop, overwhelmed by the warmth and brightness of the room. Never in my life had I been so grateful for the dawn. Turning, I threw my arms around Joe, who squeezed me tightly.

"You okay?" I whispered.

"Always," he replied, but his cheeks were wet and his eyes puffy. I wondered what he had seen while we were trapped inside the manifestation of my soul.

Questions for another time.

We turned toward the giant gold double doors that loomed ahead. Unlike the smooth doors through which we'd entered, these were etched with symbols and pictures—a blend of cuneiform and hieroglyph that felt both familiar and alien.

We shared a look and then turned to the last pair of canopic jars. The final plague of Egypt. Glancing behind me, I was surprised to see an empty hall and tiny doors at the other end of this nightmare. No locusts, no darkness.

Joe squeezed my hand. "Ready?"

I shrugged. "How much worse can it get, right?"

His grim smile didn't reach his eyes. I nodded, and we ran toward salvation.

As we passed between the last two jars, they dissolved into waterfalls of liquid gold that pooled between us and the exit.

"Faster!"

We sprinted for the exit, but we couldn't outrun the liquid metal. As the last of the jars reached the pool, the liquid flowed up, solidifying into a faceless figure: Egypt's Angel of Death. We skidded to a halt.

"Fuck," Joe said.

"Agreed."

"What the hell do we do now?" He didn't take his eyes off the golden figure. His chest heaved as human lungs gulped for air.

I pulled my khukuri from its sheath. "Your guess is as good as mine." I tried to tug Joe behind me, but he resisted. I risked a quick glance his way. "Whatever this is, you're no match for it."

"I'm done being the damsel in distress." He reached for his Glock, smiling when I would have protested. "Remember what I said about arguing?"

"You'll just do something to piss me off."

"And probably get myself killed."

"Together, then?"

"Together." He drew his gun and fired round after round as we charged. Where each bullet struck, the figure became liquid gold, sucking the lead into its body before solidifying again. Various weapons shifted through its hands until it settled on a wicked-looking dagger with a hooked end, meant for sliding into a body and pulling everything out.

The figure lunged for me, its body shifting between liquid and solid as needed to take a blow, a bullet, or a swipe of my knife. I tried to use my power to slow it but failed. Everything felt too distant, my powers locked away by whatever barriers existed here.

Death moved fast, almost like *blinking*, and I struggled to keep up. I tried to keep both it and Joe within sight as Joe made his way to the door. My heart pounded when he reached out to touch the golden surface. Distracted, I missed a parry and took a slice to my shoulder from the hooked dagger. The figure's next slice came too fast. I blocked but lost my balance and went tumbling across the marble floor.

"There's no handle, no release!" Joe yelled.

The figure's empty face turned toward Joe, and it advanced on him while I pulled myself from the ground. My khukuri rested a few steps away. Blade or Joe? I didn't think I had time for both.

Making my decision, I raced for my reaping blade and then sprinted back to Joe. As he had said, he wasn't a damsel, and I definitely wasn't a hero.

The figure raised its dagger to strike just as I reached the pair. Joe turned, Death sliced, and I hooked its arm and pulled—all three at the same time. It turned and swiped at me, and I blocked, pushing it back away from Joe as best I could.

Joe coughed. "Keres."

I turned back to him. A red line of blood seeped through a gash in his shirt. I hadn't been fast enough. Icy tendrils of fear clutched my heart as I tried to defend us both from a stronger, faster attacker.

How do I keep him safe? How do I set him free?

I threw my fear at the unseen barrier blocking me from my power. I clawed and pounded against it, until only the cold resolution that we were going to die remained. It seeped into the invisible wall that denied me my power, like canned air sprayed onto a bike lock, and the wall shifted and became brittle. I slammed my will—everything I had—against the barrier until it cracked and gave way.

My fear became a conduit, and I couldn't contain the rush of power. I screamed pain as my body burned with a frostbite that came from within.

I turned toward the figure and redirected the flow.

At first, nothing happened. I'd hoped for a shockwave, like the one I'd created in my apartment, but Death didn't even stumble. Instead, it stepped forward.

Once.

Twice.

When the figure's shoulders twisted for a third step, its feet remained still. It looked down, where an icy fog poured off its body as though it had been dipped in liquid nitrogen. Lunging forward, I stabbed my khukuri into its center. A spiderweb of cracks splintered across its torso and limbs. Yanking my blade free, I struck the crackling warrior in the chest with a spinning back kick. It exploded into golden shards.

Racing to Joe's side, I ripped off the bottom half of his shirt and pressed it against the open wound. His blood felt hot against my cold hands.

"Hold this," I told him.

As he pressed his hands against his shirt, I helped him slide to the floor with his back against the door. I glanced over my shoulder; the golden warrior had already thawed, its bits and pieces flowing back together.

Sadness wafted from Joe. "I'm sorry, Keres."

"Save your pity." I looked around for some clue as to how we were supposed to open the damned door. It had no knobs, but perhaps there was a switch somewhere.

"You always assume the worst."

"In my experience, I'm usually right." I pushed up from the ground to get a better look at the picture carved into the center of the two doors. It depicted a woman, hands held out as if offering me something. Rivers of water fell from her hands and gathered in a basin below. I looked around for water, keeping an eye on the slowly forming Death.

"I don't pity you," Joe said.

"Then don't apologize for things you can't control."

He winced and inhaled sharply. "Am I not allowed to feel bad for not being able to help?"

"I'll let you know when we get out of this." *Damn it! Where is the water?* I returned to the carving and stared. *What am I missing?*

Recalling the first jars, I gasped. Not water. Rivers of blood.

The liquid poured from small openings in both hands—a sacrifice. Reaching up, I touched the wounds with tingling fingers. Then I glanced over my shoulder. The last of the liquid gold flowed up to form Death's head; its wicked dagger gleamed in the light.

I was out of time and options.

I handed my khukuri to Joe. "Hold this as tightly as you can."

He smiled. "You've decided to leave me after all?" How in the world could he smile while bleeding out as some demon warrior hunted us down?

"Hold it!"

He grabbed the hilt of my knife, and I wrapped my hands around the blade. Joe's eyes widened in shock as I pulled up, efficiently slicing open my hands.

"What the hell!" He dropped the khukuri and stared at me in disgust.

Without explaining, I stood back up and reached up on tiptoe, placing my hands in the ones etched on the door. My blood ran down the golden surface in crimson streams, some catching in the grooves of the image and the rest flowing freely down the door.

"Keres!"

I didn't dare turn or let go. Even if I was correct, I still didn't know how much blood would be needed.

As the wicked dagger pierced my back, I screamed in surprise. The golden figure used its hook to pull me away from the door and to my knees. I screamed again when it twisted the blade, pulling at my insides.

My blood flowed.

My screams intensified.

And shots rang out as Joe emptied the last of his clip into my faceless Angel of Death.

A click echoed through the vaulted room, and a sliver of dull light appeared down the middle of the image where the door swung open. The tugging stopped, and I turned to see the golden figure and its weapon disintegrate into nothingness.

I moved slowly toward Joe, half dragging my body across the cold floor. The wound where Death had played tug-of-war with my insides had healed, but my hands still bled. I tried ripping my own shirt to create bandages for them, but I had to settle for grabbing the fabric and scrunching it in my fists. Every part of my body screamed for sleep.

I leaned against Joe, and he leaned back. After a few breaths, I turned my face toward him. "Joe?"

"I know." Without looking at me, he reached into his pocket and pulled out the piece of my *abba*'s shofar. His eyes closed in pain, but he managed to choke out, "As promised."

I waited for him to look at me. When he didn't, I pulled his face around with one bloodied hand and kissed him, quick and easy. Then I took the shofar and shoved it into my khukuri sheath.

When I looked back at him, his eyes were wide.

"For pissing off that guard earlier," I explained. "I never got to say thank you."

He smiled to his dimples. "Feel free to thank me anytime."

I laughed. "Let's go before you pass out from the sight of all this blood." It was my turn to wink. The moment felt foreign, and I blushed.

Sheathing my reaping blade, I stood, pulling Joe up with me and wrapping his arm around my neck so I could support his weight. Hooking my foot in the door, I swung it open.

"Please let this be the end," I said.

"Agreed."

Together, we stepped through the door and into an empty foyer. The same foyer we had left an eternity ago.

"So much for the welcome wagon." Joe coughed on the last word.

I'd been ready to be done with the gauntlet when I stepped through this last door, but it wasn't over yet. It didn't matter that I'd passed their test. It didn't matter that I'd almost died—that *Joe* had almost died. Like the Guardians, they still wanted *more*, and I hated them for it.

Tension built at the base of my skull, and adrenaline chased the painful exhaustion from my limbs. Small tremors grew in my chest and arms. How long would they wait before descending from their lofty perches? How long would they ignore me?

"Cowards!" I shouted at the alcoves. Their collective fear oozed down the pristine walls of their precious hall. "I'm here! I've passed your test!" Disdain wafted from a few of them, contempt for a dog who thought she could speak above her station.

"You pretend to be superior. You're supposed to have the answers and offer wisdom and lead your people." I was assuming a lot based on the little I knew of the Guardian hierarchy, but the rising anger I felt from them meant I'd hit the mark.

"But you're—"

Joe cried out in pain. "Keres?" He stared at me, eyes wide, as he coughed up blood and then collapsed. I fell beneath his weight.

"Joe. Joe! *Frat Boy!*"

What had he done but desire to help me? And what had they done but watch him bleed out? As his life force weakened, the insatiable hunger to destroy awakened within me, thirsty for souls. My khukuri sang, and the runes glowed brightly. I fought against it, the push for release, the animal clawing for freedom.

Perhaps this was what they'd wanted all along.

The Bloodlust.

"You are no better than the Guardians," I whispered. I tried to empty myself as J-Man had said, but it didn't work. I was too far gone.

A woman appeared in front of me, her rage a toddler tantrum compared to what fought for release inside me. Others followed, popping into view, until seven people stood before me: three women, three men, and the boy who looked like Raven.

"The Council," I spat. I gripped my stomach as it churned in pain. I couldn't hold on much longer. I need to get away. I needed to make Joe safe. But they only stared, masking their terror with anger and self-righteousness.

‹I can feel your fear,› I projected.

‹And I can feel yours.›

The boy stepped forward. "Hello, Keres. I'm Adi."

TWENTY-FIVE

Every muscle in my body contracted, until I writhed on the floor, pain streaming down my face. I'd put so much into finding Adi—to making it here and surviving—only to find a child standing where my savior should be.

"Not. Possible," I forced out through clenched teeth. I couldn't accept that this tiny figure held all my hopes in his too-small hands. How in the hell could *he* help *me*? What had Ielu been thinking?

"I am as I say," he replied.

Not possible. The words looped through my mind, fanning the flames of my rage, until my insides burned. Blood pounded in my ears, and I clutched my chest. He'd been so close the whole time and hadn't helped.

"Fire . . . in her eyes," a woman whispered, her fear pouring gasoline on my fury. The ground shook beneath me, and heat poured off my skin. It took everything I had to keep it from touching Joe.

Everyone but Adi retreated. The boy stepped closer.

"But . . ." The wildfire raging inside overtook my vision.

Whatever this is comes from you, Joe had said. He was right.

My fault, my fault, my fault, always my fault.

I screamed, long and loud. I forced all my anger into that scream, hoping I might expel it from my body with my breath. Instead, it fed the monster pulling against its chains—links of hope and fear woven together to keep the Bloodlust from breaking free. The chains groaned.

Tug. Wrench. Twist. Tug.

Please, God, don't let it free.

Snap. The chains broke.

Gasping and convulsing, I curled into a tighter ball and pressed bleeding hands to the sides of my head. I stared up at the small form leaning over me and raised a hand, a beggar pleading for alms. I'd arrived too late. The Bloodlust roared free. Only one option remained.

"Please," I sobbed, "destroy me." *Save me.*

Adi took my hand, and my body recoiled from the power of his touch. His spirit raced through me, faster and fiercer than Ielu's, creating an almost instant connection.

We stood inside my mind, two figures in a long hallway surrounded by scorching flames. Everything here felt *tangible,* as if this were reality and the other place a dream. We stepped forward, and our presence rippled down the corridor. The ghosts of my past roiled and shrieked, drawing together to form a ravenous, multi-faced monster.

Sergio, Olivia, Kaylee, Alyssa, Matt, Nathan, Julie, Henry—all the way back to Maahir. I could name all my marks from last to first. I relived their crimes and heard the cries of their victims mingled with their own death screams. Other faces surfaced in the heat, people I could not name because they hadn't mattered, their lives labeled collateral in my pursuit of justice. They wailed, and I cringed from their hungry stares.

Adi stepped between us. His power became a tidal wave, pushing back the fires. The Bloodlust howled, lashing out with razor-sharp teeth. Their energies battled, the cool waters of Adi's peace against the inferno of my rage.

The boy—calm, centered, and unafraid—released a burst of controlled power, which roared down the hallway of my consciousness, shattering the Bloodlust into the separate flames from which it had come.

He walked forward, reaching for the monsters that reached for him. I flinched, expecting them to consume him. Instead, he quenched the fires, leaving behind dying embers of black laced with hot orange.

"What are those?" My voice echoed down the hallway, above the crackle of the retreating blaze. "Souls?"

"The souls you've reaped are inseparable and indistinguishable from your own. They are part of you, as you are of them. These"—picking one up, he looked it over—"are echoes of the former souls. Memories, if you will."

Using the lower half of his tunic as a pouch, he collected the memories and placed them gently into the cloth. The more he collected, the more the terrors retreated before him, back through the twisted door carved with tangled bodies that clamored to be free.

"They feel . . . tangible," I whispered. "Powerful."

"Memories often do. Sometimes more than real life."

When we reached the door, his impromptu pouch overflowing, he paused. "Did you open this?"

"Ielu," I said.

He sighed. "I am sorry for you both." He looked down at the dying embers held in his shirt. "Though it couldn't have held forever. It isn't enough."

"I never am."

"You and this"—he waved at the carved wood—"are not the same. Do not confuse them."

I nodded toward the door. "Can you fix it?"

"You don't want to die?"

I stared at the ground. "I should die. How can I ever make this right?"

"You can't."

Heat from the hallway beyond the door pressed against my flesh. I leaned closer, both wishing and fearing it could burn me alive. Adi waited.

"I don't want to die," I said finally.

"Good." He stepped through the door and waited.

"I'm afraid."

He shifted the weight of the memories so he could take my hand. "It's okay to be afraid." He continued forward, dragging me behind him.

Rather than a hotel hallway lined with wooden doors, this area reminded me of a horror-flick psychiatric hospital. Light flickered in sickly green hues as screams ricocheted down the hall, bouncing off tiled floors and dirt-smeared walls. The gaping doors looked like metal teeth ready to grind us between them.

The remaining nightmares retreated into their cells as Adi pulled me along, stopping at each door to glance inside. If it was empty, he deposited an ember within it. Once certain the cell was occupied, he locked it and moved on to the next. This continued until his hands were empty and all the doors were locked shut.

Twisted faces pressed against glass windows, wild eyes watching us—wary of Adi, ravenous for me. Some of the doorknobs turned slowly as monsters tested their prisons, but none made a sound. Water dripped somewhere in the distance, maddening in its incessant *splish . . . splish . . . splish* that echoed in the tight silence.

"Let's go." I tugged Adi toward the black door I could no longer see.

A desperate wail punctured the emptiness, freezing my already-clenched muscles. All eyes turned toward the sound, and my gaze followed to an offshoot of the main hall that ended in blackness.

The cry came again, more intense.

Adi cocked his head to the side. "This way." He pulled me toward the sound.

"Shouldn't we leave now?" I didn't want to be here any longer.

"Not yet." The wail turned to a shriek, and I clenched Adi's hand. He squeezed gently but pulled me forward.

"Please, don't make me see this." The growing darkness reminded me of the pitch black of the Hall, and I never wanted to be without light again. Panic shifted in my belly, and my feet stopped moving.

"You will never be free unless *all* of you is free."

I glanced back the way we'd come. "But we locked away all . . ." I waved a hand, unable to find the right word. "Those. How is this different?"

"This isn't a memory." A small flame sprouted from Adi's free hand and grew until its light exposed a windowless, double-barricaded door an arm's length from me.

I pulled him away as more shrieks pierced our ears. "But you saw what happened," I whispered. My throat burned, and my chest hurt from the tension held there.

He set the flame off to the side as if lighting an invisible torch on the wall. "And what will continue to happen unless you stop trying to lock this part of you away. I'm here to help you. Let me."

He pulled his hand gently from mine and stepped to the door. I wrapped my arms around myself as he lifted the first plank of wood, more easily than his little body implied. Whatever lurked inside threw itself against the metal and screamed. I backed away.

"Trust me." Adi removed the second bar. As he opened the door, the monster shrieked, and I vomited from the putrid scent of burnt flesh and urine.

Hunched over and half in the dark crouched a young woman with wild eyes and translucent skin that barely stretched over her bones. She clung to the doorframe with gnarled hands and yellowed fingernails twisted with age. Her long, black hair fell in a snarled mass down her naked body, and the shiny shells of dark bugs roaming her scalp reflected the light that spilled in from the hallway. She seemed more animal than human, more dead than alive.

"Yaffa." It took all the air in my lungs to say that one word, leaving me breathless. Cold tingles raced beneath my skin, raising the fine hairs on my arms and neck.

I'd expected to see anything . . . anything but me.

Yaffa's gaze burned as a low, guttural growl churned in her throat. Her hate reached out with razor-sharp tendrils that slashed at everything, thousands of paper cuts to the soul. Adi didn't seem to notice. He wasn't afraid, only sad. A sorrow so deep, I struggled not to drown.

He stepped closer to the girl and crouched down. She swiped at him with a clawed hand, and sparks flew where it connected with an invisible barrier. She whimpered and retreated into the darkness behind her. Adi walked farther into the cell, carrying his light with him.

Yaffa curled up in the muck in the back corner of the room, her old clothing long since becoming toilet and bed. A bony arm draped over her face in an attempt to hide from the world as she whined softly.

Adi touched her leg, and she flinched, screaming as if he'd burned her. I thought of Luke's punishments. She looked up at me, eyes pleading.

Adi tried again, but I stopped him. I didn't know what to say, how to explain, so I only said, "It hurts."

He nodded and turned back to the girl. "It's going to be okay." He beckoned me closer, but I shook my head. I didn't know if I could. She was so foul and hideous.

So weak.

Adi pulled me down next to him. "She needs hope. I can't give it to her; it must come from you."

I stared at her, with her face covered and her body shaking. "What do I say?"

"Tell her everything's going to be okay."

"Is it?" I asked.

"You tell me. You decide."

I looked at him sharply. His words echoed the voice in the Hall. That had been my voice, hadn't it?

"Any change, Keres, must come from you. I might be able to light the path, but you are the one who must walk it."

"But I don't know . . ."

"You don't have to know. Can you hope?"

Could I? If I hadn't been able to, I wouldn't have left Luke, fought Daemons, and walked that damned Hall.

Okay. I could hope.

"Everything will be okay." The words tasted wrong, but I didn't know how to make them taste right.

Adi nodded toward the huddling creature. "To her."

Staring at Yaffa, I tried to see beyond everything that said she was too animal to be human. I tried to remember her before her death, when she smiled and laughed and played. I tried to remember when she had been confident and brave, using her voice to ask questions and pushing the boundaries of both her desert and her tribe.

I paused in reaching for Yaffa. Until then, I hadn't realized how much I'd lost when I chose my life as an Aod. I had physical strength beyond anything I could have imagined, but was it worth losing my voice, losing myself?

All I'd lost in my choice—it was time to get it back.

I touched her leg. "Everything's going to be okay." She whimpered but didn't pull away. I moved my hand back and forth, trying to console her, and repeated the words. "Everything is going to be okay."

Her arms dropped, and she stared at me. Then, shifting her weight, she dived into my arms. I froze as her body pressed against mine. It was the first time in a thousand years she'd touched another soul in this forsaken place. My humanity locked in a cell—tired, broken, starved, and yearning for a freedom that also frightened her.

Wrapping my arms around her, I held on tightly and rocked us both. So many confusing emotions flicked through me. Anger I knew—what it was and how to use it. The others made me feel vulnerable and uncertain, yet strong and determined. "I don't know how, but it's going to be okay. I promise. I'm going to free you, to free us."

"But monsters must die," she said.

Crying tears I didn't understand, I buried my face in her ratty hair. "But you're not a monster, Yaffa. You never were." *Please, God, let me be right.*

When I opened my eyes, I was back in the foyer of air and light. I cradled Adi in my arms, his head against my chest, warming my heart with peace. I cried harder and hugged him tighter. He was Emily and Uri. He was my father and mother, my siblings, my people. He was every person I'd ever wanted to save but had always been too late to, all rolled into a tiny body of warmth and light.

He was Yaffa and Keres.

I held onto him, and for one small moment, I felt strong enough to hold my pain in the light instead of keeping it buried in the shadows.

He hugged me back, patted my face, and then stood. As he grasped my hands again, a tingling spread through them. When he released them, I stared into healed palms, wondering at the wholeness I felt inside.

When Adi walked over to Joe, I wiped furiously at my tears, embarrassed by the rabid display of emotion. "Is he going to be okay?"

Adi didn't look up, too focused on Joe to meet my gaze. The others hovered around us in an uncertain stupor. Their anger had receded into curiosity tinged with fear and disdain—a kind of peekaboo, where their emotions brushed against me and fled. Nothing indicated the Council knew what had happened inside me.

Beneath the boy's hands, the open wound on Joe's lower chest stopped bleeding, and invisible threads sewed it shut. A heavy weight pressed against my chest as Joe's body heaved and rocked from the pain of a quick mending. His eyes remained closed, his breathing labored.

Adi motioned to the Council, and one of the six, an elderly woman, stepped forward. "He needs more rest. Take him to our home," he told her. She nodded, gathered Joe into her arms, and *blinked* away.

"Will he be okay?" My voice sounded strained and foreign.

The boy smiled. "As healthy as ever." Adi nodded to the remaining council members, who all left.

I looked around the empty foyer. I no longer desired to paint it. Every part of it reminded me of death.

Adi glanced around. "Not so beautiful when you know what happens here."

"Then why make it like this?"

"To make it bearable, I suppose." He held out a hand. "Let's go."

Rising from the floor, I took it. "What now?"

"We talk."

TWENTY-SIX

Answer the question, Adi," I repeated. "I have a right to know how to break the Contract."

We rode along a paved street in a graceful, low-sitting phaeton that, while drawn by a single horse, reminded me of the vintage car that shared its name. Despite the light design made for breakneck speeds, Adi never pushed the horse faster than a walk. I suppose riding in the sleek car following behind us wouldn't have gotten us to our destination any faster. Transportation seemed to be an accessory here, like a purse or a necklace, chosen more for its appearance than its function.

The crawling pace and excessive joy surrounding me grated on my tired nerves. I wanted to be somewhere with four walls and fewer people. Instead, I watched warily as thousands of slightly glowing faces journeyed wherever Daemons had to go, no one rushing or pushing their neighbors to get one step ahead.

"Odessa," Adi said.

"Excuse me?

"The city. Its name is Odessa."

"Not what I asked." Using the numbness floating inside me, I squeezed out irritation like juice from a fruit. Emotion spilled to the ground beneath me, leaving an invisible trail that led right back to the monstrosity these Daemons disguised as a wondrous temple. I didn't want a repeat of the Hall. Ever.

I took a deep breath. I had to stay empty, like J-Man.

"You can't get where you're going until you know where you are," Adi said.

I massaged my forehead. "Fine. Where am I?"

He smiled. "One of the few Daemon cities on Earth."

I raised an eyebrow. I'd assumed we were in another layer, like the Echo and wherever Ielu had taken me. Not . . . *here* . . . on Earth.

I tried, unsuccessfully, to get my bearings. The city was a melting pot of architecture and culture. Yet instead of looking like a world history of architecture had puked on the landscape, the structural elements flowed together to create a breathtaking vista of spires, columns, domes, and pagodas. Splashes of culture also ran over each other in dress, color, and style, mixing at the edges like dyes on a T-shirt during Holi.

"What part of the world?"

"Nowhere, for now—tucked away in the folds of a discarded blanket."

Adi reined in the horse, allowing a stream of people to cross the road in front of us. A little girl slowed as she passed, staring up at me with wide eyes. The woman holding her hand glanced in my direction and then scooped up the girl, tendrils of fear clutching the child more tightly than her physical embrace.

I tried not to take it personally.

"It never occurred to me that Daemons might have children. I thought you were monsters, not people."

"Even monsters have offspring. Good is not a prerequisite for procreation."

"So you *are* monsters?"

"As you see, so we are."

"You make zero sense. You know that, right?"

"A teacher never does until the student understands." Adi smiled at the woman and child and waved. The woman's fear eased as she smiled at him, but her eyes remained tight at the edges. Once they had passed, we moved forward again.

"How do I trust a cryptic child who's barely potty-trained?"

"How has trusting adults worked for you?"

"Touché."

"Ask more powerful questions; get more powerful answers."

"What's more powerful than 'how do I break the Contract?' It's the only reason I came here!"

Numbness. Squeeze. Release. Breathe.

"Your perception is more powerful. If all you can see are monsters, that is all you'll ever find. In you, in others. But if you can see humanity, you will find humanity. *Daemon* is a very old word in this layer that refers to a spiritual being less than God but more than human. But at their core, they are simply individuals doing the best they can as they navigate their own hopes, dreams, and fears."

Fear. I turned and stared into the crowd, studying everyone and no one. I watched the mother's fear spread, as fear always did—a light mist crawling through the crowd, touching this person, chilling that one, whispering alongside the carriage. My back stiffened under the scrutiny.

"Why do they fear me?" I spoke lowly, hoping my words wouldn't travel beyond the turning wheels and *clickety-clack* of horse hooves.

"The child wasn't afraid."

"Not her. *Daemons*—the big ones." *The scary ones. Numbness. Squeeze. Release. Breathe.*

He gathered the reins in one hand and grabbed mine with the other. His warm, tiny hand felt comfortable in mine, and I never wanted to let go.

The feeling worried me.

"Because they don't understand," he said. "Isn't that always the beginning of fear?"

"Understanding that the snake has venom doesn't make it less dangerous."

"But knowing how to handle it does."

I stared down at the boy sitting next to me in a white tunic and baggy, white pants that were tucked into his socks and shoes.

"Fallen! Fallen!"

My stomach flipped as a man rushed Adi's side of the phaeton. I had to stay calm and not react.

Numbness. Squeeze. Squeeze. *Release. Breathe.*

Adi stopped the rig, and I wished someone would honk or yell, anything to get us moving again.

"Fallen." The man beamed, his chest rising and falling quickly. He held out a small box, crimson wrapped in a golden bow. I eyed it but didn't reach for the package. He made a motion encouraging me to take it. "For you."

"Why?" I couldn't handle another Daemon surprise.

Pulling the box back and holding it close to his chest, he bowed his head—a reverent gesture. "To say thank you and welcome home." When he looked back up, his eyes were wet with unshed tears. "I've waited my whole life for the return of your people."

"Thank you, Omyhn." Adi took the box and handed it to me, and the man stepped back from the carriage. Adi clucked at the horse, and I nodded at the man as we rolled forward. Omyhn smiled and drew his shoulders back to stand at full height, as if I'd knighted him. The light of his gratitude cut through the shroud of fear surrounding us.

"What just happened?" I glanced back and then shifted my gaze to Adi when he didn't answer. "Why parade me through the city when you could have *blinked* me anywhere?"

He smiled. "Your questions are improving."

"So should your answers."

"I'm testing."

I frowned. "Another test for me."

"And them," Adi replied. "They are afraid, Keres. Even the ones like Omyhn who have been waiting for the return of loved ones worry about what this means. They need to see you as safe—and you them—if your return is to be as peaceful as we've always hoped."

"My return? Like prophecy?"

Adi shook his head. "Not at all."

We turned into a large park, where green lawns stretched lazily through several city blocks. Adi climbed down from the phaeton and motioned for me to follow, leading us to a secluded bench. The sun continued to sink below the buildings, and the sky shifted colors, painting golden rooftops and shining walls with the soft pinks and oranges of sunset.

"We expected the Fallen would return someday—a hope, not a prophecy. We just didn't expect it now."

"Why do you call me Fallen?"

Sadness seeped from the boy, and he let out a sigh too big for his little body. "A story too long for today." He touched my face when I opened my mouth to push, his hand soft and warm against my skin. "I promise," he said. "Tomorrow."

"Adi, please, how do I break the Contract?"

"Tell me, Keres, who are you?"

"This." I unsheathed my blade. "This is who I am."

"Violence is what you do, not who you are. It is a face, like the many I have." To demonstrate, he changed into an old man, head bald and long, white beard brushing the ground. He looked like he'd lived in a monastery for over a hundred years. "This does not define me." Even his voice sounded deeper and smoothed by time.

"Perhaps."

"Or this." His form shimmered again, and a woman sat next to me, shorter than me but with the same choppy, black hair. "The faces we wear can be changed—used and discarded as needed to conceal and even protect."

I averted my gaze. She looked and sounded too much like Raven for my comfort.

"We must look past the faces—our own and others'— if we are ever to truly see."

He had returned to being a seven-year-old boy, which I appreciated. I found comfort in this face, more than the old man or the young woman. For better or worse, he didn't seem capable of lying in this form, which could be why he preferred it.

Wake up, Keres, I chided myself. *Everybody lies.*

"Not everyone," Adi said.

"Must you be in my head too?"

"Never without your permission. I only catch the thoughts you release into the world, like a radio broadcasting intermittent phrases amid the static. Your thoughts speak loudly of distrust."

"Do you blame me?"

"I think the better question is, do you blame yourself?"

I didn't answer. Instead, I sheathed my blade, and he slipped his small arm beneath mine and cuddled close.

His warmth spread through me, softened me, and I released the numbness. Released everything but his peace.

For this moment, I promised myself. *Just this moment.* There would be time for death, stress, anger, and pain in the next heartbeat.

Adi's hand brushed down my forearm. "Tell me your story."

So I did. Recited to him what I'd explained to Ielu and Joe, and then some. I told him everything. He felt safe, and the words tumbled out of my mouth, weak, frail, and begging for mercy. Begging for redemption. His sadness deepened as I described the Contract, the tortures from Raven, the isolation, and the nightmares that only intensified the longer I lived, until I couldn't hold the weight of his sorrow.

Emotion burned my throat where I choked it back. "Please stop."

His brow furrowed. "Stop what?"

"Feeling so sad. I can't hold mine and yours. It's too much, too heavy."

He nodded. "You can feel the emotions of others."

I bit my lip. The one secret I hadn't meant to share. "You're not surprised?"

"You'd already told me you could feel our fear. This only confirmed my suspicion."

"I call myself a Reader."

"Can you read thoughts too?"

I shook my head. "Mostly I feel emotions, but sometimes I see images. Your thoughts are the only ones I've heard."

"That's different. It's connected to my power, not yours." Adi stiffened. "Does anyone else know?"

"Not sure. I never told anyone, but . . ." I shrugged.

He relaxed back into me. "Wise to keep it a secret."

I hesitated. "Is *reading* common among Daemons?"

"Not at all."

"But you—"

"Are an exception to the rule," he finished.

"What does that make me?"

"Too early to know for sure."

Always different. Always alone. I shivered despite the warm air.

"Not always. Not anymore." He squeezed my arm and pressed his little body more tightly against mine. I rested my cheek on his soft hair but straightened as soon as I realized what I'd done.

If he noticed either movement, he didn't react.

We sat in silence, both lost in our thoughts. A couple crossed the park, elbows linked as they whispered together. Their love felt new and exciting, like the adrenaline of skydiving.

"Am I safe?" I wondered aloud as the couple disappeared around a bend in the path.

Adi smiled. "They won't hurt you."

"I meant for them. How long will . . . *it* . . . hold?" I looked inward at the black door in my mind. It felt strong and solid, but it had felt that way before Ielu.

"That's up to you."

I frowned. "Then it's not permanent."

"Whatever held you together was already weakening when Ielu stumbled upon you. That was the only reason he broke through."

I swallowed down bile.

"And it will happen again," he said.

"That doesn't make me feel better."

"It wasn't supposed to."

"Can I ever be free?"

"What do you think?"

I shrugged. "I don't know."

"Keres, what are you hoping for on the other side of all this? What does that future look like to you?"

"I'm hoping I won't feel this anymore." I circled my hand over my heart. "The pain, the gut-wrenching heartache, the visions and nightmares—I'm hoping all of it will die with the Contract."

"And if it doesn't? If breaking the Contract doesn't release you from the demons it created?"

"But we freed Yaffa." That meant something, didn't it? Meant I could be freed from the demons?

"We opened the door, but she isn't free."

I watched the rivers of orange and pink flow over the buildings until they faded into the deep blues of twilight. "I don't know," I whispered when the silence became unbearable. "I don't want to believe that future exists."

Adi pulled me from the bench and led me across the park to a lane of small mansions, their architecture as eclectic as the rest of the city. His question burned within me, manifesting as dull pain in my upper back as we walked the tree-lined street. Like my heart, the overhanging branches drooped with the weight of spring promises. I reached up and pulled a flower from one—beautiful and unfamiliar.

What would I be on the other side of this? I pressed my shoulder blades together and then stretched them apart, but the burning remained. I didn't even know what breaking the Contract meant beyond not having to kill again. Would I pass on? Would I stay here, all power with no direction? J-Man had remained on the Earth, but he hadn't been released from the need to kill. He'd only found a way to keep it at bay.

"Adi, what will happen to me once we break the Contract?"

We passed one house and then a second and a third. Adi opened his mouth a few times to speak but then closed it again. Eventually, we left the lane and turned into the courtyard of one of the grand houses. I pulled him to a stop partway up the path.

"Adi, what happens?" A thought dawned within me, slow and cold. "Can you even break the Contract?"

He inhaled and held the breath for a few seconds before exhaling slowly. "I don't know. Before Ielu's death, we didn't even know your kind existed . . . as this." He waved his hand toward me.

"What the hell does that mean?" A bubble of anger popped inside me, followed by heart-racing panic. I clung to the numbness. I wouldn't explode again. I wouldn't. Even if it meant I never felt again.

Numbness. Squeeze. *Release. Breathe.*

Breathe.

Breathe.

"Being a Fallen and being an angel of death, as you call it, are not the same thing. And we know *nothing* of the latter."

"Then what am I doing here?"

"Fighting for your freedom," he answered.

"You just told me you didn't know how to break the Contract." We were talking in circles.

"There are many things from which you need to be liberated. Your Contract is only one of them."

"What good will any of it do if I can't stop killing?"

I laughed—a short burst that sounded sharp and brassy, at odds with all the soft edges around me. It twisted inside me, and more manic laughter bubbled up from my chest and flowed out my mouth. I collapsed to the ground, hugging my knees as I cackled and rocked, until there was nothing left but a gaping hole inside me.

Adi studied me for a long time. My body screamed to run, but I forced myself to hold.

"May I?" He pointed to my weapon.

I placed my hand on my khukuri. "Why?"

"I'm looking for answers. May I study it for a time?"

"How long?" I asked.

"Tomorrow. Maybe the next day? Is that okay?" My hesitation must have spoken volumes. "I wouldn't take it if it weren't absolutely necessary."

Reluctantly, I nodded and handed him my blade.

He received it gently, holding my weapon with reverence rather than fear. "Keres, there is a chance I won't be able to help you with this Contract. I will try, but it is possible I will fail."

What could I say to that? Nothing. So I focused on breathing instead. *Numbness. Numbness. Numb . . . numb . . . numb . . .*

"Head inside. Dinner will be waiting."

I nodded, turning robotically toward the house as he *blinked* away.

Squeeze.

I trudged up to the house and let myself in.

Release.

What would I do if Adi failed me? Had Ielu put too much faith in this small child?

Breathe.

I stepped into a sitting room off the main hall. "Excuse me . . ."

My words disappeared as Daliah turned her gaze from the flames dancing in the oversize fireplace and stared daggers at me. I moved to leave, but she *blinked*, appearing in front of me, blocking my retreat. Rage burned though her aura, but it seemed contained—a forest fire burning itself out.

We stared at each other for a very long time.

"This isn't over, Fallen." Her rage spiked, but she brought it back under control. I understood her pain. She needed someone to hate, and I was the best candidate. As long as she hated me, she wouldn't hate herself. That was when it really got ugly.

"Original," I replied, stoking her fire. I would do everything I could to keep her hate directed at me. My penance for taking Ielu.

She slapped me hard across the face. It didn't even register; I'd been slapped before with greater conviction.

"Daliah." The voice sounded like sandpaper blocks rubbing against each other. An old woman stepped into my periphery—her simple white dress cut in at her waist and flowed to the floor, where it pooled slightly—but I never took my gaze off Daliah.

Daliah stiffened and turned, bowing her head. "Yes, Adyti."

"Keres is our guest. You will show her respect while she is in this home."

"It's okay." I turned and immediately recognized the older woman. She was the council member who had *blinked* away with Joe.

"I don't need your permission or your pity!" As Daliah fled the room, my eyes widened. Hadn't those same words tumbled past my own lips before?

"Please forgive Daliah. She's struggling without Ielu. He was balm for older wounds." She gazed after the redhead, sadness in her eyes.

"I am sorry." I didn't know what else to say.

"I'm not." I stared at her blankly, and she motioned to the couch. "Please sit." When I did, she claimed the chair closest to me.

"Ielu had his reasons, and I trust him implicitly. If he

gave his life, it mattered. We all make choices. Sometimes they hurt us, sometimes they hurt others, and sometimes they do both. But if you make a good choice, it has meaning in the end. His choice has meaning."

"You think I'm special."

"Doesn't matter what I think. It matters what you think."

"You sound like Adi."

"I learned from the best."

"You're *younger* than him?" I couldn't believe it. While her skin was flawless and beautiful, her silver hair was swept back in a loose bun and her eyes held a certain wisdom that only came with age. I stared into her eyes—mother-of-pearl outlined in gold.

"Those of us like Adi take the form most comfortable for us."

"Then not all Daemons can shift?"

She smiled and shook her head. "Daemons can't shift at all."

The knot in my chest eased. I didn't want to imagine a world where monsters could change their faces.

Then I caught the nuance of her answer. "If not Daemon, what are you?"

"Ai'Yang Kulyt," she said. "A vessel of light and knowledge."

"You sound like a hippie."

She rasped out a laugh. "They did get a few things right."

"How many of you are there?"

"Two in each Daemon city."

Joe's laughter sounded from the hallway, and my heart leaped. *You're being ridiculous. He's not mine.*

The doe-eyed barmaid from Jakarta walked into the room with Joe, their arms linked. I stared at their interlocked elbows, and rage burned through the numbness and then turned to ice.

Mine.

"Having fun?" I asked icily.

Joe frowned. "We both know that question's a trap, K."

"Is having fun wrong?" Adyti asked.

"I'm more interested in finding a way to live," I retorted.

When Joe's eyebrows drew together, I remembered he didn't know. "What is that supposed to mean?"

Ignoring the question, I stood to leave. "This is useless! Why did Ielu send me here?" Adyti remained calmly sitting but reached out and lightly grabbed my hand. Her warmth poured into me.

"Keres, Adi has much to offer, but he can't add water to a full jar."

"I'm already dead inside." I thought of the Bloodlust breaking free only hours before and what Adi had said in the park. "My soul may have days, maybe weeks, but the rest of me . . ."

I couldn't finish. My emotions were so twisted and overwhelming, I couldn't distinguish between them. The room was too hot. *I* was too hot. I pulled at Adyti's grip, but she didn't let go. Did she want me to break down and shatter into little pieces in front of her?

"How much emptier do you want me to be?" I whispered. I swallowed, trying to add moisture to my very dry throat. I was falling, falling, falling—and inside, Yaffa huddled in the corner, crying.

Even when Adyti released my wrist, her pity continued to hold me. I moved to leave—to go somewhere, anywhere but here. Before I could, Joe stepped in front of me, alarm rising within him.

"What do you mean, 'days'?"

"I'm dying, Joe." I thought of Adi's I-don't-knows. "And there may not be a cure."

A chill swept over me that had nothing to do with what I felt. It wafted from Joe, a winter's frost that seeped through my skin, under my bones, and straight to my heart. His mountain aura darkened as clouds of fear blotted out his usually bright-blue skies and everything that made him feel alive seemed to wilt and die before the approaching storm.

"Stop. Stop!" I couldn't take his concern and fear.

Joe's lake of emotion spilled from his body and pooled on the floor at my feet, accusatory in its despair. Adyti's willingness to understand, to hold my pain and rock me through it, only made things worse. Her love cut where it should have healed, carving out the strength that kept me standing.

I didn't know what to do with it—with any of it. What did they want from me? What did one do with compassion instead of criticism?

I ran from the room before their pity could make me fall.

TWENTY-SEVEN

Morning light roused me from a restless slumber. My body felt recharged, but my mind longed for a dreamless night—and perhaps a less cheerful sun. I flicked off the lamp nearest my bed and went to wash away the nightmares with hot water and a long shower.

Stepping from the shower stall, I couldn't help but notice my body in the full-length mirror. I gasped. Luke's handprints on my arms and neck were gone. Was this from Adi's healing magic?

I dressed and left in search of answers and food.

Joe sat alone at the grand dining table, his back to me, where I stood in the doorway, and his head lowered over the meal in front of him. I tried to back away before he could notice me—I didn't want a repeat of last night—but I stopped when I heard Daliah's voice.

"What do you even see in her?" She walked into view and sat down next to Joe, digging into a large bowl of exotic fruit.

My heart pounded in my chest as I awaited his response.

"Give her a chance."

Daliah shook her head. "You're a fool."

Joe laughed. "My mother called it impulsive."

"I call it stupid."

Agreed.

He shrugged. "You look at her, and all you see is a murderer. It's the role you've given her, the only one she's allowed to play in your world."

"But she—"

Joe held up a hand, then rested it on Daliah's shoulder—a comfort she leaned into instead of pushing away. Jealousy churned in my gut—not for their connection but for the way he always won people over. His talent impressed me, which made it all the more maddening.

"I'm not saying she didn't kill your mate, Daliah, or that Ielu's death isn't a tragedy. It is. I'm only pointing out that a killer is all you can see when you look at her, which means she can never be anything else. When I look at her, I see her grief as she cradled a cup and called it Uri. I see a woman willing to fight for the people she loves . . . even if those people are only here in memory. I see someone who refuses to back down, even when threatened with torture and violence. She has conviction. And when she looks at you, she has a way of making you feel—"

"Can I help you?"

I jumped. I was so intent on Joe's answer, I hadn't noticed the servant walking up behind me. I pulled my hand back from my empty scabbard, suddenly grateful Adi had my reaping blade. I didn't need any more misunderstandings. Ignoring everyone's stares, I turned back to the room and moved to the large buffet.

"I've lost my appetite." Daliah threw her fork down

with a clang and stormed from the room, the servant following in her wake.

Joe carried over Daliah's breakfast things and placed
them on a nearby dish cart. "Can I get you anything?" he
asked without looking at me.

"I got it."

He returned to his chair as I picked through the buffet. Awkwardness stretched between us and only intensified when I couldn't pick a seat. There were twenty of
them. Did I sit across from Joe? Next to him? Did I pick
a seat farther away? What did he want? What did I?

I walked toward him, but as I set my plate at the place
where Daliah had sat, he stood up.

Message received.

I sat down and stared at the star fruit on my plate,
pushing it around with my fork as he cleaned up his own
dishes. Normally, I liked silence. I could sit in it for hours
with Raven. Now, my stomach twisted and churned.

"How are you feeling?" I finally asked.

"It only hurts when I move."

Glancing toward the dish cart, I caught a peek of his
dimples before refocusing on my plate.

"What's wrong?" he asked.

"Not much. Just everything."

I refused to look when he passed behind me. I didn't
need him to stay. It was better like this, wasn't it? Safer for
us both.

So when he pulled out the chair next to mine and sat
down again, my fork screeched against the plate.

"You don't want me to leave, do you?"

Yes . . . no . . .

He touched my arm lightly, leaving his hand against
my skin like we did this kind of thing every day. "I told
you: where you go, I follow."

"Even with everything you told Daliah, it doesn't make sense. I'm *dangerous*." My chest tightened, and air caught in my throat.

"Something tells me I'm exactly where I need to be. I have faith in that."

"You shouldn't." Guilt crawled through my belly. That *had* to be the seeding talking, didn't it?

Joe brushed the hair out of my face and hunched over so he could look into my eyes. "Tell me."

"What is there to say?"

"How about everything?"

"There isn't much left." I took a bite of food and chewed slowly. "The contract I told you about? It's killing me. I can't hold all the soul energy the reapings have given me. So maybe the next reaping or the one after that . . ."

I grasped the shofar now hanging from my neck and took a deep, steadying breath.

"From what I've learned, I'll enter something called the Burn Cycle and go on a mass killing spree, until all that soul power finally overwhelms me and I explode into energy. Not that the Guardians will let it get that far. They'll capture and kill me. Either way, my soul is forfeit for eternity."

"But Adi—"

I pushed my plate away, folded my arms on the table, and laid my head on them. "He doesn't know how."

Joe's emotional landscape spun so fast, it left me nauseous and disoriented. As seconds stretched into minutes, I wasn't sure whether I would puke or pass out.

"It'll work out," he finally said.

His spinning world crashed into mine. I slammed both hands on the table, standing so I could yell down at him. I needed to feel bigger, stronger than all this. I needed to not break.

"It'll work out? It'll work out! How the hell do you see that happening? Please, enlighten me."

"I trust—"

"What, Joe? You trust what? A Daemon kid who talks in circles? A group of immortals out to kill me? An Aod without a reaping blade? What do you know about any of this? What the hell, out of everything we've seen, do you trust?"

"You."

I laughed. "You don't know me. Don't even begin to think you do." I pushed past him, but he chased after me, grabbing my arm and forcing my back against the wall.

"That's it, then? Done. Over. You're giving up?"

Ice crawled up my spine, hollowing me out before settling in my throat. "What more do you want from me? What more am I supposed to do?"

"Find another way."

"There *is* no other way. This isn't one of your manhunts—"

"Another door. Another option." He poured belief into those words, as if saying them could make them true. "We can figure it out—"

"There is no 'we,' Joe." *There can't be.*

Adi stepped into my peripheral vision, and I glanced in his direction. "It's time we go for a walk," he said. "All of us."

I pushed Joe away and left without looking back. Could Joe put back the pieces of my heart that he held in his hands? Did he even know they were there?

TWENTY-EIGHT

Adi led us along twisting paths that split off and multiplied the deeper we walked into the forest he called his backyard. Where did they lead? Could any of them take me to the end I wanted?

Despite my sullen cloud of emotional turmoil, Adi grasped my hand, holding tight as if I might try to escape.

Maybe I would.

I glanced back at Joe, who trailed behind us.

"I hope you don't mind me inviting him along," Adi whispered. "Our human friend should hear this too, and it's such a waste repeating myself."

"Do I have a choice?"

"He's a good man."

Looking away, I shrugged and tried to reclaim my hand, but Adi held firm. Of course Joe was good. I secretly loved and hated him for it. His joy both soothed and aggravated my battered soul. "I wouldn't know."

"You know," he corrected. "You just wouldn't say."

"He's human. He doesn't belong in our world."

"Humans *are* our world."

Adi stopped near a marble statue and turned to wait for Joe. I focused on the naked man carved from stone. Stretched out, he would have been tall and lean, a muscled runner's body. Instead, he lay in a fetal position, one arm raised above his head in defense. Hurt and anger twisted his beautiful face. The detail was stunning.

"Why make sure Joe would follow when he only gets in the way?" I asked the boy.

"Do you think it was *your* faith that held the blessing so long in the Hall?"

He held my gaze until Joe arrived. Then he stepped closer to the stone man and tenderly touched a marble cheek, sorrow filling his tiny body, crushing in its weight.

"The son of God," Adi whispered.

"Jesus?" Joe asked.

"That is one of the human stories, but not this one."

"So not Jesus." Frat Boy studied the statue's face.

"Most refer to him as Satan or Lucifer. During the War, he called himself the Dragon."

"And according to you guys, my boss," I added.

"Yes."

"Is this an exact likeness?" I asked.

Adi nodded.

I leaned close, trying to memorize every aspect of the supposed father of all my lies. He had strong, angular features, full lips, and curly hair—gorgeous by any standard. His eyes, though, were cold yet compelling. I saw in them the same hurt I felt. The same rejection.

"He looks so sad."

I noticed Joe watching me. He frowned.

"I love this statue," Adi said. "One of my favorites. It reminds me of his youth, when he could still be guided, when he still loved his family. I miss that boy. Full of energy and passion, like water roaring down a mountain."

"You knew him?" I struggled to connect the pieces.

"I served him, loved him."

"Then why aren't you with him now?" Joe asked.

"He changed. We all did. So many souls lost on both sides just to tame the Dragon."

"What does this have to do with me?" I asked.

Adi walked on without answering, and I followed, Joe falling into step beside me.

Joe opened his mouth to speak, but I cut him off. "I'm sorry," I said quickly, not looking at him.

"You stole my line."

I shrugged. "You shouldn't apologize for things that aren't your fault." Stealing a glance at him, I blushed. *Real* apologies felt alien, but the appreciation in his eyes should not have made me feel better. Didn't apologizing mean feeling bad?

"I'm sorry I upset you, Keres. It wasn't my intention."

I inhaled deeply. "It's me. I don't know how to process all this. It's a bit—"

"Overwhelming? I know the feeling."

I smiled slightly. "I'm sure you do."

"In more ways than you know."

Adi stopped at the next set of statues—women and men caught midstep on their journey. Each stood alone atop a dais, garbed as a warrior with weapons hanging from their hips and back. Most peculiar were the veils hiding their faces, rippling as if made from cloth, not stone.

"Soul Reapers," Adi said. "Special warriors created to fight the Dragon."

Kneeling before the nearest dais, he whispered a few words in Daemon, kissed his fingers, and touched them to the white stone. "Do you see the diamonds?"

I glanced over the daises. The base of each was encrusted with row upon row of small diamonds.

"What do they represent?" Joe asked.

"Lives lost during the War," Adi replied.

There were too many to count. "Tell me this is a one-to-one ratio." It was probably closer to a hundred to one, but I could hope.

"One million to one," he replied. "Seven billion souls destroyed."

Adi's sorrow grew into a lead sphere—dark green, almost black. As the ginormous globe darkened and solidified, the boy's shoulders sagged beneath its mass. Surprised, I stumbled from the sheer weight of the vision, and Joe caught my elbow to steady me.

"That's the entire population of the Earth," Joe whispered. He felt sick. I felt sick.

When Adi looked up, tears filled his eyes. "And then some. Many belonged to the Dragon's army. They'd captured cities, tortured men, women, and children to the brink of madness. The atrocities were endless." Adi stared at me. "You know of what I speak. The immortal body heals, but the spirit breaks."

Dropping my eyes, I shifted away from Joe, rubbing my elbow where my skin buzzed from his touch. Every Daemon had seen what Luke had done to me, even if they hadn't known what it meant, and Adi knew the rest. Shame colored my cheeks.

Adi reined in his sorrow. Whether he did it for my benefit or his own, I was grateful.

"God had to act," the boy continued. "He'd hoped Lucifer would come around, would drop the rebellion. He loved him. He'd believed . . . well, it didn't matter. He had to protect his people. So God created the reaping blades, gave them the ability to take soul energy, and asked his strongest warriors to do what needed to be done. They saved us—and destroyed themselves in the process."

The small boy cried openly now. He hadn't learned this from a history book; he'd lived it.

"The veils were meant to protect them, but we should have known they wouldn't be enough. Some were lost to madness, others to guilt. They'd reaped former friends and family—brothers, sisters, sons, daughters, fathers, mothers. Lucifer's rebellion touched every part of our world, and the Soul Reapers paid the heaviest price of all."

"What happened to them?" Joe asked.

"Fear gripped our people, and it wouldn't let go."

I stared at the veiled faces. People like me who had done what God asked, their sacrifice for the greater good.

"What happened to them?" I echoed Joe. I turned back to Adi and held his gaze, steeled by a quiet rage for these lost warriors. He looked away first.

"Some begged for, and were granted, release at the hands of their fellow Soul Reapers."

I pictured my *abba* holding out a blade to me. *Please, Yaffa, allow my torment to end.* If he had asked, could I have said no? I tried to stuff the image away, but it sang to me from the back of my mind.

"Why them? Hadn't they endured enough?"

"Only a Soul Reaper can wield the blade. Only a Soul Reaper can grant release."

"In Heaven," I added.

Adi bowed his head as his shoulders dropped.

"You mean 'in Heaven,' right? Only a Soul Reaper can wield a reaping blade in Heaven. Here on Earth, Lucifer is transforming humans to use them."

The boy looked up at me. "You aren't a Soul Reaper because you use the blade. You use the blade because you are a Soul Reaper."

"Then why is she here?" Joe asked, an edge to his voice. Anger for me, not at me.

Adi stood and turned. "When the fear turned to out-rage among the Daemons, those who hadn't already sacrificed their souls chose to fall to Earth. To live among the mortals in a cycle of reincarnation until their sacrifice became a distant memory to the people they'd saved."

Invisible tumblers shifted and clicked into place inside me. "Then I'm a—"

"Fallen angel. A soldier in the army of God who threw Satan from Heaven and then, abandoned by your people, left to find a different home."

"God rejected me." *Damned before I even came to Earth.*

The doors inside me bulged. I fell to my knees, grasping my stomach as it churned in pain. My muscles pulled in on each other, and I gave myself over to the convulsions. J-Man had said we had to ride them out, and I had no desire to fight. Crouching beside me, Joe placed an arm around me. His calm drifted over me, and I gulped it down greedily.

Adi laid a hand on my shoulder. "The *people* did—"

"And God did nothing to stop it." As rage surged from Joe, animalistic howls rose behind my black door.

I tugged on his sleeve. "Please, I need your calm." He eyed me questioningly but relaxed his anger and recentered himself. I drank until the shaking stopped.

Adi pulled his hand back. "I'm so sorry, Keres."

"It's not your fault," I said. "I was born a monster." *At least now I know why.*

"You're not a monster," Joe whispered.

"Please understand," Adi tried.

"Understand what? That I'm expendable? I already knew that. What need is there to break a contract for a Soul Reaper? If what you say is true, then the Guardians are only finishing the job God started."

Adi flinched. "That's not what's happening."

I laughed at the absurdity of what I had done—risking everything to run to the very people who wanted me dead. Luke had been right. "So Lucifer is King of the Fallen, and I'm a pet for a new master." I laughed until I cried. Laughed to push away Joe's concern and Adi's sorrow. I'm sure I looked crazy, but what did it matter?

What the hell did it matter?

I stood slowly and brushed gravel from my clothes. Joe's hand slid into mine, and I didn't let go; his weak mortal flesh was the only thing keeping me on my feet.

"God of the Damned," Adi corrected. "He is *not* your king. The Fallen can return to Heaven once it's safe. The Damned—those who fought *for* the Dragon—will be stripped of their power and returned to Darkness."

"Goody for us. We *Fallen* will line up to lick the boots of the God who used us and tossed us away."

White-hot anger engulfed Adi. "Enough! You don't know *his* suffering on your behalf. The heart shattered into pieces that can never be gathered. He lost his children, his people, and the warriors he loved. You know so little. Do not allow your own sorrow and pain to spurn the suffering of those you don't know."

I flinched, my cheeks heating with shame, then anger. "How could you know my pain?"

Adi breathed in calm, but his aura still burned. "Because you are not the only Reader here. The Ai'Yang Kulyt feel everything—you, Joe, the Earth—*every* creation. I even feel God—his heart, his fears, his hope."

"Then why won't you help me?"

He stepped toward me, and the fire of his righteous indignation winked out. "I'm trying, Keres. You want a change-by-numbers, but I can't give you that. This is a process—*your* process. It'll be different from anyone else's.

Growth is abstract, messy, and hard, harder than reaping souls. In reaping, you steal; now you must learn to let go."

"I don't know how," I whispered. "I'm fighting this demon inside me in an endless tug-of-war, and I'm afraid it's winning."

Adi grabbed my free hand. "Drop the rope."

"What?"

"Your anger isn't a monster; it's an emotion. Drop the rope. Stop fighting it."

"And what? Let it devour me and anyone nearby?"

"Listen to it. What is your anger trying to tell you?"

"That I'm fucked!" Dropping Adi's hand, I pushed past him, dragging Joe behind me. Adi let us go.

I followed the path, picking our turns at random, until I led us into a dead end. In the center of the clearing stood another statue. This one seemed to be a family portrait, a man looking over the shoulder of his wife, who held a baby. A small boy huddled close, his face caught for eternity in the moment of deciding whether he liked the infant as a tiny hand reached up from the blankets to grasp his. A family lost during the War, perhaps? I wondered about their story and if anyone remained to tell it.

I breathed deep and slow, but my heart continued to race. Letting go of Joe, I sat on the nearest bench and shoved my face in my hands. "What do I do?"

He sat beside me. "Do you have all your answers yet?" I shook my head. "Then you play nice with the Daemons until you do. *Then* decide your next move."

I glanced at him and nodded. "Smart."

He smiled. "I try."

I looked back at the statue. How much more didn't I know?

"Keres," Joe said.

When he didn't continue, I looked at him. "Yeah?"

"What the kid said about . . . emotions . . ."

I sighed. It didn't seem to matter how hard I tried; my secrets seeped from me like water from a broken pipe. "I'm a Reader. I can't feel the emotions of plants, animals, or the Earth, like Adi, but—"

"You can feel people."

I nodded, and he took a turn staring at the family. He remained calm—not as much screaming as I'd anticipated. Breathing deeply, I decided to push while I could. Perhaps if he knew everything, he would run from me as he should. God knew, I was incapable of running from him.

"You should also know I can seed thoughts."

"As in—"

"I make suggestions to humans that become their reality. I can't force them to do anything against their ethos, but you'd be surprised what most humans are okay with."

"That's not funny," he said.

"It wasn't supposed to be."

"And me? Have you . . ." He waved his hand in front of my face.

Inhale. "Yes, but it didn't work."

"You tried to control me?"

"I tried to get rid of you in my apartment, and you shut me down. Then again in the cell. I needed . . . a release, but you had to be the good guy."

Anger skimmed his calm. "So what inside me is me, and what is you toying with me?"

"I don't know. You've resisted everything, but . . ."

"But what?"

"I can't help but think that the 'something' you talked about earlier—your need to follow me—might be an unintended side effect."

"Is that all?" he asked.

"Isn't that enough?"

"What aren't you saying, K?"

I paused, chewing on my words before spitting them out. "If I could, I would send you away. I'd use you, discard you, and make sure you stayed as far from me as possible. I'm not nice, Joe, and I wasn't raised to play with dirt." He had to go. I didn't want to let anyone inside my heart. I'd done that with Luke. No thank you. Not again.

His fingers brushed mine, and my heart raced. *Traitorous heart. First Luke, now Joe. I should cut you out—*

Joe's lucky eyes churned with the heat of anger and passion. I breathed it in and licked my lips as he leaned toward me. It tasted so good.

I should let you win.

"You can feel what I feel right now?" His breath skimmed my lips, and I closed my eyes.

"Anger," I whispered.

"Yes." His lips brushed mine.

"Hunger." The word came out a moan.

"Yes." He ran his mouth softly along my jawline and back again.

"L—"

My eyes widened, and I backed away.

Joe slipped an arm around my waist and pulled me almost on top of him. "What?"

I was saved from having to answer by a small cough. A young man stood blushing at the entrance of the clearing, looking anywhere but at us. "Sorry . . . the Council . . . you . . ." He coughed again to clear his throat. "The Council is waiting."

I swear Joe growled right before he turned to the kid and smiled. "Of course they are." Letting go of me, he stood and held out a hand to me.

Why wouldn't he run?

TWENTY-NINE

Silence yawned, filling the whole room. The council members stared at me long after I'd answered them with a final "I don't know." Some nodded, as though they had already imagined the worst. Others held perfectly still, as if the truth couldn't find them if they didn't move.

I sat between Adi and Adyti at what I assumed was the head of the ring-shaped table. In the center of the ring burned a blue flame, like the one that had protected Joe and me as we walked the Hall.

Joe observed the proceedings from a seat in the corner nearest the main doorway, his countenance darkening by the minute. He'd been able to maintain his calm, but his patience for the Council had thinned to rice paper as he studied their reactions to my answers.

I hated reciting my story, reopening barely healed wounds every time someone wanted to know about me and my kind. To Ielu. To J-Man and Joe. To Adi. And now to the Council. This telling, especially, had laid me naked on the table before my judges—their words, tone, and angry eyes violating my most intimate parts.

I wrapped my arms across my abdomen as I listed off the atrocities done to my family, my transformation, and my life since as if reciting a grocery list. Murder: check. Assault: check. Torture: double check. And loneliness . . . so much loneliness.

But they didn't care. All they could focus on was *how many Aods are there?*

Finally, the one called Malik spoke. "How is this even possible? I thought the blades had been altered and hidden away?"

I'd hated him and his self-righteous arrogance the moment I'd stepped into the room, and I knew he felt the same. "Apparently, your God isn't good at hide and seek."

Malik's gray-blue eyes became an ocean sky right before a storm, roiling with anger and judgment. Chains of distrust reached for me, wrapping themselves around my throat, until I almost couldn't breathe. I returned his gaze with my own, allowing death to seep from the hollow center of my body and into my stare. Yaffa growled inside me, at this person who reminded us of the men who had murdered our family. I pushed the emptiness toward him, a sliver of shadow snaking across the table to brush against his fingers. Malik's eyes tightened, and he flexed his hand.

Adi's foot brushed against my leg. ‹Not now.›

I released the shadow, and Malik inhaled deeply.

"Our best guess? There is a traitor among us." As Adyti spoke, all eyes shifted to me. "Someone who secreted the blades to Lucifer before the gates were sealed."

"Regardless," Malik replied, "she shouldn't be able to use them. The blades were altered to be useless to Daemon and Damned, and mortal flesh is too weak."

"It may have to do with her unique makeup as both Fallen and mortal, but we won't know until we can examine more angels of death."

I winced internally at the word *examine*, and Adyti gently grasped my hand. Adi had said all Ai'Yangs Kulyt could *read* emotions. I had to be more careful with what I revealed.

‹I'm sorry,› she said inside my head.

"How did they find her?" Suri had beautiful, ebony skin and hair cut almost to the scalp, with a beautiful S-curve design shaved into it. Silver bands ringed her muscular arms and tall neck. Her full lips and lavender eyes looked accustomed to smiling, all corners turned slightly up, yet she held no smile for me.

"Find me?" I turned to Adi, confused.

"God shielded each of the Fallen who came to Earth. He altered how you look, sound, and feel to each other and to immortals like the Daemons and Damned. In your mortal skin, you are undetectable and unable to access any Eternal power."

"Then how could Ielu and every Daemon since him tell I was a Fallen?"

"The only time a Fallen can be detected is during the brief transition of reincarnation, from death to life and life to death. We don't know how they found you—whether by pure chance or some indicator they've discover that we've missed—but I am sure that would be why your 'Gabriel' approached you at your death."

"That doesn't explain why *you* see me."

"Lucifer has found a way to hold your people in that transition state between life cycles," Adyti replied. "You aren't exactly dead, but you aren't exactly alive either, allowing your true essence to shine through your mortal soul. Like the sun shining on your skin."

My eyes widened. "But I've never seen that on myself or any other Angel of Death."

"I have," Joe said.

Adi grasped my hand. "It's hard to see the light within when you're convinced you are only darkness."

"It's why humans are drawn to you," Adyti added.

"I repel mortals."

"Only because you choose to," Joe said. I wished he would stop taking their side. "You push people away, K, but that doesn't change the desire to be near you."

I stared through him, trying to see what he saw—a current of humanity being pushed away rather than repelled. I thought of the drunken monkey at the club and the others on the dance floor. When I wanted them, people came. When I didn't . . .

I refocused my gaze on the one human I'd failed to repel. "Only idiots fall for an Angel of Death."

Joe spread his hands. "I prefer the term *daring.*"

"Any chance Lucifer—or any of the Guardians, for that matter—knows each Aod's true identity?" Suri asked.

"We don't think so," Adi said.

"But you just said they could tell I was Fallen."

"But not *which* Fallen."

I frowned. "But why does that even matter? We all fought against him; we're all fucked."

"There are key leaders among your kind who were instrumental in defeating the Dragon's army, like a Joan of Arc or a George Washington. I can see that you *are* a Fallen, but I cannot discern your power and rank."

"Thank the heavens," Adyti added, and most of the Council nodded. I pictured Luke's response if he ever discovered an Aod to be one of those commanders, rather than just a soldier, and shivered.

"How does killing make you feel?" Malik asked.

Joe started from his chair. "Bullshit! You can't—"

Guards prevented him from nearing the table as Adi called out "Joe" and Adyti said "Malik!" The Ai'Yangs

Kulyt quickly had emotions back under control. Joe reclaimed his seat, though he stayed on the edge of his chair.

"Keres passed through the Hall. Does the Council doubt the outcome or what it means?" Adyti demanded without raising her voice.

An elderly man, Lahk, answered. "Of course not, Ai'Yang. We meant no disrespect. I'm sure Malik only seeks to understand."

The man with the gray-blue eyes frowned. "I seek to know if we are in the same situation we were after the War. We could not trust the stability of the Soul Reapers then, and I have little hope we can trust them now." His gaze turned back to me. "You can't disagree that their banishment made Heaven a better place."

"Which had nothing to do with the Soul Reapers and everything to do with the people hating them." Adi stood, planting his hands on the table as he leaned toward the other council members. He didn't grow any taller, but his presence filled the room. His authority without threat confused me. I hadn't known the two could be independent of each other. "Do not shame yourself by bringing that same fear to this room."

While Adi spoke, Adyti calmed the room. I caught flashes of a soft, green fog weaving intricately around and between each person.

Malik nodded. "I am sorry. I still have much to learn." Inside him, the branding iron of his self-righteousness cooled to curiosity rather than the shame I would have expected after a correction. Either he had an amazing ability to display counterfeit emotion or he truly sought to humble himself and see the world in a new way.

Either way, I knew he'd be watching me.

"I agree, Adi," Suri said. "But I am concerned by the reaping the Soul Reaper detailed. Our warriors never entered such trances, nor were they ever as violent as Daliah described. Now, Keres, you're requesting we find a way to free you from whatever force controls you. We may have been in the wrong when we forced your kind from our world, but can you blame us for being cautious when there are so many questions and too few answers?"

I remained silent. No, I couldn't blame them. Not even Adi knew how long his fix would hold. Rocking ever so slightly in my chair, I focused on the dancing blue fire.

Tired. So tired.

Rock. Rock. Rock. Forward, back. Forward, back.

I reached for Joe's calming essence but was surprised to find solace in the aura of the older man, Lahk.

He reminded me of an ancient guru: Wild gray hair hung in thick waves down to his shoulders, framing a long, thin face, the flesh of which hugged every curve and crevice of the skull beneath. Heavy eyebrows hung over brown eyes, seemingly in competition with the full beard growing from his cheeks and chin. The coarse curls faded from black to gray the farther they extended from his face. Yet for all his imposing appearance, his gaze was kind, and his emotions read like a warm blanket on a chilly day. I wanted to wrap myself in it and sleep for a very long time.

He noticed me studying him and smiled.

"Seven hundred thousand."

The soft voice drew my attention, and I turned to see poison-ivy eyes widen in fear. The woman's face, paler than its initial creamy color, was a dense galaxy of freckles that crossed the bridge of her nose and thinned down to smaller constellations toward the edges.

They reminded me of Ielu. I looked away.

"Let's not do the math, Eibhlín," Lahk said. "Conjecture won't help us." He scratched absently at his face beneath the beard.

"She is right, though," said the man at the end of the table—Rheobim, Adi had called him. He seemed out of place amid this collection of ethereal beauty; with his sable hair and strong features, he was handsome but ordinary. "Worst-case scenario, but still possible. I hate to think what that means for the Daemons captured by the other side. Seven hundred thousand—it changes everything."

Guilt and fear swirled around this Daemon. My face surfaced every so often in the current, and he couldn't—or perhaps wouldn't—look directly at me.

"What are they talking about?" I whispered to Adi.

"The number of Fallen who joined humanity," Suri answered. "All potential angels of death, as you say."

I tried to think of our regions—assigned areas where we worked and lived. We didn't share those. They kept us separate. Solitary. I could count on one hand the number of other blades I'd heard besides Raven's, the number of Aods I'd met besides J-Man. Could hundreds of thousands of us exist without us ever knowing one another? I wondered if Raven knew these things or if she stood in the same darkness I did. How many Angels of Death did she oversee? What about Luke?

"Surely Daemons outnumber the Aods?" I offered.

"Whatever our numbers, they won't matter against a Reaper. The War proved that. When only one side can die . . ." Rheobim shrugged.

"As Lahk pointed out," Adyti said, "conjecture won't help us. We have Lucifer stealing soul energy for some unknown purpose, Soul Reapers operating on Earth, and this child searching for freedom. What is our next step?"

"Rheobim," Adi said, "I need you to speak to your contacts. Find out why we haven't learned of this sooner."

My eyes widened. "You have spies among the Guardians?"

Rheobim shook his head. "More like traitors, and there are never enough. Finding a Damned is difficult, but convincing them to turn? Almost impossible."

I snorted. "And you trust them?"

"Of course not." Malik's gaze bored into me. "Just as we wouldn't trust you but for the Hall. But their information is the best lead we have. Sometimes it works out, and we banish a few more Damned; sometimes it doesn't."

"Why not put them through the Hall?" Joe asked.

Rheobim turned to look at him. "Think of the Hall as an instant reaping blade for the Damned. There is zero chance of survival for them . . . or for any who fail."

I remembered the power I'd felt there, the "it" pressing against me. "Then I could have—" I pictured Ielu and Sergio, and my mouth went dry. Every council member, other than those squeezing my hands, averted their gaze.

"Best not to think about it, dear," Adyti said.

‹I don't have that luxury.› I pulled my hands from hers and Adi's and folded them across my stomach. I wanted to go—anywhere but here.

Rock. Rock. Rock. Forward, back. Forward, back.

Eibhlín shifted, uncertain. "You're unconscious during a reaping? That's never happened before."

"How would you know?"

"We have records," Suri replied.

"Records?" I shook my head. "Let me guess. Reports created by people like you. People who study a Soul Reaper as if they were a bug pinned and wriggling on a table. Dissecting them. Judging them. Not considering for a second how it feels to take a life and then a soul, and then wake up the next morning—and for the rest of your life—with their memories, thoughts, feelings, and death swimming around in your head as if you had lived them— as if you had *committed* the atrocities."

Anxiety gripped the room, constrictive and suffocating, but besides the Ai'Yangs', none of it was for me.

I leaned forward. "Your recordkeepers never discovered that, did they? They didn't care to. They just followed their stupid checklists and waved us off flippantly. 'Thanks. Goodbye. Have a nice Earth life.'"

Eibhlín stared. "You shouldn't have their memories."

I scoffed. "I shouldn't have a lot of things."

Adyti grasped my knee tightly. "Do you have Ielu's?"

I swallowed against the uneasy tightness building in my throat. "Forget I said anything."

"We have to know!" said Suri.

"Our people's lives depend on it," said Rheobim.

Their people's lives. The distinction cut deeper than my khukuri. I pulled myself free of Adyti and stood. "I used to be one of those people."

I left, and they didn't try to stop me.

Joe followed me out and across the bridge that connected the Council's island to the lakeshore. We walked awhile in silence before Joe finally asked, "You okay?"

"I'm fine."

He grabbed my wrist, gentle but firm. When I turned, he had *that look*—the one that said he was *in it* with me.

I threw my arms around him and sobbed into his chest. I felt weak, like Yaffa, and hated myself for it, but I couldn't find the will to be strong. So I clung to him, staining his shirt with snot and grief.

Enveloping me in human arms that felt stronger and safer than they should have, he gently ran a hand through my hair. "I'm sorry, Keres. I'm so sorry."

The Guardians had always painted these people as demonic monsters who would devour my soul, but all I saw were impotent men and women.

It was time to leave Odessa.

THIRTY

*S*lam. *Slam. Slam.*

I pounded the sparring dummy, grateful it didn't give way beneath my fists. My jaw ached from clenching, teeth grinding as if I could crush what happened on the bridge into nothingness. I swallowed thickly as a new wave of heat spread across my neck and cheeks.

Death didn't cry.

Raven's laughter in my head sounded real enough that I turned to scan the room for her languid form as I listened for her reaping blade.

Nothing.

Of course.

I leaned my head against the dummy, my heavy breathing dampening its face. There was no way she could be here. I'd *blinked* away after my episode with Joe and hadn't been able to get past the edge of the city, as if Odessa were the beginning and end of the entire world.

Raven couldn't get in, and I couldn't get out.

"I'm an idiot."

Yes, you are, replied the voices in my head.

I laughed at my own insanity, and somewhere beyond the doors that Adi had locked, the Bloodlust growled. I needed to kill something, anything. My legs and arms became a whir of kicks and jabs as I tried to release the intensity building within me. I only succeeded in making it burn hotter, like dousing a fire with gasoline.

Unable to appease it, I screamed and pushed myself harder, faster, quicker. I couldn't stop. Didn't want to. I yearned to destroy the dummy, just as I yearned to destroy my Contract. And—

Luke. *Slam-slam-slam.*

Raven. *Slam-slam-slam.*

The Council. *Slam-slam-slam.*

Me. *Slam-slam—*

My fist finally gave way, the bones fracturing and mending. My breath caught. It felt . . . *good.* I wanted more, *needed* more.

Harder.

Slam. Fracture, mend.

Harder.

Slam. Fracture, m—

Harder.

Slam. Break—

Harder.

I kept ahead of the mending, forcing myself to feel the pain, the relief. My skin opened long enough to spill blood, and I inhaled the coppery scent of life and death.

"I'd be happy to help you with that."

I froze, my brief flash of ecstasy licked up by Kai's hungry gaze. Ielu's younger brother leaned against the doorframe of the rectangular room's only exit—not counting the windows on the opposite side. Otherwise, floor-to-ceiling mirrors paneled the long wall nearest me, and a range of weapons and supplies lined the other.

I watched him via the mirror as the Bloodlust howled for more blood. Mine or his, it didn't care.

Slam.

"I'm good." *Draw them in, make them comfortable, and* then *attack.* That's how I'd been taught.

Slam.

Kai's reflection smiled, wide and menacing, as he stepped farther into the room. I returned the smile, insanity dancing in my eyes. Excitement raced along my skin as I watched the white-haired, hot-tempered Daemon. We could spill so much blood between us.

So very delicious.

He strolled along the weapon racks, touching a handle here and a blade there, as if deciding which to choose. "*Good* isn't a word I'd use to describe you."

"Depends on the context. Some things I'm very good at."

His mouth twisted into a grimace, and his gaze flicked to my waist, where my khukuri usually rested.

I sauntered to the weapon rack, pushing my hunger for pain toward him with each step, a lust that begged for savagery over sex. He licked it up, shivering in expectation, and I breathed it back in. Together, we created a dark, insidious loop that left us both breathless with the promise of violence. I reached past him, my lips only a breath from his, as I grabbed a dagger and drew it across his shoulder on the return. It shimmered with his iridescent blood, and I licked the blade.

"What do you want most, Kai?"

He smirked. "Your death." He grabbed the wrist of my knife-wielding hand. "Is that so much to ask?" He *blinked* us across the room, slamming me against the mirror. Small shards of glass sliced my scalp, and I breathed in the pain as monsters raged inside me.

I laughed. "Again."

Kai released me slightly and then shoved me back into the mirror. More dark laughter spilled from my lips. Delicious. *So very delicious.*

His nostrils flared and his scowl deepened as veins popped at his neck. He slammed me harder against the shredded glass before throwing me across the room into the weapon rack.

Standing up, I pulled a piece of glass from my arm, before crouching. "My turn."

I *blinked,* shouldering him into the mirror and dropping quickly, making sure to slice his belly and legs on my way down. He roared and fell on top of me as I tried to roll away. Nothing would kill either of us—our bodies healed too quickly—but I reveled in the recklessness. We grappled across the floor, exchanging blows, dislocations, and broken bones as we wrestled for dominance. My blood splattered the ground and walls; his sparkled where I tried to keep a wound from closing.

He won.

Or I let him win.

Either way, I didn't really care; the pain felt too blindingly good. My body tightened with anticipation as he leaned his weight against my throat. I stared into his eyes, his veil of anger flickering between hate and hurt. My wild smile faltered.

"He was my *brother,*" Kai said. "And you laugh!"

His grief did what his anger couldn't. It cut through the Bloodlust, silenced it, and pulled me back from the brink of the abyss. Staring deep into his grief, I added it to my own. What was *wrong* with me?

"I'm sorry," I whispered.

Releasing my throat, he began pummeling my face, beating me as I had the sparring dummy. I tasted blood, felt every break and mend. He howled like an animal, hitting harder and faster, just like I'd wanted. But the pain no longer felt good; it frightened me.

I frightened me.

What was I becoming?

I gathered power inside me, drawing in the pain, sorrow, and fear until they built into a small bomb. I released it all in a surge of power that sent Kai flying back into the mirror.

We needed space. The blood on us both was making me heave.

Oh God, who am I?

We both stood crouched, our arms outstretched. He stared at me for a long time, forcing away all his emotions. I tensed. A less experienced me would have *read* this as calm—a situation de-escalating into walking away—but I knew better now. Raven and the Guardians had made sure of that.

When nothing remained in him except the slight scent of decay, Kai pulled a small knife from his boot. "You don't get to say you're sorry."

We circled each other. "You can't kill me, Kai."

He smiled, twisted and terrifying, as he dragged the dagger across his palm. Instead of immediately healing, the wound remained fresh and open, dripping iridescent blood as he stepped toward me.

I didn't understand his plan. "A khyabadian blade will make it harder for me to heal, but it won't take my life."

"There are worse things than death." Images flickered around him like silently screaming faces pressed against fabric. In them, I saw darkness—*more* than darkness, heavier than what I experienced in the Hall. An inky black so thick, it pressed against my chest, threatening to fill my throat and lungs as it drowned my screams. I gasped, gulping down air, and stumbled back. Whatever that was, I'd reap myself before I went there.

"Kai!" Mr. Narcissist, the Daemon who had tried to take me from my apartment, stood in the doorway, still smelling of cheap perfume and dead skunk. "Gotta go." When Kai continued staring at me, he shouted, "Now!"

"This isn't over, Fallen." Kai *blinked* into me, crushing my windpipe with his forearm as he slammed me against the wall, and *blinked* away.

My windpipe healed before my lungs could miss the air, but I still slid to the ground in a fit of coughing.

Stupid angel. What was I playing at?

"I think Joe would call it impulsive." Adi entered the room, Adyti right behind him. They both frowned, taking in the broken mirror and my bloodstained face.

"Get out of my head. Both of you."

Adyti knelt before me and grabbed my chin, staring into my eyes as she turned my head from side to side.

"I can't get a concussion."

"Who was here?" she asked.

"I slipped."

"Who, Keres?" Adi demanded calmly.

"Doesn't matter."

"How can we protect you—"

"You can't. And not because I won't tell you a name." I pulled Adyti's hand gently from my face and stood. "Odessa isn't safe. Your *home* isn't safe." *For me or them.*

They exchanged a look, a whole conversation passing in the blink of an eye.

I spoke before they could. "I'm leaving."

Adi sighed heavily. "I know." He met my gaze, his young face tired. I felt the weight he carried, and I wished I could lighten it rather than add to it.

"Poking around in my brain again?"

He shook his head. "I would do the same thing in your shoes. I'd hoped they would be different. Hundreds of millennia and the fear still exists, a cancer for which we refuse the cure. Instead, we pass it on to the next generation. I only hope the new ones are smarter than the old."

I stared at the broken glass on the floor, not sure whether to pick it up or walk away. "I don't know that fear and hate can be cured."

"Love—"

"Don't. Love is just as dangerous as hate. It can make us hurt, make us kill, make us lose everything we think we are in hopes of having that love returned."

"You don't really believe that," Adi replied.

"Because you think you can *read* me?"

"We don't have to be Readers—"

"To know how big your heart is." Adyti stood next to Adi and took his hand in hers. "One only has to watch you interact with others. Dominance, in the guise of love, may have taken from you, but it hasn't broken you. Your entire being resonates with love."

Adi pointed at the shofar hanging from my neck. "Otherwise, you wouldn't be wearing that. You wouldn't cry over the Emilys of this world. You wouldn't care what happened to Joe."

My chest tightened.

"Can love save Lucifer?" I countered. "Will it restore his former life?"

"If everyone had selfless love, including him, it could. But it won't."

I yanked a towel from a stack that had spilled to the ground and shook it at the small boy. "Because that kind of selfless love doesn't exist." I wiped sweat and blood from my face.

Adi shrugged. "Because it doesn't exist *in everyone*. But unconditional love *does* exist."

I threw the rag at the bin across the room. "Do *you* still love him?" The thought hurt, especially when, according to them, Lucifer had caused me so much suffering.

Walking over to my fallen towel, the small boy picked it up and carried it the rest of the way to the bin. He sat on a nearby bench and hugged his legs to his chest, resting his chin on his knees. "I've accepted he's lost forever." He looked up at me. "I'm more concerned about those he's broken in his fall."

Adyti wrapped an arm around me. Her skin felt impossibly soft, as if time had sanded away the rough spots and blemishes to reveal a kind of human cashmere. I imagined my mother's arms would have felt similarly had she lived to greet old age. "Would you reconsider staying with us? Let us help you figure this out. We can protect you while you're in Odessa. Our options are few once you leave the city."

"Can you protect me from your own people—the mob who called for my death in Jakarta or the ones who found me here? Even members of your Council see me as a threat. You felt what I did. Fear spreads like a plague. It won't be long before this city tries to put me in a cage."

Adi sighed sadly, as though to say, *You're right, but I don't like it.* "Not all of them are that way."

"They don't have to be, Adi. Only the loudest do."

I pulled Adyti over to Adi and sat down next to the boy, curling my legs beneath me and hugging my body. We remained quiet, watching through the windows as the sun set. The changing light reminded me that time never stopped. I couldn't remain still. Yet I clung to each second with Adi as if I were drinking all the water I could at an oasis before heading back into the desert.

We watched the light and colors shift until they finally gave way to the dark.

"Better go find Joe," Adi said. "You'll be leaving in the morning."

"I can be ready in an hour."

"I can't." Adyti's sadness shimmered in the low light, beautiful and tragic.

Adi reached across me and squeezed Adyti's hand. "Besides, the gates to the rest of Earth won't reopen until tomorrow."

"Is that the only way to get me outta here?" I asked.

"The city is shielded, and we only open the gates at certain times. Precautions implemented centuries ago. We couldn't risk the Damned popping in whenever they liked." He smiled. "See, you *have* to stay."

I couldn't resist his seemingly genuine desire to have me around. It felt nice to be wanted. I tussled his hair. "Okay, then. Tomorrow morning it is."

The small boy, full of emotion and love and everything I wanted to have forever, leaned in and hugged me.

"Adi." He let go and looked at me. I wanted to tell him about the Bloodlust and losing control with Kai. Instead, I said, "I'll need my khukuri."

"That gives me one more night to make some progress. I'll have answers for you before you go." His face took on an endearing, determined look. "I promise."

He stood and *blinked* away. Adyti walked me back to servant-filled hallways. I hoped that would be enough to protect me from meeting the fate worse than death that Kai had planned.

THIRTY-ONE

Joe and I hunched over the stone balustrade of the balcony outside his room, staring out into the night. Propping my head on my hand, I watched firelight from the garden torches caress his almost-beautiful features. Joe seemed to have aged since we met, from cocky Frat Boy to pensive Atlas. His emotions flickered between resolve and doubt like the flames that danced below. Even knowing I could *read* him, he didn't try to hide.

It felt vulnerable . . . *intimate.*

I took a deep breath and leaned closer to him, a black witch moth attracted to his light. *I'll try not to hide from you either, Joseph Fitzgerald.*

"Kai came for me."

Joe broke from his thoughts and turned toward me. "Wait, what? That guy from the bar?"

"Yeah. Though in his defense, I didn't exactly encourage conversation."

Pulling me around to face him, he examined my arms and face, looking for any sign I'd been hurt. "Are you okay? Did you tell Adi?"

I shrugged off his searching hands, which burned hotter than fire. "I'm fine."

He frowned. "Like you were after the Council meeting today?"

"Fine, as in nothing permanent happened."

The muscles along his jawline twitched. "Nothing permanent?"

"And he isn't acting alone, Joe. One of the Daemons from my apartment showed up."

"Too many variables, K. I don't like it."

"Me either."

"Did you tell Adi?" he asked again.

"It's not Kai's fault," I replied. "I know what he's thinking—what he's feeling . . ."

"Your Reader ability?"

"Experience. He needs time, not more people telling him he's wrong to hate me or to let it go."

Joe glanced aside, his hand gripping the edge of the balustrade. "Then why tell me?"

"I want you to know it won't be easy if . . ." The words caught in my throat.

"If what?" His gaze settled back on me, penetrating and intense. He leaned closer; I leaned back. Micro movements, the slightest dance. "If what, K?"

"If you decide to go with me," I whispered. Without even trying, he'd captured me, entranced me, filled me. He was so human and frail, yet he was stronger, more immovable, than a mountain.

Than Luke.

"I'd assumed you would make the decision for me and try to send me home."

"You'd just do something stupid and get yourself killed." I half smiled at our inside joke, and his lucky eyes danced. I held my breath as he leaned even closer.

"You see their memories."

I blinked in surprise. Not the response I'd expected.

Joe pressed his hip against the balustrade and hooked a thumb in his pocket. My stomach tightened as the desire to lean into him crashed through me—to feel the length of his body against mine and the warmth of his arms around me. I missed those moments when I would be tucked perfectly in Luke's embrace, his chin resting against my head, and the outside world would disappear. In those moments, only we remained—our breath, our heartbeats. Would it be the same with Joe? Did I want it to be?

Exhaling, I turned back to the balustrade. Gazing down at the garden paths twisting below us, I finally realized what Joe was hinting at.

"Sergio? I don't have any leads for you."

"Just a face or location."

"I have thousands of faces, but none will help you."

"Can't you . . . ?" He shrugged, uncertainty swimming through his aura.

"It's not a full-length movie. I get blips and images. Mostly emotions so vile you'd be puking for weeks. Sometimes, I see entire scenes, like when I dream of Emily—"

I stopped as her screams and terrified eyes shattered my thoughts. Joe reached for my hand and, turning, pressed the side of his body against mine. I lost myself for a moment in his emotional aroma. He always read the same: water, mountains, and pine trees. Now, remorse drifted across the lake like an early-morning mist, accompanied by a heartbreaking cello melody that mourned for us all. It didn't obscure the landscape so much as enhance its beauty.

He squeezed my hand. "I get it. I have a brother who—" He coughed uncomfortably. "Whose memories I can't forget."

"Is that what you saw in the Hall?" He flinched, his hand tightening around mine. "Damn it. I'm sorry. I shouldn't have . . ." It made me one of *them*—the Daemon questioners. "I'm sorry."

A smile tugged at his lips, even as he blinked tears from his shamrock eyes and stood to his full height. "We made it through; that's what matters. Things that come from the darkness should be left in the darkness."

Digging my toe into the base of one of the carved balusters, I stared at the solid stone beneath my arms. "Is that how you feel about me?"

Turning, he wrapped his fingers around my arm and gently pulled me to his chest. I froze, not knowing whether to give in to my head or my heart. As he grasped my other arm, my breath quickened, and warmth flooded my body. "You're the Reader."

His hands slid to my back, fingers tracing the angel wings beneath my shirt. I struggled to block out his emotions. I didn't want them changing me, taking away my ability to think and breathe as Luke's had, lost in the maddening swirl of sweet chaos.

"Not hiding" wasn't the same as choosing to drown.

Yet his aura tasted so good—fed me, held me.

I gripped the shofar hanging from my neck until it dug into my palm. What to choose, what to choose, what to choose? I pulled away, another micro movement that fractured the bigger moment.

Joe let go. "Yes, I'm going with you. Just because you haven't seen Quinn doesn't mean you won't. You're still my best lead." He grabbed my shoulders before I could turn from him and ducked his head to make sure I stared directly into his eyes. "More importantly, you're my friend. We're in this together, remember?"

"But I'm so broken."

"Aren't we all, K. Aren't we all."

Before I could change my mind, I hugged him. "Wait for me, Joe. I'm trying to let you in. I really am trying."

He hugged me back, and it felt like his arms were made for me. I let go before I couldn't.

"So, where are we headed?" he asked, breaking the awkward tension.

"Home."

"Baltimore?"

"The Middle East." His eyebrows shot up, but his inner lake remained still. "I need to go somewhere. Why not the desert where Death was born?"

"How long since you were last there?"

"For as long as I've been an angel." *Forsake everything.* "As if handing them my soul wasn't enough, I had to leave behind everything attached to my former life."

He glanced at the pendant I unconsciously stroked. "But you kept your father's shofar."

"Some things are too important to give up."

He stared at me, intense and determined. "Exactly."

THIRTY-TWO

Small hands shook me from dark dreams. Shooting up, I reached for a reaping blade I didn't have as Adi ducked behind the foot of the bed. He peeked around the bedpost he clutched.

"You were whimpering," he whispered.

"What were you doing in my bedroom that you could hear me whimper?"

"I wanted to show you the stars."

I shook my head. "I could have hurt you."

"You could have tried." He winked. A Joe wink.

I pressed my hand against my eyes and thought about ignoring him, but I knew what awaited me in sleep. At least tonight I hadn't dreamed of dying.

"Fine." I slid on a pair of slippers and followed the boy toward the door.

Abruptly, he stopped and I almost fell over him. "Keres, why do you have the light on?"

"So little boys who shouldn't be in my room will ask me silly questions."

He waited.

I sighed. "Because your Hall did what a millennium of Guardians could not; it made me afraid of the dark."

He took my hand and squeezed.

We wound through deserted streets, always climbing up, as though we were destined to walk off the edge of the world. He didn't stop until the houses had given way to a large, isolated field that felt more mountain meadow than city park. Out here, it was quiet—peaceful, rather than lonely, with the stars to keep us company.

Two swings rocked back and forth in the cool breeze, their chains squeaking softly against the metal rings that held them aloft.

Adi sat on one of the swings. "Push me."

"Seriously?"

He motioned for me to come push. Too tired to fight, I gave him a couple of quick pumps and then sat in the other swing. He used the initial momentum to push himself higher and higher, giggling as the wind blew across his face and tousled his hair.

I turned my gaze skyward. Without the light pollution I'd become accustomed to, it looked like someone—probably Adi—had spilled a bottle of glitter across a dark-navy blanket and hung it above us. The stars were bright, intoxicating, and they made me think of Ielu—a terrible beauty.

Beyond the silhouetted mountains, the sun crept into the sky, its light outlining the peaks in turquoise.

Adi slowed until he could look straight at me. "I love swings. Best invention ever."

"You're weird."

"I'm also happy."

I kicked at the sand beneath my slippers. "We should get back. I'll be leaving in a few hours."

He sighed heavily and turned his gaze to the mountains and the sunrise. "Darkness can be beautiful."

I thought about the Hall and the inky black reflected in Kai's aura. "Without light, it's oppressive. Suffocating."

"Exactly." He twisted in his swing. "Do you understand what I'm saying?"

"Not usually."

He reached up as if grabbing a star between his fingertips. When he held out his hand as if to offer me his prize, I opened my own. A speck of blue light dropped into my palm, illuminating our faces. I stared at him, eyes wide.

"Keres, you are the light, not the darkness."

I glanced up to where he'd snatched it from the heavens, but the star still danced and winked in the brightening sky. When I looked back at my hand, the orb had already dissolved into the nothingness from whence it had come.

Adi shifted his weight so one foot could reach the ground and took my hand in his tiny one, leaning against the chain as he looked at me. "I have news."

"Good or bad?"

"Just news."

"Adi, I'm tired and working off the empty sleep of nightmares. Can we skip the cryptic speak?"

He shrugged and looked back to the mountain range. Yellow now tinged the horizon, and the turquoise yawned until its greenish-blue hues covered half the sky. "The journey to be free of your contract is like the night. You cannot force the sun to rise; you can only have faith that the night will end and the light return."

"I don't understand."

He took a deep breath and squeezed my hand. "As far as I can discern, there is no escaping the requirements of the Contract."

"You are sure?"

"As much as I can be, not knowing how Lucifer managed all this."

"How sure is sure?"

"Mortals and their stats."

I waited.

"Ninety-nine percent."

I slumped from the swing and fell to the ground. Acid burned my throat as I heaved until my body had nothing left to give. My hands clutched the sand, but it escaped me as the earth fled from beneath me.

I was falling . . .

Falling . . .

Falling . . .

Adi's small arm around my shoulders pulled my mind back to the playground.

"What am I to do now?"

Holding me tightly, he flooded me with peace, which I soaked up greedily.

"Stay with us, Keres. Learn to control your emotions and powers."

I laughed and pulled away, leaning back against one of the poles. "What does it matter if I can't be free?"

Adi squatted in front of me, drawing idly in the sand. "I never said you couldn't be free."

"You said it can't be broken."

"It can't, but I think it can be managed. Here, in the safety of Odessa."

"There's no safety here. We both know it. I'm out of options."

"You always have options."

"You sound like Joe."

The boy shrugged. "He does get some things right."

"But not this," I said. "There is no back door to *this*."

"The requirement can be met."

"You're talking about reaping my soul . . . forever. There's no coming back from that." I gripped my hair and tugged. Not enough to rip it out, only enough to feel the pain and remember I wasn't dead yet.

"Forever isn't as long as you might think."

"Stop talking in riddles!"

"Plain words won't help you. You do not understand even the basics of this world you've been dragged into. You want me to explain calculus when you haven't yet learned to add."

I stopped tugging and stared. "Adi, I will do whatever you ask."

He reached into the air and pulled out my reaping blade. Its death song shattered the silence and filled my ears. He held it out to me, his gaze burrowing into me. "Then take this and plunge it into your heart."

"You can't be—"

"Serious? You said you'd do whatever I asked."

"But . . ." I stared at the khukuri, weighing his words. I grasped the handle and shifted onto my knees. The story of Abraham and Isaac flashed through my mind. Would Adi stop my hand at the last moment, after I'd proven my faith? Or did he seek to prove I wasn't willing to do *anything* to be free of the Contract?

"There is no other way?" I looked to Adi for help, but he didn't respond.

I raised my blade, and the runes glowed brightly.

I turned my gaze to the sky, where the stars dimmed as dawn crept forward—disappearing as if they had never existed. I thought of Ielu and the countless other souls who had all ended in an explosion of stars and black holes. Maybe some after-afterlife existed that Adi wasn't telling me about. Maybe somewhere beyond here and God, Ielu still drew breath.

Do it, Keres. Do it. My hands shook. My heart pounded. *Monsters must die.*

I screamed.

And buried the blade in the earth rather than my heart. I couldn't commit to that kind of maybe.

"I am a coward." I fell back against the post and bawled, gut-wrenching wails that shook my body and left my throat sore and burning.

Once I'd quieted to stuttering breaths, Adi pulled my weapon from the ground and handed it back to me. He pushed my hair from my eyes and dabbed my cheeks with his sleeve. "You are a girl unsure of which sacrifice is the right one. Which leads to freedom, and which leads to more pain and suffering under the guise of freedom?"

I nodded. He spoke to my soul and pain, his understanding a balm for my festering wounds. I buried my face in his tunic and cried as he rubbed my back.

"Don't mistake uncertainty for cowardice. Real courage is making a choice every day to not allow your past to dictate your future. You are no coward, Keres."

I sat back. "I wish I could believe you." I wiped the snot bubbling from my nose on the sleeve of my shirt.

"You waste a lot of time deciding whether you should believe others—me, Joe, Ielu, the Damned." Adi's mouth twisted with the last word. "What you need is to believe in yourself. You have all the power and answers you need."

If I'd had any of what he said, I wouldn't have risked everything to find him.

"Where does a Soul Reaper belong when she is rejected by Heaven and hunted by Hell?"

He slipped a small hand into mine. "With me."

I offered a squeeze in reply.

Standing, Adi pulled me from the ground. He turned us toward the rising sun, which now peeked above the ridgeline. Its brightness had chased away the black of night, even if it couldn't fill the growing chasm in my heart.

"There's no hope, is there? I'm chasing nonexistent answers around the world."

"There is always hope." Turning back, he pulled something from his pocket and held his fist out to me.

"Will you accept it, Keres?"

"What is it?"

He smiled. "Does it matter?"

I bit the inside of my cheek. *Trust.* He wasn't Raven; this wasn't a trap. "Fine. Yes, I receive the gift, Adi."

He motioned for me to bend closer. As I did, he grasped the shofar hanging from around my neck with both hands. Blue light flashed from between his closed fingers, and a loud pop rang in my ears. When he released the shofar, it had a solid center.

I held up my memento of Abba, which was now infused with a token. "Ielu's?"

He nodded. "And a little something extra from me. It won't protect you from Daemon or Damned, but it should camouflage the song of your blade. They'd have to be practically on top of you to know where you are."

The homing signal had been one of many flaws in my desperate plan. But this . . .

I wrapped him in my arms and held him for a long time. "Thank you, Adi." I squeezed him harder. "This just might work."

Ninety-nine percent, he'd said. That meant there was a one percent out there somewhere for me to find. I opened myself to the song of my blade and let it fill me.

"Let's go."

THIRTY-THREE

Our small party stood before an arch in the Gate House—the grand central station of Odessa. Some arches held the shimmering liquid of a crossing gate, while others, like ours, reflected an image of some place on Earth. The former, I'd learned, worked like a tunnel, connecting two dimensions several layers apart. The latter was simply a secure doorway, controlling travel in and out of the Daemon strongholds hidden across the planet.

Joe and Adi flanked me, while Adyti and the ancient-looking council member, Lahk, chatted a few steps away. Acting as our Gatekeeper, Talon stood closest to the arch, the other side of which he'd already secured.

Down the corridor, Daliah and Kai fumed. They'd been exchanging angry glances and terse body language since she'd learned of her assigned penance—to protect me from harm—and had broken off from our party as soon as we entered the Gate House. Her wrath burned around her, leaving behind dark smoke that mingled with the blackness emanating from Ielu's brother. He scowled at me, and gooseflesh raced across my skin.

I turned my gaze to Adi. "Don't force her. No one should ever be forced."

Adi studied me for a moment. "Very well."

The boy must have whispered to her mind, because Daliah abruptly turned from Kai and moved in our direction. Kai gripped her arm and held her until she gave the slightest of nods. Then he disappeared into the current of people, and she made her way toward us.

"Do you trust me?" Adi asked as she arrived.

She stiffened but remained silent. Adi held her gaze until her shoulders slumped and her head bowed. "Yes, Ai'Yang Kulyt. I trust you."

"Then receive this assignment for *your* sake. I will not force you to protect Keres, but I ask you to journey with her and covenant that you will not harm her ever again."

Daliah bit her cheek.

Adi clasped her hand. "This is your price."

She glared venom at me. "And *her* price?"

"Will be hers to pay. Do you accept?"

"Fine." She pulled her hand from his and stormed toward the arch, pausing in front of me along the way. "I won't kill you, but that doesn't mean I'll save you either." She stepped through the arch without looking back.

"This is a bad idea," Joe told Adi as Adyti joined us.

The older woman stared at the arch. "There are things she needs to learn that only our Keres can teach her. She loved Ielu, and his capacity to love all others helped her. But without him, she is lost and her heart is shriveling." She glanced at me. "She needs someone who can show her how to love despite the pain."

"Surely you have someone better," I said.

Adi took my hand. "No one who understands her like you do."

I did understand her, perhaps better than she did.

Definitely better than she wanted me to. She was me as I had been a millennium ago; I knew where that could lead.

"I'll do what I can."

Joe's hand brushed against mine, giving it a quick squeeze before letting go.

I tried to keep my focus on Adi rather than the butterflies in my stomach. "And *my* price for stealing so many other souls?"

Adi's stare focused beyond the doorway, beyond layers and time and futures. When he spoke, his voice rang deep and hollow. "You will pay, little one. And the price will be greater than anything Daliah can imagine."

I shuddered. "Sometimes, *little one*, you terrify me."

Pulling me down, he cupped my face in his hands. "Be safe." Then he let go.

Not exactly reassuring.

The others said quick goodbyes. Adyti hugged me, Talon slapped me across the back, and Lahk waved from a distance.

"Ready?" Joe asked. I nodded. He crossed through first—his idea—and I hesitated just before the clear liquid of the doorway could touch my face.

Leaving should have been easy. It had always been my favorite part of any city over the last thousand years, but I didn't want to let go of the little boy who was more than a boy.

⟨Don't worry. I'll be here when you get back.⟩ I glanced at him, and he smiled. "But you gotta promise to swing with me next time!"

I left without making any promises.

As I stepped from Odessa into a tiny, dilapidated shack, an onslaught of foreign emotion rushed over me. I tried to block it out, but the feelings were too overwhelming for me to filter and too oblique for me to identify their sources and release them. Anxiety churned in my gut, stoking the small flames of rage lingering in my heart.

Trying to release the tension, I rolled my neck and shoulders as I exited the shack. I'd never realized how potent human emotion could be. Even with all the Daemons right on top of me, Odessa had never felt this intense.

Noting the barren landscape around the shack, I eyed Daliah. "This isn't Jerusalem."

"Was the princess expecting door-to-door service?"

"Call me Keres."

Her aura burst into red flames, and she stalked toward me. Joe stepped between us, but rather than push him out of the way or throw a punch, she simply touched us both and *blinked*.

As Daliah stalked off into the crowds of newer Jerusalem, Joe watched her thoughtfully. "Makes sense."

"What's that?"

"Hiding their doorways in out-of-the-way places—root cellars of abandoned buildings and tiny shacks in the middle of nowhere. Especially when they can *blink* anywhere without being seen coming and going. That's what I'd do if I wanted to stay off the Guardian's radar."

I shrugged. "All this cloak-and-dagger shit really isn't my thing."

He smiled. "I know."

I raised a brow. "What's that supposed to mean?"

Joe grabbed my hand and pulled me after Daliah. As we weaved through the crowds, my gaze swept back and forth. I'd forgotten how hot the desert was. Summer lingered here, its intensity a heavy shroud that couldn't be shrugged off or left behind. I inhaled dust and heat and exhaled more of the same.

I had thought being here would feel different. More *meaningful.* I had expected to resonate with the bodies overflowing from buildings as everyone gathered to celebrate the Jewish high holidays. These were my people—distant family connected to me through the blood we once shared. Shouldn't I feel *something*? Shouldn't they?

Emotions shouted from behind passive faces as I stretched my *reading* ability to its limits, hoping to *feel* any Aods before they were close enough for me to hear their reaping blades. Despite the increased danger to both the humans and us, I was grateful for the extra bodies packed into the streets. Dressed in conservative western clothes, the three of us blended in nicely, making us harder to find.

I touched the token hanging beneath my shirt. At least I *hoped* it made it harder.

Please, God, let Adi's protection work.

Though why I kept praying to a God who, thus far, hadn't answered even one of my prayers was beyond me. Habit, maybe? Hope?

"Where to?" Joe asked.

"Stay here."

Leaving him with Daliah, who had stopped to wait for us, I pushed through the mass of bodies into a nearby building and climbed to the roof. Hotels were out. They already bulged with humans, and while the crowds were nice for walking through the streets, I wanted more privacy for our living arrangements. Without Adi's influence to keep the Bloodlust in check and with my emotions already surging, I had no idea what to expect. Accidentally reaping a hotel full of people wasn't a risk I wanted to take.

From the roof, I could see most of the city. Ancient stone domes and arches gave way to cement complexes and towering buildings as the city flowed down each fold of the hills and splashed back up the other side. Homes sprouted from rock wherever there was a view to be had. I picked a random ridgeline and went to retrieve my party.

Joe frowned as I returned, but I spoke before he could lecture me. "It's easier for me to move through the crowds without you. There is barely enough room for one body to move quickly here, let alone three."

Daliah shrugged, unconcerned.

I sighed. Maybe I should have told Adi to keep her. "We're going to take a house on the hill."

"Kidnapping?" Joe asked. "Or do you know an empty place?"

"Neither. The owner is suddenly going to feel the need to visit family elsewhere."

"And if he doesn't?"

"We'll find one who does."

We *blinked* to the ridge I indicated near the outskirts of the city and, skipping the established apartment and condo buildings, began our search in a new development. Less was more right now, and this place only had a couple of completed buildings. I *read* through walls as we wandered the site, until I found what we needed: an isolated location with a lone occupant. Built on the corner of the hillside, it was the last tower of concrete before a sharp drop to more streets and housing far below.

As we ascended to the top floor, I pulled my scarf over my head and motioned for Daliah to do the same. An older man answered our brief knock with a wary hello.

"Moadim l'simcha." My Hebrew wasn't rusty so much as my dialect was extremely old. However, I easily picked up on his inflections, and soon, mine matched his perfectly, as though I'd grown up in his neighborhood. As the man's trust grew, I shepherded his thoughts, coaxing them in my favor, until he believed me to be some friend's relative all grown up. I smiled and nodded, until we were welcomed warmly under his roof. A few minutes later, he had the sudden urge to visit family elsewhere.

Joe stared at the door after the man had waved good-bye and left. "Where's he going?"

Daliah chuckled. "She convinced him he needed to visit his family's sukkah in Haifa before Sukkot begins." When Joe's brows furrowed, she waved a hand dismissively. "Jewish holiday stuff."

We took a quick tour of the luxury condo. A modern kitchen nestled at the back flowed into a living room with large windows and a balcony overlooking the city. Stairs ran up the far wall, leading to an open loft and two bedrooms with en suite bathrooms. It wasn't as much floor space as my place in Baltimore, but the view was breathtaking and our stay would hopefully be short.

"I'll take the room on the left," Daliah called from the loft before disappearing into her claimed space.

Joe stared after her. "Do they even sleep?"

"No idea." I collapsed onto the sofa with a huge sigh and stared out over the city.

Shrugging off his jacket, Joe sat beside me, though not too close, and focused on the window. Immediately, anxiety—excitement?—twisted my stomach, and I couldn't keep my gaze on the vista beyond the glass. Instead, it swept down the curve of his shoulder, across his forearm, to the stretch of his pants over the lean muscle of his thigh.

"What did it look like when you lived here?" he asked.

I turned back to the window, my face warming as though he'd caught me studying him. "I never lived here."

"You must have visited. I mean . . . it's *Jerusalem*."

I glanced back at him and raised an eyebrow. "Have you visited Ireland, Joseph Fitzgerald? The land of your people, yes? I mean . . . it's *Ireland*."

He nodded sheepishly. "Point taken. I'm sorry for assuming."

"I think my parents meant to bring me here, but they died before . . ." I coughed uncomfortably and stood, crossing to the window. Placing a hand on the glass, I tried to picture this place without all the modern buildings and people in jeans and T-shirts.

It felt too far away.

Daliah *blinked* into the living room, an arm's length from me. "I'm leaving to make sure the city is safe."

"It is." I'd been checking with every heartbeat.

She ignored me. "We'll leave before dawn tomorrow to find your . . . place. I assume you know where it is."

I nodded. Jerusalem and its people didn't resonate with me, but a small tug in my chest pulled at me from beyond the city limits. Even my khukuri responded, humming louder the closer we came to my birthplace.

"Then rest, Fallen. You're gonna need it."

I caught her arm before she could leave. "Do you know what's going to happen?"

She yanked free, eyes narrowing. Radiating distrust and anger, she seemed to consider lying, but in the end, her aura burned white with truth. "No. But I'm praying to all that's holy it's something awful." She *blinked* away, probably to stomp out her anger at the edge of the desert.

Joe came up behind me and massaged my shoulders. It felt so good, I rolled my shoulders into his circling thumbs and dropped my head slightly. His fingers moved up my neck. "I wouldn't worry about her."

"I'm not."

"But you *are* worried."

I put a hand on top of his and tapped lightly before pulling away. "Yes, Joe, I'm worried. About this contract, my death, the Guardians, the War. All of it. It still doesn't make sense to me. Everything feels so clouded, like I'm chasing a firefly at night. It lights up long enough for me to catch a glimpse but disappears before I can grasp it in my hands."

"You'll get it."

"You can't know that."

"But I trust it." He leaned against the wall of windows. City lights flickered in the distance as the sun set behind the hills, its rays splashing oranges and reds across the sky. The view was beautiful.

He was beautiful.

"That's incredibly annoying, you know," I said.

"What is?"

"Your unwavering faith that everything will work out. Sometimes, it makes me want to scream."

He smiled. "An improvement, then." He brushed his fingers against my cheek. "I believe I used to make you want to scream *all* the time."

"Be serious, Joe."

Resisting the urge to touch him back, I returned to the couch and sat with my arms folded. Closing my eyes, I inhaled deeply and released my tension along with the breath. For the first time since leaving Baltimore, we were alone—no Xiiph, no Guardians, no Daemons, no Aods.

Joe sat in a nearby chair and leaned toward me, hands clasped in his thinking position. "I am. Working through anger takes time. Forgiveness even longer. But it's doable, and you're strong, Keres. One of the strongest people I know."

"Because I'm an Angel of Death."

"Because you are you. I'm not talking about physical strength. You're strong at your core. It's why Adi paired you with Daliah. At your core, you are strength, resilience, and power."

"I don't feel strong."

"They never let you. You're not just fighting yourself; you're trying to overcome a thousand years of lies and abuse."

I laughed.

"It *is* abuse, Keres. Mental, physical, emotional."

"Stop saying that."

"Why?"

"Because the people I killed for—*they* were abused. *They* were hurt. I can't be one of them, Joe."

"Are you saying abused equals weak?"

I hesitated. There was an intensity to Joe's voice that made me think of the slow burn that preceded a forest fire, which could either die out or burst into flame. Should I heed the warning or speak the truth? I studied his emotions as the moment stretched in silence.

"You're trying to trap me," I finally replied. "Without even realizing it, you're leading me into a trap."

"Get out of my head, Keres."

"I'm not in your head, but I can't help seeing the emotions wafting off you. Why set me up to fail?"

He stared at me. Then he shifted closer, to the edge of his chair, and pulled his hands through his blond curls.

"I'm sorry. I didn't mean to."

I hugged my knees. "I *do* think the abused are weak. If they weren't, these things wouldn't happen to them. They would fight. I was weak once, Joe, and I lost the only family I've ever had. I can't be that again. I can't."

I squeezed my legs harder, trying to suppress the angst welling in my chest. I sought the numbness I'd found in Odessa, inviting it to fill me.

To feel everything or to feel nothing seemed my only options.

"He was barely six."

I opened my eyes to find Joe staring at his hands as he brushed them back and forth across each other.

"My brother. I was twelve and was supposed to be looking after him. Mom had a double shift that night. Same tired story of a single mom working to raise two kids. Only to me, it isn't a story; it's my life." He sighed heavily. "Anyway, he was taken, molested by some local pedophile, and returned."

My gut twisted into a knot. I thought of Emily tied up in the hotel closet, her eyes wide with terror as tears streamed down her face. Joe's brother would have been a few years older than her, but the terror would have been the same.

"Joe, I—"

His pain-darkened gaze met mine. "Patrick was never the same, K. Never the same. He jumped at every sound, clung to us wherever we went. His whole life changed because I'd been too caught up in my own games to watch my little brother."

Joe's glass lake burst into a geyser of emotion, spewing pain, heartache, and overwhelming guilt. In the depths of his waters boiled a rage I'd only known in myself.

I only caught a glimpse, though, before his normal serenity returned.

"It's not your fault," I said. He looked away, and I resisted the ache to grasp his hand, to force him to believe me. I wasn't designed to comfort, only to kill.

He chuckled darkly. "I'll believe that when you believe the same for yourself."

He took one of my hands, prying open the pretzel I'd folded my arms into. The knot in my belly jumped into my throat as the numbness melted beneath the heat of his touch. I almost couldn't breathe. I didn't want to. I didn't want to shatter our moment. The whole world froze, and everything disappeared—reaping blades, contracts, war. I exhaled slowly, relishing the intensity prickling my skin.

He held my hand in both of his and traced the back with one thumb. He studied the bumps and divots of my veins and bones, as though through them, he could divine the future or make sense of the past.

"He wasn't weak, Keres. He was the strongest kid I knew. The trauma changed him and how he interacted with his world, but it didn't defeat him. It could never take from him his joy for life. I saw him, a little boy, fight back against the hurt with laughter and the darkness with love. Every day, he fought. I believe he still does. Some trauma doesn't go away; you only get better at managing it."

I tried to pull away, unsure if this was what I wanted, but Joe held firm. He turned my palm face up and continued tracing, brushing every so often against the soft, sensitive flesh at my wrist. Heat crept through my body.

"I will never forget the day Pat learned of the man's death," Joe continued. "The bastard had been shot a few blocks from home. Pat cried. I thought they were tears of relief. Instead, he said, 'I needed more time.'"

"More time for what?"

"To stop hating him. To learn to forgive him. That's all Pat said." Joe wrapped both hands around mine and squeezed. "I'm not saying you have to be Patrick. We all have our own paths. I'm only saying being abused isn't a sign of weakness. Surviving abuse is strength. Keres . . ."

He waited until I met his eyes, which were tight and wet. "You are not weak. You are one of the strongest people I know."

I glanced away. He pulled me closer, and my body complied, until our faces were breaths apart. His thumb brushed gently against my cheek and traced my jawline. He opened his hand, his fingers spreading fire as they swept across my face and traced the edge of my ear. He smiled and playfully tugged on my earlobe.

Just like Luke.

I inhaled sharply and *blinked* to the other side of the room. "Joe, I can't do this." My chest tightened against the desire churning inside me, and my lungs screamed for air.

Standing, Joe approached me. I retreated until my back pressed against the glass wall, which had been overtaken by the night. I could have *blinked* anywhere, but a stronger, more primal part of me begged to feel him close, to know his taste as well as I knew the center of his calm.

He placed a hand on the glass beside my head and slid the other gently up and down my arm. "If I let you, you'll run forever. And I'll wait for you, K, if that's what you want. But that's not what I want. I want *you*. I *need* you. But only with your permission." He leaned closer, his hand spreading fire as it moved to my waist and pulled me into him. "May I?"

His question held everything: Desire. Longing. Passion. Yet still he waited.

"Yes," I whispered.

He brushed his lips against mine—tender caresses that deepened into hard pleas, begging me for more.

God forgive me.

I parted my lips to taste him.

THIRTY-FOUR

As my tongue slid across his lips, he moaned and pushed me back against the glass. He pressed the hard lines of his body into the soft spaces of mine. Jumping slightly, I wrapped my legs around his waist. I needed something—anything—between them.

No, not anything. I wanted *him*—Joe—a human.

As Joe steadied me with one hand beneath my upper thigh, his fingers brushed against the edges of my sex through my cotton pants.

I opened my mouth, willing him to reach in deeper with his tongue. I loved the feel of it, commanding and begging as it moved against mine. When I tilted my head back, he answered my unspoken desire, lips and tongue kissing and flicking over my chin and down my neck.

I wanted more. I needed more.

I wrapped my fingers in his hair and pressed him against my neck. As I moaned with pleasure, the gentle nip of his teeth turned to a hard bite. Still lodged between his body and the windows, I pushed my hips against him as his nibbling moved down my throat.

I loved this part: The anticipation. The almost but not quite. His tongue danced along my collarbone and dipped into my cleavage, and I tore my shirt off to give him full access to my breasts, now only covered by my lace bra. I sank my fingers into his shoulders, begging with lips and body and voice for more.

When his free hand moved up my waist, however, I grabbed it before he could grope my breast.

He leaned his forehead against my chest, breathing heavily. "Do we need to stop?"

I wrapped my arms around his head and kissed his curls before dropping my legs from around his waist. Lifting my arms, I rotated them back and forth and rolled my fingers through a fire only I could see.

The flames engulfed me—the deep reddish pink of Joe's passion tinged with wisps of yellow joy. They didn't carry the sting of anger that had always accompanied lovemaking with Luke. His emotions had always burned a hot crimson orange and charred the soul like a branding iron. Lovemaking with him had hurt at first, but I'd grown accustomed to it over time. Luke's heat had been exciting and deadly all at once.

But this? This was different. Joe's heat warmed me slowly, like a sunrise chasing away the dark of night. Powerful enough to coax life from the cold ground of a harsh winter, it thawed every layer of my body, melting me and holding me.

It felt safe, and I wanted more. *Needed* more.

"What do you see?" he breathed.

I touched his face and smiled. "You. All of you."

Flashing his dimples, he pulled me back in. "I'll show you all of me."

His gentle caresses melted into deep kisses. Crushing, commanding, taking. The kind that made me want to cross my legs. As I hooked a leg around his, he spun me around, and I *blinked* us into the extra bedroom upstairs.

We toppled onto the bed. Grabbing Joe's shirt, I pulled it over his head and tossed it aside. He kissed me again—long and deliciously—then stood, quickly tugging our pants from our bodies. As he did, shadows rippled across the lean muscles of his torso and legs, shifting as he moved and touching everything I wanted to touch.

He climbed atop me, licking here and nibbling there as his fingers brushed against the thin layers of fabric separating me from him and ecstasy. My hips rocked against whatever part of his body they could find as my fingers raked his hair and shoulders.

But he wouldn't be rushed. He seemed to savor the exploration, pushing my body to new heights with each kiss, with each stroke. I felt delicate by the time he finally removed my bra and panties in slow, careful movements, treating the moment like it was almost . . . sacred. He made me feel like I was more than my power. With him, *I* was enough.

Joe gently spread my legs. Just as he would have entered me, he hesitated, fear and shame contorting his face.

I retreated slightly within myself, ready to slam my walls back up between us. "What is it?"

"I don't have any protection."

Smiling, I pushed up onto my elbows so I could lick the sweat from his neck. I loved his salty taste. "I'm not human, remember?"

"And?"

"You can't give me anything."

He smiled to full dimples as his aura burst into bright flames of passion. "Let's see about that."

He pushed inside me with more force than even his kisses had held. I enjoyed the pounding against my thighs.

There would be time for soft later, but for now, I wanted hard. I wanted someone else to be in control.

"I want to let go," I whispered unconsciously.

Lowering his body on top of mine, he caressed one of my breasts. As he wrapped his tongue around the nipple, I arched my back and pressed his head down. His other hand grabbed my thigh, digging his fingers into my flesh, so close to everything I wanted him to touch.

By the time he finished with the first breast, my chest heaved and my hips ground against his. He lifted his head and held my gaze. "Then let go. I'll catch you."

"I believe you."

I gave him everything I could. It might not have been the smart move or the right one, but it had been so long since I felt like this—safe and warm and human.

I could have had any man I wanted, strumming their desire until they were willing to pleasure me forever. Even Luke, immune to my *seeding*, had been more than willing to satiate his lust with my own.

But no matter how passionate the sex, I had always felt empty afterward. We'd only known how to take, feeding off each other like the parasites we were.

Tonight, though, as Joe moved inside me, our bodies hot and sticky and moving in unison in the ugly yet beautiful dance that was sex, I felt connected. We were giving to each other. Or at least, *he* was giving, his emotions enfolding us both, caressing me as surely has his hands did. I wasn't sure if I knew how. But I tried.

My cries of ecstasy mingled with his deep moans, a harmony of body and soul, as we climaxed together. His eyes closed, and his emotions burst like little stars around me. He pushed a few more times, long and slow, to make sure I'd ridden my climax all the way to the end.

He smiled and leaned down to kiss me slowly. I

wrapped my arms around his back and pulled him down. I loved this part too. The holding—the feeling of another person on top of me as their roaring emotional blaze retreated into glowing embers. There was magic in that moment. Magic in *this* moment, in being completely enveloped in the calm of Joe's inner glacier lake.

Closing my eyes, I inhaled the subtle smell of pine and smiled.

"Keres, we have a problem."

And just like that, the moment shattered.

I turned my head aside, looking away from him and our still-entwined bodies. I didn't want problems. It should have taken longer for him to see the mistake.

I let my arms fall from his body as cold crept from my center out. "We have a lot of problems."

He grabbed my chin and caught my eye. His gaze was serious and nervous. "Are you okay?"

"Yep, great. Now if you'd kindly get off me . . ."

"That's the problem."

"What is?"

"I forgot to grab a towel."

"A towel?"

"No condom? No towel? This could create quite the mess."

I'd forgotten. Guardians didn't have this issue. And it had been a few hundred years since my last human interlude. I laughed. "*That's* our problem?"

"What did you think it was?"

"But it's so . . . so . . . human!"

"So am I. I can show you again if you'd like." Grabbing my hand, he pulled it down between our legs. He was already hard again.

"Yes, prove it to me."

He claimed my mouth with his own.

THIRTY-FIVE

A chill had crept into the bedroom while we slept, exhausted from stress and physical exertion. I'd almost forgotten how much of an emotional release sex could be.

Daliah slept in the room across the hall, her anger present but muted, allowing her sadness to seep out from wherever she kept it buried. She whimpered, and I sighed.

How do you replace murdered loved ones? How do you repair broken souls?

I glanced at Joe. His naked body was barely covered by the thin sheet on our bed. *Our* bed. Was it ours? Were we a "we" now? I could feel his emotions, but right now, I wished I could read his mind.

Carefully untangling myself from Joe, I walked to the window. The place of my rebirth filled me with a growing thirst that begged to be satiated. I considered *blinking* to the source, but that didn't feel right. This wasn't a bandage to be ripped off; it was a bullet to be carefully extracted from among internal organs.

Not enough time.

Lights winked on around the city in the predawn

gloom as I tried to divine the future from my window. Together or alone? We or me? If something other than the past waited for me in the desert, would it be our death or mine? I knew what Joe would say. He'd want to go with me, but . . . what?

I looked back at Joe. He'd whispered "I love you" into my hair last night while in that space between consciousness and sleep, exhaling it as he wrapped an arm over my torso and snuggled closer to me for warmth. I didn't even know if he'd been aware of saying it.

Luke had said he loved me, too, but his love hurt. It required submission and sacrifice and giving him all of myself. Would Joe require the same? Bending and twisting me until I became the Keres he wanted instead of the Keres I already was or the Keres I desired to be?

Luke said love changed people. Sharing oneself with another person created a covenant between them, a promise to put the other person before oneself. Only later, I discovered he'd meant me putting him first. I had done all the changing, the begging, the serving, and somehow, he'd convinced me I liked it.

I *had* liked it. His love was a drug, and it had taken me too long to figure out it was wrecking me, devouring my identity and soul.

I watched Joe's chest gently rise and fall. I didn't want to believe he would require that of me. He wouldn't take until I had nothing left. But what *would* he expect?

More concerning, what would *I?* What would I give, and what would I take? What would my desire to have him close, to feel his calm, to laugh and smile again cost him? Would I become Luke as I had become the raiders?

What have I done?

Crossing the room, I pulled a blanket over Joe, replacing the warmth of my body with cotton and wool.

This isn't a price I'm ready to pay, Joseph Fitzgerald.

Locking away my worries, I turned back to the window. Messy feelings would have to wait. I couldn't fix a damn thing if I didn't save myself first. I dressed quietly, grabbed my reaping blade and a bladder of water, and left to find the place where I'd died and been reborn.

It didn't take long for the crescent moon to give way to a too-bright sun, turning the desert into an oven that baked the water from my body. I gulped messily from the bladder, enough to keep my throat wet as I ran. My fingers brushed a large phantom braid away from my hot skin—a habit from another life. I'd left all hints of civilization miles behind me, along with the car I'd borrowed to make better time. I was grateful humanity and industry hadn't infiltrated my former home, even if that meant the last leg of the journey had to be made on foot.

The desert remained empty of anyone but me and the occasional lonely olive tree. I watched their shadows shift across the rocky floor as the sun crept first toward and then away from me, minutes stretching into hours. My heart raced faster than the drum of my feet against the rock as I ran toward the pull I'd first felt in Jerusalem. It intensified with each step, until it had become so strong, I couldn't have turned back if I tried. Gravity seemed to increase, pulling me toward an invisible epicenter as it also pulled me toward the ground.

Doubling.

Heavy.

Tripling.

So heavy.

Its crushing weight grew exponentially as I struggled to breathe, to walk, to think.

Almost . . . there.

The air pushed, and the Earth pulled, until I fell to my hands and knees.

Death.

I felt it. Right here, beneath my fingers. My blood still seeped through layers of the dry desert floor. Screams and images flickered through my head as everything shifted from now to then and back again. I couldn't discern the difference between past and present, between reality and memory. In both, I suffocated, my breaths shallow and rapid as my brain begged for oxygen.

"Run, Yaffa! Run!"

"Abba!"

Strange men laughed.

I screamed—then or now, I couldn't tell. Perhaps both. My head . . . my body . . . were torn apart and pressed through the eye of a needle all at once. I collapsed to the ground, a forever fall, and tasted sand as I reached for ancient ghosts.

THIRTY-SIX

"Not much left for us," says the taller of the black-booted men after having dragged me behind a horse through the desert. He stares at my torn flesh, as shredded as the remnants of my clothing. He says more, but my understanding of his tongue is limited. Part of me is grateful.

The shorter man reaches for me. "There's enough."

My heart pounds, and I try to yell, but instead, I cough up sand and blood—too much sand, not enough blood. Laughing, they pull at the cloth scraps clinging to my bloody skin. I swipe at their hands and try to crawl away, but my body is too weak.

The first forces me onto my back and kneels on my arms as the second tears away what remains of my dress. Once he has me naked, he gropes one torn breast, then the other, like an old woman choosing a melon.

I scream.

He grasps harder when he makes his decision. "One is all I need."

Blood and saliva spew from my mouth as a racking cough forces my ribs into places they shouldn't go. The man on my arms grabs a fistful of my matted hair and yanks my head back, forcing me to look at him. Speaking brokenly in my tongue, he tells me what he has in mind for my body and tries to shove his uncircumcised *zayin* into my mouth as his companion holds my legs. After a couple of unsuccessful attempts, he leans closer to tell me to be still, and I spit blood in his face. His hand slams against my cheek, but I don't feel it through the numbness of my face.

Too tired and broken to fight, I do the only thing I can think to: roll my eyes back, hold my breath, and empty my bowels.

The men flinch away, but they quickly return, shaking and kicking me. The violent strikes make me want to curl up and cry, but I remain limp, hoping they'll stab me just to be sure. I welcome death.

"Leave it!" The first commands when the second pushes my legs apart. "Even you won't defile yourself with the dead."

The second man gropes my torn breast one more time. "Shame." He stands and mounts his horse. "But I'm sure there's more back at camp."

They laugh and thunder away, and I hold my breath until I pass out.

I wake to the sun burning my bare skin as sand crawls in and out of open wounds. With consciousness comes images of my *abba* and *immah,* of little Uri. I try to push them away but can't. My mother's screams, my father's gurgling breath, and my own cries for the men to stop are the only sounds I hear in the desert now. So many people running and screaming and dying.

We never stood a chance.

"Dear God, *why?*"

I sob. Broken bones press against skin and organs, and pain explodes throughout my body. For a long time, I scream at the desert and at God. I scream through the sand still clinging to my throat. I don't have strength to move, only to cry and scream and breathe.

I don't want to breathe, but my lungs inhale without my consent, so I keep living and burning beneath the sun.

Grief eventually gives way to uncontrollable rage. I should have been stronger when it counted. I should have saved the others when I had the chance. But I had trusted God and his commandment of *thou shalt not kill*. In the end, both failed me, and my people did all the dying.

"I'm so sorry, Abba. So sorry."

I claw at the ground, fingernails digging into rock and earth, until the broken flesh of my fingertips tears away.

"Please. Please let me kill them! God, hear me! *Hear me!* Please. Please. Make them pay and let me die."

I mumble pleas to God and apologies to my father for eternity. Prayers for justice, death, and release tumble incoherently from my mouth.

"Why don't you hear me? Why don't you love me?"

No one answers, and I wonder if God ever has. Perhaps all those answered prayers were simply faith-filled mirages fooling the thirsty. I cry as my hope dies before I do, my faith a crumbling carcass, blown away like sand.

"I hate you!" I finally shriek. My new truth. The only one that feels tangible now. "I. *Hate.* You."

Still, he does not answer, so I open myself to the fury within and allow it to consume me. The empty voices of my dead people shout to let it go, but it masks the pain and blurs the memories, so I draw it in until their voices are silenced. I continue to babble, slipping in and out of consciousness, and my prayer for justice becomes a thirst for vengeance. I scream for it when I have the energy and dream of it when I have none.

Day becomes night, and still I beg. Night births another day already pregnant with heat. I lose all sense of time, though my waking moments seem to grow shorter. Will he take me now?

"Please, God. Please. Please, please, please . . ."

I repeat the word until I once again black out.

I wake to a man's voice asking, "What do you desire?"

I cannot lift my head to see anything more than sandaled feet. "I will kill you," I whisper. I picture myself as a snake sinking poisoned fangs into his leg.

"Silly child, I am not of the men who did this to you."

"Silly man, I am of age."

"All are children in God's eyes, and I am his messenger. You have been heard."

"God does not hear his children. He is deaf."

"Yet I am here."

"Who are you?"

"Call me Gabriel."

"Gabriel?" I couldn't have heard him correctly.

"Yes, you did. I am a messenger from God. Ask and you shall receive."

"Where were you when my family begged for their lives? Where was God then?"

"God must allow the wicked to act so the demands of justice can be satisfied. One cannot be held accountable for something that has not been done."

"So God offers justice?"

"Ask and you shall receive."

"Give me the strength to rip the life from their bodies and send their souls to hell."

"There is a price to be paid for such a request. Are you willing?"

"What more can be taken from me?"

"Will you pay the price for your request?"

"Yes! Yes! Whatever it is, I will pay." I cough up more blood.

"Where much is given, much will be required."

I sob. "I don't care!"

"What you ask is to become an Angel of Death."

"Then give me wings and the power to destroy." I use the last of everything I have to raise my head so I can stare into his eyes.

He is beautiful!

His eyes darken as he holds my gaze, ignoring my broken and bleeding body. "Are you willing to accept the price of being the left hand of God? An eternity of killing those marked for the reaping in exchange for the chance to kill these few today? Your soul is forfeit. Forever. No end. No release."

I say yes—*scream* yes—unconcerned about what he means or how long eternity could be. All I see are the faces of the men who haunt me. All I taste is the salt of their blood on my lips. Later doesn't matter. I need now.

He gives me now. "Choose."

My head falls back to the desert floor, and I'm barely able to keep my eyes open. Before me, rock and sand rise from the earth and meld together to form the shape of a bladed weapon. Before I can wrap my brain around its intricate, cruel curves, it shifts into another weapon, and then another. Some I recognize; most I don't. The flickering sand speeds up, weapons flashing so quickly, I almost can't tell one from the next. I worry I will make the wrong choice, if that even matters, or miss my chance altogether.

A soft note whines from the shifting blades, calling to

me. The song crescendos in my ears until it is deafening, and black creeps along the edges of my vision. My heart pounds, waiting . . . waiting . . .

There!

With barely the flick of a finger, I reach for the blade I didn't even know I was waiting for. Sand and rock hold firm in the shape of a simple but powerful blade.

My hand crawls toward it and brushes against the tip that hovers a whisper above the ground. My touch turns sand to steel, and the metamorphosis races up the blade and through the hilt, which points skyward. It's beautiful. Flawless. I stretch to hold it but only have the strength to brush against it with the same finger.

Gabriel squats, his gaze shifting from the blade to me and back again. When he frowns, I fear I've made the wrong choice.

"What . . . issit?" I slur.

"They will call it a khukuri."

He grasps the hilt and stands, rolling me onto my back with a sandaled foot. In one swift motion, he slices open his palm, and a thick, iridescent liquid seeps from the wound. Whispering words I cannot hear, he squeezes the iridescent blood over the weapon. It sizzles like acid as it crawls down the blade.

When his immortal blood drips from the blade onto my face, I flinch, but nothing happens. "I don't . . . under . . . stand."

"You don't have to," he replies and stabs me between my torn breasts.

The transition to angel of death is more painful than all my dying has been. I feel each bone shift and mend as invisible needles prick and pull at bleeding organs, sewing them back together. Fire burns through me, hotter than the sun, boiling my blood. My heart pounds so furiously,

I expect it to burst, but it continues to hold strong as it circulates lava through my veins.

As my insides broil, I screech and sob and plead, and Gabriel does nothing but smile. I feel a foreign stab of satisfaction, but it's quickly lost among the pain. I beg for unconsciousness—for relief of any kind—but none comes. In this state halfway between human and angel, all the pain of mortality cycles through the enduring body of an immortal.

Oh God, what have I done?

The pain climaxes as an explosion in my brain. I am both dead and alive as the tissue splatters against the inside of my skull and reforms into something new. I lose sense of everything but the pain as I writhe in the dark, screaming and crying and begging for it to stop.

"Remove the blade," Gabriel whispers, almost too faint for me to hear.

"I can't find it."

"You must, or you will never be free."

I search blindly with twisted limbs that defy my will. Twice, I almost get it, but my fingers struggle to bend. When I finally force them closed around the unseen hilt, lightning surges through me, but I maintain my hold, afraid that letting go means never finding it again. Bright blue fire pierces the thick night of my vision and burns my eyes. Howling, I pull the blade from my body.

It's over. Breath rapid and shallow, I lie on my back beneath the fiery sun, as if I weren't just lost in darkness.

"You have been born again," Gabriel says. "Now, your task is to overcome the world. Destroy the wicked to justify the righteous."

I look at the blade clutched in my hand, its shimmering surface now etched from hilt to tip with faint markings I do not comprehend. I want to hate it, but I can't. My soul rejoices in its song. We are connected, more tightly than my *abba* and *immah* ever were. It is my father, my mother, my self, my god—the only family I have left.

I inhale deeply to slow my breathing and stand, flexing my new muscles and feeling my new body. Everything is strong and perfect. My dry, matted hair is silky. My breasts are full and lifted. My stomach, thighs, shoulders, arms—everything is the same but better. Improved. Flawless. Powerful.

Like my blade.

I glance around, slightly disoriented to find the desert alive with the movement of insects and animals. When I focus, I can hear and smell them, regardless of whether they are at my feet or a horizon away.

"You are now shadow, touching everything and nothing," Gabriel whispers into my ear. "You are power and darkness. Use both well. Embrace them, and they will help you; ignore them, and you will fall."

Power courses through me, along with a hunger to do more. To be more.

"Follow your instincts."

I follow the path of the darkness tingling inside me until I reach the edge of my shadow on the ground. Forcing it to stretch, I snake across rock and sand. I am myself and the shadow, seeing from both perspectives, feeling from both experiences. The rock is rough against our belly as we—the shadow and my intelligence—flow across the desert and wrap around an olive tree in the distance.

"What now?" asks Gabriel.

"Death." I clench my fists, and my Shadow power cinches against the bark. The olive tree moans beneath the pressure. A quick twist and the tree snaps, splinters flying from each breaking point as a thunderous crack rolls across the rock floor.

"Good angel," Gabriel says.

The adrenaline makes me bold, and I correct the messenger. "My name is Yaffa."

"You are no longer human, and that name is no longer yours. Someday, you may be allowed to take a new name—if you prove yourself."

"But angel is meaningless. It's—"

"Nothing. Just like you."

"But—"

Gabriel pulls all the light from the sky, growing to tower over me. "You accepted the Contract. You will obey without question or be destroyed." His words crush me, and tortures more terrifying than fire and brimstone flick through my head. Unable to stand against the weight of such things, I fall to the ground.

"Will you obey?" he asks.

"Yes," I choke out.

"Yes what?"

"I will obey."

The weight disappears, and light returns to the sky. Gabriel stands over me, human sized, as though nothing happened. "Your first task awaits you."

"Where?"

"You already know. This is your first and final test. If you pass, you will be accepted as an Angel of Death."

"And if I fail?"

He grabs my wrist, the one holding the khukuri, and pulls me to standing as a child would a rag doll. "Do not fail."

In his eyes, I see him peeling my skin in pretty, delicate curls.

THIRTY-SEVEN

The sun still crept toward the horizon as I came to, my arms tingling with the phantom sensations of my skin being sheared. I'd forgotten the details of my transformation, only remembering the pain, fear, and power. Even now, the details were illusive, lost among a mental fog.

Slowly, I sat up and massaged my limbs and neck. Everything ached, the way it did after a reaping. Unsheathing my khukuri, I turned it over in my hands, trying to recall the already-hazy details. I ran my fingers over the runes.

"What am I not supposed to see?"

The runes flashed, quick and hot, burning away the fog encasing my brain. The blade, the blood, the runes. I stared at my reaping blade with a new awareness.

"I've had the answer this whole time."

I *blinked* back to the condo, breathy with excitement. I appeared next to Joe, who was hunched over the island separating the kitchen and living room. "It's the blade!"

Jumping back, Joe drew his weapon. He relaxed as his gaze met mine but tensed again, slamming his Glock back into its holster. "Where the hell have you been?"

"I figured it out."

"You've been gone for more than three days, Keres. *Three.* Daliah hasn't stopped searching for you, and with the whole damn country shut down for the holidays, I've been stuck here unable to do jack shit."

"The Contract, Joe. It's the blade! The runes didn't appear until *after* . . . until his blood and my blood—"

Joe grabbed my shoulders. "I thought you were dead." Black clouds filled the sky of his inner mountain landscape, and lightning flashed through sheets of rain that poured down fear, anger, and impotence.

I slammed my khukuri onto the counter, willing him to understand. "I might know how to break the Contract."

"Fuck the Contract!" Joe stepped back, releasing me. "You can jump from Baltimore to Jakarta in a heartbeat, but you couldn't find a damn second to let me know you were okay?"

"I'm sorry. I wasn't exactly conscious."

His eyes bulged, and I winced. "What if Guardians had been there? What if you'd run into another Aod?"

"Exactly why I didn't take you with me!"

"Wait . . . so being completely defenseless is one step *up* from having me around?"

"Can we fight about that later? *This*"—I grabbed my khukuri—"is more important." I wanted to shake this human, make him *see* what I was trying to say. "We've gotta go back to J-Man."

Emotion drained from Joe as his professional mask slid into place, creating a wall between me and his mountain lake. Jarred by the loss, I touched his arm. "Have you even heard a word I've said?"

He stared coldly at me until I pulled away. "Loud and clear. You don't give a damn about anyone but yourself." He shook his head. "I'm a fool."

I stumbled back as if his words were a physical blow. Mentally steadying myself, I nodded. "On that we agree."

Daliah *blinked* into the living room, her arms folded tightly across her chest and her jaw clenched. "Where the fuck have you been?"

I stepped toward her. "The runes. They didn't exist on the original blades, did they."

Her eyes narrowed. "Perhaps, but I didn't know the Soul Reapers. *Ielu* did." She wielded his name like a knife, slicing open the deep wound of my regret.

"I take it *our* conversation's over." Joe moved toward the entrance, trailing little pools of rage and hurt behind him like footprints.

Ugh! "This isn't the time—"

"It never is." He grabbed the door handle.

"Joe—"

The song of another reaping blade filled my ears, and my focus snapped to the hallway beyond the front door.

"We've gotta go," I whispered.

"Then go. It's what you're good at." He yanked open the door, and blue light poured into the room.

"No!" I *blinked* in front of Joe as an Aod sliced for his throat, catching their blade with my own.

Fear shattered the tenuous hold I had on my emotions, which exploded into a vortex that sucked up every shred of energy in the room. At the center of the vortex, I felt raw, as though my skin had been peeled away and blasted with sand. Emotions both pelted and fed me as images of Joe's sliced and bleeding body slammed against my brain. The black door in my consciousness bulged, and the Bloodlust howled.

The Earth answered—walls trembling, floor shifting— and I shook with it, my stomach churning and chest tightening until I could hardly breathe. With one small push,

I could have sheared the building from the rock and sent it tumbling down the hillside. With one push, I could have freed the Bloodlust and reaped every soul in the room.

The Bloodlust purred.

What the hell is happening to me?

I had to get rid of it. Had to get it out of me. I hurled the power at the Aod who had tried to hurt my Joe. It slammed against him and the Guardian who had appeared behind him, and they flew backward, crashing through the door into the condo across from ours.

The Bloodlust howled again, and I gulped down air, forcing myself to breathe. I had to stay calm.

I stole a quick glance over my shoulder. Other than the breath held in his lungs and the Glock in his hand, Joe showed no signs of distress.

He's okay. Joe's okay.

The building shivered once more, then stilled as my inner demon returned to pacing behind the black door.

Pulling Joe with me, I stepped through the rubble to get a closer look at the unconscious Guardian, a lean man whose tight shirt accentuated an even tighter body. Unfamiliar tattoos covered his left bicep. He didn't belong to Luke, which meant someone else was hunting me.

I shuddered. Even unconscious, this Guardian felt dangerous, cold, calculating. Which meant he could probably provide the answers we all needed. I turned away from his sharp eyebrows and chiseled jaw. "Daliah—"

The words died on my lips. A second Guardian held her, a golden cord encircling her neck and Shadow constricting her body. She might as well have been human.

"Wanna play?" the Guardian taunted. His blond hair fell to his shoulders in soft waves, reminding me of a trashy romance cover model, but his eyes gleamed like a wild animal that hadn't eaten for weeks.

"What do I do?" Joe whispered.

"Stay close and remember you're human." I gave his arm a quick squeeze. Stretching my senses as far as they could go, I stalked toward the Guardian.

Daliah threw her head back, smashing Goldilocks's nose with her skull. It mended instantly, and he laughed. His wide eyes brightened as he licked her face. "I like mine feisty."

I heard the blade before the next Aod finished materializing. "Drop!" I yelled, and Joe dove to the ground. I parried and kicked the other angel in the sternum. He stumbled back but smiled, revealing sharpened teeth.

"An actual challenge. It's been too long," he purred.

He lunged. I parried again but had to retreat from his kick. When the Bloodlust growled, I tightened my grip on my emotions. I didn't dare use any more raw power, so I reached for the Shadow instead. This power I could control, and with it, I would destroy.

I whipped a tentacle of shadow toward the Aod. It wrapped easily around his wrist, but other shadows, sharp as knives, cut through it. I tried again with another tentacle, but he blocked it before it even reached him.

"Very good," he said. "How do you like this?"

Spikes shot up from the floor, slicing my leg as I pushed Joe out of the way. Hardening my Shadow power into a steel bar, I swept it around me, shattering his spikes like ice. He nodded in approval and *blinked*, blade already slicing as he reappeared. I caught it with my own before he could sever Joe's head.

Goldilocks watched us fight, breathing heavily as he pushed his face into Daliah's hair. Lust flowed from him, a river of refuse pouring over her shoulders and down her body. Burning with anger, she shot blame at me like incendiary bullets. I'd add it to her list of grievances later.

Moving around the room, the Aod and I fought blade to blade and Shadow to Shadow. I couldn't keep this up, not with Joe as a handicap, which the Aod used to his full advantage. After another close call, the Guardian cheered, and the two men smiled stupidly at each other as if they already held victory in their hands.

Forming another whip of darkness, I flicked it. The Aod dodged, but he wasn't my intended target. Instead, the tendril encircled the leg of the Guardian, and I pulled.

Thanks for the idea, Luke.

Goldilocks stumbled, losing his hold on Daliah. As the binding cord fell away, she exploded from the Shadow wielding whips of light. Together, we fought back, a dance of light and dark that grabbed limbs and opened skin.

The Guardian tried to recover, but Daliah was a lightning storm—brilliant, breathtaking, powerful, and deadly. I tried to focus on taking down the Aod, but the incandescent current of her rage set the room ablaze, drawing my attention again and again. When Goldilocks fell, I missed the subtle shift in my opponent's tactics: A step back when he should have stepped forward. A dodge when he should have parried. It was the tiniest of retreats, but it drew me forward, giving him space to *blink* past me, knife descending toward Daliah's back as she knelt on the Guardian's neck, binding his wrists with her golden cord.

"*Daliah!*" I *blinked*, folding my arms around her shoulders as I slid between her and the other Aod. As his reaping blade slid into my back, she turned, her eyes burning. The Aod yanked his blade free and disappeared, just as a flame burned up from the floor where he'd stood.

The air stilled, the only sound my labored breathing.

I slid from Daliah's back onto my hands and knees. The knife wound screamed in protest as my body tried unsuccessfully to mend it.

Joe rushed to my side, pulling his shirt off to help stop the bleeding. "Shit," he whispered. He was so human, and I loved that about him.

I looked at Daliah, who stared at me openly. Her anger burned like the sun, too bright and hot to be near, but questions shimmered in the heat. Confusion. Disbelief. I nodded toward the hole in the wall. "The other one needs to be bound."

She quickly finished hog-tying the blond Guardian, hands and feet bound behind his back, and rushed toward the other one. When she reached the opening in the wall, her anger shifted inward.

"He's already gone."

She tied up the unconscious Aod, abandoned by his coward of a master, before returning to Goldilocks, who was already stirring. She stared down at him, hand tapping her leg feverishly, as her emotions twisted into knots.

"I need to banish him."

I groaned as Joe pulled me to my feet, pain radiating from my shoulder. "Let's take him with us."

The Guardian pulled against his bonds, testing his restraints. He smiled up at Daliah. "Yes, do. Take me with you." He ran his tongue slowly across his lips.

Ignoring him, she knelt and pulled a small vial from her pocket, pouring its contents on her index and middle fingers. Goldilocks paled and tried to scoot away, but Daliah pinned him with bands of light.

"But the Council—"

"It's too dangerous! They found you once; they'll find you again. I can't risk leading them to our city, and I refuse to let him go."

She began chanting in the Daemon tongue, dragging her fingers across Goldilocks's head and neck. He struggled and hissed with each pass of her hand.

"We don't have time!" I shouted. They'd be back in force at any moment.

She turned to me, nostrils flaring. "We make time."

The hum of reaping blades sounded loud in my ears. Stilling, Goldilocks smiled. "They're here," he said, just as I yelled Daliah's name again. Five different blades circled the building and crept closer, though more could have been hiding within the sweet harmony.

"One more second." She dumped more liquid on her fingers as the hums grew louder and footsteps echoed from the hallway.

Joe glanced at the open door. "Keres," he said tightly.

I grabbed Daliah's arm and forced her to look at me. "Keep him safe."

She yanked her arm free. "Do it yourself."

"Please." The word, thick and heavy, fell helplessly to the floor, trembling as it waited for her to receive it. "They want me, not him. I'm the liability."

Joe dropped his arms from around me. Shaking out his wadded shirt, he pulled it back over his head, indifferent to the blotches of blood that dotted the fabric. Scowling, he turned to Daliah. "Let's go."

Daliah stared at me as Goldilocks giggled. Standing, she took Joe's arm. "Fine."

"I'm sorry," I told Joe.

He shrugged, refusing to look at me. "I get it." But I couldn't tell if he really did.

Five Angels of Death appeared, blades drawn and muscles flexed. Daliah looked between me and the laughing Guardian, anger and gratitude warring within her.

"Consider this my payment of Adi's price." She *blinked* away with Joe.

I sighed deeply. *I finally made the right choice.*

I turned to confront death and smiled.

THIRTY-EIGHT

Dropping to the floor, I placed my khukuri to the Guardian's throat. I could barely hold the knife, but the Aods stopped advancing.

Goldilocks threw his head back and laughed. "Daemons. You can't trust them, can you?"

"Guardians aren't any better," I replied.

"What next, Pretty Girl?"

"This."

I slit his throat and *blinked* into the streets below. If Ielu had told me the truth, it wouldn't reap him, only slow him down, and I needed all the advantages I could get.

Out here on the streets, the wind whipped between buildings in cold, icy gusts, tugging at anything it could grab. Humans ran for cover in nearby doorways and taxi cabs, shouting to one another about a freak storm.

A couple more steps and I could *blink* again, creating enough distance between my jumps that they might not be able to follow the traces I left.

Glancing back, I threw myself into a roll as an Aod appeared, blade swinging. She pressed her attack, and I sprang to my feet, catching her wrist and twisting it with a futile crack. She'd heal as quickly as I would.

Wide-eyed mortals looked on as the howl of the wind swallowed the clang of our blades. One particular gust threw the Aod woman off balance, and I kicked hard, sending her flying into a car across the street.

I didn't wait for her to react, just *blinked*.

I made small jumps at first, disappearing from one corner and reappearing on the next. Human eyes widened as I seemed to wink in and out of existence, like a glitch in their mortal software.

More Aods followed, which probably meant Goldilocks would join the chase soon. Some kept my pace, while others *blinked* ahead, all trying to anticipate my next move. They *blinked* in waves, reaching me, slicing at me, and falling back as I fended them off with my khukuri and little spurts of power. I raced through the streets and between buildings that cascaded down the hill, leading us deeper into the heart of the city, where high-rises butted up against pockets of Palestinian villages.

One Aod appeared before me, knife ready to slice me open. I veered left, off the street entirely and onto the rooftops below. People screamed and scurried as I rolled off the ledge and onto the next street. The fall reopened my wound, and blood dripped down my right arm.

I looked back over my shoulder, wondering if I had enough space, enough time.

Darting behind a row of homes, I *blinked* to Paris—a city laid out like shattered glass and paved with old stones soaked in revolutionary blood and secrets. I hoped to lose them in the fractures Parisians called alleyways, but the Aods burst through from Jerusalem, reaping blades reaching for me as we raced through the rambling streets.

When a disfigured Aod appeared ahead of me, I

dropped and slid beneath his blade, slicing his ankles as I passed. He turned to follow me and fell, his blood mingling with the crimson streaks left by my open shoulder. Grabbing my arm, I stood and pressed forward through twists and turns, trying to get farther ahead.

Humans dotted the streets, staring as forgotten monsters fought an ancient battle. I pushed them out of the way with Shadow, sending them screaming into nearby shops and diving beneath café tables. Those who didn't move fell before the wave of death that chased me. I tried to block out the shrieks and gurgling last breaths as I ran—tried to seek comfort in knowing they were killed, not reaped—but it didn't settle my churning stomach.

I'm so sorry.

Turning, I threw a wild energy burst at the nearest Aod. It missed, exploding the wooden sign above him, but it distracted him from the human who had inadvertently stepped into his path. The Aod *blinked* to me, forcing me back against a stucco wall, which crumbled around me. I winced as pain raced up my shoulder and down my arm.

"Traitor!" he spat.

"I'm not a traitor! *They* are. They lied to us." Pressing my hand to his chest, I released a tiny bit of the power I'd been collecting, fingers crossed I didn't stir the Bloodlust.

He flew through the glass window of a shop across the way, and people screamed and ran.

I considered running too, but he'd only follow if I didn't do something. *Blinking* into the shop, I scooped up his reaping blade and placed it against his throat, reminding myself he'd take my life if given the chance.

He stopped moving, stopped breathing.

A week ago, I would have destroyed his soul in a heartbeat—probably without regret. But I'd seen too much since then. He didn't know, just as I hadn't.

"Kill me and be done with it. I die for God."

I let the runes of his blade flicker and go dark. "You kill for Satan."

He wouldn't understand, but I hoped I could make him doubt enough to ask more questions. I released pulses of energy into him until his body went limp and lowered him to the ground. Tossing his reaping blade into J-Man's Echo, I turned to leave.

"V . . . Guardian V . . . V . . ."

My stomach dropped as I caught his barely conscious ramblings. Despite my limited knowledge, I knew *that* name. V wasn't someone I wanted looking my way—*ever*. She was a high-ranking Guardian infamous for her cruelty and twisted pleasures. I'd crossed her path only once, but she had left an impression; the depravity of her emotional aura made Luke's seem like sunshine and puppies.

I shivered. *Why the hell is she after me?*

Something wasn't right. Guardians didn't bother with other Guardian clans. Or had that been a lie too?

The hum of reaping blades grew louder. Closer. I had to go.

I *blinked* to a nearby rooftop and kept running, kept *blinking* farther away from the pack of death hunting me, until only two songs remained. They grew a little more distant with every jump, but I couldn't shake them.

Leaping, I *blinked* in midair, landing in London, Rome, Johannesburg. I bounced all over the world, to every city that came to mind. If I created enough distur-bances—those "shaking beads" in the doorway of every *blink*— quickly enough, maybe they wouldn't know which to follow.

Luck seemed to be on my side, because they fell far-ther behind with each *blink*. I finally stopped in Tokyo to see if anyone still tailed me.

Even late at night, people crowded the streets of Ka-bukichō, an entertainment district like New York's Times Square, only the digital signs here flashed in the too-bright colors of hot pink, electric blue, and neon green. The city pulsed with light and information, the motherboard of a giant computer laid open for the world to see.

I backed into a side street, covered myself with Shadow, and waited.

And waited.

And waited.

I inhaled slowly, afraid any sudden movement would bring the world crashing down on me. Seconds ticked into minutes. Goldilocks appeared in the middle of a sur-prised group of Japanese men, his tall, broad frame tower-ing over theirs. People pulled out phones and began snap-ping pictures. He glanced around, hand fidgeting with the bandage at his throat, and disappeared again, leaving be-hind a vapor of fear.

V would not be pleased he had lost me.

I grabbed the token-shofar hanging from my neck and kissed it, grateful for the protection it had provided me tonight.

"Thank you," I whispered.

"Don't mention it." Before I could *blink*, a large hand engulfed my wrist and whipped me around.

The other Guardian from Jerusalem!

"I like to let Jilian do all the work," he whispered. The sex lacing his British accent would have made even Queen Victoria cross her legs. "Makes him right mad when I swoop in at the last second and nick his prize."

Pushing away his emotions, I reached for my blade, but he grabbed my neck with his other hand and slammed me into the wall, digging my injured shoulder into the con-crete. Pain from the wound melded with the shower of electricity pulsing from his hands, its current forcing my muscles to spasm. I grunted but refused to scream.

His eyebrows climbed high, and his lips split into a predatory grin of perfect white teeth. The same depravity I'd felt in V wafted from her servant—immense in its perverseness, cold in its concern for nothing but self.

"I can see why Luke fancied you. Surprising, cagey." His gaze burned with violence as I twisted in his grip, and his lust seeped through my clothes—not for me but for the pain. Images flickered around him—scenes of stiletto stomping creatures, body mutilation, and more—and I immediately wished I could burn from my brain everything to do with V and her palace of sadistic pleasures. Torture was this Guardian's drug, and I dry heaved, shuddering in his grasp. He leaned in and inhaled my scent, exhaling warmth against my neck as I continued to convulse.

"If Jilian only knew how to wait and watch. He's too impatient, but it's fun to watch him try. To watch him fail." He let up on the electricity for a moment, long enough to let me breathe, and I kicked at him blindly. The crunch of his knee echoed through the alleyway. "Come on now. All I wanted was a little chin-wag. No need to get physical." More electricity burned through my wrist, popping blood vessels and charring the skin.

Clenching my jaw, I focused on pulling in every drop of emotional power I thought I could hold without breaking. This was what I'd been waiting for, the live-or-die situation that would require everything I had and then some.

I released the full force against him, smiling in satisfaction at the thought of his body flying.

For a second, we were wrapped in a glow brighter than the digital ads flickering in the streets, as my power collided with whatever barrier he held between us.

It didn't work.

He chuckled. "Fool me twice." Then all I saw were his eyes, bright white globes smiling wickedly from the shadows as his electricity burned me from the inside out.

Worse than Luke's.

My organs burst, and I screamed.

The current stopped, and he threw his head back and laughed. "V will be chuffed. *So* chuffed. Shame on Luke for keeping your power a secret for so long. They could have enjoyed you together. The fun. The fun."

His aura whirled with ecstasy. Releasing my wrist, he reached into his pants. Electricity beat through me in time with his racing pulse, as he gripped my neck with one hand and worked himself to climax with the other.

I pushed against the current, but it was too strong. The bolts cut through my resistance, following whatever paths they wanted to my heart. Burn, mend. Burn, mend. A terrible circuit I couldn't interrupt.

A circuit!

My eyes widened as his closed. Reaching for the current inside me, I shifted the flow, giving it new paths to follow, until it raced through me and back into the Guardian getting off on my pain. As it left me, I magnified the lightning with the few shards of power I could pull into me.

It shot back into his fingertips and up his arm, engulfing the entire limb in a flash of fire. Screaming, the Guardian pulled his hand back, eyes wide as he took in the mess of charred and healing flesh.

Unfortunately, the pain wasn't the hindrance I had expected. He studied the well-done remains of his arm with sickening fascination. He liked it. Liked the burning, the charring, the regrowing of flesh. He relished the pain.

He closed his eyes, his rapture heightening, his emotions intensifying as he healed. "So good. So good." His head fell back, his lips parting. Suppressing the need to vomit, I reached for my reaping blade, but he clicked his tongue. "Naughty, naughty." Shadows weaved around me, pressing my hands to my sides and locking me in place.

He stepped closer, leaning an elbow against the wall next to my head as he played with my hair. "Want to know a secret?" he whispered. "I like you." His lips pressed against mine, and his lightning electrocuted us both.

I screamed—a hollow sound that echoed in his throat. A thick heat, wet and heavy, crawled from his lips, filling me with anger, surrender, and fear. More horrific, twisted images flickered in his arousal, and as the scenes of vorarephilia, ederacinism, and sadistic torture bored into my head, I suddenly knew something worse existed than a soul-splattering death-by-Contract. This. This was worse. *V* and her people were worse.

The burning stopped. He leaned back, wicked eyes heavy with want. "The trick is knowing when to stop, how much to give without draining your strength to scream."

I tilted my face up to the sky. "Please, God."

The Guardian ran his lips along my jaw and chuckled darkly. "They usually call me Elijah."

Please, God.

I didn't know how to call for Adi or Daliah, or any Daemon for that matter, which left me one choice.

Electricity rocked my body.

‹Raven!› *Please. Please.* ‹Raven.›

Would she even hear me? Could she, while I wore Adi's protection around my neck?

Please let her hear me. ‹Raven.› *Please.*

"Raven." Her name escaped my lips.

The Guardian smiled wickedly. "No one here but me, love."

That's when I heard it.

The one blade song I knew, besides my own.

THIRTY-NINE

Elijah flinched as Raven's sickle sliced clean through his neck, but he never stopped smiling, not even as his head slid from his body and thwacked against the concrete. The rest of him collapsed at my feet.

"Raven!" I threw my arms around her without thinking. "You heard me."

Wrapping an arm around me, she rested her head against mine. "Like you were calling me through water."

"And you came."

"No matter how a daughter disappoints, a mother will always answer." Giving me a quick squeeze, she released me and tapped Elijah's head with her foot. "Keres, what have you done?"

I crossed my arms. "I ran." As if that explained anything.

"You were supposed to wait for me."

"I couldn't. Luke . . . and then Daemons."

She shook her head. "Must you always be so stupid?"

"So, I shouldn't have done anything? Just sat around waiting for the Burn Cycle?"

"You sure as hell shouldn't have attacked Luke! What were you thinking?"

"They lied to us, Raven!"

She laughed. "Truth is deceptive—like the ancient dragon changing its color to blend in with its surroundings. Change the surroundings, change the truth."

"I don't get it."

"Of course not. You act; you don't think." She knelt next to Elijah's body and raised her sickle above her head.

I dropped to my knees beside her. "What are you doing?"

"He *must* be reaped. We can't leave Elijah around to tell them I'm helping you."

I placed my hand on her thigh. When she met my gaze, I searched hers for the strings that had to be attached. All I found was pain, compassion, and hope as she slowly lowered the sickle to her side. Leaning in quickly, she grazed my cheek with her lips.

"Of all the dirt, I have loved you the most." Truth. Not even a speck of deceit, just white-hot flame.

I let go, stunned. "You've changed."

"You weren't the only one being lied to, daughter."

"The blade and the Contract are the same, aren't they?"

She pursed her lips and turned back to Elijah's body without answering. "Reaping a Guardian or Daemon is different from reaping a human."

"I know." When she raised an eyebrow, I muttered, "Ielu."

"How much did he tell you?"

"Only that his body and spirit were one, and that it's the same for the Guardians."

She nodded. "Each soul has a crystal at its center that houses the soul's energy."

"Including humans?"

She pursed her lips, annoyance wafting from her aura. "Because the body and soul of an immortal are one and the same, this crystal is accessible here." She tapped the tip of her sickle against Elijah's chest. "But that doesn't hold true for humans. While weak, mortal bodies aren't fused with their souls and thus act as armor of sorts. We destroy the armor, remove the soul, and reap it." She touched my arm briefly, enough to make me look at her. "I know how much you hate the violence of it, but the throat is the only access point. Otherwise, the soul disappears before it can be reaped."

"Why are you telling me this? Why now?"

"You ran before I could tell you more."

Always too hasty, Keres. What-ifs swam through my head, but I pushed them away.

"You must pierce the soul crystal with your reaping blade to draw out the energy." Her grip on her sickle tightened. "Once I do this, I won't be able to protect us. You'll have to keep us safe until I wake." She hesitated. "I've never reaped a Guardian before."

"Will they know it was you?"

She smirked. "But it wasn't me, daughter; it was *you.*"

I stilled beneath her intense gaze, not even breathing. There it was—the iron string wrapping around my throat. "Should we leave him?"

She peered at me, weighing me and her future on the internal scale she always kept balanced. Looking back at the Guardian, she raised her reaping blade. "We're dead either way." She plunged the sickle into Elijah's heart, and glowing orbs blossomed beneath his skin.

"Will you tell me everything, Raven?" I whispered.

"When we are safe in Kazakhstan. You remember our home?" I nodded. "You'll take us there until I wake."

"But—"

"You must learn and adapt quickly if you are to run from the Guardians." Placing her hand on the body, she closed her eyes. "Lesson one: when we don't have time to wait for the soul to find us, we must show it the path."

While Ielu had seemed to take hours to break down and expand, this Guardian took mere seconds. I tried to follow Raven's power as she sped up the disintegration of the soul and drew it into herself. Rather than exploding into a galaxy, the stars raced through the Guardian's body and marched up her outstretched arm in blue-hued columns. Even the soul energy contained within his head danced across the pavement and up through her fingertips. When she opened her eyes again, the irises glowed the blue of the orbs before fading back to brown.

She took one deep inhalation and collapsed. Pulling her into my arms, I tucked her sickle into my belt.

"Leeaff," she slurred. "Go . . . now." She tried to open her eyes, but they rolled back under heavy lids.

"We're working for the wrong side." Tension almost strangled the words before they could escape my lips, but confessing to an almost-unconscious Xiiph would be easier than telling one in her full power and glory.

"I . . . know . . ." She reached for my hand and rested her head on my shoulder.

"Do you know how to free us? The blade is the Contract, isn't it? Isn't it?" When she didn't answer, I shook her slightly. "Raven. Raven!"

Her eyes fluttered open, then closed. "So tired."

"Do you know how to free us from the Contract?"

"Nnno . . ." She tried to say more, but it came out as gibberish, her consciousness slipping beneath the pressure of her reaping. Her head fell back, and her body went slack.

"Shh . . . it's okay. Sleep. Sleep." I patted her hand and brushed her hair away from her face. "I'll keep you safe," I promised, even though I didn't know if I could. Lifting her over my shoulder, I stood.

She wanted us to hole up in Almaty, but that would have to wait. I only wanted to go to one place right now, and I hoped the Aod there had more answers than Raven could give me. If not, perhaps he needed me more than I needed him.

I *blinked* to Jakarta.

I appeared in J-Man's living room just as the Aod grabbed Joe by the collar. Anger filled the room, seeping into innumerable cracks and crevices. Shamrock eyes widened as Joe spotted me over J-Man's shoulder. At the same time, the former Xiiph turned. His normally empty emotional shell filled instantly with fear, anger, and hatred as his gaze flicked from my face to the unconscious Raven draped over my shoulder, her long, inky ponytail whispering against the floor.

"You made it!" Joe said at the same time J-Man yelled, "Leave, now!"

"Why the hell are you here?" I shouted at Joe. Pushing past the two men, I laid Raven down on the ratty couch. When frustration swirled through Joe's mountain landscape, I grabbed his arm before he could turn away. "I didn't mean it like that. I just don't want you caught up in my mess."

He quickly embraced me and let go.

I turned to J-Man, who struggled to control his emotions. His usual drain seemed clogged. New fears layered atop existing ones, until his emotional container overflowed and he reached for the sickle at my hip. Drawing my khukuri, I pressed it to his chest as Joe leveled his Glock at the Aod's head. Neither would kill him, but now I knew the khyabadian of my reaping blade could at least do some harm.

J-Man froze, his fingertips a breath away from the sickle. As he shifted carefully away from my khukuri, I frowned. I shouldn't have been able to draw my weapon before he could grab Raven's. He was better than this—than me. Had fear made him slip?

Wrapping my free hand around his wrist, I pulled it gently away from the sickle. "Joe, where is Daliah?" I asked, my eyes never leaving J-Man.

"I'm here." She stepped out from the bedroom area. "Your human insisted we wait."

"How soon can you get us back to Odessa?"

Uncertainty wafted from her. "I'll have to check the gate schedules."

"Do it."

She scowled but disappeared.

I looked back at J-Man. "I just need information, and then we'll be out of your life."

Distrust crawled down his arm and bit my hand where I held his wrist, a thousand needles drilling into my flesh. "I should have abandoned this place after you left the first time."

"I'm glad you didn't. I need you."

"Do you even know who she is?" He nodded toward the space where Daliah had stood. "Who they both are?"

"Daliah is a Daemon who helped us. And this"—I looked at the unconscious woman on the couch—"is my friend."

"She is Raven."

My eyes widened. "You know her?"

"She is *dangerous.*"

"She reaped a Guardian to keep him from taking me to V."

All color and emotion drained from J-Man. "*V* is chasing you?" He whispered her name, as if the woman could hear it across the world and whatever dimensions interlaced with this one.

Maybe she could.

"Who is V?" Joe asked.

"Later. I'm here about the Contract." I kept my gaze on J-Man. His eyes were tight, his jaw clenched. I sighed. "I get it. You don't want anything to do with this. But I need answers. *Please.*"

The ex-Xiiph collapsed into a nearby chair, and I released his wrist so he wouldn't pull me down with him. It might mean he could *blink* away, but I didn't believe he'd abandon his *kota* with two Aods and a Daemon nearby. Besides, he could probably pull me into the Echo regardless of who held whom.

I decided to keep my khukuri drawn, just in case.

Seeming to understand the energy of the room, Joe holstered his weapon and sat at the table. I studied the slow rise and fall of his chest as he centered himself in peace, and let his calm wash over me.

Exhaling slowly, I knelt in front of J-Man. "Please."

The Aod slumped forward, staring down at his empty hands. "It's not what you're hoping."

"Tell me."

He sighed. "Our Contracts aren't like humans' paper ones. You can't sneak in, set fire to all the copies, and declare yourself free of the mess you created when you signed up the first time."

"Then what *is* it like?"

"Our blades were merely the catalysts for creating the bonds between us and whatever power holds us to the

Guardians—the pen used to sign the document, not the document itself."

"And when they're destroyed?"

He turned his head away, and his hands clenched into fists. "Not freedom. The longing for death, the need to kill, the anger bordering on rage—all of it remains, intensified in the absence of reaping souls."

My stomach somersaulted with his. "But that isn't why you're afraid."

J-Man looked at me, eyes tight. Ice crawled from his emotional aura and settled in my chest. "Torture and death await every Aod without a blade. You don't gain immunity. You lose the only protection you have."

"I don't get it," Joe said.

J-Man didn't even glance at Joe. "You wouldn't. You are human."

Understanding dawned slowly within me as J-Man held my gaze. "An Angel of Death who can be killed by *any* reaping blade. *Fuck.*"

"K?"

I turned to Joe. "Right now, the only reaping blade that can take my soul is my own. While any reaping blade wielded by any being, immortal or otherwise, can hurt me—as Daliah so graciously demonstrated—it won't *reap* me. Only mine can do that, and only if held by another Angel of Death."

Joe snapped his fingers. "So destroy the blade, and you destroy the condition that keeps you safe from other blades."

J-Man nodded. "It's its own kind of hell."

I grasped his hand. I could only imagine the intense anxiety he'd been living with—a kind of drip torture where every sound could be an Aod coming to reap your soul. His life of hypervigilance and anxious anticipation would wreck anyone mentally and emotionally. No wonder Raven had cowered before Luke's threat. I shuddered.

My eyes widened as another thought hit me. *I could have accidentally reaped him!* Raven had explained humans and Guardians, but where did that leave the Aods who lived between humans and gods? I quickly sheathed my reaping blade. "I'm so sorry, J-Man."

J-Man leaned toward me. "Freedom is a myth."

"What do we do now?"

He nodded toward Joe. "Protect them from us. For as long as we can."

"There has to be more," Joe said. "Something we're missing."

J-Man shook his head, and I wondered if death really was the only answer. Adi's ninety-nine percent . . .

I stood, numbness creeping through my insides. I had to get back to Adi. Maybe I could hide among the Daemons, living a half life like J-Man.

"Let's—"

My head exploded with pain, a geyser of information jetting through what felt like a pinhole in the side of my skull. Falling to the floor, I clutched my head as my vision swam with image after image, blocking out the rest of the world.

An older man cowers on the ground before me, so ordinary he could have been any man. Skittish eyes flick around the street while snot runs over plump lips pleading for me to stop, to spare him. Anger and fear roil inside me so strongly, I puke.

"Keres!" Joe's voice climbed through the chaos, begging me to come back. I couldn't, not once it had started.

"What's happening to her?" Daliah asked.

"Leave her," J-Man said.

He smiles and wipes the snot away with his sleeve. "You're too green for this."

Raising the gun, I aim it at his face. It's too big for my hands. Too heavy. It has five bullets in the clip—my shaky hands couldn't add any more—but I only need one. I pull the trigger, and he flinches, covering his face with fleshy hands. An empty click echoes in my ears. I forgot to rack the slide. It's stiff, difficult to pull back with sweaty fingers.

"You don't want to do this," he coos. "You're young, too much life waiting for you."

My hands shake. I almost drop the gun, but I'm able to catch it and finally get a bullet in the chamber. I want to run, but I point the gun at him instead.

"She's dangerous right now."

"What's wrong?"

"What's wrong?" he asks again, a smile spreading his lips. "Harder than you thought?"

I hesitate. *What am I doing?* I lower my gun. I can't do this. Not even for him. I am a coward. I hate myself.

The little pig chuckles and starts to back away. As he turns, I hear him say, "If he were just a few years younger, I'd have taken him instead."

I take a few quick steps, put the gun to the back of his head, and pull the trigger.

Only one. I stare at the brain matter and blood spewed across the pavement, like the snot spread across his sleeve. I vomit again.

And I cry.

But it is done, and I am better for it.

I vomited on the floor as the vision subsided, the smell of fresh blood still clinging to my nostrils.

"What's wrong?" Joe's concern reached for me, tried to hold me, but I pushed it away. Daliah stared as Joe grabbed a glass of water and brought it to me. I took it but shied away from his touch. He squatted near me, face pale and lips tight. "How can I help?"

"You can't." No one could.

Joe looked over his shoulder at J-Man. "What is it?"

The Aod watched me knowingly. "She's been scheduled for a reaping."

Joe turned back to me. "Who is it? Maybe we can get them protection."

"There is no protection from an Aod," J-Man said. "There is only death."

The muscle along Joe's jawline danced with tension, but he kept his gaze on me. "We have to try, Keres. Who is it?"

Tears ran down my face as the pit in my stomach opened wide.

He reached for me. "Who?"

I pulled my arm away. "It's *you*."

FORTY

Joe's hand froze before it could touch mine, shamrock eyes draining of color until they looked gray. "What?"

I *blinked* away from him, reappearing in the kitchen; the urge to kill already built inside me with my mark so close.

Joe . . . mark. Funny how fast that changes from one to the other.

But no one was laughing.

"Keres—"

"Don't! Don't talk. Don't breathe."

"You don't have to kill me."

"If you were meant to die right now, you'd already be dead. The only reason I'm not tearing you apart is because it isn't time. But that doesn't mean the Bloodlust doesn't want to be free."

He tried to approach me, but J-Man stepped between us and grabbed his shoulders. "Don't make it harder for her—harder than it will already be."

"You don't have to do this," Joe said. "You can *choose.*"

"Like you chose?" I folded in on myself, laughing because it was easier than breaking. "All this time, you've been counseling me, *judging* me, telling me *I'm selfish* and that I can make better choices, and then *this.*"

Joe stopped fighting J-Man and stared, shame wrapping his chest like a hungry python. Constrict. Exhale. Constrict.

"He was the man who molested your brother, wasn't he?"

"Yes."

I slumped down the wall, a crooked smile on my lips as I shook my head. "I'm so *sick* of everyone lying to me."

"I never said I didn't have a past."

"No. You just pretended to be someone who doesn't choose anger or revenge."

"Patrick changed that."

"I'm glad you had a second chance, that *your* mistake didn't lead to this." I pointed at myself. "But mine did."

"We all get second chances."

Unshed tears blurred my vision. "Not all of us, Joe. Not all of us."

As Joe stepped toward me, the front door exploded inward. I screamed as wooden shrapnel flew toward him. J-Man knocked my human to the floor and covered Joe with his own body. Splinters of wood peppered the Aod's back and the floor like tiny daggers.

Leaping to my feet, I turned to the source of the explosion and recognized the darker-than-black aura before I saw the face. "Kai."

"Knock, knock." He stepped through the rubble as the dust settled, his emotions a slow, thick churn of hate-filled sludge. Mr. Narcissist followed closely behind, a human in tow—the drunk I'd met outside J-Man's front door.

"I tried," the old man said to J-Man in Betawi.

The ex-Xiiph's eyes narrowed, anger wafting from him as he stood. "The end comes for us all." I knew his words were meant for me, though he kept his gaze trained on the Daemon holding his human friend. "The only thing we can control is how we spend our final hours."

Mr. Narcissist's gaze barely flickered to J-Man before refocusing on me. "Blah, blah. Let's get on with this."

I wanted nothing more than to beat the confidence out of him, but for the second time in our acquaintance, his arrogance worked in my favor. He either hadn't noticed or didn't care that J-Man was Fallen.

"Don't come for me again, Aod, or I *will* kill you." J-Man radiated truth and intent as he *blinked* to his friend and, grabbing both men, pulled them into the Echo.

"What the fuck!" Kai yelled.

I smiled and hoped to everything J-Man could trap Mr. Narcissist in the Echo forever.

Stay safe, I prayed. *And let us never meet again.*

Three shots deafened me for a split second as a rapid succession of bullets slammed into one side of Kai's skull and exited the other. Kai's face was whole again before his iridescent blood and tissue had even splattered the wall. His rage turned toward Joe, who still lay on the floor. The room buzzed with energy as Kai drew in power and launched it at the mortal.

"No!" Not trusting myself to get any closer, I threw Shadow between Joe and Kai, but Daliah was already there. Catching Kai's lightning bolt, she absorbed its power until nothing was left.

"Thank you," I breathed.

She frowned at Kai. "Leave the human alone. I brought you here for the girl."

My whole body tightened as if I'd been struck by Kai's lightning bolt. "But your promise to Adi . . ."

Joe scrambled to his feet. "You fucking b—"

Light silenced him as luminescent chains bound us both. Joe collapsed back to the ground and glanced at me apologetically.

I'm the one who should be sorry, Joseph Fitzgerald.

Kai *blinked* behind me, his breath hot against my ear. "She only promised *she* wouldn't hurt you." He laughed, savoring his "gotcha" moment, but doubt cut in and out of Daliah's aura like white static on a television. It was the last thing I felt before Kai slipped a golden cord around my neck.

"No!" I screamed. "*Nooo!*"

I *knew* what came next. Knew where Kai wanted to send me and the Darkness that would ultimately destroy my sanity. I'd tasted it in the Hall. No light, no candles, no dawn. Only me and the crushing blackness suffocating my life but never taking it, leaving me alive to remember everything I'd done.

I fought frantically, pulling and twisting within my chains as he forced my hands behind me and bound them with cords. When my head connected with his nose, Kai swore and swept my legs out from under me, pushing me to the floor. My head bounced as it collided with the ground.

I looked up at Daliah as Kai knelt to bind my ankles. "Please don't let him do this."

She frowned. "If Ielu had said the same thing, would you have listened?"

I rested my forehead against the ground. "No."

"It's over, Fallen," Kai said.

"Then why can't I give up?" Everything pointed to death, but some primal instinct kept me fighting for survival. If I'd truly wanted an end, wouldn't I have given myself over to be reaped ages ago?

Kai leaned over me, his face twisted in a beautiful, horrible smile. "Don't worry. I'll help you."

He pushed me onto my back and tore my T-shirt from collar to sternum. Slicing open his hand with a small knife, Kai dipped his fingers in the thick iridescent liquid and wiped them across my brow.

Yes, whispered hissing voices through black doors.

I cried.

When he reached toward me again, I flinched away from his touch, whining like a terrified dog as he drew a second line in blood across my throat.

Yes! they screeched.

Tears continued to spill down my cheeks as Joe struggled silently against the chains of sunlight. Ignoring it all, Kai drew a third line over my heart.

So close. So close. The Bloodlust screamed defiance and victory. I screamed with it.

Kai chanted . . .

"Daliah!" She stared down at me, chewing her lip, but did nothing. I gritted my teeth against the power building inside me. Sweat beaded on my forehead from the strain as, deep within, the Bloodlust thrashed against its cage.

Kai chanted, his words popping locks and breaking bolts a thousand years old . . .

"Stop! Stop!" I heaved deep breaths through my teeth, as if I were birthing a baby rather than a monster. My body rocked with the effort of keeping it contained. "You don't . . . know what . . . you're doing."

"What the Council never could," Daliah replied.

Kai chanted, his spell wreaking havoc as the Bloodlust swelled with his song . . .

The lines he'd drawn heated, sizzling on my skin, and I cried out in pain. The dark door bulged beneath the pressure, and ancient powers pushed to be free. How many lives would I take before the Burn Cycle destroyed me? Joe, Daliah, Kai, and Raven were certainties, unless the Daemons *blinked* away. But beyond them? Would I take the building? The *kota*? The whole damn city?

I thrashed within my bindings and tried to roll away from Kai. He simply extended his chains of light to pin me to the floor. My heart raced as I strained against the hold, black spots appearing in my vision. Tight, tight, tighter—until I almost couldn't breathe.

Kai stopped chanting; my inner restraints barely held.

"Please!" I begged him, just as I'd begged his brother. "Please stop. I don't want to hurt you. Ielu . . ."

He grabbed me by the shoulders and slammed me into the ground over and over. "You don't get to speak his name!" Spittle dribbled from his lips.

I sobbed. "He wanted to help me."

"You only have me now. *Elystial.*" Kai passed his hand over the burning line on my forehead.

My inner door splintered, and I screamed. "Can't hold" and "Please" spilled from my lips.

"Kai! Stop!" Daliah yelled.

He ignored her and made another pass across the line at my throat. "Elythrall."

My neck, wrists, and ankles burned where cord met skin, and the Bloodlust pushed at the door, almost breaking free. I thought of Joe and Raven and all the innocent humans in the building around me and braced everything I had against my inner door. The Bloodlust pushed again, and I screamed.

"Kai, stop!" Daliah wrapped him in a choke hold and pulled him away from me. "We have to stop."

"I thought you understood."

"I loved him too. But we have to stop."

"I *still* love him!"

I opened my eyes just enough to take in the room before shutting them again. Tears streamed down Kai's cheeks, and Daliah stared down at me, regret in her gaze. I heard the scuffle but couldn't watch. All my concentration focused on the doors. I tuned out the bone-crunching *oomph*s as hands and feet connected with flesh.

One body fell hard.

"Why, Daliah? This is *sanctioned!*"

"I'm so sorry, Kai."

"That doesn't bring back my brother."

"Neither will this. It will only destroy you."

"Too late."

Daliah cried out, and opening my eyes, I saw her tumble, Kai's khyabadian blade protruding from her chest. He lunged toward me and passed his hand over my heart. "Elyhyyl."

"No!" Daliah's voice was more gurgle than word.

Kai's last word decimated my inner door and destroyed the ancient bindings tempering the Bloodlust—bindings I hadn't known existed until they disappeared.

Power unlike anything I'd ever felt before rushed out to fill my entire body. I screamed as it roared inside my head. So loud. So incredibly loud, as pressure pushed against skull and skin. It needed a release.

Daliah crawled over to me. "The ropes are disintegrating!"

"Impossible," Kai said. "Impossible."

The pressure at my neck, hands, and ankles gave way, and emotions rushed through me, adding to the chaos churning in my soul. Shadow destroyed the chains of sunlight without my conscious bidding, and I dragged my body away from Daliah and Kai. Pulling my legs into my chest and covering my head with my arms, I rocked and rocked, trying to calm the power surging within me. My body twisted in on itself, my stomach muscles clenching as my fingers curled in and my limbs shook.

"Daliah," I gritted out through clenched teeth. "Save . . . them."

Kai turned his rage and frustration on Daliah. "This is *your* fault! You shouldn't have interfered with the banishment."

She ignored him, her eyes glued to me. "What are you?"

"Death."

Rock. Rock. Rock. Breathe.

Rock. Rock. Rock. Breathe.

Rock. Rock. Rock. Breathe.

Too much. Too much. Too much.

I screamed. "Go. *Now!*" I screamed again, but neither Daemon moved. I was a train wreck just before impact, and they couldn't look away.

Breathe, Keres. Breathe.

Too much emotion. Too many people. I shifted, afraid to let go, afraid to stay. Screaming, I clawed my way upright using whatever furniture I could grasp, and tore open the fabric between here and any place devoid of people, not even sure where I'd end up. I stumbled forward.

You can stop this, I told myself.

Liar, the Bloodlust replied and obliterated my final hold.

FORTY-ONE

I hit the ground hard as power rocketed out of my body and up into the sky as a beam of light—a volcanic eruption of fear, hate, rage, lust, and greed. I closed my eyes against the brightness, but not before witnessing how it expanded around me, disintegrating everything in its path.

I screamed loud and hard as rage that wasn't my own fed me or fed on me—I couldn't tell which. Its source was too far away for me to recognize but close enough to drown me in its coursing river of dark emotion.

Too much. Too much. Too much. Like burning alive but never dying.

I pushed the power of the Bloodlust into the Earth, and the ground shook. I poured all my emotion into it—my fear, anger, sadness, and defeat. It felt good to give the pain to something else. I pulled in more power, bundled up more emotion, and pushed it into the planet itself. If there had been anyone here, I no doubt would have taken from them too. Without thinking. Without remorse.

I tore at the Earth with my power, reaching deep into her cracks and ripping her apart. I shook anything I could grab hold of, trying to break her spirit as the Guardians had broken mine. All the while, light pulsed from my body, walls of destruction rippling out in every direction. The entire planet shook beneath my force and screamed at me to stop, to be done, to be over.

But I couldn't stop.

"Take me!" I screamed. "Let me die."

Surely suffocating in darkness would have been better than this. The light was searing—hotter than my anger, hotter than Luke's punishments and Elijah's electricity. My flesh melted and healed in a never-ending cycle, until I thought I would both liquify and explode. I shrieked until I became nothing but light and pain and screams.

And Death.

I approach the dead man. The bite on his leg looks swollen and painful, and desert insects already crawl across his skin. I lean closer. I have never seen a dead body before, and I am curious.

His eyelids shoot open, revealing dull eyes the gray blue of an approaching storm, and I stumble back, heart pounding.

"Please . . . help . . ." The two words are all I understand from his parched, broken lips. Abba has only taught me a little of this language so far.

There is no need for you to speak it, Abba said. *Only men trade with men.*

Teach me so I can listen as well as serve when we host your guests.

So he did.

Now I listen, trying to understand this foreign tongue, but the man slips back into unconsciousness. His body is heavy, awkward with weight and slipping limbs, but with

Atira kneeling, I manage to pull him over the horse's back and return to the tents of my *abba*.

"What have you done!" Abba yells before I can even dismount.

"We help the injured." I slide from Atira's back, leaving the stranger on my horse, and stare at my father. I don't understand what I have done wrong.

Abba swears, displaying an anger I've rarely seen in him. I lean into my horse's side. "His people are dangerous, Yaffa! And you bring him here!" As he swears again, other men gather around us. They discuss whether to kill the stranger or let the desert do the work.

"We do not kill!" I shout, emboldened by outrage. First Abba shames me for doing what is right, and now he speaks of doing what is wrong to fix it?

Abba turns a cold gaze on me, as if I were a stranger. "Do not speak of things you do not understand, girl. We protect our people. We give this one man back to the desert so others may live."

The depth of his disappointment breaks my heart, and tears burn in my eyes. I cannot stay a moment longer among these men's tight eyes and angry whispers. I glance at Immah, who stands at the door of my *abba*'s tent. I beg silently for her to defend me, but she shakes her head.

I am alone.

Before the tears can fall, I remount Atira behind the stranger's body and ride hard into the desert, the cries of angry men trailing behind me.

Once far enough away, I stop, dismount, and lightly slap the stranger's face to rouse him. "Where? Where are your people?"

I continue patting and asking until I make sense of his mumbles. Remounting, I ride until I reach the area I seek. It is almost dark, and evening fires have already been lit, winking in the distance.

"This is as far as I can go." I don't bother speaking his language. The words are for me, not him. "May the desert keep you safe until you are found."

My beautiful Atira kneels for me, and I slide the man to the ground. "May God hold you."

When I return to the tent of my *abba,* well into the night, I expect to be shamed again. Instead, Abba throws his arms around me. He was scared, and now he is sorry. I tell him not to worry; I returned the man to the desert. He tells me I am strong as he cries into my hair.

I cry too.

He tells me it is okay to cry because I have done a hard thing in giving the stranger to the desert. But I don't cry for the stranger or myself. I cry because my *abba* isn't the great man I thought he was. That Abba died today, and I mourn him.

FORTY-TWO

Death should have been nothingness, an end, a forgetting.

Instead, every nerve felt raw as a hammer pounded out a desperate rhythm inside my skull. The shattered grief left behind by a waning Bloodlust cried out from my core, a beacon for darker emotions that gathered in silence and waited. At least shape and shadow existed in this black. It wasn't the Hall; it wasn't Kai's Darkness.

Light eventually pierced my closed eyelids, sharp and unforgiving, and I struggled against the sleep restraining the rest of my senses. Low, terse mumbles floated along the gray before finally forming into words I understood.

". . . Burn Cycle . . ."

My eyelids fluttered. *Open . . . close . . . open.*

Blurry figures stood nearby in a world once again turned on its side. My fingers twitched against something soft and fine. Dirt, maybe? Mentally shrugging, I tried to focus on the pair in front of me. When my vision remained blurry, I closed my eyes and listened.

". . . should have been reaped—"

"Not your concern."

"It's *all* our concern when your pet loses control."

"Then why not tell your fellow Conclave members, *ma chatte*?"

Luke? I should have panicked, but only a yawning emptiness filled me.

Large hands scooped me up like a rag doll, my limbs deadweight as my head bobbed against hairy flesh.

"Put her down." Luke's silky tones turned deceptively friendly. "*Gently, bon ami.*"

Hairy Man hesitated, then gasped and set me back down. I peeked through heavy lids. Dozens of blurry figures stood around me, connected by a tight emotional string, ready to snap. I remained still.

A woman tsked. "I thought you knew me better than that." Her curvy blob leaned into the tight blur of my Aishah. She seemed friendly. *Intimate.* "I like a good chase." I blinked a few times, trying to focus.

Luke chuckled. "Too bad Elijah turned out to be more mouse than cat."

V? The name bounced slowly around my consciousness. I should have felt fear, but I didn't and that worried me. *Wake up, Keres.*

Red-hot flares of anger burst around the female Conclave member as she moved away from Luke, her bare feet stopping in front of my face. Her feet were beautiful, sensual. Milky curves and soft lines that caressed the ground rather than walked on it.

A pang of jealousy worked through me, separate from the numbness, almost silly in the way it stumbled around inside me, trying to find purchase.

"Another reason to settle this without Conclave interference: I'd like some . . . *time* . . . with your pet before we reap her."

My brain thought we should find my reaping blade, and I agreed. Opening myself to its song, I discovered it humming at Luke's hip.

Damn.

"I'm not playing," Luke told V. "As his second and head of the Conclave, I am in command."

Shit. Of *course* he led the Conclave. *So naive, Keres.*

V returned to him, her figure brushing his as her hand reached for his face. "I seem to remember liking your head very much, and you never used to complain about my playing with it." Her voice dipped huskily, breathless and sultry.

Luke grabbed her wrist, and I smelled searing flesh as he pushed her away. Her head tilted back, and she moaned, sex dancing among the flares of her anger. "You remember how I like it."

With a quick twist of Luke's hand, the crack of V's wrist breaking pierced the air.

Hissing, she snatched her arm back and cradled it against her chest. "Bastard!" It would have healed instantly, but she continued rubbing it. "Your hold on the Conclave isn't as sure as you think it is."

Luke drew in Shadow, filling the entire space with his dark presence. He seemed to be everywhere all at once: in the ground, in the sky, in the air. The tension wound tighter as the other Guardians struggled to breathe.

Even V bled fear, inky tar slicking across her skin as she coughed and clawed at her throat. The lack of oxygen wouldn't kill any of us, but it sure hurt like hell.

Luke grabbed V by the throat, digging in with his fingers. "Don't cross me. Forgiveness is not my strong suit."

V nodded, and Luke shoved her away, releasing his power. As we collectively inhaled, V slunk back to him, wrapped her body around his, and kissed him hard.

And long.

And he let her.

"No one has ever pleased you like I have. Not even *her*. Not then, not now. Your words, remember? I'll be here when you decide to crawl back, and your penance will be delicious." She licked him, then nodded to her men and stepped back as they gathered around her.

Luke smirked. "Be careful, V. This isn't a game you can win."

She laughed—full, deep, delicious. "I play the long game, *doudou*. And I *always* win." She glanced at me, her smile twisting with unspoken promises of horror. "Your pet is stirring." She *blinked* away with her entourage of wicked men.

"Ah, *cher*, you're awake."

"Luke." I coughed and swallowed against the pain in my throat.

He squatted beside me, pushing matted hair away from my face. "Shh . . . I'm here." He motioned to one of his men, who handed him something as Luke sat down and lifted my head into his lap.

"Drink." Stroking my hair, he held a bladder of water against my broken lips. I swallowed what I could, but most of the liquid sloshed down my chin. I tried to pull away but couldn't even roll my head from his lap.

"Why am I not dead?" I whispered, too hoarse to speak any louder.

"If it only took once, we wouldn't call it the Burn *Cycle*."

My guts finally had the sense to twist. *This would happen again?* "But Raven said—"

"Raven knows just enough to be dangerous, *cher*—to herself and others. I've been slack in my duties as Aishah, it seems—a problem I'll remedy as soon as we find her."

"She's missing?" *Please, God, let her be okay.*

He shrugged and caressed my face, tracing my cheek and jawline with his fingertips. I tried to pull away again, but my muscles wouldn't respond.

"I can't move."

"You worked hard, *cher.*"

Tiny icy tendrils seeped into my heart. "Where am I?" I tried to raise my arm, move my head, shift my weight—but nothing. Tears trickled from my eyes.

He gently wiped them away as he smiled down at me. "You're safe."

"I'll never be safe."

"You've always been safe, *cher.* It's everyone else who has to worry."

I frowned. "I don't understand." *Damn this brain fog!*

"Though perhaps I *should* give you to V?"

Elijah's vision of him and V "playing" with me flashed through my mind. I couldn't unsee that. Ever. More tears gathered in my eyes.

"Even *I* didn't think you were stupid enough to go home." He adjusted and straightened my clothes as if I were some delicate porcelain doll. "Point to V. But you should have come to me first, instead of running all over the world." He almost seemed hurt—almost—and his hand paused on my cheek. "I have everything you need."

"I can't trust you."

"I've never lied to you, *cher.*"

I rolled my head away from his hand. It took all my energy, but I did it. I laid there, breathing like I'd lifted a mountain but grateful I'd been able to move at all. He pulled my face back around with one finger.

I held his gaze without flinching and spoke in a voice thick with accusation. "We serve Lucifer, not God."

Smiling, he leaned closer. "Lucifer *is* my god."

My brow furrowed, and my mouth fell open.

"You've heard a few stories, Keres, but not ours. Daemon hands are just as dirty. I'm simply willing to acknowledge my deeds. So yes, we serve Lucifer. And if you hadn't been so caught up in yourself, you would have figured it out sooner, like Raven did. In fact, part of you probably did. *He* gave you a choice in the beginning, and *you* chose. That's no one's fault but yours."

No one's fault but mine.

"Do you think your life would have been so easy without me? That you'd have had other Guardians without my approval? Or so few reapings? Or such an easy mentor?"

"What are you talking about?"

Wrapping around me, Shadow lifted me from the ground like a marionette with shadowy strings. My limbs burned with pins and needles, and my fingers twitched.

Luke stood and stepped in front of me, holding my gaze. "Aods are disposable. We use you fast and destroy you when you become too dangerous. Where others would have days to recover, you had months . . . years. I protected you. Sheltered you. Kept you hidden from the Conclave and safe from a more *exacting* Xiiph."

"Have you met Raven?"

"She wasn't Elijah." He reached to stroke my face.

As I pulled away from his touch, I finally noticed the fine dirt covering every part of me that I could see and every part of Luke that had touched me. More words spilled from his lips, but I couldn't hear them as my brain struggled to grasp what some part of me already knew.

"Cher?"

I rubbed the dirt between my fingers. No, not dirt. *Ash.*

Luke gripped my chin. "Even the Daemons have allowed lambs to be led to the slaughter. We're at war, *cher,* and sacrifices must be made. Yet I risked everything—my seat of power, my *life*—for *you*."

The scene behind him drew my gaze, and I gasped. Miles of charred earth stretched in every direction, surrounded by toppled trees. I rubbed my fingers together again, recognition dawning slowly. "What have I done?"

Luke released me and stepped back, arms spread wide. "Impressive, right? This is where I found you, curled up and unconscious, the last of your blackened flesh sloughing to the ground." He tsked as if correcting a naughty child. "You've been holding out on me, *cher*."

"You're a monster."

He flashed a sharp smile, his gaze dark, intense, *feral*. "Sick, perhaps. But *I* am not the monster here." The earth rumbled beneath us, and Luke stared at me, grinning wickedly, until the ground settled once again. "You did this, *cher*. Instant. Precise. Beautiful destruction."

"Stop it, Luke." I almost choked on the fear crawling up from my belly. The crater stretched for miles. Nothing within its charred edges could have survived, and everything beyond them was a mess of fallen trees and shifted earth. I'd tried so hard to stop it from happening—Jakarta, the Hall, Jerusalem—yet here we were, at the epicenter of my destruction. I didn't want this power; it terrified me. "Take it back, Luke. Take this—whatever it is—back."

He shook his head. "I am just the witness. *You* are the weapon, Keres."

The Shadow holding me up disappeared, and I almost collapsed from the weight of my own body. I took a few timid steps on wobbly legs, one tiny hope burning through the tears spilling from my eyes. "Tell me there weren't people here."

"Only forest."

My strength gave out, and I slumped to my knees,

unconcerned about the ash as I curled in toward the earth, my forehead touching the ground. *Thank you, thank you, thank you, thank you, thank you.* I couldn't say the words enough. I *had* done it after all. Even while falling apart, I'd managed to save everyone. I laughed through my tears as they watered the ash. *Thank you, thank you, thank you.*

"I did it." I sat up and turned my face to the sky. "I DID IT!"

I wiped my eyes with the back of my hands and smiled up at Luke. "I did it, you horrible bastard! I did it!"

He smiled back as if he'd won a prize, effectively dousing my joy. He stepped up to me, blocking the sun as he leaned close. "Oh, Keres, this is just the beginning." He turned to his entourage. "Leave us."

As the Guardians disappeared, Luke grabbed my wrist and pulled me to my feet. "Remember those words, *cher. You* did this."

FORTY-THREE

I stared down at the sprawling city of Santiago and wished the entire mountain Luke had *blinked* us to would overturn and bury me alive.

Ravaged buildings cowered among the green. Some jutted out like broken bottles, jagged edges where their tops had been. Others slouched as if they'd been seized, twisted in two, and dropped on crooked foundations.

I swallowed down bile. "No."

We *blinked* again, and the need to vomit intensified as we emerged in a decimated neighborhood. Luke let go of me as we walked through the rubble of broken buildings. I could have *blinked* away, tried to run, but I didn't. Instead, I listened in horror as wails ascended to the sky. They asked God why, but it wasn't his fault.

It was mine. *I did it.*

"It's been over three days, Keres, and the earth still shakes from the remnants of your power. I only wish I'd been here to see it."

"You're disgusting."

"Says the girl who has killed *hundreds* of innocents."

I hugged myself, but it didn't stop the slice-slice-slice of his words against my heart. "Hundreds?"

"For now. They're still searching."

He turned down a side street, where a little girl sat crying next to a large chunk of broken cement. Clutching a doll in her hands, she sobbed, "Papi, Papi," over and over, her cries for her father as endless as her tears. Beneath the concrete next to her lay a man.

I *blinked* to his side and lifted the cement, but his body was crushed beyond human repair. There was nothing I could do. Lowering the large chunk back down, I knelt at his side. The man's gaze turned toward me, but his eyes clouded over with confusion and the beginnings of unconsciousness. I looked to Luke. "Help him!"

Luke squatted next to me. He looked like he was about to speak, but he stopped and cocked his head to the side. Abruptly, he grabbed me and pulled me back into J-Man's Echo. I gasped—*Luke knows about this place?*—and the Guardian covered my mouth with his hand.

"I don't think we're alone," he whispered. The tear he'd made in the fabric between the two dimensions began to collapse, until all that remained was a limited view of the little girl and her dying father.

"Help them," I tried to say again, but it came out as wet mumbles.

Shadow gathered around us in the Echo as Luke breathed words into my ear. "I promise to help him as soon as *they* do."

I followed Luke's gaze as a solemn, little boy and a fiery-haired woman stepped into view. My eyes widened, and I struggled against Luke, but he tightened the Shadow until I couldn't move, couldn't breathe.

‹Please help him,› I sent to Adi. He glanced toward us, even took a step in our direction, before Daliah cut in.

"I'm sorry, Adi, she's not here. You saw the crater. I don't think she survived. I'm so sorry." And she was; the deep strains of her sorrow reached me even in the Echo.

Adi's face fell, his shoulders slumping. "Then more is lost than you can imagine." Stepping over to the father, Adi gently closed his now-dead eyes and whispered to the little girl. Her wails turned to hiccupping sobs.

Daliah stepped up beside him. "We must go." He nodded, and they *blinked* away.

I died inside. I stopped fighting the Shadow, and Luke released me as he returned us to the Earth layer. "Why didn't he save him? If you're all so powerful, why didn't someone save him."

"We didn't make the mess, Keres."

I slumped to the ground near the dead man. He wasn't marked. He'd committed no crime. And *I* had killed him. "I didn't mean to . . ."

"He's still dead." Luke's voice sounded right next to my ear. "Killed by your choice, just like your *abba*. You are destruction, *cher*."

His words wrecked me. "And death."

"Yes, and death."

I'd saved one little girl's daddy because he'd looked like mine, and I'd killed this little girl's father because I'd chosen *my* freedom at all costs.

I did it.

"If only you'd followed the rules." He shifted as he crouched next to me, his breath hot against my other ear. "Can you say it was all worth it now?"

The void yawned inside me, and I climbed into it. Pulled it around me until I couldn't feel a thing. "You can't let me live."

"I won't let you die." He stood, pulling me up with him. "I protect what's mine."

I turned to face him. His gaze was so cold and intense, I flinched.

"And you don't want to leave me. Not *really.*"

I *blinked* a few feet away. "Adi can help me." But the words died as they passed my lips. *He should have saved him.* Was no one who I thought?

Luke shrugged. "He can cage you." He moved to my side but kept his hands clasped behind his back. Shoulder to shoulder, we watched the little girl. "But he can't save you. No one can. No one but me. You can't escape what you've become, *cher.* Any intense emotion will trigger this from now on."

The girl stared past us, her sobs increasing the longer we stood there.

"I can stop feeling." I could empty myself like J-Man, right?

"What are you waiting for, then?" Luke held out my reaping blade, and I hesitated. "Take it. Go."

He forced it into my doubting hands and stepped up to the little girl, leaning down to gently wipe away the tears streaking her small cheeks. Her cries stopped abruptly, and she gazed ahead vacantly as Luke stroked her hair. The ugliest side of *seeding.* I'd blanked adults before, wiping memories and emotions as needed, but seeing her like this horrified me.

Still petting her, Luke looked at me. "Lose control once, and this *will* happen again."

I looked down at my reaping blade. For the first time ever, it felt . . . *wrong* . . . in my hands.

"Besides, you can't escape your next reaping. And the more you reap, the harder you'll be to control."

Heat drained from my face. *Joe.*

Luke *blinked* behind me, gently cupping my shoulders. "*I* can save him."

"You can't cancel a reaping."

"I can shift it."

I pulled away and turned around. "You what?"

"Ah-ah-ah." Luke nodded toward the little girl and her dead father. "Feelings, remember?"

I swallowed down the anger burning my throat. "What will your help cost me?"

Luke smiled. "Choose me; that simple. Choose to do what I say when I say. You give me so little—only you—and I give you everything you desire."

"Everything but my freedom."

He *blinked* to the top of the cement block that had crushed Papi and gestured to the girl, then to the city. "Do you call *this* free? Aren't you tired of running? Of being *afraid*? Not ever worrying again—I call *that* freedom."

"And the reapings?"

He hopped down from the block and crossed over to kneel in front of me, taking my hands in his. "I promise you: only two more reapings. This one now, and one more in the future."

"Who?"

"Doesn't matter."

"*Who*?" I pressed.

Luke frowned. "Not Joe."

"Ever?"

"Ever."

"And if I don't agree?"

Shrugging, he stood. "Joe dies, and you destroy another city." He strolled back over to the little girl and, sitting on the ground beside her, pulled her into his lap and rocked her gently. "And I'll let you do it again and again and again. I'm a patient man when it comes to you learning your lessons."

I stared, weighing my limited options.

Luke frowned. "Am I really so awful that you'd rather murder *thousands* of innocent people than spend a bit of eternity with me?"

"I choose the mark."

His eyes narrowed, and he stopped rocking. The silence stretched between us. I held still under his scrutiny.

Finally, he shrugged. "Whatever *cher* requests."

I looked at the little girl. "Then I am yours."

"And the new mark?"

"Not here."

Luke set the girl down like a rag doll next to her father's body and stood. "Then let us leave this place."

I refused his outstretched hand. "She needs help."

His jaw clenched, but he smiled tightly. "Fine." Grabbing my arm, he tugged me back the way we'd come. At the main road, Luke called out in flawless Chilean Spanish to people in neon *Manos que Ayudan* T-shirts and pointed them toward the girl and her dad. He held me as if I'd been injured and, wishing them well, walked me down the street before *blinking* us back to the mountains.

"Now . . . the mark."

I closed my eyes. "Sergio's boss . . . Quinn."

A raging river raced through my skull, washing away the memories of Joe's first kill and replacing them with the sickening torrent of violence Quinn called life. I collapsed into Luke's arms as disturbing memories of rape, murder, and torture soaked up my sanity. I screamed, even as I searched for anything that could help me.

Please, God, let me find something.

As the last of the images flicked through my brain, I saw it. I laughed through my tears, almost delirious with pain and joy. My final amends—a puzzle piece to help Joe get to Quinn before I reaped him.

Thank you, thank you, thank you.

I pushed away from Luke, still laughing, at least until the Bloodlust roared inside me. Inhaling sharply, I scowled at my new master. Luke had changed not only the mark but the timing. Quinn would die *tonight*.

"No!" I stepped back and punched Luke in the face. "You can't reschedule a reaping!"

His shoulders tensed, and the muscle along his jawline bounced, but he didn't retaliate. He smirked. "New mark, new rules. You should have asked more questions, *cher*. Always leaping before you judge the distance."

He grabbed me and kissed me, hard and unrelenting. Yaffa hissed within me, but I didn't fight back. This was our agreement. My life for Joe's. I reached for the vast nothingness growing inside me.

When he finally released me, Luke was breathless. He leaned his forehead against mine. "Then again, that's what I like about you. Now, shall we go tell Joe?"

My eyes narrowed. "You knew."

He chuckled. "Why else would you pick Quinn?"

"None of that matters now."

He grinned. "Disappointing your *couyon* matters to me."

I swung at him again, but he grabbed my arm, searing the flesh as we locked eyes. "Be careful, *cher*, or there will be new lessons to learn."

I dropped my gaze. "Yes, Aishah."

"Good girl."

Luke's underlings appeared, probably called by Luke the way Raven called me. "Place lookouts at Quinn's place for his reaping. We can't afford to take any chances, even if the Daemons think she's dead. Keres and I will you meet you there."

He turned back to me and smiled. "Let's go chat with your human."

FORTY-FOUR

Joe sat in a chair near the overturned bookcases, facing the window. The rest of my apartment looked exactly as I'd left it, except for the broken police tape hanging from the front door and the large plastic sheets covering the shattered window frames. Those were new.

"How'd you know he was here?" I whispered.

Luke chuckled. "Turns out, I had my people watching the wrong home. Should have put them in the desert."

"Stay here."

Luke raised an eyebrow.

"*Please.* Out of sight."

"As *ma cher* wishes."

Walking down the hall, I silently crossed the living room, until I stood directly behind the human who had shifted my whole world. I placed a hand gently on his shoulder. "Joe."

He glanced back over his shoulder. Dark circles sat under his eyes, and his hair was a mess, as though he'd dragged his fingers through it a hundred times too many. In one fluid motion, he stood and embraced me.

We fit together perfectly, his body complementing mine. As much as I wanted to relax into his embrace, though, I held back, hoping to make this easier for the both of us. Even as his body shook with sobs, I kept my arms pinned to my sides.

"I'm so sorry," I said.

"You're not dead." He squeezed tighter.

I pushed away from him before I changed my mind and got us both killed, but he grabbed my shoulders and ducked his head to look into my eyes. "What's wrong?"

I surveyed the mess we'd left behind only . . . what? A week ago? Two? I'd lost track of time. "I don't have to kill you anymore."

"That's great news, K!"

"Why are you here, Joe?" I kept my voice flat.

His smile faltered. Instead of answering, he took my hand and pulled me into the kitchen, where he wet a towel and began wiping down my face and arms. It felt too intimate. Dangerous, even. I pulled free, and we stared at the floor in awkward silence. I glanced at the ash smeared all over him, hating how I dirtied everything I touched.

Joe threw the towel in the sink. "I didn't know where else to go when Adi told me—" He coughed, swallowing down grief. "I couldn't stay there. Not with Daliah constantly underfoot, as if servitude could make amends for helping Kai destroy you."

The muscle along his jaw twitched as he ground his teeth. Sadness, grief, gratitude, and more swam in his eyes, in his heart. "This was all I had left of you."

His face softening, he enveloped me again in those strong, tender arms of his and laughed. "But you're *here*. You're alive!"

I was leaning my head back to tell him I couldn't stay when his lips crushed down on my own. They were fire to the ice inside me, melting me, healing me. My mouth yearned to respond, to give as much as I received. My fingers ached to reach up, grab his messy hair and unshaven face, and pull him down on top of me.

But I gripped the shirt at his waistline to keep from responding and pushed him away, our moment shattering into tiny shards of glass that cut as they fell at our feet.

Luke had promised to stay out of sight, and I would not give him a reason to change his mind. Yet . . .

Kiss him, take him, leave him. I could still save it. I only had to lean in and take what I wanted.

Instead, I asked what the small human girl inside me wanted to know.

"Had you known about everything, would you have made the same choice? Followed me to Jakarta? And everything after?" I considered what I'd put him through—things that, all together, should have earned me scorn instead of kisses.

He tensed. I wanted so much to touch him right now, to be touched in return. "I've asked myself the same question." Turning his back to me, he leaned over the counter.

"And?"

"I decided the answer doesn't matter. We can't go back. Can't unchoose. I made a decision, and I don't regret it. It was the right choice at the time with all the information I had. Would I do it again? I don't know. Would I have tried to find another way? Hell yes. But it doesn't change the past."

I crossed to the overturned dining table and righted it, brushing my hands along its beautiful wood. "Could it have changed the future?"

"Old choices don't make the future, Keres. New ones do."

I paused. "Then we were never guaranteed to stay

together." The words should have brought me peace for what I had to do next, but instead, they cut me.

"We're not a solar system—planets orbiting a sun in predictable patterns. We're messy, chaotic humans who can choose to change course at any time."

"Then what keeps people together?" For all the power Luke and I held in our bodies, it couldn't prevent our relationship from exploding into a storm of fire and ash, and the future Luke clung to was nothing but smoke.

"The same thing that pulls them apart. Choice. And hard work. Eventually trust and maybe someday . . ."

I turned around to face him, gripping the table at my back. "What?"

He crossed over and brushed his hand along my cheek. "Maybe someday, it'll feel more natural to be together than apart."

I shook my head. "Why did you choose me, Joe? It doesn't make sense."

He smiled sadly, his gaze shifting from my cheek to my eyes. "Because you can't see yourself the way I do."

Even though he'd said all the right things and touched me in all the right ways, my sadness only deepened. I only wanted tomorrows with Joe in them, but now . . .

Fuck.

"Joe, don't waste your life chasing after me."

He smiled, lucky eyes shining. "You think I'd miss the part where you kick some Guardian ass?"

"This isn't a joke."

He took my face in his hands. "It never was." He kissed me gently, and I let him. Let those soft caresses turn to ash and die on my lips when I didn't respond.

He stopped and slowly pulled away, his brow furrowing as his gaze searched my face. "What happened?"

"I destroyed a city." Abandoning him at the table, I

grabbed a piece of paper and pencil from the mess and crossed to the bar. I scribbled down places and names—every detail I could remember from my Quinn download.

Joe followed and stood over my shoulder as I wrote. "K, what is this?"

"It's Quinn. Not exactly the way I wanted, but it's all I can give you."

"What are you saying?"

"I'm sorry. For everything. It'll all make sense tomorrow. None of this information will help you until then. So wait. Please, Joe. You can't save him now. No one can."

"Shit! You're talking about a reaping. Kai's thing didn't break it?" I could see the computations in his eyes. Already trying to figure out how to save the world.

I shook my head.

"Then why is it not me?" He reached for me, but I stepped away.

Luke suddenly appeared in the kitchen, smirking as he leaned nonchalantly against the fridge.

So much for staying out of sight.

Joe's gaze flicked to Luke, and his face darkened before he turned back to me. "You *can* stop it, Keres. You are stronger than them." He tried to take my hand again, and I pulled it away.

"No. I'm not."

"Don't do this," he pleaded.

"As you said, new choices make our future, Joseph Fitzgerald, Field Recovery Agent." I held my hand out to Luke, and he *blinked* to my side. "And I've made mine."

Joe looked from me to Luke and back again. His lips pursed into a hard, white line. No lucky eyes, no dancing dimples, and my heart broke. He grabbed the paper off the countertop and, crumpling it, threw it across the room. "Fuck you."

Pushing past us, he left.

Luke tsked. "Humans. You sacrifice *everything* for them, and you're still never enough." He stepped aside and gestured at the doorway. "You can still back out, *cher*. Run after him, convince him you're worth it."

Inside me, Yaffa screamed and pulled her cell door closed. I settled back into the void. "I am dirt."

He brushed his fingers against my face and gave my ear a gentle tug. "Now, you are ash."

And ash doesn't cry.

FORTY-FIVE

While Luke checked with the elite squad of Guardians here to protect us from Daemons, I sat on a bench, waiting. Turning my khukuri over in my hands, I wondered if he would keep his promise: just two more reapings if I would share his life, his future . . .

His bed. My stomach lurched.

Any Guardian in Luke's clan would have given their soul to be in my place. With both power and skill, Luke could fulfill every desire and bring one to climax in ways I doubted Joe ever could. But physical pleasure would never compensate for the loss of what I felt with Joe: the emotion, the vulnerability, the absolute giving.

Shuddering with remembered pleasure, I slammed my khukuri into its sheath. Wouldn't it have been better to have never known such intimacy than to ache for it every day forever? I would be Luke's, however he wanted me, for the rest of eternity.

As if reading my thoughts, Luke appeared next to me and, pulling my face around, kissed me. "Ready, *cher*?"

I stood and shrugged. "Whatever makes you happy."

"Exactly." Taking my hand, Luke led me to the tallest Art Deco building in Baltimore. Quinn would die tonight, and with him, the lead Joe needed to take down his trafficking ring. I hoped to God the information I had written down would be enough to guide him somewhere.

If he ever goes back for it.

You tried, I argued. But my efforts felt overwhelmingly inadequate when I thought about Emily's fear and the hurt in Joe's eyes.

The Bloodlust stirred, and I quickly pushed the grief away. I had to be empty.

Empty kept me in control.

Empty meant I could serve Luke.

Empty would keep Joe safe—even if he never knew.

I inhaled and exhaled slowly, deeply.

"Stop being afraid," Luke said. "It doesn't suit you. This will make you powerful."

"I'd rather be free."

"Aren't they the same?"

"As alike as sex and love."

Luke yanked me closer and turned us into the stone framing the large glass door of the building. His body felt harder and less forgiving than the rock at my back. He slid his muscled thigh between mine and pressed against me.

"Perhaps we should have brought your human as well? I can still make him my pet."

Anger rolled through me, and my Shadow power cracked against his.

He smiled. "*This* is the Keres I want. Defiance and fire." He pushed my arms above my head and held me there, breathing my air, searching my eyes, stroking my desire with his own, until my breathing quickened to match his. My whole body tightened as tingles rolled in waves through my intimate places. I tipped my head back as he leaned close, hot breath igniting the skin of my ear and neck.

When the edges of his passion turned sharp and cutting, I came back to myself with a start.

I had to get better at playing his game.

His lips hovered over mine as he breathed me in. "Power is intoxicating, no?"

I bit his lip, hard enough to taste Guardian blood, sweet instead of metallic. "What else is there?"

Love, intimacy, friendship, giving and receiving. Joe had shown me all of these, but Luke would never understand.

Licking my lips, I *blinked* beyond the glass and beckoned him to follow.

We made our way through now-empty offices where the mega wealthy spent their days moving pieces, collecting rent, and buying up people and real estate. Their injustices were a noxious mold that saturated the floors, discolored the walls, and infected everything it touched. At the top squatted Quinn's apartment, sprawling across a penthouse floor that dripped with dirty, ugly, awful money. The Bloodlust thrashed and growled as I stepped from the elevator, and I grabbed Luke's forearm.

"What do we do if this turns out like Chile? I could level Baltimore and pull the Chesapeake Bay on top of it." My chest tightened, and I gripped him harder.

"It won't." He removed my hand, annoyance tinging his aura. He didn't want fearful Keres. He wanted me fierce and strong.

I swallowed back my next question and continued forward, the dreaded hammer already pounding at my skull. The city shimmered in the dark beyond walls of floor-to-ceiling windows, reminding me of Jerusalem and bodies pressed against the glass—

I shook my head. *Get it together, Keres. Joe isn't an option, and Jerusalem never happened.* I had to be J-Man now—empty and focused on keeping humans safe.

We made our way across the apartment until we reached a closed door, from beneath which seeped angry reds, violent oranges, and pain-filled blues. My body became fire as the Bloodlust howled for death. I felt at least four different humans in the adjacent room, a muddle of emotion made worse by the pounding in my skull and the black swirling at the edges of my vision.

"Ready, *cher?*"

Nodding, I grasped the door handle. As I pushed the door open, I caught the crisp scent of clean mountain air and fresh pine.

No!

Ignoring Luke's outstretched hand, I flicked my gaze from surprised face to surprised face, until I found the one I didn't want to see. As Luke's hand landed on my arm, pain exploded within the back of my skull.

Sad shamrock eyes were the last thing I saw before everything went dark.

Joe.

FORTY-SIX

I floated in a void—rolled gently back and forth by an inky blackness with no shape or texture. Whether I opened or closed my eyes, the darkness was the same. Wherever "here" was, though, it felt comforting rather than suffocating, the warmth of a blanket I'd wrapped around myself thousands of times before. Even sound disappeared here, swallowed by the nothing, leaving only distant lullabies that moved with the current, rocking me into an even deeper sleep.

Rock.

Rock.

Rock.

I tried to succumb, to embrace the peaceful respite, but something *urgent* tickled my senses, keeping me in sleepy awareness. Frustrated, I opened all my senses and felt into the space around me.

Where am I? Everything felt familiar and strange all at once. I strained against the void, but it only wrapped me tighter, taking on substance the more I moved.

‹Shh, shh . . . sleep.› The soft, soothing tones of a

voice not my own drifted along my body, relaxing every muscle, until my breath became steady, my awareness grew heavy, and the void returned to its inviting embrace.

⟨That's it,⟩ cooed the voice.

A few images tried to flit through my brain, and I let them enter and leave. Mountains against crisp, blue skies. A glacier lake. Regal pines. I pictured myself floating there in the sunshine rather than here in the dark.

So peaceful and calm, I finally gave in.

Floating right up to the shore, I pull myself lazily from the water and sprawl on the grass. The sun is warm, embracing my whole body in heat. It reaches through every cold layer, even touching my heart. I am happy. So very happy. It's been so long since I've felt this . . . complete.

I roll over in this magical dreamscape—so warm, so safe. I pull at the grass around me, tugging up individual blades and releasing them into the soft breeze.

Tug, release, tug, release.

They float like dancing green fairies.

Tug, release.

Among the blades of grass dances another shape. So familiar. I sit up and reach for it, but the wind carries it away. Giggling, I jump up and give chase. At the water's edge, I leap and grasp the non-blade in my hand. We are suspended in air—the small plant and I—and I open my hand carefully to not let the wind take it away again.

A shamrock.

The color of luck.

A memory, as listless as the wind, flits around me, but I can't quite catch it. I take the shamrock between my thumb and forefinger and twirl it in the light.

Beautiful and green.

The color of luck.
Lucky eyes.
Joe!
As I inhale sharply, the wind lets go, dropping me into the glacial waters below.

I woke with a start, and the void closed around me, cutting off my air.

Joe! Something felt wrong, so terribly wrong.

I raged against the concrete coffin of nothingness, using my panic as a sledgehammer, but the void swallowed my screams and buried me in blackness that no longer felt safe. It filled my ears and nostrils, slipped down my throat, choked my lungs, and strangled every thought but one—*lucky eyes.* My stomach clenched, and I flinched, waiting for unknown voices to rob me of my sanity.

But they never came.

Just the first voice, slightly louder than before. ‹Sleep.›

I ignored the voice, too caught up in the panic compressing my chest. There were no openings, no outs. Just pressure and panic. All the while, shamrock eyes begged me to hurry.

"Keres, you don't have to do this." Joe's words, sharp with terror, pierced the void. "You are stronger than him."

Screaming silence, I threw everything I had against the invisible power holding me. Instead of shattering, it grew stronger, squeezing until I thought I would die. At the edge of my vision, a flicker caught my attention, stilling my fight—a tank emptying itself of water.

J-Man.

I imagined a stopper being pulled from my feet and all the anxiety, fear, hate, and rage draining from my body. It flowed from my skull, down my spine, through my stomach and intestines, and down my legs, where it emptied into the nothingness around me.

Empty.

Empty.

Empty.

I let the emotion flow, the power of the void flowing with it, until I stood empty in the nothing and the nothing released me, revealing an exit.

I stepped through it, appearing in a long hallway filled with doors, and the opening disappeared as if neither it nor the void had ever existed. In front of me stretched a seemingly endless corridor. Behind me . . .

I gasped.

Two sooty-black hand-carved doors. I moved to peer beyond their broken carcasses, where sickly green lights flickered and laughter mingled with screams.

I'm inside my own head!

The maniacal laughter drew closer, and I ran.

Wake up, Keres. Wake up! But the hallway didn't disappear, and my physical eyes wouldn't open.

Instead, my footsteps echoed behind me, alerting the Bloodlust to my presence, and the mass of voices—hysterical and terrifying—followed the echoes like breadcrumbs. They grew louder, stronger, closer with each footfall, and I pushed harder, racing through the maze of doors and hallways. Joe's pleas led me forward. The Bloodlust's screams chased me from behind.

Until I forced my way into a large chamber and stumbled to a stop.

Luke stood on a raised dais, his back to me. As I followed his gaze down to the round stage before him, my heart thumped heavily.

On the stage flickered two shadowy forms: Joe, his hands raised placatingly, and me.

"She can't hear you right now." Luke's lips shaped the words, but my form spoke them. He lifted one arm across his body, hand curled as if gripping an invisible hilt, and my shadowy form mimicked him, raising my khukuri to strike. "But I promise, she will hear your screams for eternity." His hand—*my hand*—sliced toward Joe.

"No!" I shrieked, and a chorus of voices howled in reply. Bursting into the chamber, the Bloodlust devoured me.

And I let it.

I am the Bloodlust.

I hurled myself at Luke, who spun toward me, eyes wide with surprise and fear.

The Bloodlust is me.

The shadowy forms on the stage wavered and disappeared as I knocked Luke from the dais—forcing him out as I had Ielu. Only this time, the Bloodlust came with me.

I am the Bloodlust.

The Bloodlust is me.

As I returned to full consciousness, wide shamrock eyes met mine. Joe gripped my wrist with one hand, while his other curled futilely around the blade at his throat. Crimson tears dripped down his hand and the side of his neck. He'd need stitches, but he wasn't dead.

He wasn't dead.

I slowly pulled the blade away, careful not to do any more damage.

"Keres?" His eyes searched mine.

I pulled him into me, hugging him until he couldn't breathe. "I did it," I whispered. "I stopped it. I stopped it." Tears ran down my cheeks.

He hugged me back. "Always knew you could."

Releasing him, I frowned at his dimples. "Don't get cocky."

Movement caught my eye, and I turned to face Luke, who was sprawled on the floor at the edge of the room. Pulling Joe behind me, I held my reaping blade ready.

I am the Bloodlust.

The Bloodlust is me.

Power raced along my skin, crying out for death. Glancing around the room, I took in the carnage left behind by the bloodbath of a reaping. I finally knew the truth: the violence *wasn't* mine.

They—Luke and his Guardians—had been controlling me from *inside* my own mind. I swallowed down the vomit burning my throat. I *wasn't* the maker of this madness, only the weapon.

"Liar." I stalked toward Luke, growling. "*Liar!*"

He clambered to his feet, hands outstretched in surrender. "Keres, I—"

"How long? How long have you been *violating* me?"

"It doesn't matter."

"Doesn't matter?" I demanded, and the floor shook. Grabbing Joe's hand, I drew on his peace. I had to stay calm.

"The reaping is done, *cher. That's* what matters. We can go." He tried to act aloof, nonchalant, but he couldn't contain his fear. The black granite of his emotional walls cracked and crumbled, eaten away by terror and panic.

"Fuck. You."

His face grew dark. He lashed out at me, and my aura crackled where his Shadow danced with my Bloodlust.

I am the Bloodlust.

The Bloodlust is me.

With woman and monster united, the speed and agility of my defenses made his attempts to overpower me seem clumsy and slow. Harnessing the violence, destruction, chaos, and decay coursing through my veins, and wrapping it in the calm I siphoned from Joe, I sliced through Luke's shields and threw him into a nearby wall.

Blinking back, he aimed his elbow at my throat, while Shadow swept our legs. Joe dove, rolling to his knees against the desk, and I *blinked* behind Luke, shoving my amplified power into his heart with a hit that sent him sprawling. Gasping, he eyed me over his shoulder. When he glanced at Joe, I *blinked* in front of the human before Luke's gaze could even flick back to where I'd been.

He feigned nonchalance as he stood, but his muscles were tense and fear slicked his skin. Even more telling was the sudden appearance of our protection detail, who mirrored their leader's air of indifference by lazily taking seats here and there around the room.

Joe stepped closer to me.

"You were *inside* me, *controlling* me," I spat, darting my gaze from one menacing smile to the next. My heart sped as my shoulders and neck tightened painfully.

Sighing, Luke leaned on an oversize chair. "When will you tire of this story? You *wanted it, cher.* You wanted it in the desert, calling for power and help. You wanted it after your first massacre. You begged for it, and I gave it to you. And you *liked* it."

"Yeah, she did," said one of the other Guardians. His words crept along the rawest parts of me, and I felt dirty remembering all the Guardians who had entered me for a reaping, interlacing with my soul.

When another Guardian snickered, I threw a wild bolt of Shadow in their direction, knocking them back into a wall. "Shut up!"

Joe touched my side. "They're goading you, K. Don't listen."

Luke's sharp smile glinted in the lamplight. "Don't you ever grow bored of hearing yourself complain? Of playing the victim? God, you're so tedious sometimes." He slashed the air with another whip of Shadow, which broke against the shields I held around Joe and me.

"Bastard."

"If it was so awful, *cher*, why didn't you fight harder? Why did you wait until today to force one of us out?"

"I didn't know—"

"You didn't *want* to know. You could have stopped anytime, but you didn't."

I threw another surge of power, this time at Luke. He dodged, but it caught his shoulder, singeing the fabric. He grinned wickedly.

"I tried," I choked out. I *had* tried. I had run. I had hidden. I had begged. I had pleaded. And every time, I blacked out and woke up amid another massacre.

"Is that what you tell yourself?"

More snickers sounded around the room.

"K, *please*. Ignore these fuckers and let's go."

I knew Joe was right and I should just take him and leave, but I couldn't take my eyes off Luke.

"Oh God, it is." He clicked his tongue. "Tell me, *cher*, when has trying ever made you enough?"

The Bloodlust screamed rage through my throat, and the Guardians laughed.

"Keres . . ."

Joe's words were lost beneath Luke's.

"You *tried* to save a dying man because you thought you were better than the rules of your people. You *tried* to prove yourself more righteous than your *abba* and instead left a perfect trail for the raiders to follow back to your tents. And when all that holier-than-thou blew up in your face, you *tried* to make amends by slaughtering a whole tribe and bathing in their blood."

Flashes of blood-drenched clothing surfaced in my

memory. I felt the blood on my face, warm and slick, and it felt *good.*

"No." I shook, and the building shook with me, my power surging as the Bloodlust and I drew from the world, hungry for more.

It's happening again.

"Don't listen, K," Joe pleaded.

My Guardian held my gaze. "It's true, no? Even now, I can see how much you like it." He stepped closer, power and lust reaching for me, overloading my senses.

"Get out of my *head!*" I threw power everywhere, and Guardians *blinked* out of the way, reappearing closer to me.

"I don't have to be in your head. Your whole body shakes with the Bloodlust, like the first time. You didn't even fight the instinct to kill then. You *slaughtered* them."

"*No!*" I screamed.

"Poor, fucked up, little Keres who has murdered more innocents than all other Aods combined. Yet *you* keep claiming to be the victim."

I gathered all the energy I could—Shadow, Bloodlust, emotions, *all of it*—and released surge after surge of power at Luke as he raced across the floor. His entourage *blinked* in and out, fighting with Shadow as I tried to destroy them and their master.

"You put yourself there, *cher.* No one's fault but your own."

We all stumbled as the rumbling of the building grew stronger, and I strained to contain the rage to this building, rather than letting it spread across Baltimore. A particularly violent shake sent everyone except me to their knees.

Joe struggled to stand near my feet. "Stop, K. Stop!"

Luke smiled up at me. "No one forced you into it. You could've gotten out. You simply chose to stay."

Joe lunged toward a headless body, grabbing for the gun still holstered there. He squeezed off a couple of wild shots in Luke's direction, and I raised my hands to destroy the Guardian with the calamitous power raging through my body. I let go, and the Bloodlust shredded the fabrics of reality as it went, leaving a weird mix of Quinn's office, an X-ray replica, and a too-bright duplicate in its wake.

Luke's face twisted in fear.

Joe yelled my name. Just as my gaze flicked to him, Luke's man—the one who had come for Raven—dragged a knife across Joe's neck.

"No!"

I *blinked* to Joe's side but was too late. I caught him as he slumped to the floor, a waterfall of crimson already washing down his front. Joe's eyes widened as air gurgled from the gaping wound. I watched, helpless, as human hope dissolved into fear—so much fear—then into death. His body strained and shook with the lack of oxygen, until his lucky eyes finally went dark.

"*Nooo!*"

I reached for his glacier lake, for his emotional core, but felt only death—a tangible emptiness that spread and consumed anything it touched. It ate up all my thoughts and feelings, leaving me a cold shell that quaked with energy I couldn't contain.

Luke grabbed my arm. "Keres—"

I released everything I had through his touch and into his soul—cold fury rather than volcanic anger. Flying backward, he crashed through the office's wooden panels and slammed into one of the living room's outer glass walls.

The other Guardians glanced between me and Luke, before *blinking* away, Joe's murderer grabbing Luke's unconscious form. I let them go. I would reap Luke later.

Right now, there was only Joe.

And death.

Though I'd spent a millennium as death's maiden, I hadn't known the depth of its abyss until this moment.

Of its emptiness.

Of its cruelty.

More than the deaths of my father and mother. More than the deaths of my people. Those had left me rage and vengeance.

Joe's loss left me nothing.

I closed his eyelids, unable to handle the sight of the dull eyes that death had robbed of their luck.

"I'm so sorry, Joe. I'm so sorry."

After all the lives lost and taken by my hand, I didn't have the right to mourn this one, but I couldn't stop the grief. Tears dripped off my face as I cradled Joe's body against my chest and howled. I screamed until my voice shattered the glass walls of Quinn's apartment and shook the Earth.

I wanted the world to feel his loss, but killing more innocents wouldn't honor him. Releasing my hold on the Earth, I tore open the skies with lightning and thunder.

And let my heart die.

FORTY-SEVEN

"Fix this." My voice sounded robotic as I stared past outraged council members, directly into Adi's eyes. "Bring him back to me."

I'd gone to Oscar's on Blok M and been both surprised and relieved to find Grease Man—Talon—waiting for me in the empty space.

I didn't think anyone would be here, I'd confessed. I'd tried to say Joe's name, but I choked on the word and could only add, *Said you thought I was dead.*

Yet you're here.

It's the only place I know.

That's what Adi said. Come. I'll take you to him.

With Talon's help, I'd entered Odessa and forced my way into the council chamber. Indignation, sharp as spears, stabbed me from the front, while a hostile army gathered at my back. Neither mattered.

"What have you done, Gatekeeper?" demanded Suri.

"What I instructed him to do." Remorse and sorrow wafted from Adi, but they died in the void that filled me.

I didn't want emotions—mine or others—ever again. Adi stepped around the table and reached for Joe.

I hesitated. "He's mine to carry."

"Not even you are strong enough to carry this death alone." He took the weight of Joe's body in his arms, and I let him—let my arms fall, my body sag.

Malik mistook defeat for defenselessness and rushed toward me. "How dare—"

My reaping blade flashed from my sheath to his breastbone, and he froze. Talon moved to intervene, but Adi shook his head slightly and the Gatekeeper shifted back into his original stance.

I stared directly into Malik's eyes. "Back off, or I will reap your soul and burn Odessa to ash. I wouldn't even have to leave this room." Doubt wafted from him. "Ask Adi about Santiago."

Adi's eyes widened. "You *were* there. By the man and his child?"

Malik stepped back into the fearful crowd of council members and guards, and I looked down at Adi, who kneeled with Joe in his arms. Tears ran down the child's face, their weight heavy against the void, but I didn't care.

"You do not get to cry for him. You do not get to mourn. I saw. I *know*. I thought you were different, but we are nothing but dirt to you." I pointed my khukuri at the boy. "This time, you will *not* do nothing."

Adi reached out with compassion and love. "None are insignificant before God."

"Tell that to the child in Santiago who lost her dad because you wouldn't help him." Despite the empty shell of my heart, tears slipped down my cheeks. "You could have saved him."

"I could have saved the whole city."

My detachment shattered, and I stumbled back, eyes

wide. *They didn't have to die.* Emotion rushed me before I could stop it. Before I could reclaim the void.

"You are no better than the Guardians," I whispered. My stomach churned, and my muscles contracted. Tremors spread through my chest and arms as pain seared my abdomen like a red-hot dagger scrambling my organs.

Looking down at Joe, Adi gently touched the dead man's face. "I simply honor the choice humans made to experience mortality."

Clutching my stomach, I struggled to stay standing, to keep from imploding like a dying star. Malik shouted, and a guard lunged for me, wrapping me in a bear hug and knocking my weapon from my hand. Rheobim rushed to pick it up while Talon wrestled with the guard holding me.

"Let her go!" shouted Adyti, but no one heard her among the chaos.

Inside, I burned, counting the last moments of their lives in breaths.

Inhale. Fire.

Guards rushed in and grappled with Talon, trying to pull him off the nameless guard holding me.

Exhale. Love.

Lahk argued with Malik as Suri and Eibhlín rebuffed the guards who wanted to take them to "safety."

Inhale. Rage.

Rheobim backed away to the farthest side of the room, holding my khukuri like a dangerous animal.

Exhale. Forgiveness.

All of them—little children playing dress-up in a world they couldn't control.

I listened to the yelling as I stared down at Adi and Joe. They had one last chance. ‹Save him.›

Shrugging off his robe, Adi used it to cover the upper half of Joe's body before looking up at me. ‹I cannot.›

‹Cannot or will not?›

He stared at me, searching my eyes. Then, finally, he breathed, "Will not."

Inhale. Death.

My rage gave birth to the Bloodlust. It screamed inside me, the high-pitched screech of metal on metal, and pushed against my skin from within, as if it would tear free and walk into the world on its own legs.

I bled death from every pore as power pulsed from me, knocking everyone over like dominoes and silencing the room. They all turned to me, eyes wide with fear. All except the Ai'Yangs Kulyt, whose eyes held sadness.

"Impotents, all of you." My voice rang hollow and terrifying as it echoed throughout the small chamber. "You play at being saviors, yet you are powerless to protect." Energy pulsed again, stronger this time. Some of the guards who had been trying to stand collapsed, unconscious.

The Bloodlust held me, spoke for me. I felt nothing—*was* nothing—but power and death.

‹Stop her.›

Snapping around, I glared at Adyti, furious. But both Ai'Yangs looked surprised, and I realized the words had not come from Adyti or anyone else.

They had come from deep within me.

Yaffa? I snarled. *Even you betray me?*

‹Do not speak to *me* of betrayal.›

Her sharp retort spurred me to draw in more of this sacred space's abundant energy, feeding the inferno I had become. I would burn them all to ash. Every. Single. One.

Before I could release the firestorm, Adi sprung over Joe's lifeless body and tackled me. As we tumbled, he *blinked*, forcing me through a pair of double doors and into a cell. The walls pressed in, cutting off my power with a shocking suddenness. I screamed and the Bloodlust screeched, but Adi just waited outside, slumped against the door of my cell as he wiped at his wet eyes. Eventually, exhaustion extinguished the flames of my fury.

Struggling to breathe, I collapsed to the floor. "What . . . is in . . . these walls?" Like before, I couldn't access any of my power, Shadow or otherwise. This cell must have been stronger than the one I'd shared with Joe, though, because I couldn't even feel Adi's emotions.

Only mine.

The grief pooling within me like a black abyss scared me more than what I'd almost done to the Daemon city.

Entering the cell, Adi grabbed a glass of water from the sink and made me drink. "The same material the rope bindings are made from. It suppresses or cuts off one's powers, depending on the concentration."

Clinging to the small boy as if he were my sanity, I sipped from the glass between coughing fits. "I hate you." I sobbed and curled in on myself. "I hate you."

"That's okay." He ran a small hand through my hair. "It's okay to hate me."

"I hate me too." I cried harder, feeling the truth of those words. "I wanted to save him, and I ended up killing so many more."

"You tried, Keres. I saw the crater and its distance from every human settlement. You did everything you could to mitigate the damage."

"But it wasn't enough."

"Trying is *always* enough," Adi replied.

"People still died!"

"Even God lost people he loved by trying to do the right thing."

"But you have the power to save them. All of them. Why didn't you?" I sobbed snot and tears into my shirt. "Why didn't you save him?"

Grabbing my hand, Adi pressed it to his forehead and closed his eyes. In my mind, a spool unraveled, impacting the world in big and small ways as its thread wove in and out among people and events. It disappeared into a nothingness that was neither good nor bad. It just was.

When the images disappeared, Adi opened his eyes. "Can you see where Joe's death leads?"

I wiped my face with my shirt. Grief tugged at my soul, but I said nothing.

"I won't say his death was necessary, but its impact is already rippling into a future I cannot see—a current I'm unwilling to change. For better or worse, he's dead. We must accept it. Feel through it. Grow with it. We'll create meaning on the other side."

"Feeling through it could mean the death of everyone in Odessa. In the world." I shuddered. So many souls to reap, and the Bloodlust hungered for the chance.

"I believe in you."

"So did Joe, and look where that got him."

"You put the knife to his throat?"

I tried to forget the red smile cut into Joe's neck. "I might as well have."

"Is Emily responsible for Sergio's death, then? If she hadn't been so alluring to a pedophile, if she hadn't gotten caught, if she hadn't been used the way they used her, you wouldn't have killed that man, right? So it's her fault."

"You know it's not! She was a child, used by people who should know better. I am—"

"Also a child, used by people who knew better."

"It's diff—"

"Enough! Let others answer for their actions. As long as you insist on being responsible for others' choices, you will never be empowered to take care of your own."

"And Santiago?"

The child-leader stood, kissed the top of my head, and moved toward the cell door. "Rest. I'll come back for you. I need to talk with Rheobim about bringing his informants in. It's time we had answers."

"Unless you've turned a member of the Conclave, you won't get what you need from your spies."

He peered at me intently. "We have to try." He stepped out of the cell, closing and locking the gate behind him. "For your safety."

"And yours."

Daemon guards dragged Raven, kicking and screaming, into the cell across from me, Chinese curses filling the air. "*Cào nǐ zǔ zōng shí bā dài*! Fuck your ancestors!"

She spat the last insult through the metal gate they'd closed behind her, and I laughed. She turned to glare daggers in my direction but relaxed as soon as she saw me. Sitting down, she leaned her back against the wall with one shoulder against the bars.

"To the eighteenth generation? You must be pissed." I moved to the door of my own cell and mirrored her position. "I'm glad you're okay. I was worried."

"I raised you better than that."

"Than to worry?"

"Than to run from Guardian arms straight into Daemon ones."

I laughed. "Then what are *you* doing here."

"You abandoned me, remember? One minute, some Daemon healer is treating me; the next, guards are dragging me here, shouting nonsense about Soul Reapers."

I blushed.

"Shit, Keres." She turned to meet my eye, one eyebrow raised high. "What were you thinking?"

When I couldn't hold her stare any longer, I looked away . . . and told her everything. I explained Jerusalem, V, Daliah, Kai, the attempted banishment, the Burn Cycle, and Santiago. She stopped me here and there to ask questions and clarify. She seemed especially interested in my vision in the desert of choosing my blade and becoming an Angel of Death. She skimmed over Chile, Luke's request, and Quinn's reaping as if none of it surprised her, and barely reacted at all when I mentioned, through choked words, Joe's death.

"Who?" she asked.

"Joe—the blond human with the green eyes."

She rolled her eyes. "Not him, the *Guardian* who slit his throat."

I flinched. "The one who came for you in Baltimore."

"Ah, Seth." She shifted her weight a few times and picked at invisible specks on her clothes. "I'm sorry," she finally said, "about your human."

"Don't lie, Raven." She didn't know how to be sorry.

She shrugged. "Fine. I don't know why you got so attached anyway."

I smiled. "There's the Raven I know." She was hurtful and spiteful and would never win any mother-of-the-year awards, but she was mine and she felt like home.

"Luke?" she asked. "He let you go?"

"He wasn't in any condition to stop me."

Her face brightened, a smile playing at her lips. "Dead?"

I shook my head. "Unconscious. The other one—Seth?—grabbed him and disappeared while I was . . . distracted."

Raven stood and paced. She had that look—the one that meant she would either praise me for exceeding her expectations or string me up and stab me for insubordination when she was done. As she returned to the bars, the fire in her eyes made me grateful we were both in cages.

"Keres, I think I know how to break the Contract."

Oh. It was *that* kind of fire—just as dangerous, but it wouldn't have me bleeding . . . yet. I turned toward her, gripping the bars.

"I think if we reap the Guardian who turned us . . . I think that will break it. There can't be a contract without both parties."

I stared at her, trying to find the loophole but coming up empty. Her idea was ludicrous and insanely problematic, but logical. "You're talking about reaping Lucifer. How could we even get close to him, let alone reap him?"

She shook her head. "Lucifer didn't offer us our Contracts. Luke did."

"What?" I yelled.

I paused, waiting to see if the guards would come storming in. When no one did, I turned back to Raven and whispered, "What are you talking about?"

"Each Conclave member is responsible for finding and creating their own Angels of Death. They create the bonds. *They* are the other side of our Contracts."

"But it wasn't Luke who appeared to me; it was—"

"Luke disguised as Gabriel."

"You knew?" I held up my hand. "Wait, of course you knew."

"*Some of us,* daughter, grabbed at scraps where we could, discontent with the offerings of our Guardian masters, not succumbing to them." She crossed her arms over her chest, her lips pressed into a flat line.

I ignored the insult. "What aren't you telling me?"

She leaned against the wall, pulling her face back into the shadows. "Much, but none of it matters right now."

I moved to my knees, gripping the bars so hard, my fingers turned white. "It all matters."

"More than the death of your human?"

I sat back on my feet, leaning my forehead against the warm metal. "You're sure you're right?"

"Of course not. But it's worth trying, isn't it? If nothing else, shouldn't Luke pay for what he did to *Joe*?"

Her words resonated. *Yes*, Luke deserved to die. Even Yaffa, locked deep inside me, called for his blood. For the first time, all the pieces of my fractured soul seemed to agree.

"All right, I'm in. When Adi comes back, I'll ask to speak to the Council. We'll convince them Luke is their only option for answers and we're their only option to get to Luke. I'm assuming you know how to find him?"

She nodded. "There's only one place Seth would take Luke: the Nether. If we're lucky, he'll still be there."

My smile felt wicked and terrible. "And I'll make sure he never leaves."

FORTY-EIGHT

I had given up on sleep—and Adi—hours ago. I may not have expected to be freed, but I had thought he would update me. I needed the chance to convince him that capturing Luke warranted releasing me. Then I would kill Luke, break my Contract, and disappear like J-Man had.

Let these fools fight their own war.

Sighing, I rolled onto my back and stared up at the blank ceiling. That wasn't what Joe would have done.

Then again, when I closed my eyes, all I saw were his dead green eyes staring back.

It no longer matters what Joe would do.

My cell door squeaked open. Snapping my gaze to the entrance, I tensed when I spotted a tall silhouette that was definitely not Adi.

"Keres."

I recognized the voice instantly. When the figure reached for me, I grabbed their hand and rolled out of bed, pulling them to the ground beneath me. As I settled atop them, the tiniest bit of light gathered around their face, highlighting Daliah's fiery hair with gold.

"I should kill you," I hissed, reaching for her throat. I couldn't reap her without my blade, but I sure as hell could rip out her windpipe and make breathing difficult for a while.

She didn't move as my hand closed around her flesh, didn't try to stop me. She just stared up at me, her eyes swimming with emotions I couldn't *read*.

"I'm sorry."

I stilled.

Two words. The same two words I'd offered her for reaping Ielu. Beyond the emotion, I saw my reflection in her eyes. What had she done that I hadn't? Angel of Death and Daemon—we were more similar than different.

Releasing my hold on her throat, I climbed to my feet. As I did, something deep within me unclenched, like an invisible hand loosening its grip.

"Why are you here?" I didn't bother to whisper.

She stood slowly. "Adi."

"Why you?"

Her gaze flicked to the cell's entrance. "Releasing you is . . . unsanctioned . . . and the penalty for anyone caught setting you free is steep." She crossed back to the open cell door, peered both ways down the hallway, and motioned for me to follow.

I didn't budge. "What aren't you telling me?"

She hesitated. "You're officially prisoners of war."

"What?" The word came out in a breathy hiss.

"The Council was split, but those against you won out."

"I bet they did."

"Adi will explain." She stepped out into the light of the hallway. "We're running out of time."

Walking to the doorway, I hesitated at the threshold and thrust my chin at the double doors Adi had brought me through earlier. "How do I know Kai isn't waiting for me on the other side?"

"You don't. All I can offer is this." She held out her hand, closed in a loose fist, and waited for me to place my open palm beneath it. When her fingers opened, a small coin the size of an amusement park token fell into my hand. My mouth dropped open. "To keep you safe from Daemon power until you reach Adi."

Nodding, I tucked her sacred token in my pocket and stepped out of the cell. When she turned to leave without opening Raven's cell, I grabbed her arm.

"Daliah." I pointed at my mentor, who watched us silently from the shadows. "Not without my Xiiph."

"Adi sent me for you." Daliah didn't protest, though, when I crossed to her and pulled the keys from her hand.

"All or nothing." I released Raven from her prison and tossed the keys back to Daliah. "Let's go."

We went not to Adi's house as I expected but to the Gate House, where row upon row of empty arches supported the balconies above. There were no shimmering-liquid crossing gates, no scenic doorways to earthly locations. Only the songs of our reaping blades echoing through the otherwise silent, empty building.

Tensing, I reached for the void within me where the Bloodlust slept, careful not to wake it until I needed it.

Daliah held up a hand, and we stopped. As she disappeared around the corner, I touched my Xiiph's wrist and leaned in close. "Adi can read thoughts and emotions."

"Who is he?"

"Head of the Daemon Council." I squeezed her arm when she opened her mouth to ask more. "We don't have time. Stay neutral while we're with him, or he'll know."

Reappearing, Daliah motioned for us to follow and led us to the small group of Daemons who waited for us, Lahk and Adi at its center. I handed Daliah back her token and moved toward the group.

As we approached, Adi offered up both my khukuri and Raven's sickle. I wondered why he had brought both blades when he'd sent Daliah to fetch only me, but I didn't bother questioning him as Raven and I sheathed our weapons. A current of fear wound its way through the group, but no one objected.

"Come," Adi beckoned. "Time is running out."

"Where's Adyti?" *If she's not here, does that mean—*

"Home trying to make everything look normal." The boy led our party to one of the empty arches. "Let's get you safe."

"Why aren't we *blinking* the hell out of here?" Raven whispered from behind me.

Adi looked up at her, tilting his head to the side as he studied her. "Daemon cities are shielded through all layers. No one can *blink* in or out. We must use a doorway."

"But I thought these all stayed closed at night."

"I happen to know the guy in charge." Adi winked—a *Joe* wink—and my chest tightened. Talon stepped from behind one of the columns and nodded, before turning toward the opening and raising his hands.

"Where are we going?" I whispered. Raven muttered something in Chinese about hell, and I glanced at her sharply. We needed them to trust us, and for that, we needed to stay neutral.

"I have a few places that can keep you safe from these Daemons until they come to their senses." Adi's voice was tight, and for the first time, I realized his little neck and shoulders were rigid, his small hands clenching and releasing. I'd never seen him like this.

"Daliah tells me Aods are enemies of Odessa right now."

Adi's gaze flicked to Daliah, who blushed and looked away. "For now."

"Running won't prove we're not."

Beside me, Raven almost choked, but I held my calm as Adi peered at me, gaze sharp and unrelenting. I emptied my mind and heart, careful to speak only truth.

"Wouldn't it be better to offer a sign of good faith? Like bringing in a member of the Guardian Conclave?"

Everyone turned to face me. Even Talon stopped chanting to stare openly, gaping slightly.

"Who would you suggest?" Lahk asked before Adi could respond.

I kept my eyes on the boy as I answered. "I know him as Luke." Adi frowned. "Head of the Conclave."

"You're sure he's the head?" Lahk asked. When I nodded, his eyes widened. Meanwhile, Raven paled, her emotional aura shrinking in on itself.

The aged Daemon man pulled at his beard. "If we'd known, I'm sure Rheobim would have sent more than Ielu and Daliah." The seemingly ancient man crossed to the red-haired warrior, who couldn't hide her flinch at the mention of her mate. "I am sorry, dear girl. Our lack of insight caused you great harm."

"We both knew the risks." Despite the assurance, her gaze was distant in a way I knew well. What-ifs were already tumbling through her head.

"It's too dangerous." Distrust shrouded Adi as he studied me, but nearly everyone else had already grasped the promise of sweet fruit. If it worked, my suggestion could turn the tides in the War, and we all knew it.

"Do you have a plan?" asked Talon. "One does not simply ask a Damned to dinner."

"I wish Rheobim were here," Lahk interjected. "This feels like a suicide mission at best."

Ignoring the interruption, I continued to address Adi. Lahk and Talon could debate all they liked, but the real power rested in the boy's tiny hands. "That force you felt in the council chamber? The one that knocked out a few guards and immobilized the rest of you? That was nothing. A heartbeat of energy. I hit Luke with all of it, everything I had. He fell unconscious and had to be carried away before I destroyed him."

Talon grunted, raising his eyebrows at Adi. "He's probably down, but that already-small window is closing."

Adi wavered, and I pressed my advantage. "Which means we have one chance to take him. His people will have moved him to his estate by now. A place in what he calls the Nether Layer, with one gate in and out, defended by his elite."

I left out that all my information came from Raven. They didn't trust her yet, and I didn't have time to convince them.

Talon shook his head. "Then all is lost before you begin. I would have to know *exactly* where the gate is tethered, down to a pinprick of precision, to force it open."

I smiled at the Gatekeeper. He'd solved the one part of our plan we hadn't worked out. I'd worried we'd have to wait for someone to open the gate from the other side.

"Then we're in luck. We have someone who knows exactly where that prick is located." I chuckled darkly.

"We do?"

I nodded toward my Xiiph. "Everyone, meet Raven. Raven, meet everyone. She's Xiiphronai—a type of general among the Angels of Death—and one of Luke's most trusted Aods. She's been to the Nether often and knows what we're looking for but not how to open it."

Talon studied Raven, frowning. She scowled back. "Then how can we trust her?"

"Perhaps she should ask the same question of you?" I held up a hand when he tried to ask another question. "Look, neither of our kinds are super excited about the other, but we're wasting time. Either you want Luke or you don't. I'm tired of running, tired of hiding, and tired of people hating me for who I am. If giving you Luke stops that, then I'll do whatever it takes to capture that bastard and bring him to you."

My heart pounded, and passion buzzed along my skin. *I* almost believed myself.

Lahk approached Adi. "The plan has merit. And the Council will have to rescind its decision if she returns with a Conclave member in tow, head or not."

Adi reached out and pulled me down to his level. Placing his hands on either side of my face, he peered intently into my eyes. "What aren't you telling me, Keres?"

"That I'm terrified," I answered honestly. I let the fear pour from me. I truly was scared. Scared that this wouldn't work, that Adi would learn the truth before I could try, that Luke wouldn't be where we thought, and that I'd never have my chance to avenge Joe.

Adi stared at me for an eternity, and everyone else seemed to hold their breath, even Raven.

Finally, he nodded. "Then I will go with you."

"No." The entire group whisper-shouted.

"We can't allow that," Lahk added.

"I've already confirmed it with Adyti. It is done." Adi stared down each individual until they nodded or turned away. Then he looked at me. "If two Soul Reapers are willing to risk their lives to save the people who once rejected them, then surely this humble servant can risk his to make sure they return."

‹*No!*› I projected to Adi.

‹I go, or no one does.›

I couldn't say anything more, not without spilling the truth, so I nodded.

"Let us at least send you with more warriors," Talon insisted.

Adi shook his head. "I don't want to divide our people any more than I already have. I won't make soldiers choose between love for me and loyalty to the Council."

"Then let me go," Daliah said. "I've already chosen."

Raven rested a hand on her sickle. "More Daemons, more problems."

Daliah nodded. "A small party is more likely to go undetected. We don't have time for reconnaissance—not if Talon is right and our window is closing. Ielu—" The name caught in her throat, and she coughed. "Ielu and I almost took him alone. If we can catch him unconscious, we'll be able to bring him back without casualties."

She turned to Raven. "Surely one Daemon escort would not go amiss."

I placed my hand on Raven's. We couldn't afford any more of Adi's suspicion. "Thank you, Daliah . . . if Adi approves." I looked at the small boy, one eyebrow raised. Before he could respond, Daliah knelt before him.

"Please, Ai'Yang. Ielu would be so ashamed of me." She bowed her head, staring at the floor. "I have so much to atone for."

Adi looked at me. He would feel the same emotions I did—confusion, love, despair, resolve. The rock of anger she'd been clinging to had finally dissolved into a mess of grief and shame. She needed somewhere to direct her emotion, some action to take, or she would be lost to whatever cause came next.

Grabbing her hand, he helped her rise. "Daliah—"

"Please."

He nodded, and she threw her arms around him.

Returning to her usual stern posture, spine straight and shoulders back, she turned to Raven, all business. "You know the layout and guard positions?"

"A small but elite welcoming party just inside the gate. Luke thinks he's safe in his Nether Layer, and his pride will be his downfall. As long as they don't sound an alarm, the walk between the gate and his house will be empty."

"And inside?"

"Trickier. But he doesn't keep a lot of warriors there, so it can be done."

I glanced out the large windows of the second floor to a lightening sky as dawn drew closer. "I vote we discuss specifics when we get to Luke's crossing gate. We settled, then?" I looked around the crowd, and each conspirator nodded, Adi the last to agree.

I turned to Talon and adopted the most patronizing voice I could muster. "Gatekeeper, take us to Boston."

"You'll get a door to wherever I damn well want to send you." Despite his bluster, the area between the columns wavered and solidified into a large park next to a giant parking sign that read *Boston Commons.*

Perfect.

I stepped through with Raven, followed by Adi, Daliah, and finally Talon. Lahk and the remaining Daemon guards clung to each other—a collective of hope, fear, and uncertainty—until the doorway winked out of existence.

"Where to next, girl?" Talon asked gruffly, belying his fear.

I rolled the khukuri in my hand, admiring the soft blue glow of the runes. When I smiled at Raven through the darkness, she smiled back.

"Show them, Raven."

FORTY-NINE

Once Raven had shown Talon the tether he needed, she gripped her sickle. "Open the gate. I'll go first."

I touched her arm. "You shouldn't go alone."

"We need a plan," Adi said at the same time.

She shook her head. "I've been summoned enough that the guards on that side shouldn't question my presence. I'll take them out and return when it's safe."

Daliah stepped closer. "Is that wise, Fallen? There's a reason we always send at least two Daemons to confront a Damned."

Raven laughed. "Your"—she waved her hand at Daliah's face—"*glow* will have them sounding the alarm before you've even stepped from the gate."

Frowning, Daliah nodded. "And the landscape once we're inside?" She looked at the horizon. "We don't have much time until dawn."

"What happens at dawn?" I asked.

Talon's eyes narrowed. "The Daemons will hunt us, if they haven't already started. And this time, you'd go straight to the Hall."

I shivered. Raven didn't know to be afraid, but I doubted she would survive the Hall. I certainly wouldn't a second time.

Raven grabbed a stick and began scratching out a scene in some nearby dirt. "Then don't make me repeat myself." Once done, she used the stick to point at the drawing as she explained. "Luke's part of the Nether Layer: gate, trail to the house, and manor. I'll take out the three guards at the crossing gate. We'll find another two at the front of the house and another two at the back."

Daliah studied the drawing. "Not a lot of protection."

Raven shrugged. "Guardian pride." She dragged her stick from the gate to the open area around the manor house. "Together, we follow the trail, skimming along the tree line to approach the house from the far side. Best point of entry is the conservatory. From gate to door will be a good ten-minute run."

"No *blinking*, I assume." No way Luke would allow that in his stronghold, but it didn't hurt to double-check.

The Xiiph shook her head. "No anything. According to our *Aishah*, he sealed off this part of the layer. Even if someone found their way to the Nether, they wouldn't be able to find him."

"Why would he tell you this?" Daliah's face stayed neutral, but distrust seeped from her aura.

Raven turned to her. "The hunter does not worry about what the tiger hears when she is already in his trap." Anger and fear warred in the Xiiph's emotional aura as various images grew and popped like bubbles around her: running through a skeleton forest under a blood-red sky, falling, spikes piercing her thigh, wrenching free and running again, and overlying everything, Luke's warped smile.

Adi stepped up to her, placing a small hand on her forearm. "I am so sorry."

She flinched as though he'd bitten her. Her face twisted into a sneer as she forced her emotions back into a chaotic neutral. "Everything comes at a price."

Adi sighed but left her alone, squatting beside the drawing instead. "We'll have to cross in front of guards to get to the conservatory. Why not enter the house through the same side as the trail?"

Raven frowned. "Closest entry point, hardest fight to Luke's room."

"Will the front sentry be missed if we take them out?" Daliah pointed to the front doors. "Otherwise, we're trying to sneak through a forest hauling a lifeless body on the return."

"We're wasting time." Raven pointed at the conservatory again. "We avoid the front guards and go through here. It's an easy shot to the back stairs, with only a couple of rooms and a small hallway between us and the quick climb to the third floor. These back stairs are rarely used." She glanced at the redhead. "You can take out the sentry on the way back if you're so clumsy in the woods."

Daliah's lips settled into a hard line, but she didn't say anything more.

When everyone nodded, Raven drew a series of lines inside the house. "The third floor. Luke's quarters span the back of the house, but the entry is here." She drew a couple of marks about halfway down the long hallway.

My eyebrows rose. "You've been to his bedroom?"

She met my gaze but didn't answer. "And beyond that,"—she circled the rest of the floor—"his elite. He usually doesn't have more than a dozen or so at a time in his house, often less. But I'd recommend we don't find out."

"Then back down and out the way we came," Daliah said. "So, ten minutes to the house, ten to get in and out, and fifteen back to the gate. Sound right?"

Raven nodded.

Adi's emotions were unusually quiet as he looked up at the Gatekeeper. "Does that give us enough time?"

Talon stared back. They didn't speak aloud, but Adi gave the slightest of nods. The Gatekeeper returned to the tether point Raven had indicated, opening a gate of liquid silver that shimmered in the shifting darkness.

Raven turned to me, her emotional chaos flickering like the runes on our blades. "Impress me," she breathed. Glancing at the others, she stepped through the gate.

"What if she fails?" Talon asked.

"She doesn't know how."

But as a few minutes stretched into five and then ten, my confidence wavered. After the incident with Elijah, I knew she didn't need to reap anyone to incapacitate a few guards, but what if they'd added more guards to the gate because of Luke's condition? What if they'd captured her, imprisoned her? What if they were gathering a small army in the Nether to come after us?

I would do many things to slaughter Luke like the pig he was, but I would *not* sacrifice these people who'd become my . . . *friends?*

"Adi—"

Raven's head poked through the shimmering wall of liquid, delight racing across her skin. "It's done. Come." Her head disappeared.

Our small group released a collective exhale. Holding up a hand for us to wait, Daliah stepped through the gate. She quickly reappeared and gave the okay. Adi went next, but Talon grabbed my arm before I could cross.

"I don't trust her. Your Raven."

I pulled my arm from his grasp. "She doesn't trust you either. I don't know if our two kinds ever will."

He humphed but didn't argue. "I'll open the gate

again in thirty-five minutes and hold it for one minute. I'll open it for one minute every five minutes after that for as long as possible. Which won't be very long."

"You should have told Adi."

"I did. I wanted you to know. Because after that, you are on your own."

"You would leave Adi and Daliah?"

"I won't have a choice. The Council will come, and I will be stripped of my power." His chest and stomach abruptly tightened—I felt it as if the sensations were my own—but just as quickly, he shrugged away the fear. "We all knew the risks."

"Come with us."

He shook his head. "Every layer has its quirks, meaning I may not be able to open a gate from that side. Besides,"—his smile didn't reach his eyes—"who will stop the wave of Damned if they call for reinforcements?"

My eyes widened. "You would give your life to protect our gate?"

Nodding, the large man embraced me roughly, awkward but fierce. "You have won me, Soul Reaper. Bring the Damned back, and you will win more. Not even Malik will be able to refuse you."

I hugged him back and stepped through the gate without reply. I couldn't let him see my shame.

FIFTY

A silver sun peeked out over the tree line, bathing everything in metallic light and making the crossing gate almost invisible—a rippling shadow rather than a door to another world. A large elm-like tree dominated the clearing we stood in, its black skeleton stretching long fingers into a sky so thick and red, I reached up to see if I could wipe blood from the heavens. My hand came away clean.

"Where are the guards?" I whispered. It didn't seem right to talk here.

Eyes wide, Raven pointed at Daliah.

"Banished," the Daemon replied.

I shuddered.

Adi glanced around. "This place feels wrong."

I nodded. "Let's hurry."

Raven led us through the dense forest as the silver sun set, leaving a thick, oppressive night in its absence. My heart pounded in my throat, and for a split second, I believed I was back in the Hall.

It's not thick enough, I told myself. I could still make out my hands and the shapes of my companions. Inhaling deeply, I kept running, following Raven down the trail and along the tree line. We only slowed once to avoid drawing the attention of the two guards chatting at the front of the house.

When we were sure no one was watching, we dashed to the glass wall of the conservatory and made our way to the door, which didn't even have a locking mechanism. With a turn of the knob, we were inside.

"I don't like it," Daliah said. "This whole place is too . . . empty."

"What do you suggest?" I asked.

"We turn back," Adi said. "Hide you."

"We are too close to turn back now." My heart beat heavily, and I prayed he wouldn't hear it. I *needed* this, but once it was done, I knew there would be no Daemon to protect me from the Guardians and no Guardians to protect me from the wrath of betrayed Daemons.

Just me and my Xiiph. Avoiding both sides. Forever.

I swallowed hard, locking down those thoughts, and Adi frowned at me.

"I *must* see this through to the end," I whispered. "There is nothing left for me if I don't."

"I could force you to leave."

"But you wouldn't. You're not a Guardian." He did not force; he invited and led.

Finally, he nodded.

Raven's emotions were a mess, her whirling chaos disrupting my focus as we crept down the short hallway between the conservatory and the house. She stopped at the end of the hall. Based on her crude drawing earlier, we should go right, pass two rooms, and take a quick right into the next hallway, which had the stairs we needed.

"Any chance one of your powers is seeing through walls?" she asked Daliah, who frowned.

I reached out with my Reader ability. Two people. Their emotions grew stronger with each second, which meant they were walking toward us. I opened my mouth to share but shut it again when Adi shook his head slightly.

‹No one can know.›

I nodded slightly.

"Two," he whispered.

Raven raised an eyebrow.

The boy stared back, giving nothing away. Instead, he crept to the edge of the hall, pushing Raven behind him. When the voices were almost on top of us, Adi stepped out, wrapped both men in his power, and pulled them back into our hallway before they even knew to open their mouths. Daliah made quick work of binding their hands as the two Guardians gaped at our band of four.

When Daliah produced a vial of clear liquid from one pocket, Raven turned her back, vomiting fear like a child with the flu. My stomach churned. After all we'd seen, what could affect a powerful Xiiphronai this way?

Morbidly curious, I focused on Daliah as the Guardians thrashed against their restraints, screaming silent protests that couldn't break through her light. The Daemon warrior moved through the banishment ritual quickly. As she whispered the last words and passed her hand over each Guardian's heart, black claws burst from each of their chests, folding around each one's body as though reaching for a bear hug.

The Guardians' silent screaming grew more frantic as the claws pierced their backs, ripped them open, and pulled the two halves back toward their hearts. Slick crunches mixed with the popping of bones as the claws continued reaching and pulling, the monster inside each immortal scraping him open in layers, until nothing remained but a black stain where the Guardian had once sat. The dark blotch slowly disappeared, like fog from a window.

I shuddered. It had only taken seconds, but the image had seared itself upon my soul.

I stepped up beside Daliah. "And *this* is what you and Kai had planned for me?" I didn't know whether to be pissed or terrified. Maybe both.

She dropped her gaze. "I wanted you to feel what I felt when Ielu died." When she looked back up, tears filled her eyes. "I am sorry, Keres. I was wrong."

I squeezed her shoulder but said nothing. I didn't trust myself to not throw up. Instead, I turned to Adi, whose sadness brushed against me.

‹Why?› I projected to him. ‹Why so awful?›

‹A banishment only releases truth and ushers the soul to where it belongs. They received what they created.›

‹Your grief is *wrong*. You can't have it both ways—awful end *and* sadness that they're gone. It's twisted.›

‹Mourning their pain, no matter how terrible their existence, does not lessen the need for justice. It aligns me to love. I am not sad they are banished. I am sad their hate became too strong to overcome.›

Aloud, Adi added, "Lead on. We are running out of time."

Raven led us through the house, past two rooms, down the longer hallway leading to the back of the house, up the servant stairway, and out onto the landing of the third floor. We only met two other Guardians along the way, poor creatures who were more servant than power and whom Daliah banished as well.

After the last—a servant girl who simply knelt and cried silently until the claws took her—Raven turned on Adi. Her whole body shook, anger rearing as she tried to control her fear.

"Where do they go?"

Daliah stepped between my Xiiph and the boy. "To the place of endless night and torment."

"What the hell is that supposed to mean?"

I shuddered. "You don't want to know." I tugged her away from the Daemon woman, channeling calm in her direction.

Still, Raven's emotions danced on a razor's edge as we traversed the final hall, a wide, ostentatious corridor that offered little in the way of protection or cover. Her tension heightened my own, until I thought I would snap.

"Finally!" Releasing a huge breath, Raven motioned us toward a short entryway, bringing our group face to face with a large pair of sooty-black wooden doors.

I gasped. I *knew* these doors.

They were *my* doors.

The ones Ielu had broken when he set the Bloodlust free.

FIFTY-ONE

Twisted, broken bodies climbed over each other, their faces turned up with mouths opened in endless, silent screams—identical to my inner doors, which had been damaged by Ielu and obliterated by his brother, Kai.

My stomach churned. Had my internal doors somehow molded themselves to reflect these, or had he commissioned these based on the manifestation of my madness? Bile climbed up my throat, and I turned away to keep from vomiting as strange tingles, like bugs crawling beneath my skin, spread from my fingertips, up my hands, and into my arms.

Raven tried to open the doors. "Locked."

Daliah tried opening them, without success. "Strange that the only locks in this house are on his bedroom."

Raven tried again. Even Adi brought his power to bear against the wood, but they wouldn't budge.

The tingles racing up my limbs intensified into sharp needles as they rushed over my shoulders, up my neck, and into the back of my head. I stretched my neck and flexed my hands, opening and closing my fingers.

"Damn it!" Raven whisper-yelled.

"We'll have to find another way in," said Daliah.

"We don't have time," Adi replied.

"Maybe we should have kept one of those Guardians," Raven spat.

Ignoring the growing tension, I stepped forward. As I reached out a shaking hand, my heart beat erratically.

The moment I touched the wood, a soft click cut through Raven and Daliah's whisper-fight, and all eyes turned to me. Swallowing hard, I pushed open the doors.

I'd expected opulence, grandeur. Something of the arrogance and power Luke embodied, like the home we'd shared in New Orleans. But this room held nothing—no paintings, no mirrors. Just two pieces of furniture: a king-size bed squatting atop a large dais opposite us and one oversize chair far to the right, turned to face the window. The whole room felt sad . . . *intimate* despite its size, as if I'd been given a glimpse into Luke's barren soul.

Adi grabbed my hand, his gaze darting around the empty space. "I don't like it."

I reached out with my Reader ability, sensing only one person: Luke. "This is what we came for." I pulled my hand free and continued inside, a dark pit growing in my stomach. I hustled across the floor and up onto the dais, pulling back the sheer curtain surrounding the bed. "It's him," I confirmed for everyone else.

Luke's chest slowly rose and fell as his face twisted with emotions muted by sleep. Despite my better judgment, I reached into his madness, peeling back the layers. Fear blanketed everything. Beneath that, anger, hurt, and . . . *loneliness?* His painful emptiness surprised me, reached for me, begged me to relieve it.

Not an insight I wanted right before reaping him.

I looked up when Raven and Adi joined me beside

the bed. Daliah remained near the entrance, watching the hallway.

Adi's concern brushed against me from the right. "What is it?"

To my left, Raven's whirling chaos quieted to dark determination. "Remember Joe."

I reached for my anger and my grief and let them devour my compassion. The rage stirred the Bloodlust and became my shield and sword against Luke's internal abyss. I pulled my khukuri from its sheath, the runes already glowing a soft blue.

"You came to reap him." Adi spoke the words as a statement of confirmation, not surprise, and my cheeks burned. Shame chewed through my belly, heart, and throat, chilling the vengeance pounding through my body.

"He deserves it." I stared at Luke's chest. One strike and all my problems would be over—my contract terminated, my vengeance claimed. I only had to forsake my yearning for this child's acceptance and love.

I hesitated.

Raven leaned closer, her shoulder brushing mine. "Do it."

"We all deserve something," Adi replied.

I peeled my gaze from Luke to stare at the boy, pleading with him to understand me, to support me. "Don't I deserve freedom?"

"Is that what you think this is? Kill him now, and you'll be trapped in a prison far darker and more eternal than your Contract has ever been."

"How would you know?" Raven almost yelled.

"Keres . . . *Yaffa* . . ." Adi placed a small hand on my forearm, and I trembled. "What about all the lives preserving his could save?"

"You mean all the *Daemon* lives his knowledge could

save. Why should I care? What have *your* people ever done for me?" Tears burned my eyes.

"What about other angels of death? What about the humans? His knowledge could help us save and protect so many more."

I thought of Frat Boy and his lucky eyes. All those children he'd tried to save but couldn't because I'd murdered his only lead. What had he said? Something about children being prostituted around the city? Like the Aods being prostituted through the centuries for darker thirsts. What Emilys and Jameses could be saved if I let Luke live? What other Aods? I thought of the angel in the Parisian alley. Who would save him? Who would save me?

All of it came with a sacrifice.

My life for theirs. My vengeance for their salvation.

"But Joe . . ."

"Is already dead," Adi replied. "Killing Luke won't bring him back."

Raven hauled me out of the way to confront the boy. "Letting Luke live won't either." She pulled her sickle from where it hung at her hip.

Daliah raced toward us, ready to attack, but Adi waved her off. Grunting her disapproval, she stopped at the foot of the dais, back stiff and muscles tight.

Raven glared at Adi. "Luke is too dangerous. Hell couldn't hold him; what makes you think Daemons can? Nothing you do will make him talk. Luke. Must. Die."

The song of her blade crescendoed, filling me with its song. She had a point. And what would happen if he broke free? I wasn't safe while he lived. No one was.

Raven glanced at me, fire burning in her eyes. "Save us, Keres. Save us all. Kill him."

Daliah moved toward Raven again. "We're taking this Damned back to Odessa."

When Adi touched her arm, the Daemon warrior stopped and stared down at him, questions swimming in her eyes. Her mouth dropped open. "You're kidding!" She pressed her lips into a fine line, her nostrils flaring. "Fine!" She crossed back to the open door, her hands clenching and unclenching as she glanced between the hallway and my Xiiph.

Adi focused on me. "I won't stop you." Sadness filled his gaze, and his disappointment hurt more than I would have thought possible. He stepped down from the dais.

Catching his eye, Daliah jerked her chin toward the hall impatiently, and I had to agree. We had two, maybe three gate openings before the Council caught Talon.

Adi nodded and looked at me. "The choice is yours."

"Will you hold the gate?"

Stepping past Raven, he threw his arms around my waist, squeezing so tightly, it hurt. "I will *always* hold the gate for you." Suddenly, we were no longer talking about interlayer travel. "And I'll never stop believing that one day, you'll step through." Releasing me, he joined Daliah and grasped her hand. He watched me for a moment longer before turning to leave.

Love emanated from him even as he left. It wrapped me up and swallowed me whole. Yet I didn't feel trapped; I felt free. For the first time in forever, I felt free. Because no matter what I chose, this tiny little being would love me. Forever. No conditions, no rules, no strings. Just love and acceptance . . . and forgiveness.

When Adi turned away, so did I. I lifted my khukuri high above my head, ready to sink it into Luke's sad and twisted heart.

"For us," Raven whispered.

"For all of us." I plunged my reaping blade toward Luke's body.

Only to bury it in the mattress beside him.

For all *of us.*

Silence lay heavy over the room as I hunched over the bed, gripping my blade. Even Raven's whirling tornado of emotional chaos had shattered, leaving behind only a harsh emptiness.

"What are you doing?" Raven asked, voice flat.

I remained still, breathing until the runes flickered and went dark. Straightening, I pulled my reaping blade from the mattress and slid it back into its sheath.

Instantly, the fire of Raven's rage reignited, like a welding torch ready to liquify anything it touched. She grabbed my arm. "Keres, what are you doing?"

Laying my hand on hers, I squeezed. "Trust me." She might not understand now, but this would be better for us.

I gently removed her hand and called to Adi. ‹Wait!› Grabbing one of Luke's limp arms, I pulled his body over my shoulder and rushed off the dais.

Raven followed, grabbing my arm again and spinning me around. "Explain yourself!"

"I'm giving myself time."

She gaped at me. "For what?"

"To stop choosing hate." I thought of Joe's brother, Patrick. I wasn't sure it was possible, but I wanted to try. I wanted to be capable of the love Adi gave so freely. And I wanted—someday—to feel that love for myself and Yaffa.

Raven howled in frustration as Daliah and Adi re-entered the room. As her howl morphed into a rage-filled scream, she rushed me, sickle raised to strike and runes glowing a bright, hot blue.

"No!" Daliah threw herself in front of me as the reaping blade descended. Time seemed to slow, as it had on the rooftop a million ages ago. I caught every detail yet had no power to alter events.

Daliah threw up a shield made of light, and in this extended time, it blossomed like a flower opening its petals to the sun. Raven twisted to avoid it, her sickle descending—*tick-tick-tick*—like the second hand of a clock. Adi ran to help me as I shifted Luke to keep him from the bite of Raven's blade. We all moved too slowly, our bodies dragging through the resistance of time.

Tick.

Tick.

Tick.

Until with a final twist to her sickle, Raven plunged it into his chest.

Not Luke's, but the boy's.

Too slow, Keres. Always too slow.

FIFTY-TWO

Can't breathe. Can't breathe. Can't breathe.

As Raven unhooked her blade from Adi's tiny chest, Daliah, Adi, and I collapsed like puppets whose strings had been cut. Luke rolled from my shoulder as I pulled the small boy into my lap and stared up at Raven.

"What have you done?"

She bared her teeth, the curve of her mouth as sharp as her sickle, and glared down at me with wild eyes. "You were supposed to choose *me*."

Daliah sobbed uncontrollably at my side, speaking the words I sought. "Don't go, Adi. Don't go." Anger slid out with her tears, sizzling as it hit the air—a stark contrast to the cold that now filled us both.

When Raven laughed, Daliah's anger surged, and she lunged for the Xiiph, just as a band of Guardians raced into the room. Light fiercely fought Shadow, but Daliah's hatred and rage made her sloppy—feinting instead of parrying, attacking when she should have defended. Her gaze never left Raven's face, not even when Guardian shackles clamped around her wrists.

Seth stepped into my line of sight. "Take her to V. The Conclave Mistress is looking forward to her new pet."

Daliah thrashed against the chains as the Guardians pulled her backward. Headbutting one, she pulled free and lunged forward to spit in Seth's face. Two more Guardians raced in to secure her. As one grabbed her in a choke hold, Seth landed a jab to her gut and a hard left hook to her jaw, dazing her while other Guardians enclosed her in Shadow.

Seth sneered. "V likes feisty."

With vile grins, his men dragged Daliah from the room. Meanwhile, I just sat there, impotent, as she fought and lost and was taken away like garbage.

"The rest of you take care of the Daemon at the gate."

We'd lost—and my friends had paid the price.

"It's not your fault," Adi whispered. Though something moved beneath his skin, it looked different from Ielu's reaping.

Seth turned to Raven and frowned. "What now? This isn't what we discussed." His voice sounded more whine than command.

I stared at the too-small form in my lap. "Please." Tears burned down my cheeks, and I ran a hand gently over Adi's face and through his hair. "Please stay. Please, Adi, please." I rocked him, just as I had little Uri, holding my heart in my hands. The last twelve hours had done more to break me than the last thousand years. "I am so sorry I did this to you."

"Shut up," Raven spat at Seth. "It's not too late to fix this."

Their argument became white noise as Adi laid a hand on my face and brushed away my tears. He pulled me closer. "Please, Keres," he echoed. "You have everything you need."

"I am exempt from grace, remember?" I tried to smile but didn't succeed.

"You only have to claim it."

"I don't understand."

Storming away from Seth, Raven turned her roiling anger on us. "Sweet, really, but let's speed things along." When she reached for Adi, I tried to stop her, but Seth yanked me back by my hair. Adi slipped from my arms with a thud, and I screamed as Seth's Shadow power climbed over my body, crushing me to the wooden floor.

Raven rolled Adi onto his back and placed a hand on his chest.

"None of this is what you think," he told her.

"Everything is just as I want it." Her gaze flicked to me. "Almost."

I tried to yell his name, but it came out as a strained whisper—not enough air in my lungs for the two tiny syllables. I tried to rouse the Bloodlust, to access the Death power it had granted me, but it seemed indifferent to my plight. I wasn't angry; I was empty—so lost to the void of grief and failure, the Bloodlust remained silent.

Defeated, I remained still as the ripples beneath Adi's skin sped up, moving back and forth across his flesh like a typewriter pressing letters against the ribbon of his body. Throughout it all, he held my gaze, peace and love flowing from him—until everything paused.

He smiled. "You are a most beautiful star."

Abruptly, the ripples rolled back, as if erasing what the invisible typewriter had written. The faster they rolled, the more transparent Adi became, until the final particles of his being fell to the floor like grains of sand. A gentle breeze blew them away, curling around me as it passed.

"Don't let them make you feel that you are the night," the breeze whispered, before the air once again fell still.

"What the hell was that?" Seth demanded.

"You're the Guardian," Raven replied.

"*You* said he was part of the Daemon Council."

"*You* said you could guarantee Luke's demise at Sergio's reaping! I've been planning this for *centuries*, and you fucked it up."

I stared at the spot where Adi had lain, my shattered heart darkening without the boy's light. The void widened inside me, and I became lost in its nothingness.

She planned this.

Seth stepped in between us. "*We*, Raven. *We* have been planning this for centuries. I am going to be your new Aishah when he's gone. Don't you forget that." He tried to imitate Luke, pulling light from the room to make himself seem bigger, but he failed to impress. He'd even released his Shadow hold on me in the process.

Raven shoved past him and kicked me in the ribs. "Why can't you ever just do as you're told?" She kicked me again, and my body flopped across the floor like a rag doll. "The raider. The reapings. Baltimore. Tonight. If"—*kick*—"you'd just"—*kick*—"listened!"

A broken rib pierced my lung, and I gasped before it mended. Finally interested, the Bloodlust purred.

It watched her.

And I watched it.

She pulled a small knife from her belt, one she'd used on me countless times before, but I wasn't afraid anymore. What was the point?

"What about *Luke*? If he wakes, we're fucked." Seth frowned at me, his bravado dissolving into the stench of fear.

She ignored her simpering Guardian and dropped to her knees, pushing me onto my back. "All you had to do was run!" She stabbed me in the abdomen.

The Bloodlust smiled, and the corner of my mouth turned up.

"Stupid . . . fucking . . . bitch!"

She dug in and twisted, reopening the wound over and over. The Bloodlust licked its lips; my tongue moved across my own.

"All you had to do was *not* choose *Luke.*"

She lost control, the knife popping in and out too many times to count. Blood covered her hands and face. The Bloodlust chuckled, and I laughed up at her.

She buried her dagger in my right eye. When that didn't stop the laughter, she pulled the blade out and stood, using her boot to wreck my face.

"*Always* him. *Always* choosing *him.*" Her whirling chaos engulfed her in a grand storm. Lightning slashed the air as I continued to laugh, a strange, distorted sound that wheezed through my broken bones and mending teeth.

"Enough!" Seth yelled. "She's all we have left to reap Luke, and I *refuse* to fall because of your shit plan!" When she didn't stop, Seth grabbed her arm. "I command you to stop!"

Raven's reaping blade flashed through the air in the space of a breath, and Seth's severed head thudded to the floor, rolling toward me, eyes wide. Raven didn't like to be touched, but maybe he hadn't known that.

I licked the blood from my teeth. "He didn't realize he was *your* pet, did he?"

Returning her sickle to her belt, Raven bent over and grabbed my face. "Would you keep choosing Luke if you knew the truth?"

"There is nothing left to know."

Her smile grew sharper than her blade. "Your raider? The one you saved. He didn't die." She leaned close, her lips brushing my ear. "I killed him. At Luke's command."

Dread blossomed in my stomach, and my head spun. "What?"

"You keep saving him. *Choosing* him. But *Luke* was the one who ordered your family's murder."

"I don't—"

"I slit the man's throat. I tossed him to his people. I led them straight back to your camp. I suggested they drag your body through the desert, and *I* watched until Lucifer came to grant you your immortality." Tears gathered in her eyes, but she held my gaze, lifting her chin against the hurt that raged in her emotional aura. "But it was *Luke* pulling the strings. *Luke* whispering the commands. All I could do was make you strong. Keep you safe. Love you more than he ever could! But you kept *choosing him.*" She released a string of Chinese curses. "All you had to do was stay away."

"Gabriel wasn't Luke?"

"*That's* what you got from what I just said? No, Gabriel wasn't fucking Luke. Lucifer is the only one strong enough to create an Aod. But *Luke* is the reason for all this! And I could have saved us." She grabbed my shirt, pulling me toward her. "I still can. I only have to dispose of Luke, and Lucifer will make me a Guardian. He promised. Then I can save you." One bloodied hand brushed my face and hair. "But I'm not allowed to touch him, Keres. Part of my bargain. I can't reap Luke. I *need* you. Do this one small thing for me, and then *I* will save you. *I* will love you."

I pulled back, crawling away. "You've been working with Lucifer. All this time. And . . . *my family* . . . you knew." I felt sick. Hollow. A thousand years of blame I never deserved for an outcome I never could have altered. And Raven didn't just know, she'd *made it happen.*

I rolled to my knees and vomited. When she reached

out to brush my hair back, I flinched. "Stay away from me."

She snatched her hand back and crossed to Luke's bed. "Will you reap him?"

"Your deal with Satan? Before or after my people?"

She shrugged. "Luke *had* to have you, and that gave me power over him."

"Before. Or. After?"

She met my eyes. "We all make sacrifices."

I screamed into my vomit, banging my fists against the floor. The Bloodlust danced around my grief, lapping at the edges and begging for rage and anger to feed it power. "I hate you! I hate you!"

Raven's whirling tornado of chaos broke open, unfurling into a tidal wave of darkness. "You still choose Luke, then?"

Click. The furnace of my rage ignited, and the Bloodlust howled. I stood, wiping vomit from my lips with the back of my hand.

"I choose me."

FIFTY-THREE

In the space of a breath, I inhaled all the energy I could reach—from the once-blood-red skies above to the molten core of the world below—and exhaled a rushing river of *ending* power aimed straight at Raven. It exploded around her, shattering the bed into less than splinters and showering the trees outside with plaster and glass.

My chest heaved from the effort, and my legs shook. As I stepped forward to grab her sickle and reap her, an unseen force gripped me, tossed me into the ceiling, and slammed me down on the floor.

Raven stepped from the cloud of destruction I'd created, smiling tightly. "You didn't think you were the only one to harness Spirit, did you?" She swiped her hand through the air, and I flew across the room, knocking over the chair and crashing into the wall.

Grabbing the Shadow at her feet, I pulled, sending her sprawling, and raced back toward her, throwing spurts of the power she must have been referring to as Spirit—that extra force I'd been using since holding back the ocean. I packed away the zillion questions crowding my brain and focused on killing my Xiiph. Before I could reach her, I slammed into an invisible barrier and staggered backward. Driving a shadowy spike into her wall, I hammered at it until the barrier shattered, and groped for her legs with dark tendrils.

Raven rolled toward me, throwing sharp slices of Shadow as she came to her feet. Her form became a whirl of knees, elbows, and hands intermixed with bursts of power. My Bloodlust screeched, and I countered with shadowy whips, daggers, and spears. Shadow and Spirit broke across Spirit and Shadow as we each used all our power trying to defeat the other. I struggled to do more than defend myself as energy built inside her aura, the same way I collected it in mine.

I would only have one chance, and I didn't want to use it to shield.

I punched, a hair slower than I should have, and she grabbed my wrist with one hand, pulling me toward her as the other brushed up my arm to chop at my neck. There, as her hand passed my shoulder, was the opening I'd wanted. Releasing all the energy I held, I screamed as cold fury shot through our arms and hit her in the chest and chin. She flew backward onto the dais that had contained Luke's bed.

The house shook, and the Nether Layer screeched in protest, but no one came. I strained deeper, clawed higher, drew in everything I could, until I reached the brink of the Burn Cycle and had to fight back the Bloodlust as it screamed for more.

I have to be stronger. I have to be stronger.

Forcing the power away, I collapsed to my knees, exhausted. Raven lay face down on the floor, unmoving. Her chaotic aura flickered but never went out. Falling back, I stared out the hole I'd created in the back side of the house. A handful of stars bled light into the horrid darkness of the inky-black sky.

Laughter came from Raven's direction, and I turned my head tiredly. She was pushing up from the ground.

"You are a fool, Keres. You always go all in without thinking." She lifted my khukuri, and my hand flew to the empty sheath at my side.

My eyes widened. "When—"

"*Zhǒng guā dé guā, zhǒng dòu dé dòu.* It's time to reap what you've sown." She stalked toward me. The khukuri's runes glowed bright blue as it sang of death.

Shit.

She sliced the blade down, and I raised my hands to protect myself.

‹Claim the price.›

The soft voice spoke in my mind, and suddenly, I sat on a hill under a sky littered with stars.

"The requirement can be met," the boy says.

"You're talking about forfeiting my soul," I reply. "Forever. There's no coming back from that."

He shows me the cycle of the sun and moon, of the day and night. "Forever isn't as long as you might think."

Then I'm in an unknown room, sitting across from a giant of a man with blazing-white hair. One eye is purple, the other blue. I want to cry because I know he's dead.

"Who gets the soul, Keres? Who?"

Understanding creeps over me like the rays of a rising sun. A cycle. It's a cycle. I don't have to destroy *his* end of the contract.

I have to destroy mine.

"But will it work?" I ask.

"You are everything you need."

❦

I wrapped one hand atop Raven's on the hilt of my khukuri and grabbed the sickle hanging from her hip with the other. Using a quick scissoring motion, I yanked her blade up from her belt as I pulled down on mine, severing her hand at the wrist just before my reaping blade plunged into my chest.

The runes glowed the brightest blue I had ever seen as the khukuri slipped into my flesh with ease.

"No!" Raven pulled the knife from my chest with her remaining hand. "No!" She stabbed me with the blade. Once. Twice. Several more times, but my blade remained quiet and dark.

The reaping was already complete.

I chuckled. *All that time spent running from this moment . . .*

Searing lights swirled beneath my skin, chasing each other through my veins and organs, disintegrating both spirit and flesh. I smiled. My tormented birth as an Angel of Death had burdened me with darkness and shame, but now, as my fiery death burned those away, I felt only lightness and hope.

As Raven raged beyond my collapsing vision, I pressed my hand to my chest and drew as she had taught me. Energy raced through my body in an infinite loop, accelerating with every circuit. Overwhelmed by the lack of an exit point, my soul exploded into a galaxy of stars.

FIFTY-FOUR

My intelligence swam among the stars. I was all of it and none of it, everywhere and nowhere, beautiful and glorious amid the darkness of life.

Was this what Adi had seen all along?

Beyond the span of my galaxy, Raven stood frozen, her face contorted by the chaos that defined her, her soul a shattered glass glued together with hate and self-loathing.

Here in this space, I saw everything, could *be* everything, if I chose. Layers were meaningless here, time non-existent. Had I wanted, I could have moved forward into could-bes or backward into yesterdays. I stood in the past, present, and possible futures, all at once. They all overlaid each other, shifting as people chose, acted, and chose again. I couldn't change anything, but I could see and, maybe one day, understand the patterns.

I wanted to stay here, detached, where things simply *were*—the all-seeing eye with no emotions clouding my vision. But the slight tugging I'd felt since being born as an Angel of Death grew stronger. Glancing around, I discovered that each star of my soul was tethered by an almost-imperceptible thread—an umbilical cord taking, rather than giving, nourishment. Raven had one as well, though hers was dormant, as if waiting to be fed.

As the pull grew incessant, my galaxy collapsed into a tiny cluster of stars. The tethers collapsed together as well, forming a single tube that sucked me down a path my curiosity encouraged me to follow. I didn't feel fear, not really. Fear didn't exist in this state, but I also knew I wasn't free.

Free. Freedom. Need to be free.

My light shone brighter at the thought. But I wouldn't *be* free as long as these cords existed to siphon energy from my soul.

I turned toward the pull instead of fighting against it and sped faster along the tether. Other lines soon intersected mine. Some dormant, others carrying energy. They wrapped around each other—threads forming strands that twisted into thick ropes.

I passed other Aods frozen in this in-between space and time. Some had dormant cords like Raven, but those in the process of reaping were bright with energy, their cords feeding both the Guardians wielding them *and* this thing that drew me toward its center.

They lied to us. They all *lied.*

My collective of stars raced through layers I knew, but most I'd never seen. I flew across a foreign landscape and into a majestic building, through carved doors and towering pillars, until I passed into a massive room filled with people who couldn't see me. On a throne at the end of my line, his torso writhing with innumerable tentacles of energy, sat the man Adi had shown me in his garden.

Lucifer.

Too many ropes to count carried an unending supply of power to the God of the Damned, shifting and moving as if alive.

My curiosity satisfied, I fought against the momentum pulling me toward him. I reached back along the tether to my reaping blade. I tried to use it as an anchor, to wrench myself back, but the pull was too strong—a current careening off a cliff.

My power felt insignificant against the enormity of his. Worlds would fall into orbit around him.

Perhaps they already did.

Someone in the room fell, and the prince smiled. For a moment, I saw him as the center of the Universe—bright, powerful, shaping the course of everything. I *wanted* to follow wherever he led. I wanted him to see me, to love me. I would have done anything to have him smile at me in praise.

But then I remembered Adi, Daliah, and Joe. Even my broken, terrible Xiiph, more afraid than angry when seen from this space. I thought of my family, sacrificed upon the altar of *his* lust for power. Power taken through the Angels of Death, bled from each of us until, empty, we were discarded for the next.

The more atrocities I cataloged, the more his allure faded. He remained breathtaking of face, but his soul radiated a darkness deeper than black and more terrifying than the Hall. I shuddered.

I reached for the power I'd used in my previous life, but everything was too disjointed. I could slow my movement but not set myself free.

Yaffa, I called. The stars shifted, and her face, made of light, turned to my awareness, connected but separate. *We need to be one.*

Yes.

I pictured her huddling in the cell I'd forced her into when everyone else had died. Locked there for being too weak to slay a raider. Too weak to save her people when the raiders eventually came. Too weak to say no when vengeance was offered in place of humanity. I had blamed her, hated her, buried her so deep, I had thought I would never have to see that part of myself again. Yet I could never escape myself.

Perhaps I never should have tried.

But I don't know how, Yaffa. I'm so sorry.

Her constellation of stars reached for mine, a hand extended in friendship. I took it.

I know, she replied. *I forgive you.*

Yaffa reached for the Bloodlust, the part of me I'd labeled a monster, and it turned toward us, its mutated face a constant shifting of grotesque forms. I flinched away and it howled, but Yaffa kept reaching. She held it, loved it, appreciated it, until I saw my own face reflected in its stars.

I am so sorry, I said to that form. To the thing that had only tried to protect me and save me. *I am sorry I hated you.*

I know, she replied. *I forgive you.*

What's next? I asked them both.

You must forgive yourself too.

With Yaffa guiding, we held each other close, pouring all the darkness from our past into a river that carried it away. We poured and poured until three became one—Yaffa, me, and the Bloodlust as one whole instead of three separate parts.

I was humanity, uncertainty, and death.

And hope. I was also hope.

My disjointed star cluster melded into a single beaming light, burning brighter as judgment and guilt gave way to acceptance and mercy. I finally felt whole and complete.

I pulled energy from this layer and every other layer I could reach, almost limitless power pulsating from my tiny, beautiful star. As I neared Lucifer's chest, I released it all, and light exploded through every energy-sucking tentacle attached to his soul.

All energy traveling toward him slowed to a stop, like a rubber band reaching its apex, before shooting back toward its starting point. Lucifer's eyes widened, and he stared down at his chest, running his fingers through lifeless, severed cords. His face twisting in anger, he shifted his gaze to mine, as though he could see me as a fully formed being rather than an invisible pulse of soul energy. The anger faltered as his eyes widened further, recognition and surprise sparking within them like fireworks.

He reached for me, but as his fingers began to close around me, my tether snapped back, pulling me out of his grasp and through the layers that kept him separate from my world. His rage echoed in my soul, and I was gripped by a fear unlike anything I'd ever known.

A problem for tomorrow.

Back in Luke's bedroom, my light grew and took shape, until I stood whole, all my parts connected as one. There was no longer a me and a them, only an us.

Only myself.

Raven's eyes finished their blink, her face still twisted in rage, though it quickly melted into fear when I pulled my khukuri from my chest. Its song still filled me, but the runes had disappeared.

"Impossible," she whispered. "I saw you explode."

I flexed and moved my body, and Raven stumbled back. I couldn't have been gone long, but it felt like an eternity. I loved being back in my Aod form.

Raven's eyes darted around the room, and her hands shook. "What—"

"We are no longer bound to Lucifer." I searched inward for that pull. Incredible, hungry power still lingered there—mine from all the souls reaped and energy taken—but the thirst for *more*? The insatiable need for death? All gone. "I broke the Contract, Raven. *All* the Contracts."

"Not possible."

"Look for yourself."

Her eyes unfocused for a moment before she backed away from me. "No. No!"

"It's over," I said. *Finally, it's over.*

"Tell me you killed him."

"I destroyed the tethers binding us to him."

She shook her head. "You don't know what you've done."

"I freed the Angels of Death."

Fear climbed like a snake up from her belly and wrapped around her throat. "You woke the Dragon, and now our blood will run like rivers!"

As I gazed into her swirling chaos, I saw—as I had when I was just a galaxy of stars—the past, present, and future overlaid on each other. The promise of a prince, her current plans undone, and the terror of her future—an image of curled shavings scattered around the floor beneath a table where she lay skinless, bleeding and broken.

My eyes widened. "Raven, run."

She turned and leaped through the opening in the wall. Despite myself, I hoped she could find a place to hide from the monstrosity who sat atop his throne. Not even Raven deserved him.

I sheathed my khukuri and hooked Raven's sickle through my belt. Grabbing Luke's still-unconscious form, I raced to do whatever I could for Talon. By the time I arrived in the grove, the gate was already too small for me to climb through and closing.

No. I refused to accept defeat.

I reached into the gate with Spirit power, as Raven

had called it. I had no idea what to do, but I felt around for anything that might reverse the closing. Pushing as far as I could, I bumped into a barrier that was moving toward the Earth layer. As it retreated, the tunnel allowing travel slowly collapsed behind it.

Grabbing it, I yanked it toward me. For long moments, it hesitated, stuck between layers. Finally, though, it gave in to my power, racing back to the Nether. Once the gate was fully open, I crossed everything and, hoping this wouldn't plunk us in the empty expanse of space or worse, stepped through.

Talon stood on the other side, surrounded by a small group of Daemons headed by Malik. I watched as the last Guardian screamed his way into Darkness, earsplitting without Daliah's power muffling the sound.

I stepped up beside the Gatekeeper. "I'm back."

He glanced at me and then back at the point where the gate had been. "Remind me *not* to ask you how you managed that. I don't think my delicate sensibilities could handle it."

Malik shot toward me, but Talon stepped between us. "The others?" demanded the council member.

I placed my free hand on Talon's shoulder. He glanced at me questioningly but moved to the side.

"Sacrificed themselves to bring you him." I laid Luke at Malik's feet. "The head of the Guardian Conclave."

The Daemons eyed him warily, the soldiers tense. Malik's brows rose high as he frowned, but he didn't argue. Instead, he snapped his fingers, and the closest set of warriors surrounded Luke. "Take him to Odessa before he wakes."

As they wrapped him in golden cords, Malik turned

to Talon. "Gatekeeper, can you open a door straight to Odessa?"

Talon opened a portal, and the warriors carried Luke through.

Malik placed a tentative hand on my shoulder. "We have misjudged you, Fall—Keres."

"There is still much for both of us to learn."

He nodded. When he moved to step through the doorway, I touched his arm. He stopped and turned back to me.

"I've freed the other Aods. I don't know what that means."

He nodded. "I'll talk with the Council. We'll need you on our side." He stepped through, leaving Talon and me alone in the cold morning.

"Talon. They have Daliah . . . *alive.*" My tears began to fall. "I couldn't save them, any of them. All the power and I still couldn't save them." *Does it matter that their sacrifice allowed me to save my own kind?*

He pulled me into a rough embrace. "It's not your fault."

I paused, searching for my truth. "I hope to believe that someday. I just wanted so much for this to turn out differently."

Releasing me, he stepped back. His aura swirled with determination and wonder—oranges, yellows, and purples twirling like autumn leaves. "All is not lost. We will find Daliah, and your offering will turn the tide. That must be enough for today. Come with me to Odessa and rest."

I handed him Raven's sickle. "Keep it safe."

"For your friend?"

"For all of us. One less blade is one less threat."

"So you won't come?"

"I have some things I have to do first."

He grasped my forearm. "No peril in the fight."

I returned the gesture. "No glory in the triumph."

He entered the portal, and the window to Odessa closed behind him. Whatever bubble we'd been standing in burst, and the sound of early-morning traffic crept into the silence.

I *blinked* to Baltimore—*my* damn city. The place that would hold my heart for as long as I held my soul.

Because of *him.*

Because of Joe.

I crouched on the rooftop where Raven had once threatened to kill me as the rising sun peeked between buildings and glinted gold off skyscrapers.

Night had ended.

Dawn had come.

Thank you, Adi, for guiding me through the darkness.

I didn't know where to go from here. I'd freed the Aods from Lucifer's Bloodlust, but not from the Guardians' hold. I'd made a tenuous alliance with Daemons who feared us as much as Aods feared them. And I'd fucked with the Dragon's plan.

Somehow, I knew, Aods and humans would pay the price.

A death light lit up the Baltimore skyline, and I smiled grimly.

I couldn't save the world, but I would be her tourniquet.

I dropped from the building and *blinked.*

EPILOGUE

Talon let me know when they gave Joe's body to his family so I could watch for his funeral. His family made it simple but beautiful, just like Joe. My breath caught the first time I saw Pat. Not because he resembled Joe—because he did, though shorter and stockier—but because of those eyes.

Those damn lucky eyes.

I had to leave before Joe's friend Tony finished his ridiculously irreverent graveside speech. My broken heart couldn't hold anymore grief, but Joe would have loved it.

I wished I were one of them, mourning alongside the others. People who could have known me as Joe's girl, who would have put their arms around me and cried with me. But our worlds were different, and in their world, I couldn't exist.

In my world, Joe never should have come.

What could I have said to them? What would have been my words at the casket if our worlds had been the same?

"Joseph Fitzgerald, Field Recovery Agent. You've left

a hole in the heart of every person present, including me. And I don't even know your middle name or if you even have one. I don't know where you grew up or who your people are. I don't know your favorite color, ice cream, or sports team. Did you even like sports? Did you like evenings or mornings or afternoons? Did you like naps? Holidays? Vacations? What did you dream of, Joe—besides saving the world? What did you secretly desire that you would have told no one but me? I should know these things, right? As the woman who loved you and killed you, I should have known at least one thing.

"But I don't. I only know your character and the way you made me feel. I know your heart is bigger than the whole world. I know you always put others first and are the best of people. I know you tried every day to be a better person than you were the day before. And I know you loved your brother fiercely and endlessly. I know you would do—*did* do—everything for the ones you love, even giving your life for a friend. I know because you gave it for me and for the children you wanted so desperately to save.

"Dear God, you're so annoying! Why couldn't you think of yourself for once? Why couldn't you walk away? Then I wouldn't be hurting. I wouldn't be missing you like this. You were my air, Joe; only I realized it too late. My air, my sun, my light, my life. And now I can't breathe. I can't breathe.

"You were spring breezes and summer sunlight. You were cool nights filled with fireflies and red wagons over-flowing with childhood magic. You were the peace of a glacier lake tucked away in snow-capped mountains. And you were laughter and dimples and lucky eyes.

"Thank you for saving me—just some girl who first mistook you for a frat boy and then an enemy before finally accepting you as a friend and lover. Thank you for choosing me, for loving me, for forgiving me, and then choosing me again.

"I don't deserve you. I never did. But I choose you too, Joseph Fitzgerald, always and forever. I choose you too."

That's what I would have said at his casket . . . if I were just a girl, rather than Death.

I wandered the cemetery for a while, not even sure of my direction until I came across a gravestone with a name I recognized.

Sergio Ricci. Born. Died. No epitaph. Just a name and dates.

It seemed wrong to have people like Joe and Sergio buried in the same ground, sharing the same space. But perhaps they needed to be—a balancing of the ledger. We all have sins, Joe told me once. We all were in need of some kind of redemption.

Turning to leave, I bumped into a woman who'd walked up behind me with her head down. She looked up, revealing a tear-streaked face, and blinked a couple of times to clear away both tears and fog.

She pointed to Sergio's headstone. "You know him?" When I nodded, she threw her arms around me and thanked me for visiting.

She was the widow.

"I'm sure he was . . ."

"A monster." Her words were woven with a bitterness that soon dissolved into sadness and self-loathing. "But he was all I had." Her eyes begged for forgiveness and peace, neither of which I could give her. When I didn't speak, she added, "I should have done something . . . anything . . ."

"You should have." She flinched, but when I placed a hand on hers, she grasped it as if it were a lifeline. "But you can't change the past. You can only choose something different in the future."

"Something different?"

I looked at the grave and then back at Sergio's widow. "We all deserve second chances. Do something meaningful with yours."

I walked away.

"Unexpected," called a familiar voice.

My heart jumped into my throat as I turned. He leaned against a tree, lucky eyes dancing as the wind tugged at his hair.

"Joe?"

I *blinked* to him, threw my arms around him, and almost pulled him to the ground in my need to prove he was real. Eventually, I released him so I could take in every one of his features. I traced his eyes, nose, lips, dimples, and jawline. My fingers traveled up into his hair and tried to undo the tousle caused by the wind.

"It's not possible," I whispered, terrified I might be hallucinating. "How?"

He shrugged. "Not sure. But I'd bet my life a certain kid had something to do with it. Some nonsense about the end of a thread."

I punched him in the chest. "You're not betting your life on anything. I just got you back." He tried to look sorry as he rubbed his chest, but the corners of his mouth danced and his eyes gleamed mischievously.

"Adi?" I asked when my brain caught up with the rest of what he'd said. "He's dead, Joe. Reaped by Raven."

"I wouldn't tell him that. I understand he's having a great time stirring up trouble in . . ." Joe hesitated.

"Heaven?"

He struggled, trying to find the right word. "More like a waiting zone."

"Like a terminal for the departed?"

Joe laughed. "Think less airport and more European village. Or at least what I *think* a European village might look like. I've never been to one."

I smiled. "I could fix that."

He held out his arm for me, offering me our own little world within a world, and I took it. This was the world in which I always wanted to be.

"There is a war coming," Joe said as we walked toward the cemetery gate.

"I know. I can *feel* it."

"You have a plan?"

I shrugged. "Sort of."

He smiled to his dimples. "My favorite kind."

It wasn't really a plan, though. Just a hope.

ACKNOWLEDGMENTS

Behind every book is an army of people. Thank you to that army.

To my hubs, Joe, thank you for holding my pieces together and beating your "write the story" drum every time I wanted to quit. Ours has been a journey for the ages, and I know I wouldn't have made it here without you. (But could we *pretty please* have a less exciting life for a hot minute? I know I'm an expert at this whole "dark night of the soul" thing, but I could really use a break. *wink wink*)

(Oh! And no matter how much you claim Joseph Fitzgerald is based on you, he's not. Fitz simply refused to pick a different name. Take it up with him. *laughs the last laugh*)

To my "wifies," Laura and Birdy, you are my ride or die (from long before I even knew what that meant). I am so ridiculously grateful to the conference that brought us together, the retreat that solidified our friendship (yay for Thai food and death rattles!), and the enduring connection that has taught me how to be a better writer, human, woman, and friend. I didn't know this kind of friendship was even possible. Thank you for your encouragement in all I do and your love for all I am.

To the early beta readers and champions of this book, thank you for bushwhacking through the first-draft messes I called a story. Even when it was ugly, you kept believing in me. While the years have taken us to so many different places, I still hold mad gratitude and love in my heart for our time together: Liza, Eve, Amina, Sierra, Kathy, Corey, Lina, China, Melissa, Kelly, and Lydia.

To my editor, Tod—damn, man! You've made *Soul Reaper* look good! Thank you for your brilliant editing and for being a cocreator at my side as we worked my garbled ideas into a cohesive, beautiful world. (I am sorry for my utter failure at grammar and punctuation.) *Soul Reaper* would not have shone this bright without you. There are still so many moments when I read something that makes me laugh or cry and I think, "This is really good. Did Tod sneak it in?" Hehe. Your editing strips away everything unnecessary and leaves the best to shine. Thank you!

To the incredible humans at Balance of Seven—Ynes, Leo, Charlene, Deana, and Roberta—thank you!!!! You are the unseen heroes behind this book. Thank you for making this experience better than I ever imagined. I appreciate your patience and flexibility with my health challenges, and your always-listening hearts that have been as dedicated to this book as I am. I had simply wanted help to get *Soul Reaper* published. Instead, I found partners and friends. You all are brilliant, and I appreciate you (individually and collectively) so very much.

To Lance, my cover designer, though we have never spoken, you created a cover that is everything. Thank you for hearing my vision and translating it into a stunning visual representation of Keres's story. (And Ynes, I know you had a huge role in this process. So double and triple thanks for helping me translate the chaos in my head into something that Lance could use!)

Finally to Annie. Thank you. You were the first to hold up your light and show me the way. Without you, there would be no *Soul Reaper.* Without you, I never would have tried.

ABOUT THE AUTHOR

D.B. Smyth is a Molotov cocktail in Hello Kitty packaging who dreams in anime and wrestles with monsters. She revels in vengeance, comeuppance, and heart-shattering dark nights of the soul, and she believes the villain is always worth the bullet. When she is not exploring the redemption found in darkness and the beauty in chaos, D.B. can be found resting and reading souls in Sin City.

For updates and extras, follow @db_smyth on Instagram.